ROSALIE UNDONE

THE SHIFTERS SERIES
BOOK SIX

ELIZABETH KELLY

EK PUBLISHING INC.

Edited by
L. Nunn Editing

Cover art by
The Final Wrap

ROSALIE UNDONE

THE SHIFTERS SERIES BOOK SIX

Falling in love was never part of the plan.

Sweet, shy and... human. Rosalie Parker wants one thing - her co-worker and lion shifter, Lincoln. There's only one problem. Lion shifters have a reputation for enjoying the kink, and Rosalie is far from kinky.

Determined to win Lincoln over, Rosalie will do whatever it takes - including stepping out of her comfort zone and into the kinky zone. The last person she expects to volunteer for kink teaching is grumpy polar bear shifter, Hudson. And why does she forget all about Lincoln when she's in Hudson's arms?

Hudson shouldn't get closer to Rosalie. Sure, her sweet nature and soft curves have him and his bear all worked up, but being anything more than friends is dangerous. He has a price on his head, and it'll be collected sooner or later.

But he can't stay away from her.

Will their unconventional friendship turn into something more? Or will the bounty on his life destroy their chance at happiness?

CHAPTER 1

"You know what isn't fair?" Rosalie sat down at the lunch table next to Bria.

"What's that?" Bria ate a bite of her pasta.

"Every day at lunch, you eat something delicious like pasta or bread. I eat salad. Yet, you look like you, and I look like me." Rosalie opened her lunch container and poked at her salad.

"Honestly, I'd kill for my chest to look like yours." Bria set her fork down and glanced critically at her small chest.

"Yeah, well, I'd kill to be a size two."

"You're gorgeous just the way you are," Bria said. "Besides, it's all metabolism. All the women on my side of the family got lucky with metabolism."

"Being a tiger shifter probably helps too, huh?" Rosalie said.

Bria shrugged. "Yes, but there are curvy cat shifters."

"Seriously?"

"Yep. It doesn't happen all that often, but you'll sometimes see a shifter who, in their human form, doesn't match their animal form. My dad has a friend, Mr. Baker, who's an

elephant shifter. When he's in his human form, he's only 5'2"
and weighs about a hundred and ten pounds. But when he
shifts, he's as big as any normal elephant. And most male
chipmunk shifters are huge in their human form. Of course,
that's because they use steroids and work out like maniacs.
They have the worst case of little man syndrome, I swear."

"Can you talk when you're in your animal form?" Rosalie
asked.

Bria grinned, and Rosalie said, "Sorry, that was a stupid
question."

"It isn't. We can't speak English or anything like that, but
if Jace is in his tiger form and I'm in my human form, I can
understand his growls or chuffs or whatever. Any big cat, I
can understand. But I couldn't understand a non-cat shifter,
like a coyote or a bear. Make sense?"

"Yes."

"Oh, and," Bria gave her an excited look, "apparently,
dragons could speak the human language in their animal
form, but they went extinct long ago."

"There were dragon shifters?" Rosalie said in disbelief.

"Yep. My grandpa said they were everywhere when his
father was a boy. But then the females started having a hard
time getting pregnant, and they began to die out. They were
extinct even before we revealed ourselves to humans."

"Why couldn't they get pregnant?"

"No idea," Bria replied. "Grandpa said some of the
dragons started talking about mating with other shifters to
try to keep the bloodlines going, but most dragons were kind
of racist toward other shifters. They wanted to keep their
bloodlines pure, but it made them go extinct."

Bria popped another forkful of pasta in her mouth and
ate it. "Oh, and snake shifters? They're, like, super messed up.
Some are normal-sized snakes when they shift, and some are

gigantic, like those stupid fake CGI snakes you see in the movies. There's no rhyme or reason to it, either. Some of them are just really big."

"Wow, I had no idea," Rosalie said.

"Hell, look at me. I'm way smaller than your average tiger shifter. Most female tiger shifters are over six feet tall and have curves for days. My hips are non-existent."

"I like your non-existent hips," a deep voice said from behind them.

Rosalie watched as a happy smile broke out on Bria's face. Jace joined them in the kitchen and sat next to Bria. He leaned in to kiss her, frowning when Bria leaned back and shook her head slightly before glancing at Rosalie.

Jace sat back in his chair. "How's the morning been?"

"Busy," Bria said. "The phones have been ringing almost nonstop."

She didn't object when Jace grabbed her water bottle and took a big swallow. "Rosalie, do you have time to meet with me after lunch to go over the Vanden's paperwork for their condo?"

Rosalie nodded. "Yes. If you can meet at one-thirty? I have to finish the budget report first."

"Sounds good." Jace stood, and Rosalie couldn't help but grin when he bent quickly and pressed a kiss against Bria's mouth before she could stop him. "Bye, ladies."

He walked out of the kitchen, and Rosalie's grin widened when Bria stared at his ass. A month ago, Bria and Jace had started dating. There was some gossip about it in their small office, but Rosalie refused to participate. She liked Bria a lot, and she was deeply loyal to Jace. She was glad they were dating. She had never seen Jace so happy.

She nudged Bria. "So, when will you and Jace get married and have little tiger babies?"

Bria blushed. "We've been dating a month, Rosalie. There hasn't been any talk of marriage or babies."

"You spend every night at his place, don't you? You're practically living together."

Bria didn't answer, and Rosalie ate a bite of salad. "You know you don't have to hide your relationship with Jace, right? We all know you're dating."

"I know. I also know Rhonda and Sam have been talking about me behind my back."

"Rhonda and Sam talk about everyone behind their backs. Did you know I'm going to die a withered old maid with eighty-seven cats? At least, according to Rhonda and Sam, I am."

"One, you're not even close to being withered or old and two, dating the boss is still a stigma. Don't tell anyone this, but I've been looking for a new job."

"What? No!" Rosalie's fork clattered to the table. "You can't quit."

"Why not?"

"Because I'm still planning on going through the real estate program to become an agent. And I know Jace will only consider hiring me as an agent if I find someone to replace me as his assistant."

"I still don't know what that has to do with me," Bria replied.

"I'm training you for my job."

"What? I can't do your job. I'm just the receptionist."

"Not yet, you can't. But after a few months of training, you will. You're super smart and reliable. You've only worked here for a few months and already know more about the business than Sam. She's been here for over a year."

"I don't know," Bria said. "Couples who work together and live together can be tricky."

"So, you are living together." Rosalie gave her a triumphant grin.

Bria blushed. "Not technically, but I can't remember the last time I went to my apartment."

"Okay, well, just think about it all right?"

"I will. But, Rosalie, Jace will still let you take the schooling and become an agent, even if he doesn't have someone to replace you as his assistant. You know that, right? He knows you'll be an awesome real estate agent."

"Maybe," Rosalie said. "Anyway, what are your plans for this weekend?"

"Ava and Bishop are moving into their new house on Saturday. I'm going over to help move and unpack."

Rosalie gave Bria a curious look. She'd met Ava and Bishop when they used Jace as their real estate agent. Ava was a curvy redheaded human, and Bishop was a massive grizzly shifter. "I didn't know you were friends with Ava and Bishop."

"Well, I've known Bishop since Kat started working at the security company with him. He and Kat are close, and since Kat and I are best friends, we end up in the same social circle. And since he started dating Ava, she's gotten close to Kat, so we've had our fair share of girls' nights together."

Bria ate some more pasta. "Anyway, Kat and her boyfriend Ronin are helping them move on Saturday, and I volunteered to help."

"Is Jace helping too?"

"He is," Bria said. "I told him he didn't have to, but he said he didn't mind. How about you? What are your plans?"

"Not much." Rosalie poked at her salad again. "I'm going to the movies on Sunday with Hudson."

Bria leaned forward. "You've been going to the movies with Hudson every weekend for the last month."

"We both like movies."

"Is that all you like?"

Rosalie sighed and pushed her salad away. "Hudson and I are just friends. You know just as well as I do that polar bear shifters prefer to be alone most of the time. He made it clear that he has no interest in dating me and, besides, I love Lincoln. Remember?"

Just saying the lion shifter's name made her feel too warm. Lincoln worked for Jace as an agent and was also his best friend. She'd been madly in love with the handsome lion shifter since the day she started working for Jace.

"I know, but…"

"But what?" She hated how defensive she sounded.

"I hate to sound like a broken record, but lion shifters are -"

"Kinky sex addicts, who like to bed multiple women and want a woman who has lots of experience in the bedroom?" Rosalie's cheeks felt like they were on fire.

"Yes." Bria's voice was blunt. "And unless you've been up to some serious kinky stuff with a mystery man, that's not you, Rosalie. You told me that yourself."

"Not yet, but I'm going to change that," Rosalie said.

"You shouldn't change for Lincoln. Not when he -"

"Not when he what?"

"Nothing." Bria put the lid back on her pasta. "Never mind."

"Say it, Bria."

"Lincoln is never going to settle down. Even if you're everything he wants in the bedroom, he'll never be happy with just one woman."

"You don't know that for sure."

"I do, honey. I'm sorry, I don't mean to hurt you, but I know lion shifters and -"

"You don't know Lincoln, not the way that I do. We're friends, and I know he's attracted to me. The only thing holding us back from having an actual relationship is my lack of skills in the bedroom, and I'm going to change that."

"How?"

"I have a plan. Can we change the subject? I don't want to talk about Lincoln anymore, okay?"

"Yes, I'm sorry," Bria said. "Hey, why don't you come to Bishop and Ava's moving party on Saturday?"

"Now it's a party?"

Bria laughed. "Well, Bishop has promised beer and pizza afterwards, so that's pretty much a party, right? There will be lots of people, so you'll probably only have to move a couple of boxes, then you can eat pizza and hang out with us."

"I don't know Ava and Bishop that well. Why would they want me there?"

"Uh, free labour?" Bria laughed again. "C'mon, Rosie-girl. Hang out with us on Saturday."

"I usually visit my mom."

"She won't mind if you skip one Saturday."

Bria was wrong, but spilling her guts about her complicated relationship with her mother to her boss' girlfriend was a bad idea. She hesitated a few seconds longer. Surprisingly, she wanted to go. She loved her mother, but spending every Saturday with her was getting old. It would be nice to hang out with people her own age. She didn't have many friends – hell, she didn't really have *any* friends if she was being truthful – and she liked Bria. Even if the others weren't friendly with her, she could have fun with Bria and Jace.

"There will be other humans there," Bria said. "You know that Ava and Mal's mate Willow are human. Plus, the owner of Bud's Bar – Porter is his name, did you meet him when you were there? Anyway, his mate is a human, too. So, you won't be the only human if you're worried about that."

"Sure, okay."

"Yeah?" Bria gave her a delighted look.

"Yeah. What time and where?"

"I'll email you the details. I'm so glad you're joining us, Rosalie. It'll be fun. I promise," Bria said.

"I'm sure it will be." Rosalie stared at her salad and ignored her trepidation at attempting to make new friends. She was twenty-six years old, for God's sake. This wasn't high school.

"WHO ARE YOU TEXTING WITH?"

Rosalie tucked her phone back into her pocket. "My friend Hudson."

"Hudson? You never told me about him. Is he your boyfriend?" The fear in her mother's voice was palpable.

Rosalie sighed. "No, he's not my boyfriend. I did tell you about him last week. Remember? He's a bartender."

"I don't like the idea of you being friends with someone like that. Who knows what trouble you can get into."

"It's fine. Hudson isn't like that."

"What do you and a bartender have in common? If he doesn't want to sleep with you, what else does he want from you?"

Rosalie tried not to grimace. Her mother meant well, but everything she said had a note of passive aggressiveness that drove Rosalie crazy.

"We both like going to the movies. That's why I was texting him. We were arranging to meet at the theatre on Sunday."

"Well, you shouldn't be talking to your friends when you're with me. This is my time with you. I barely see you as it is. You know how lonely I get."

"I have dinner with you three times a week and spend Saturdays with you."

"Not this Saturday." Her mother pounced like an angry kitten on a toy mouse. "You have plans this Saturday."

"I'm helping friends move. It's not like I'm abandoning you for a weekend in Vegas or something."

"What am I supposed to do on Saturday?"

She wanted to ask her mother why she was responsible for her social life. Guilt immediately flooded through her. "Why don't you ask Mrs. Nester across the street to take you with her when she goes to Bingo? She's always offering to drive you there. She's lonely, I think, and could use a friend."

Her mother hesitated, and Rosalie could almost see the excuses flickering across her face as she tried to think of a valid reason to say no.

"Mrs. Nester has cats. I'm allergic to cats."

"You're not allergic to cats. You hate them."

She had never told her mother about Mr. Pibbles and never planned to tell her. Her mother rarely came to her house. On the two occasions her mother had come to Rosalie's place after she had adopted Mr. Pibbles, Rosalie had locked Mr. Pibbles in the spare bedroom with his food and water and a generous sprinkle of cat nip on his favourite toys. He'd been too stoned to care that his usual run of the entire house was thwarted.

"Is this what's happening now, Rosalie? You're leaving your mother all alone because of your friends? You're my whole world, sweetheart. Don't you understand that?"

More guilt.

Guilt so heavy she could feel it weighing her down like a stone.

Her mother needed her. She needed to be a good daughter and be there for her mother. Bria would understand if she cancelled, and it's not like Ava and Bishop would even care. They didn't even know her.

Rosie, don't. It's one Saturday. You need this.

"It's only one Saturday, Mom. You'll be fine without me for one Saturday."

"Come over on Sunday then. I'll cook that baked chicken dish. I know it's your favourite."

"I can't. I have plans on Sunday, too, remember?"

Her mother's eyes welled up with tears. "So, I'll be alone all weekend?"

"Not if you ask Mrs. Nester to take you to Bingo with her."

Her mother glared at her, and Rosalie tried not to sigh when the tears disappeared and she switched tactics again. "You know, I always see Mrs. Nester's daughter's car at her house, Rosalie. All the time."

"That's nice, Mom." She gathered her purse and stood. "I've got to run. I'll come by Monday night, and we'll have dinner then, okay?"

"Maybe *I'll* be busy." Her mother sounded like a petulant child.

Determined not to give in to the guilt, Rosalie pasted a smile on her face. "Okay. If you are, call me and let me know. Love you."

She leaned down and kissed her mother's cheek. Her mom stared at the table and refused to reply. Ignoring the guilt eating away at her stomach lining, Rosalie hurried out of the house. She took a deep breath of the clean air. As always, she felt a sense of relief, and as always, the relief made her feel terrible.

She glanced back at her mother's house, resisting the urge to go back in and beg for her mother's forgiveness like a little kid. It was only one Saturday. Her mother would be fine.

HUDSON STARED FIXEDLY AT HIS PHONE. WHEN ROSALIE didn't text again after almost five minutes, he tossed it on the couch beside him and stared blankly at the television. After a moment, he reached down and adjusted the crotch of his jeans. He had a damn erection just from texting with Rosalie. He adjusted himself again, grimacing at the pressure.

The problem was that he could easily hear Rosalie's voice in his head as he read her texts. That low, raspy, incredibly sexy voice. Her voice always brought on images of tangled silk sheets, smooth pale skin with curves in all the right places, and a woman's soft cries as she climaxed over and over.

Rosalie's soft cries. Rosalie's pale skin. That little freckle at the corner of her mouth. Her perfect nipples outlined against the pink shirt she wore last Sunday.

The air conditioning in the theatre had been on the fritz, pumping out more cold air than it needed to pump. Despite wearing just a short-sleeved t-shirt, Rosalie had insisted it was fine. She said they didn't need to leave. She said she didn't get cold easily.

He always kept an empty seat between them. She thought it was because he took up more than one seat, and it was partially because of that. But it was mostly self-preservation. Having those soft curves of hers pressed up against him would have his dick so hard it would rip through his damn jeans.

Last week was no different. She had automatically sat a seat away, but an hour into the movie, he could almost feel Rosalie shivering in her seat, could see the way her nipples were hard little peaks against her shirt. The sight had made his bear so pathetically eager to mate with her that he would have been ashamed of it...if his human side hadn't felt the same way.

He should have given her his hoodie to wear – he never got cold – but he didn't.

He couldn't.

If he had her scent on his clothes, it would drive his bear insane with need. He wouldn't be able to stop himself from coaxing her into his bed to make her forget all about that lion shifter she was in love with.

He'd wanted the little human from the moment she'd bumped into him at the bar that night. Wanted her from the moment she had stared up at him with those gorgeous blue eyes and asked him to help her. She had pressed her body up against his, and he was lost.

The wolf shifter at the bar had threatened her. He'd scared and bullied her, and Hudson would have torn that fucking wolf shifter to shreds if he had taken one step closer to Rosalie. When the asshole tried to go near her again, not ten minutes later, Hudson had almost lost control. He'd managed not to kill the wolf but couldn't resist putting his arm around Rosalie, couldn't resist pulling her soft and curvy body up against his so that everyone would think she belonged to him. Ensuring some of his scent was on her so other shifters would stay away was bad enough, but the fact that Rosalie noticed? That was way too fucking dangerous. For Rosalie and him.

He muted the television and checked his phone again. Still no text. It wasn't like she had to keep texting him. They had confirmed their plans for the movies on Sunday. But, sometimes, she would ask him how his day was, and once, she had sent him a gif of a baby polar bear sliding off its mother's back.

He kept his replies short and didn't even respond to the gif. After that, she stopped sending texts other than ones related to their weekly movie plans. He was stupidly disappointed, but it was for the best. He needed to keep her at a distance.

Then why have you gone to the movies with her every weekend for the last month?

Because he was smitten with her like an idiot in one of those stupid romantic comedies that Samuel had always made him go to see. He tried to conceal it by being even more standoffish and irritable with her than with others. She seemed to accept that it was just his personality.

She was cautious around him, though. He didn't think she was afraid of him – would she go to the movies every Sunday with him if she was? But it bothered him that she made sure not to touch him and didn't talk much on their movie dates.

So now you're calling them dates?

He stood and shut the television off before stomping to the kitchen. He wasn't dating Rosalie, and saying he was smitten with her, was him being a fucking drama queen. Sure, he was interested in fucking her, but she was gorgeous and sweet, and any red-blooded male would feel the same way.

It had been almost two years since he'd mated. Of course he was interested in fucking Rosalie. He'd never slept with a human before but knew how to be gentle. Even shifter females were much smaller than him, and he was always conscious of the size difference. His first lover had been older than him with experience. She'd done a fine job of teaching him how to be gentle.

Besides, Rosalie wasn't a tiny, fragile little human. She was tall for a human female, and she had nice full curves that would cushion his body nicely if she was brave enough to try missionary with him.

If she wasn't, if she wanted to be on top like most of his partners preferred, watching her gorgeous, naked body ride him would be more than enough. He'd take her however she said.

Hell, he'd do whatever she wanted him to do.

Yeah, no, you're not smitten at all. Idiot. His inner voice sounded both smug and perplexed.

Who was he kidding? He was utterly and completely hers…and she had no fucking idea.

She never would.

He couldn't put her in that type of danger. If Corden knew, if he even suspected that Hudson cared for her, he'd use her to get to him. Corden would hurt her and torture her, just like Samuel was tortured until…

His hands curled into fists, and he turned and slammed his left fist into the wall next to the fridge. He punched through the drywall, scraping the shit out of his knuckles. He pulled his hand free and stared at the hole before moving to the sink and rinsing away the blood and the drywall dust. His appetite for supper had disappeared completely. Instead of eating, he added wall repair supplies to the grocery list stuck to the fridge and headed to the bedroom.

He couldn't tell Rosalie anything about him, let alone confess his immediate love for her. The idea of not seeing her at all sent his bear into a frenzy of panic, so he would keep going to the movies with her every Sunday. He would dream about her, masturbate to thoughts of being with her, and let her keep believing that he barely tolerated her.

What happens when she finds someone else? What happens if she convinces that asshole lion shifter to bang her? You'll rip him apart the first time you smell his scent on her. You know you will.

No, he wouldn't. He had more control than that. If Rosalie started sleeping with the lion shifter or anyone else… he'd pack up his shit and move on. He'd have to leave the city eventually, anyway. It was too dangerous to stay in one place for too long.

Corden would never stop looking for him.

CHAPTER 2

"Hi. Can I help you?" The dark-haired woman with incredible green eyes and a killer body smiled politely at Rosalie.

"Um, hi. I'm Rosalie. I'm here to help with the moving, but I think maybe I have the wrong house?"

She stepped back and checked the house number again. It matched the address Bria had given her, but no moving truck was parked in the driveway.

The woman's eyes lit up in understanding. "Rosalie! You work with Bria, right?"

"That's right."

"It's so nice to meet you. Bria's told me a lot about you. I'm Katarina Frost."

"From the security company. You're Bria's best friend."

"Yes." Katarina smiled at her and held out her hand. "It's nice to meet you."

"It's nice to meet you as well, Katarina," Rosalie said.

"Call me Kat. Come on in."

Rosalie followed the woman down the hallway. She was a

cat shifter of some kind, she was sure of it, but she couldn't remember what Bria had said she was.

"The guys are back at the old house packing the truck with the furniture and the rest of the boxes. They should be here any minute." Kat squeezed past a stack of boxes. "But we brought a bunch of boxes in our cars and have started to unpack."

Rosalie followed her into the kitchen. It was full of boxes, some half unpacked, and she smiled at Bria when the tiger shifter waved at her. "Rosalie, you made it!"

With a chubby, redheaded baby held in one arm, Ava was rifling through a diaper bag. "Hi, Rosalie. It's so nice to see you again. Thank you for helping us move. We really appreciate it."

"It's no problem." She gave Ava a bit of an awkward smile. "Your baby is adorable. How old is she?"

"Thanks. Her name is Lila, and she's three months old."

"Hi, Lila." Rosalie stroked the baby's soft cheek. She loved kids, and she was itching to hold the baby.

To her delight, Ava held Lila out to her. "Would you mind holding her for a second?"

"Not at all." She took Lila and kissed the top of her head before jiggling her lightly. The baby stared up at her, and Rosalie kissed her forehead. "Hi, sweetie."

"So," Bria stood beside her, "let me introduce you to everyone. You know Ava and you just met Kat. This is Willow, Ginger, and Maggie."

"It's, uh, nice to meet you all."

The three women smiled at her and said hello. They ranged in size from tiny to average height, and Rosalie was uncomfortably aware of her height and oversized hips.

Lila started to fuss, and Rosalie jiggled her again as Ava

dug deeper into the diaper bag. "Oh, for goodness sake, is it possible that I didn't put a single diaper in the diaper bag?"

Willow laughed and peeled off a piece of packing tape from a box. "I've got an emergency stash at my house."

"Seriously? Okay, let's take Lila over there, and I'll change her and feed her. If I'm really lucky, she'll fall asleep." Ava took the baby and smiled at Rosalie. "Thank you."

"How awesome is it that you can walk over to my house now?" Willow said as she joined Ava at the doorway to the kitchen. "Living next door to each other will be amazing."

"You won't be saying that when you hear Lila screaming in the middle of the night for food," Ava said. "Her hunger cry will echo across the neighbourhood."

Willow laughed and kissed Lila's chubby leg. "I won't hold it against you, sweet Lila."

The baby's forehead wrinkled, and she let out a screech that was loud enough to rattle the dishes in the boxes.

Ava winced. "Speaking of which."

Willow checked her watch. "It's almost lunchtime. We'll order pizza for dinner, but Ginger, if you don't mind helping me make sandwiches for everyone for lunch, I'd love you forever."

"Sure," Ginger replied.

Kat raised her voice to be heard over Lila's increasingly loud wails. "Bria and I will unpack the books in the living room and put them in the built-ins by the fireplace. Maggie and Rosalie – can you guys start unpacking the kitchen?"

"Of course. Ava, do you want stuff in particular cupboards?" Maggie asked.

Ava grinned at her. "Okay, don't laugh, but there's a piece of paper on the counter with a diagram of the kitchen and detailed descriptions of which dishes go in which cupboard."

"Wow, you guys are organized," Maggie said.

"Not me. Mal is the organized one," Ava said. "He and Bishop have been planning out the move. I've barely done anything. Hell, Willow and Ginger packed most of the house for me."

Willow grinned at her. "We're the nicest friends ever. Also, I'm starting to think that packing and moving is Mal's secret superpower. C'mon, let's go feed that kid of yours."

Maggie smiled at Rosalie as everyone else left the kitchen. "Boy, Lila has a cry on her, doesn't she?"

Rosalie nodded. "She does have a healthy set of lungs."

Maggie laughed and studied the paper on the counter before opening the box closest to her. "So, weird question, but – are you human?"

"I am. Are you?" Rosalie reached into the box and took out a paper-wrapped glass. She unwrapped it and set it on the counter before reaching for another.

"I am, and honestly, never thought I would start so many conversations with – are you human?"

Rosalie laughed and set another glass on the counter. "How do you know Ava and Bishop?"

"I'm mated to Porter, who is Mal's brother. Bishop practically grew up with Mal, Porter, and their siblings."

"Porter owns Bud's Bar, right?"

"He does. Have you been there?"

"Just once."

"Cool. How do you know Bishop and Ava?" Maggie reached into the box.

"I don't, not really. I mean, they used the real estate agency that I work for to buy their house. I'm Jace's PA and friends with Bria."

"Well, it's nice of you to help out." Maggie studied the paper. "Okay, everything in this box is their everyday dishes, meaning they go in the far left cupboard. How about I unwrap and hand the dishes to you, and you put them in the cupboard? I think that'll be faster."

"Sure." Rosalie stood next to the cupboard and lined up the glasses neatly on the bottom shelf as Maggie handed them to her. "So, how did you meet Porter?"

"I was having trouble with a hyena shifter I had dated briefly. Porter, as well as his brother's security company, uh, helped me with him."

"That's nice." She didn't know Maggie very well – didn't know her at all, actually – but even she could see that the woman was hiding something. Deciding it wasn't her business, she stared at the empty spot where the fridge should have been. "So, it's kind of weird that they don't have a fridge."

Maggie laughed. "Ava said the previous owners insisted on taking their fridge with them. Made it part of the sale agreement. Ava and Bishop bought a new fridge, which was delivered yesterday. It's sitting in the garage. When they return from the old house, Bishop and Hudson will bring it in. Whoops - careful." Maggie grabbed for the glass that was slipping out of Rosalie's hand.

"Hudson? Hudson, the polar bear shifter?" Rosalie said.

"Yes. He works with Porter at the bar. Do you know him?" Maggie asked.

"I do."

"Oh, right. You've been to the bar, you said. He's so big, he's kind of hard to miss." Maggie handed her the glass again, and Rosalie placed it in the cupboard.

Maggie was unwrapping the plates and stacking them neatly on the counter. "Porter asked him if he would mind just helping them load and unload the big pieces of furniture. He says Hudson is unbelievably strong. He says he usually unloads the entire beer shipment, and it takes him less than half an hour."

She handed the stack of plates to Rosalie. "I've met him several times when I've stopped by the bar. He's so quiet, I don't think I've heard him say more than five words, but Porter says he's a great bartender. How well do you know him?"

"We, um, we go to the movies together almost every weekend."

"Oh." Maggie handed her another stack of plates. "Are you guys dating?"

"No," Rosalie said quickly. "God, no."

Maggie glanced at her, and Rosalie blushed. "Not because he's a shifter or anything. I have no problem dating a shifter. In fact, I have a huge crush on this lion shifter at work, and I'm trying to get him into my bed and … oh my god, I can't believe I just said that."

Maggie laughed. "It's fine."

"I'm so embarrassed right now." Rosalie set the second stack of plates in the cupboard.

"Don't be. I know a little bit about having a crush on a shifter. Before we started dating, I was a total dork whenever I was around Porter."

"What kind of shifter is he?"

"Wolf." Maggie was unwrapping bowls, and she shoved the paper into a recycling bag. "Anyway, I get what it's like, so don't feel bad. You and Hudson are just friends, then?"

"Sort of?" Rosalie moved the plates to the side so she could fit the bowls beside them. "It's kind of hard to tell with Hudson. What with his preference for complete silence."

Maggie laughed again, and Rosalie grinned at her. "We ran into each other at the movie theatre once, and he suggested we go to the movies together as friends. I think he felt a little sorry for me because he'd just watched Lincoln dump me for Tori."

Maggie paused in handing the next bowl to her. "Tori, the bunny shifter from the bar, Tori?"

"Yes."

"And who's Lincoln?"

"Oh, he's the lion shifter that I like. He invited me to the movies, and we ran into Tori and Hudson. After the movie, Lincoln went to the club with Tori."

Maggie gave her a *you're kidding me* look, and Rosalie nodded. "I know. That was a total dick move on Lincoln's part. But, in his defense, he never said we were on a date or anything. Just asked if I wanted to go to a movie with him."

"I guess, but finishing the night with another woman isn't very nice," Maggie said.

"He's a lion shifter, and they're pretty flirty."

"Yes, I've heard," Maggie said.

"Anyway, so now Hudson and I go to the movies every Sunday, but we don't talk or anything," Rosalie said. "Still, having someone to go to the movies with is nice. My other friends -"

What friends?

She ignored her inner voice. "My other friends aren't really into movies."

"Oh, well, I like going to the movies, and a lot of my nights are free because Porter's working at the bar. If Hudson can't make it, I'd be in for a movie night."

"Yeah?" Rosalie gave her a surprised look.

"Yes. Just remind me to exchange phone numbers with you before we finish here. Okay?"

"Okay. Thanks, Maggie."

Maggie smiled at her. "Thanks for possibly hanging out

with me. I don't have a lot of friends and even fewer human friends now that I'm with Porter."

"Honestly, I don't have that many friends either," Rosalie said.

"Well, before we go any further with this new friendship, I need to ask you a serious question."

"What's that?"

"Do you like coffee?"

"Love it," Rosalie replied.

"Thank goodness. I work at a coffee shop and am a total coffee snob. If you don't like coffee, I spend most of my time wondering what the heck is wrong with you."

Rosalie burst into laughter, and Maggie grinned at her. "After Porter, coffee is my second love."

"Are you sure my brother is first? From what I've heard, you're pretty grumpy until you get that first cup of coffee in the morning."

Rosalie turned to see a tall, dark-haired man leaning in the kitchen doorway. He had light blue eyes and broad shoulders and wore jeans and a t-shirt that clung to his flat stomach. He was very handsome, and she could feel her cheeks redden when he smiled at her.

"Rosalie, this is Porter's younger brother, Heath. He's a lawyer. Heath, this is Rosalie. She works with Bria at the real estate agency."

"Hi, Rosalie." Heath's handshake was warm and strong, and he held on for a beat too long.

"Hi. It's nice to meet you."

"You as well."

"Is everyone back?" Maggie asked.

"Yep. Willow wants to have lunch before we start unloading the truck. But Bishop and Hudson are bringing in the fridge – and here they are."

Rosalie's eyes widened as she watched Bishop and Hudson carry in the fridge. Neither bear shifter had even broken a sweat. The muscles in their upper arms bulged as they maneuvered the refrigerator in front of the space. Bishop plugged in the fridge and nodded to Hudson.

Rosalie was suddenly fascinated by Hudson's back muscles as he pushed the fridge into the space. Lord, he was strong. He backed away from the fridge and shook Bishop's hand when the grizzly shifter held it out.

"Thanks for the help, Hudson."

"Sure," Hudson replied. "It's not a -"

His big body suddenly stiffened, and he lifted his head, sniffing the air before turning and staring at Rosalie. She gave him a small wave. "Hi, Hudson."

"Hey."

"You guys are friends?" Heath asked.

When Hudson didn't reply, Rosalie gave a nervous laugh. "Yes, we go to the movies together."

Heath glanced at Hudson. The polar bear shifter neither confirmed nor denied her statement, and an awkward silence descended. Rosalie's cheeks heated up, and she wanted to sink into the floor. If she wasn't sure about her friendship with Hudson, she certainly was now. Why had she said they were friends? Why couldn't she have said she met him at the bar once and left it at that? God, she was an idiot.

She considered bolting out of the house when Willow popped back into the room. "Ooh, the new fridge looks great. We'll have a quick lunch before we unload the moving van. It isn't much, just sandwiches, but we'll have pizza and beer for you later. Come on over to our place and…"

She cocked her head and stared at each person in the room before turning to Bishop. "Why is it so weird in here?"

He shrugged. "It's not weird, Will."

"It is. What happened?"

"Nothing happened," Maggie said. "It's all good, Willow."

"Well, I don't believe any of you fibbers, but since we've wrangled you all for free labour on a beautiful Saturday afternoon, I'll let it go. C'mon, let's eat."

"Here, Rosalie, let me take that."

Heath took the heavy box from her and set it on the dining room table. She straightened her shirt and brushed her hair back from her face as Heath grinned at her. "Starting to regret giving up your Saturday afternoon?"

"No, not at all," she said. "I'm having fun."

He laughed. "Sure you are. So, how do you know Ava and Bishop again?"

"Oh, I work for Jace at the real estate agency they used." She flushed a little. It sounded stupid that she was helping them when she didn't know them. "I, uh, I'm friends with Bria, and she asked me to help."

"That's nice of you." Heath stepped a little closer.

Even though she was just shy of six feet in her sneakers, he was still taller than her and, wow, did he have broad shoulders. He was also ridiculously attractive with his dark hair, square jaw and full lips. If she wasn't so in love with Lincoln, she might have allowed herself a completely point-less crush on the so-far-out-of-her-league-it-was-laughable wolf shifter.

She straightened her shirt again as Heath said, "You're very tall for a human."

"Oh, um, yeah. My dad was pretty tall. My mom isn't. She's only 5'2", has blonde hair and brown eyes and is super slim. People never believed that I was her kid when I was growing up. I was too tall and chubby and -"

Rosalie! Shut up!

She gave Heath a weak grin. "Uh, anyway. So, you're a lawyer?"

"I am," he said.

"And a wolf shifter."

"That's right, and you're human."

"Yes."

"You have beautiful eyes, Rosalie."

"Thank you." His gaze dropped to her mouth when she licked her lips. "Your eyes are pretty, too."

She cringed inwardly. Heath did have lovely green eyes, but most guys probably didn't enjoy being called pretty.

He grinned at her. "Thank you. What are you doing after - ?"

"Heath?" A dark-haired man stuck his head into the dining room. "Mom's trying to reach you. Do you have your phone turned off?"

Heath stepped away from her and reached into his pocket. "It's on silent. Thanks, Mal."

"You bet." Mal glanced at her curiously before leaving.

Heath pulled his cell from his pocket and read the texts before smiling at her. "Sorry, Rosalie. Could you excuse me?"

"Of course."

He left the dining room, nodding to Maggie, who was walking in. Rosalie opened the box on the table as Maggie joined her.

"Hey, need some help?" Maggie asked.

"Sure. Ava asked if I wouldn't mind unpacking some of the extra kitchen stuff in the buffet." Rosalie lifted out a large paper-wrapped glass pitcher and unwrapped it. She handed it to Maggie, who placed it on the cabinet's top shelf.

"What do you think of Heath?" Maggie asked.

"He seems nice."

"Just nice?"

Rosalie handed her a ceramic platter. "Why are you looking at me like that?"

"Heath's into you."

Rosalie stared at her. "What? No, he isn't."

"Yeah, girl, he is." Maggie laughed. "I've been in this family long enough to know when a Burke boy is interested. He's interested. Plus, I heard him asking Ava if you were single."

"Why would he be interested in me?"

"Why wouldn't he?"

"Because he's blindingly attractive?" Rosalie replied.

"He is pretty hot. Of course, all the Burke brothers are. You haven't met Ellet yet, but trust me, he's just as good looking as the rest. It doesn't seem fair that one family can have that much hotness." Maggie handed her another ceramic platter. "So, are you going to go out with Heath?"

Rosalie nearly dropped the platter. "I, well, I don't know. He hasn't asked me out. Are you sure he's interested?"

"Positive."

Rosalie set the platter on top of the first one. She had no idea why someone who looked like Heath was interested in her, but maybe she could use him to teach her some moves in the bedroom.

"Has Heath, uh, had a lot of girlfriends?" Her plan wouldn't work if he didn't have the experience she was looking for.

"I think he's dated occasionally but hasn't had a girlfriend in a while. So, he might not be the best choice if you want something serious. He works a ton of hours," Maggie said.

"I'm not looking for serious," Rosalie said.

"Right, you're in love with a lion shifter."

Rosalie flushed. "Do you think I'm awful?"

"No, why would I?"

"Well, because I'm in love with Lincoln, but I'm not opposed to, uh, hanging out with Heath."

"I don't think you're awful. You're not dating Lincoln, and if you're upfront with Heath about only wanting sex, then I don't see what the big deal is."

Rosalie's face turned bright red, and Maggie gave her an embarrassed look as her own face turned red. "I'm sorry. That was crude of me. I don't think, I mean…"

"No, it's okay." Rosalie grabbed another paper-wrapped object out of the box. "It's just that I don't usually do this sort of thing, but I'm trying to learn…"

Oh shit. She couldn't tell Maggie that she was trying to learn how to be kinky. She was nice, and Rosalie might feel an immediate connection with her, but normal people didn't just blurt out stuff like that to people they just met. She was hoping to be friends with Maggie. If she got too personal too quick, she'd ruin that.

"Trying to learn what?" Maggie asked.

Before Rosalie could reply, Porter strolled into the room. "Darlin? I'm leaving for the bar."

"What time is it?" Maggie glanced at her watch. "Holy crap, it's almost five. I'll walk you out to the car. I'll be right back, Rosalie."

They left, and Rosalie rubbed her forehead before finishing emptying the box. There was a second one on the floor, and she bent and tore the packing tape off the top. God, she needed to get better at not being so awkward around people. No wonder she didn't have any friends.

HUDSON CARRIED THE BOX INTO THE DINING ROOM, STOPPING short just inside the room. Rosalie was bent over a box, and he stared at her amazing ass encased in tight denim. His cock turned to stone in his jeans, and his bear made a happy little growl.

His urge to stand behind her, cup her hips in his hands and press his dick against her ass was almost impossible to ignore. She'd finally know just how much he wanted her, how insane she drove him with lust, how desperately he wanted to be between her lush thighs and deep inside her pussy.

She straightened, and he dropped the box down to cover his erection as she turned. She twitched a little in surprise before giving him a hesitant smile. "Hi, Hudson."

"Hey." He made himself walk into the room. He had avoided her at lunch and the rest of the afternoon, but he couldn't walk out of the room carrying a box labeled dining room.

"How are you?"

Praying she wouldn't notice the bulge in his jeans, he set the box on the table. "Fine. You?"

"I'm good."

"Good." He needed to leave. His need for her would only grow stronger the longer he stood here gawking at her. Too bad he couldn't get his goddamn feet to move. His bear wanted to stay close to the little human. It had smelled the wolf shifter's interest in her, and it didn't like it one fucking bit.

It's fine. She's in love with the idiot lion shifter. She isn't going to go out with the wolf. His efforts to soothe his polar bear weren't working.

"What are you doing here?" His voice was gruff, and he winced inwardly. Jesus, he sounded like an asshole.

"Oh, um, Bria and I work together. Ava and Bishop used our agency to buy their house because Bria is friends with Ava," Rosalie said awkwardly. "Bria asked if I could help out, and I didn't have other plans, so…you aren't working at the bar tonight?"

"Porter said I could go in a bit late today."

"Oh, that's good." She cleared her throat. "Are we still on for the movies tomorrow?"

"Yeah. Two o'clock, right?"

"Right. So…" she studied the room, "it's kind of neat to see a client's house. I mean, we help them buy the house, but I never actually get to see it. It's kind of cool to see it."

She flushed a little and bit at her bottom lip. God, she was fucking adorable when she got flustered. He flustered her a lot. He didn't mean to, but he did.

"Anyway, I'm looking forward to the movie tomorrow. I've heard good things about it."

"Yeah, me too."

"Are you -"

"Sorry, Rosalie, I didn't mean to abandon you like that." The wolf shifter strolled into the room, and Hudson's polar bear snarled. He pushed it back as the wolf lifted his head and inhaled. He stared at Hudson, a small smile curling up the corners of his mouth.

Fuck. The wolf shifter could smell his lust for the little human.

He clenched his hands into fists as Rosalie smiled at the wolf. "Hey, Heath. That's okay. Everything, um, all right?"

"Yes."

He didn't like the way the wolf stared at Rosalie. Like she might belong to him someday. His polar bear roared angrily, and he jerked his head toward Rosalie when she said, "Hudson? What's wrong?"

31

"Nothing," he bit out.

"Your t-shirt is ripping," She said. "And you, um, have a bit of a beard. Are you -"

"I'm fine," he muttered.

"Okay." She crossed her arms over her torso. The movement stretched her t-shirt tight across her glorious breasts. Hudson growled out loud when the wolf's gaze landed on them, and he smelled the faint scent of Heath's lust.

"Hudson?" Rosalie was nearly vibrating with anxiety now, and he cursed inwardly at his lack of self-control. Fuck, he was scaring the shit out of her.

"Rosalie? Could you give Hudson and me a minute?" Heath said.

"Um, sure, okay." Rosalie gave him another tentative look before walking out of the dining room.

Hudson waited until her footsteps faded before stomping toward the wolf and baring his fangs. "Stay away from her, wolf shifter."

Heath stared up at him and gave him a remarkably terror-free grin. "Never thought a polar bear would have a thing for a human."

His hand shot out and wrapped around Heath's neck. "Tell her, and I'll tear you apart."

Heath growled and bared his fangs. "Let go of me."

There was still no fear in his face or radiating from his body, and Hudson felt a grudging trickle of respect for the wolf. He released him, and Heath studied him for a moment. "If you're going to claim her, then stop fucking around and do it. A woman who looks like her won't stay single for long."

Hudson growled again, and Heath curled his lip at him before walking to the doorway. "One last thing – keep scaring her the way you are, and she won't exactly be eager to mate with you."

"Mind your own fucking business, wolf shifter."

Heath just shrugged and walked out of the room. Hudson paced back and forth in the room, the boxes on the floor shaking minutely with every heavy step. His bear was furious and wanted to tear apart the wolf shifter, but Hudson pushed it down when it tried to surge forward.

He's right. We are scaring her.

His bear made an undignified noise that was almost a whine. The thought that his mate would be afraid of him made its anger dissipate, and he soothed it when it made another dejected noise. He took a deep breath and left the dining room. He needed to find Rosalie and apologize for scaring her.

Just go over to him, Rosalie. You already know he's interested. He's super hot, and he's probably slept with a bunch of women and knows lots of kinky stuff. Plus, he's too busy to want to be in a relationship. He's perfect.

She poked at her piece of pizza as she stared furtively across the yard at Heath. She should talk to him, but Heath didn't speak to her again after she left him and Hudson in the dining room. She had deliberately stood next to him when everyone was grabbing a piece of pizza from the table set up in Mal and Willow's backyard, but he had just smiled at her before grabbing a couple of slices and walking away.

She peeled off a slice of pepperoni and ate it. Okay, so the wolf shifter's sudden interest seemed to have faded just as suddenly, but maybe that was just her weird imagination. She didn't even realize he was interested until Maggie pointed it out. She just needed to go over there and use her admittedly limited flirting skills. She was a strong, sexy woman who maybe needed to lose five or thirty pounds, but she also had great breasts, and guys loved boobs.

She tossed her paper plate with her uneaten slice of pizza into the garbage can and brushed off the front of her t-shirt.

She *should* do this.

She *could* do this.

She *was* doing this.

"Rosalie?"

"Hudson, uh, hi." She turned and stared up at the big shifter. She was standing too close to him, invading his personal space, and stepped backward so she didn't make him uncomfortable.

An odd look crossed his face - a combination of guilt and worry. Without thinking, she placed her hand on his arm. "Are you okay?"

He stared at her hand, and she immediately let go of him, tucking her hands behind her back and backing up another step. "I'm sorry, I shouldn't have touched you."

"I won't hurt you." His voice was so low she had trouble hearing him.

"What? I know that."

"You're afraid of me."

She frowned. "I'm not afraid of you."

"I scared you earlier. I'm sorry."

She hesitated. "You didn't scare me. I just – I'm not really around shifters very much, and it was weird to hear you growl. But I wasn't afraid of you."

He studied her with that same look of guilt and anxiety, and she smiled at him. "I swear I'm not."

"You sure?"

"Yes." She hesitated and then decided to ask the question. "Why did you growl at Heath?"

His cheeks turned red, and he scrubbed a hand through his short blond hair. "It was an accident."

"Oh, uh, okay."

He looked even more uncomfortable, and she finally accepted the truth about why he hung out with her. He'd felt sorry for her that night at the movies and made a rash decision that he regretted. Obviously, he didn't like being around her, but he was too polite to ghost her. Feeling weirdly upset about losing her movie buddy but hating that he was only doing it out of pity, she decided to fix the problem.

"Hey, Hudson? Why don't you stop pretending and be honest about how you feel about me?"

He made a weird full-body twitch and swallowed compulsively. "What do you mean?"

She sighed. "I know you only go to the movies with me because you feel sorry for me after what happened that one time with Lincoln. I appreciate the thought, but I don't need your pity. I'm perfectly fine with going to the movies by myself, okay? You don't want to be my friend, and I get that. So, why don't we, I don't know, lose each other's number, and you can go back to enjoying the movies."

He scowled at her. "I don't feel sorry for you."

"Sure, you don't."

"Rosalie, I don't." He shoved his hands into his pockets. "I go to the movies with you every Sunday because I want to. I like my personal space, that's all."

"I know," she said, "but I also know that polar bear shifters like to be alone and aren't friends with humans."

"So, what? I can't be different?"

"No, I'm not saying that. I just… look, I don't want to make you do something you don't want to do, okay?"

"You're not." He scowled again at her, and she gave him a look of exasperation.

35

"Fine. I'm not. We'll keep going to the movies together then."

"Good." He took a big drink of beer. "I don't know why you think we aren't friends."

"Why I would… maybe because we don't talk? Maybe because you went all weird and quiet when I said we were friends earlier in the kitchen? Maybe because if I text you for something unrelated to the movies, you don't even bother to text back?"

Now, she was certain it was guilt on his face, which made *her* feel guilty. She sighed and rubbed at her forehead. "Shit. I'm sorry. I don't mean to make you feel bad. I don't have a lot of friends, and I'm not all that great at making them, so maybe I don't understand how friendships work. You don't have to change or be different, okay? If you say we're friends, then we're friends."

"We're friends," he said.

"Okay." Her cell phone vibrated, and she pulled it out of her pocket, her eyes widening when she saw who it was. "Excuse me, Hudson, I need to take this."

She hit the answer button. "Hi, Lincoln. How are you?"

"Rosie, how's my favourite girl doing?"

"I'm great." Her face flushed at his warm purr. "How are you? I mean, what's going on?"

"Well, I'm hoping my favourite girl can help me out. My car died, and I'm stuck over on the west side. Are you busy? Do you think you could come pick me up? The tow truck is going to take a few hours."

"Of course I can." She could hear the giddiness in her voice. "Text me where you are, and I'll come by."

"You're the best, Rosie-girl. I'll take you for drinks to say thanks. What do you say?"

"Sure, I'd love that."

"Great. See you soon."

"Bye, Lincoln."

She ended the call and clutched her phone, grinning like a fool. She was about to have drinks with Lincoln. She suddenly touched her hair, which was tucked into a ponytail. Shit. Did she have time to run home, change, and maybe do something with her hair? She'd make the damn time. She was having drinks with Lincoln, and she'd be damned if she showed up makeup-less and -

"Rosalie?"

She blinked at Hudson. "Hudson, oh, sorry. I, um, I need to go. Lincoln needs me to -"

"Yeah, I heard. See you later." He turned and walked away, his big body stiff and one ham-sized hand curled into a fist.

She chewed on her bottom lip as she watched Hudson walk away. Why was he angry again? She started toward him when her phone vibrated. Lincoln had texted her with his location and she hesitated before turning away. She would talk to Hudson tomorrow after the movie.

CHAPTER 3

I t'd been months since he'd had the dream. Months where he didn't see Samuel's bruised and battered face, hear the cracking of the bones of the men who'd killed him, taste their blood in his mouth...months of peace.

Until now.

He tossed and turned, growling and whining in his sleep as the nightmare played out. His big body shuddered, and his low whines turned to angry growling as the dream drew him down into its dark depths.

"Please," the dying shifter whispered. "Please, I'm sorry."

His polar bear retreated, and Hudson studied the shifter in his grasp before glancing at his own naked, blood-covered body. He turned to stare at the four shifters sprawled on the cabin floor. Their bodies were hardly recognizable, just twisted shapes of splattered blood and broken bone.

Blood was filling the small cabin. He whined when it washed over Samuel's dead body, making it disappear like his best friend had never even existed. As the blood rose past Hudson's knees and up toward his thighs, he turned back to the dying shifter in his grip and bared his fangs at him.

"My father," the shifter groaned. "If you kill me, he'll never stop hunting you. He'll kill you, man, he'll…"

Hudson leaned close, wrapping his hand around the shifter's sweaty, blood-soaked hair. "He can try."

His fangs lengthened, and he bent his head and tore open the throat of his enemy with a triumphant roar. He drank down the blood, the bitter metallic taste burning in his belly. He dropped the dead shifter when he heard his father's voice.

"Hudson? Hudson, help me."

He turned, the river of blood up to his chest now, and howled helplessly when he saw his father standing in the middle of the cabin, the thick black blood about to swallow him alive.

"Dad! No!" He reached for his father, but the blood had turned thick. It held him back, kept his feet pinned to the floor, and he screamed again when the blood swept his father under.

"Dad! DAD!"

He jerked awake, sweating and whining and growling. He sat up in bed and fumbled on the nightstand for his phone as the late morning sun shone stripes of light across the far wall. Hands shaking, he stared at the screen.

The nightmare always ended the same: either his mother or father drowning in a sea of blood. He knew they were fine, knew that Corden hadn't gotten to them, but his urge to call was too great to deny. He hit a button on his phone as panic sang in his veins.

"Hello?"

"Mom, it's me. Are you okay? Is Dad okay?"

"We're fine, Hudson. What's wrong?" His mother's voice calmed the fear that held him in a vice-like grip.

"Nothing, I just, I…" he collapsed on the bed, staring at the ceiling.

"Was it the dream again?"

"Yeah," he rasped.

"I'm sorry, honey. We're okay, though."

"Are you sure?" His mother and father were powerful polar bear shifters, but the last vestige of his dream still clung to him.

"Yes. We're perfectly safe here. Corden is strong but is no match for me or your father."

"He has shifters," he said. "He has shifters who -"

"Yes, but we live in a community that looks after their own. We watch out for each other, Hudson. Corden can't get to us, you know that. He'd be a fool to try."

"I know," he said. "I just worry."

"You don't need to worry about us, my love. We're safe."

"I'm sorry," he said. "I'm so sorry for -"

"You have nothing to be sorry about." His mother's voice was firm. "What Corden's son did to Samuel... he deserved to die for it."

"You and Dad don't deserve a life of always looking over your shoulder."

She sighed, and he could almost see the look of disapproval on her face. "We loved Samuel like a son, Hudson. He was worth it."

There was silence, and, as stupid as this was, he could feel his mother's love radiating through the phone. He closed his eyes as she said, "You could come here."

"We've talked about this before. You know I can't do that."

"The community will protect you as well. You're our boy, and they -"

"If I go there, Corden will attack. He has men watching you in case I'm reckless enough to show up. Maybe he isn't stupid enough to try to go after you and Dad, but if I'm there, he won't care. He'll sacrifice as many shifters as needed to get to me. I'm not putting you, Dad, or the rest of the town in danger. I won't."

His mother sighed again. "I know. We just miss you, honey."

"I miss you guys too. How are things there?"

"Fine. Your dad's busy as usual. I operated on a human the other day."

"Human? Since when were there humans living there?" Hudson asked.

"Oh, didn't I tell you? Jed married a human. Her name's Barbara and she's lovely. She had a cyst that needed to be removed. Jed was worried about the others accepting her, you know how polar bear shifters are, but there haven't been any issues. She fits in just fine with the rest of us. What about you, honey? What's new?"

"Still working at the bar." He paused and said, "I'm going to the movies with a friend later today."

"Nice. What's his name, and how did you meet him?"

He could feel himself blushing like a teenage bear. "Her name is Rosalie, and I met her at the bar. She's, uh, human."

There was a pause, and his mother said, "I wish your father and I could meet her."

"We're just friends, Mom."

"Are you?" she said.

He didn't reply, and she laughed. "I'm very glad you've met someone, my love. I worry about you."

"We're just friends," he repeated.

"Of course you are," she said in the same tone she'd used when, at eleven years old, he'd tried to convince her it wasn't him who'd broken her favourite stethoscope.

"I better go," he said. "I gotta shower and eat before I leave. I love you, Mom. Say hi to Dad, okay?"

"I will. We love you too, Hudson. Try not to worry, honey."

He tossed his phone on the nightstand and stared at the ceiling for a few more minutes before climbing out of bed. Despite talking to his mother, the unease from his nightmare still lingered. For a moment, he considered canceling his movie date with Rosalie. His polar bear growled in anger, and he soothed it absently. He should cancel. He should stop talking to Rosalie completely.

It's fine. Corden has no idea where you are, and he'd never in a million years believe you would move to a big city. She's not in danger. Just fucking relax for once and live your life.

His polar bear growled in agreement with his inner voice. Hudson sighed and headed toward the bathroom.

ROSALIE TURNED DOWN THE STREET AND FLICKED THE WIPERS on. The rain was pouring down, and lightning was flashing across the sky. Thunder boomed directly overhead, and she flinched before checking the time on the dashboard. If she didn't hurry, she'd be late, and Hudson would be pissed. He was weird about being at the theatre exactly half an hour before the movie started.

She stepped on the gas and squinted through the windshield. It had started to get cloudy and grey about three hours ago, and the weather perfectly matched her mood. She sighed and tried to forget about last night. Her brain refused to let her.

She'd been so excited when she picked up Lincoln. She had raced home and changed into a skirt and pretty top before doing her makeup and putting her hair up in a cute twist. Traffic was terrible, and it had taken her almost forty

ELIZABETH KELLY

minutes to get to him, but it had been worth it when he'd climbed into her truck and given her a lazy grin.

She'd been over the moon about going for drinks with him. Until they'd gone to a bar of his choice, where she realized he already had plans with a group of shifters. She'd sat in the bar, feeling awkward and like an outsider, as Lincoln's friends talked around her and Lincoln flirted with a gorgeous blonde woman. After half an hour, she'd quietly slipped away and driven home. She'd scrubbed the makeup off her face, put on her pajamas, and curled up in bed with her iPad and Mr. Pibbles.

She banged her hand on the steering wheel. She should have known Lincoln wouldn't want to hang out with her, so why was she feeling so sick about it? Why did it hurt to –

The loud bang and the way the truck veered into the other lane made her scream. She jerked the wheel, crying out again when the tires slid on the slick road. She took her foot off the gas, steered the truck to the side of the road and shut it off. Her heart was racing, her palms were sweaty, and she felt sick. She was sure it was just a flat tire, but the noise of the tire blowing and how her truck had careened into the other lane frightened the hell out of her.

She reached into the back for her hoodie and muttered a curse. How could she have forgotten her damn hoodie? After how cold it was in the theatre last weekend, she reminded herself to bring a sweater just this morning. She should have written the reminder on her damn arm.

Steeling herself against the cold rain, she hopped out of the truck and ran to the back. The right rear tire was already completely flat, and she squinted at the hole in it. Fuck, whatever she had run over had been big. She was lucky she hadn't lost control of the truck and driven straight into a telephone pole or something.

She ran back to the cab and climbed in, staring blankly out the windshield. She had zero idea how to change the tire. She chewed at her bottom lip before pulling Lincoln's number up on her phone. Her finger hesitated over the call button.

Call him, Rosie. You just helped him out yesterday with car trouble.

She pressed the button. The phone rang a few times, and she was about to give up when he picked up the call.

"Hey, Rosalie. What's up?" Lincoln's voice was raspy like he'd just woken up.

"Hi, Lincoln. Is this, uh, a bad time?"

"Just having a nap."

Her imagination went into overdrive. Picturing a naked Lincoln in his bed and how it might feel to have her own naked body pressed up against his. Her cheeks were flushed, and she wiped away the rainwater sliding from her temple to her chin. Maybe she could show Lincoln how grateful she was for helping her by joining him for another... nap.

Where you what? Wow him with your non-existent sex skills? Reading a couple of books on how to bang a lion shifter isn't going to magically make you relax in bed or give you the ability to give a guy a proper blow job.

"Where did you get off to last night?" he asked. "I wanted to buy you another drink, but you disappeared."

"Oh, sorry, I had a bit of a headache, and you seemed to be having fun, so I didn't want to ask you to leave."

"You're a peach, Rosie-girl." He yawned. "Thank you again for picking me up and hanging out last night. I'm sorry I kind of abandoned you for a bit. It was Charlyn's birthday, and she's a good friend, so I didn't want to miss the party."

His voice was warm and sincere, and her anger with him was gone just like that.

"Oh, that's okay. I understand. I'm sorry to bother you, but," her voice sounded breathy and uneven, "it's just that I ran over something, and it blew my tire. I'm stranded on the side of the road."

"You okay?" Warmth flooded through her at the genuine concern in his voice.

"Yeah, a little shaken up. I have a spare tire but don't know how to change it. I was wondering if maybe you could help me?"

He didn't reply, and she tapped her fingers nervously against the steering wheel. "I know it's raining and gross, and I hate to ask, but I -"

"No, that's okay, Rosie. Of course I can help you. You helped me yesterday, right? I owe you."

"No, you don't owe me," she said hurriedly. Feeling stupid, she fibbed a little. "I just, uh, I tried calling a few other friends, but they aren't available to help, and -"

"Lincoln, come back to bed. I'm cold."

The woman's voice was warm and husky and dripping with sexiness. She heard a low purring sound, and her stomach churned as the woman's voice drew closer.

"Lincoln, did you hear me? I need your big dick to warm _"

"Just a second, Charlyn. I'm talking to a friend." Lincoln's voice was muffled.

"Unless that friend is willing to suck your dick, you have thirty seconds to get back into this bed, or you're going to be a very disappointed lion." The woman laughed before purring again.

Rosalie watched her knuckles turn white around the steering wheel. She could barely hear Lincoln over the buzzing in her ears.

"Rosalie, how about I pay for a tow truck for you?" Lincoln's voice was distracted.

"No, that's okay. I'm sorry to have bothered you."

"You aren't bothering me, Rosie. Really. It's just I have a friend over and -"

"It's fine. You, uh, have fun, and I'll see you at the office tomorrow," she said.

"Rosie, wait -"

She hit the end button and threw the phone onto the seat, staring at it like it was a venomous snake. Her hands were shaking, her face was too hot, and she wanted to vomit. It was one thing to know that Lincoln slept with other women. It was entirely different to hear it happening.

She closed her eyes and banged her head against the headrest. She wanted to cry, and she blinked the tears back fiercely. She wouldn't cry. She knew who Lincoln was and what she needed to do to make him hers. She couldn't expect him to sit and wait around while she worked up the nerve to get good at sex.

Next weekend, she'd hit a bar and find a shifter to have sex with. She'd never pictured herself having sex with a stranger, but if she wanted Lincoln to fall in love with her, she had to get over her shyness and her sexual hang-ups. She might be self-conscious about the way she looked, but some shifters found women with extra chub attractive.

Hey, Rosie? Think you can stop obsessing over your sex issues for two seconds and figure out how to fix the current mess you're in?

She grabbed her phone and Googled a tow truck company. Cursing herself for never learning to change a tire, she phoned the tow truck company.

Five minutes later, she tossed her cell phone on the seat beside her and tried not to burst into tears. There was no reason to cry. Sure, she had tried five different companies and all of them would be at least two hours, if not longer. But at least she had a tow truck coming, right?

She brushed away the hot tears and reached for her phone to text Hudson. Before she could start typing, he texted her.

Hudson

Hey, are we still on for the movie?

Rosalie

Sorry, got a flat tire on my way to the theatre. Will be a couple of hours for the tow truck. Watch the movie without me. Maybe we can try again next week.

She waited for a reply. After a few minutes, she set her phone on the seat beside her and stared out the windshield. It's not like she thought Hudson would rescue her, but she thought she'd at least get a reply.

Why? Hudson tolerates you and nothing more. He can tell you all he wants that you're friends, but it's a pretty goddamn weird friendship.

She sighed and rubbed her forehead. After their conversation yesterday, she was pretty certain Hudson believed they were friends. It was just that the polar bear shifter had a very different idea of friendship. That idea did not include coming to the rescue when she was stranded on the side of the road. That was fine with her. At least she was starting to have friends.

Are you, though? Maggie said she would call you, but she could have just said it to be polite. Also, if you're just friends with Hudson, why do you keep noticing his ass?

He had a nice ass. She could admire a friend's ass without making it weird.

The sound of the rain was very loud, and as the seconds ticked by, she grew more impatient. Why the hell didn't she know how to change a tire? It was one of those life skills that every woman should know, and just because her father wasn't around growing up, it was no excuse. If she knew how to change a tire, she could have changed it by this point and still made the movie.

Angry now, she quickly Googled how to change a tire and read through the instructions before tossing her phone on the seat.

She could do this.

Of course, it would be a hell of a lot better if she had a damn jacket.

She hesitated, staring at the way the rain beat against the windshield before she straightened her shoulders.

She could do this.

She leaned over the seat and lifted the back seat to study the storage area. She crowed with delight when she discovered the jack kit just like the website said she would. She grabbed it and exited the truck, slamming the door shut.

It was only mid-afternoon, but the sky was dark with clouds, and the rain made it hard to see. At least the street she was on was deserted, and she wouldn't get splashed by traffic flying by her.

She headed to the back of the truck and got down on her hands and knees. Another crow of happiness when she saw the spare tire. She stood and wiped the mud from her hands on the ass of her jeans before crouching and removing the plastic cover beside the license plate. Her entire body was completely soaked, and she was already starting to shiver from the cold, but she inserted the key in the hole and turned it. The lock pulled away from the hole, and she set it on the bumper before inspecting the rods in the tire-changing pouch.

She grabbed what she hoped was the right one and

inserted it into the hole before adding another rod to the end of it. She straightened and stuck the crowbar to the remaining end of the rod.

"P-p-please work." She turned the crowbar clockwise, huffing out a curse when it didn't move.

"N-n-no, counter-clockwise, it said." She reached into her pocket for her phone to double-check, but her pocket was empty. She'd left her phone on the front seat.

She tried counter-clockwise. "Thank God," she breathed when it turned. She squinted under the truck, pulling hard on the crowbar. The spare tire was lowering. Slowly, but it was lowering. She rotated the crowbar faster. Once she had the tire on the ground, she could use the jack to –

"Shit!" The crowbar suddenly refused to turn, and she squatted and squinted at the tire. It wasn't anywhere close to the ground, and she stood and wrapped her hands around the crowbar before pulling with all of her power. It didn't move an inch.

Panting, she let go of the crowbar and wiped the rain-water from her eyes before taking a deep breath and grab-bing the crowbar again. She pulled hard, grunting with the effort. God, what she wouldn't give for some damn muscles right now.

She made a mental note to finally join the damn gym.

"C'mon, you stupid motherfu -"

She screamed and jerked forward when the hand touched her shoulder. Her shins hit the crowbar with a painful smack, and the crowbar fell off the rod and clanged to the ground. She pitched forward, her hands flying up to try to protect herself.

Before she could eat hard gravel, an arm was around her waist and catching her. It pulled her back into a standing position, and she tried to squirm away, screaming again when the arm tightened and refused to let her go.

"Rosalie, it's me."

The familiar voice made her stiffen, and she craned her head to look at the man holding her. "H-Hudson?"

"Yeah."

"Oh my God, you scared me so bad." She turned and threw her arms around his waist, burying her face in his chest.

She shouldn't have - she knew he hated to be touched by her - but the adrenaline and rush of relief had made her almost giddy to see him. Plus, she was freezing, and he was so warm.

To her surprise, he didn't push her away. He patted her back several times, but when he moved a little so their lower bodies weren't touching, she let go and stepped away. She craved his warmth almost immediately and wanted to flatten herself against him again.

Instead, she crossed her arms over her chest and tried to smile at him. "Hey, what are you d-doing here?"

He scowled, and she watched in disbelief as he unzipped his hoodie before handing it to her. "Put this on. Your lips are blue."

"You're g-going to get soaked," she protested.

"Put it on, Rosalie." His scowl deepened.

She slipped into the hoodie, but her hands shook too badly to do up the zipper. With a grunt of annoyance, Hudson zipped it up for her and then pulled the hood up to protect her face.

"Come on." He took her hand and led her to his truck parked on the other side of the street. She climbed into the passenger side and huddled against the door as he slid behind the wheel. He turned the truck on and blasted the heat on high.

"How d-did you f-find me?" she asked.

He shrugged. "Figured you take the same route from home that I do to get to the theatre. What were you doing out there?"

"Ch-changing the t-tire."

"Where's your phone?"

"In my truck. Why?"

"I called you. I called and texted you, but you didn't answer me."

"I'm sorry." She pushed the sleeves of his hoodie up so she could hold her hands out in front of the heater. "When you didn't text me back, I thought you had gone into the movie."

"I ran into Judd and was talking to him. I didn't see your reply text right away."

"Oh."

"I thought you said you had a tow truck coming."

"I did, but it was going to be a couple of hours, and I didn't want to wait, so I Googled how to change a tire and -"

"Googled? You don't know how to change a tire, but you were still out there changing it?"

His face was so red she could almost see the steam rising from the top of his scalp.

"It didn't look difficult, so I -"

"You cannot learn how to change a tire online, Rosalie." He glared at her.

"Why are you so angry with me?"

"The next time something like this happens, you call me. If you text and I don't reply right away, you either call me or you keep your ass in your truck until I do reply. Is that clear?"

"I didn't want to bug you and -"

"Rosalie!" He leaned across the seat and, to her astonishment, cupped her face firmly as he stared down at her. "Stop arguing with me. If anything like this happens again, you are to call me immediately. Do you understand?"

"I – okay, yeah."

"Good." He let go of her. "Stay here. I'll be right back."

"What are you doing?"

"I'm changing your tire," he said.

"No, I can't ask you to -"

"Stop arguing with me." His voice was as unyielding as his giant body.

"Fine. Change my stupid tire with your stupid big muscles." She started to unzip his hoodie to give back to him, but he had already left the truck. She cleared the condensation from the window with the cuff of his sleeve and watched as he easily turned the crowbar to lower the tire the rest of the way.

"Show off," she muttered.

She sighed and huddled deeper into his hoodie. It smelled like him, and she buried her face in the crook of her elbow and inhaled. God, one thing about Hudson – the man always smelled delicious. She didn't know if it was an aftershave or just eau-de-polar bear, but whatever the hell it was, it got her motor running.

Her eyes widened. What was going on with her today? First, she was horny over Lincoln, and now she was acting like a horndog with Hudson. A guy even less attracted to her than Lincoln was. Was she purposely torturing herself? At least Lincoln occasionally acted like he knew she was a woman. She doubted Hudson would notice her tits if she stripped naked and shook them like maracas. Besides, having lustful thoughts about Hudson when she was in love with Lincoln made her a terrible person.

Or you secretly realize how hopeless it is with Lincoln.

Like going after Hudson is any better. At least Lincoln and I are friends. The jury is still out on the friendship thing with Hudson, she snapped at her inner voice.

Hudson is here changing your tire in the pouring rain. He told you that you were friends, but you're still unsure? Are you that stupid, girl?

She ignored her inner voice and peered out the window again. Hudson already had the flat tire off. His t-shirt was clinging to him like he was a contestant in a wet t-shirt contest.

She watched his back muscles ripple as he threw the flat tire into the bed of her truck. God, he was so strong. As he carried the spare tire to the side of the truck, she wiped away the condensation again and studied his ass. She would have to apologize to him for her comment. He was doing something nice for her, and she acted like a spoiled brat.

Hudson crouched and disappeared behind her truck. She turned the heat down and waited patiently. The conversation she just had with Hudson was the most he'd spoken to her in the entire month she'd known him. Normally, he grunted out one-word answers, and he never touched her. She brushed her fingers across her cheek. He had spoken in full sentences *and* touched her.

Lord, maybe she should check on him. He was probably in the middle of having a stroke.

He popped back up and gathered up the tools in the jack kit. She slid out of his truck and crossed the road to hers as he tossed the jack kit into the back seat.

"Thank you so much." She had to shout to be heard above the sudden boom of thunder.

He nodded and said, "Leave it on," when she tried to remove his hoodie.

"Hudson, I -"

"Go home, Rosalie."

She wanted to argue, but the rain was falling harder now, and water dripped from Hudson's ears, nose, and chin.

"I'm sorry," she said. "Thank you for changing my tire."

She climbed into the truck and started it as Hudson trudged across the road and climbed into his truck. She wasn't surprised when he followed her home. He did, after all, live in the next complex over. But she was shocked when he pulled into her complex and her visitor parking spot. Neither of them spoke as they walked quickly to the front door of her townhouse. He followed her inside and shut the door. She took off his hoodie and handed it to him.

"Thank you so much for helping me. I'm sorry I acted like such a brat."

"You didn't."

"I did, and I'm sorry. Could I pay you for fixing the tire?"

His angry scowl was back. "No."

"I'd feel better if you let me do something to -"

"I'm hungry."

"What?"

"I'm hungry."

"Okay, uh, I could cook you something to eat if you wanted?" she said.

"Sure."

"Did you want to go home and change first?" she asked. Hudson's t-shirt still clung to him, and water dripped down his neck.

"It'll dry."

"You're not cold?"

"Polar bears don't get cold."

"Right." She hesitated. "Your jeans don't seem that wet,

but I could put your t-shirt and hoodie in the dryer if you want?"

"Sure." He pulled his shirt over his head and held it and the hoodie out to her. "What's wrong?"

"Nothing," she croaked and grabbed the clothes. "Uh, go on into the kitchen, and I'll, uh, take this to the dryer."

She turned and nearly ran down the hallway to the small laundry room near the back door. Mr. Pibbles was in his litter box, and he gave her a look of disdain when she staggered into the room.

"Mr. Pibbles," she whispered as the cat scratched around in the litter before climbing out, "don't freak out, but there's a half-naked polar bear shifter in the kitchen."

He rubbed up against her leg, meowing his displeasure at the dampness of her jeans, before leaving the laundry room. She tossed Hudson's clothes into the dryer, turned it on, and climbed the stairs to her bedroom.

She changed into a dry t-shirt and jeans before running her hands nervously over her hair. It was drying a bit fuzzy, so she scooped it up into a bun on her head and secured it with a few bobby pins.

She stared at herself in the bathroom mirror. Her cheeks were flushed, and her chest rose and fell too fast.

"Can you blame me," she whispered to her reflection. "Did you see Hudson's six pack? His body was... well, it was really, really nice."

She groaned and slapped herself on the forehead. Why the hell did she ever think she'd be kinky enough in bed for Lincoln? Even her thoughts were rated PG-13. She'd just seen the most incredible man chest of her life, and all she could think was ... it was really, really nice? What the hell was wrong with her?

Okay, but it was really, really nice. He had the perfect amount of chest hair, and yeah, he's big and muscular but not out-of-control, steroid abuse muscular, right? His shoulders are so broad and he's pretty tanned for being a polar bear. Shouldn't they be, like, pale or something? And what about that treasure trail? I bet it leads to a really, really nice penis too.

She smacked herself in the forehead again. She was going crazy. A perfectly acceptable, perfectly reasonable answer to what was happening was that she was going crazy. Being attracted to Hudson was even more stupid than being attracted to Lincoln. Hudson was one hundred percent not attracted to her, not even a little, and just because he had a good body didn't mean she had to start thinking he was a candidate for teaching her kinky sex moves.

Nope, definitely not. Thinking she might try to have sex with someone who flinched when she touched him was a very bad idea. Sexual harassment bad.

She took one final glance at her reflection before heading back downstairs. She stopped in the doorway of the kitchen, staring in mute shock. Hudson was sitting at the table. Mr. Pibbles, who was standing on the kitchen table, purred loudly and butted his head against Hudson's chin. Hudson rubbed the cat's head, and Mr. Pibbles' purring grew louder.

He rubbed his entire body against Hudson's naked chest, his tail flicking in the big polar bear shifter's face as what suspiciously felt like jealousy trickled through her. She wanted to rub her body against Hudson's naked chest, too.

Rosalie! Knock it off! Sexual harassment, remember?

Yeah, she remembered. She walked into the kitchen, trying to ignore the way Hudson's big hands were rubbing all over her pussy.

Oh my God, Rosalie. Are you a thirteen-year-old boy?

Her cat. Hudson was petting her cat and it was totally unexpected and totally adorable that he liked cats, and she absolutely was not jealous that Mr. Pibbles could sit on his lap and she couldn't.

"Mr. Pibbles, get down," she said as the cat settled onto Hudson's lap and kneaded one thick thigh with his claws.

"It's fine," Hudson said.

"I can put him in the spare bedroom," Rosalie said. "He's friendly and won't leave you alone if I don't."

"I like cats. I don't mind petting him."

Ask him if he feels like petting your other cat.

Her cheeks went bright red. What the hell? Where did that come from? Inner Rosie had gone postal.

"I like cats too. Uh, obviously." She opened the fridge. "What do you like to eat?"

"Seals."

She turned and stared wide-eyed at him. "I don't, uh, that is, I'm not sure where I could even go to get seal meat. I have a shrimp ring I could thaw."

There was amusement in his eyes, and she said, "Are you – are you making a joke?"

He didn't reply, but a small grin crossed his face.

"Oh my God, you are. Don't take this the wrong way, but do you feel all right?" she asked.

"Yes. Why?"

"I'm worried you might be having a stroke."

He petted Mr. Pibbles, who arched his back and made a high-pitched trill of pleasure. "Why would you think that?"

"Because you helped me with my flat tire, touched me twice, and you're sitting in my kitchen while my cat gets hair all over you. And - *and* - you just made a joke."

He scowled. "We're friends, Rosalie. Friends help each other."

"I know, but…"

"But, what?"

"I didn't know for sure that we were friends."

He sighed and gave her his usual scowl. "I told you yesterday that we were friends."

"Right." She peered into the fridge again. "Well, I planned to make pasta tonight for dinner, but I can change that up if you don't -"

"Pasta is fine. I like pasta." Hudson placed Mr. Pibbles on the floor before standing. "What can I do to help?"

"You can sit and relax," Rosalie said. "You came to my rescue, remember? The least I can do is make you dinner. I don't have any beer, but I have a bottle of wine, water, or juice."

"Water, please," Hudson said.

She poured him a glass of water and set it on the table. She glanced at him, her gaze skittering away from his naked chest. The last thing she needed was Hudson smelling her lust for him.

He might consider her a friend, but today aside, his weird compulsion about *not* touching her was more than apparent. Even now, she could feel the tenseness radiating from his large body when she scooted past him to get a pot and pan out of the cupboard.

In fact, when she went to slide past him again, he stood and moved around the table to the other side. He pulled out the chair and sat down. Mr. Pibbles rubbed up against his legs before meowing and jumping into his lap. He petted the cat roughly as Rosalie put water on to boil and then put oil in the pan to heat.

She pulled some mushrooms, peppers, and onion out of the fridge and chopped them up before adding them to the pan. As they sizzled, she grabbed the ground beef from the refrigerator and a bottle of pasta sauce from the pantry.

"It's just bottled sauce. I hope that's okay," she said.

"Fine with me."

"Do you like to cook?" She asked as she added the meat to the pan.

"Not really. I eat a lot of frozen stuff."

"Well, I enjoy cooking, so anytime you want a home-cooked meal, just come over. It's just as easy to cook for two as for one."

"Okay, thanks."

"So," she stirred the vegetables in the pan before adding the meat, "do you like being a bartender?"

Hudson shrugged. "It's a job. Porter's a good boss."

"Were you born here?" she asked.

"Nah. I'm from Alaska."

"Right, of course." She felt a little stupid. "Polar bears are from Alaska. That was a dumb question."

"It isn't," he replied. "My dad and mom were both born in Canada and moved to Alaska after they married."

"Oh. Are they still there?"

"Yeah. My dad's an accountant, and my mom is a doctor. They live in a small, isolated community. My mom runs the medical center."

"How small?" She asked.

"There's only about four hundred bears in the town."

She stared at him. "It's all polar bear shifters?"

He nodded. "Well, mostly. There are a few black bears who married polar bears, and my mom told me that there's a human living there now, too."

"That's kind of cool." She added some pasta to the boiling water. "Do you have any siblings?"

"No. My mom and dad only wanted one cub."

"Are you close to your parents?" She added sauce to the meat and vegetables.

"Close enough. I don't see them often, but we text and talk on the phone."

She probably should stop asking Hudson so many questions, but she was weirdly fascinated by his life. "So, you moved from Alaska to here?"

He shook his head. "No. When I was in my early twenties, I moved to Canada. Worked construction for a while – that's where I met Judd."

"Who's Judd?"

"The bouncer at Bud's Bar."

"Oh, right. What kind of shifter is he?"

"Black bear."

She drained the cooked pasta and let it sit while she stirred the meat sauce. She set the table quickly and poured Hudson some more water before putting the pasta and sauce in serving bowls and setting them on the table.

"I'll just put Mr. Pibbles in the bedroom. I'll be right back," she said.

He nodded, and she picked up Mr. Pibbles from Hudson's lap, trying to ignore the heat radiating from the big polar bear shifter's body. She tucked the cat into the bedroom and stopped at the laundry room. Hudson's shirt and hoodie were dry, thank God. She wasn't entirely sure she could sit across from him for an entire meal while he was half-naked without feeling some kind of tingling in her girl parts.

No doubt he had an amazing sense of smell and, for some reason, Hudson knowing she lusted after him, even if it was just a 'temporary I've gone crazy kind of way', was even worse than Lincoln knowing she wanted him.

She returned to the kitchen and handed him his clothes. "Here you go. Nice and dry."

"Thanks." He dropped the hoodie on the seat beside him and she busied herself with pouring a glass of juice as he slipped his shirt over his head.

She sat down across from him. "Help yourself."

"Thanks. It smells good."

He piled his plate high with pasta and meat sauce, not the least bit self-conscious about how much he was taking. She added some food to her plate and smiled at him. "So, you were saying that you did construction?"

"For a while," he said. "Then I switched to working for a logging company up in Northern Alberta."

"So, what made you decide to move here?"

A 'closed for business' look immediately crossed his face. "Just needed a change."

"Oh." She ate a bit of pasta as awkward silence descended. She had gone too far, pried too much into Hudson's life.

"What about you?" He said abruptly. "You grow up here?"

"Yes. Born and raised here. My mom lives about twenty minutes away."

"What about your dad?" He ate another forkful of pasta.

"I don't know who he is. My mom raised me on my own."

Hudson frowned. "She never told you who he was?"

She shook her head. "No. Just said he wasn't a good man and that having him in my life would be more trouble than it was worth."

"Does that bother you?"

She blinked a little at the bluntness of his question. "I guess…it used to? Not so much now. My mom is very…stubborn. If she doesn't want to do something, you can't make her do it. You know?"

He nodded, and she ate a bite of pasta.

"You're an only kid too, then?" he asked.

"Yes. My mom never really dated. She said she was too busy looking after me, so she didn't meet anyone. We're, uh, pretty close. I spend a lot of time with her."

Hudson was studying her, and she flushed when he said, "Because you want to or you have to?"

"I want to," she said.

He didn't reply, and she sighed. "She's lonely, and I'm the only one she has. I feel guilty if I don't go over there a few times a week. She *makes* me feel guilty."

When he continued to stay silent, she said hurriedly, "I love her. I do."

"I know. Do you like your job?"

She paused at the sudden change in topic. A month of hanging out with Hudson, and in less than an hour, he was asking more questions than he'd asked her in the entire month.

"I do, actually. I like it a lot. My boss, Jace, is a really good guy. I'm just his assistant, but I'm..."

She hesitated, and he paused with a forkful of pasta near his mouth. "You're what?"

"I'm thinking of becoming a real estate agent. I mean... I'm going to become one. I'll have to go back to school, and it'll be a lot of work, but I know I can do it," she said.

"I know you can, too."

She stared at him, a little taken back by the simple declaration. Warmth flooded through her. "You mean that, don't you?"

"Yes." He gave her a puzzled look. "Why?"

She shrugged. "Sometimes the people in my life don't always think I can do... stuff."

"Why not?"

"Honestly? I don't know."

He mulled that over as he finished his plate of food. He eyed the serving bowls, and she said, "Take the rest."

"Thanks." He scooped out the rest of the pasta and the meat sauce, and they finished eating, this time in surprisingly comfortable silence.

When they were done, he wiped his mouth and said, "That was delicious. Thanks. Sorry, I ate all of it."

"It's fine. You have a big appetite, huh?"

"Most polar bears do. We need to eat a lot for all the energy we burn as humans."

"What do you mean?"

"Well," he leaned back in his chair, "my thick fur keeps me warm when I'm in my polar bear form. As a human, I'm just as warm, but my body has to work harder to be warm because of the lack of fur. Does that make sense?"

"It does. So, you never get cold?"

"No. Most of the time, I'm too hot. In the summer, I usually sit in an ice bath every night."

"Seriously?" she said.

"Yep." He stood and cleared the plates off the table. "Should I just put these in the dishwasher?"

"Sure. Thank you." She rinsed the rest of the supper dishes, handing them to him one by one so he could put them in the dishwasher. When they were done, he wiped down the table and hung the cloth over the side of the sink.

"Thank you."

"Thanks for dinner. It was good."

"It was the least I could do. Thank you again for helping me with my truck. I'd probably still be waiting for the tow truck."

"It's not a problem," he said. "If it happens again, call me, Rosalie. I mean it."

"I will. Thanks." She shoved her hands into the pocket of

her jeans. She didn't want the night to end. She felt an actual connection with Hudson for the first time and liked it. "So, um, I feel bad about making you miss the movie this afternoon. Do you want to find a movie on Netflix and watch it? I have a pretty comfortable couch and could make some popcorn."

A weird look crossed his face, and he immediately headed toward the door. "Thanks, but I need to get home. Bye, Rosalie."

She followed him to the door, smiling tentatively. "Okay, bye, Hudson. We're still on for a movie next Sunday, right?"

"Yeah, sure. Bye."

He didn't look at her, and by the time he hit the sidewalk, he was almost running. She sighed and shut the door before walking to the bedroom and letting Mr. Pibbles out.

"I screwed up, Mr. Pibbles." She returned to the kitchen, and the cat followed her. "I pushed too hard again. Why am I so bad at making friends? I shouldn't have asked him if he wanted to stay and watch Netflix with me...oh my God."

She stared down at her cat. "I asked Hudson to stay and watch a movie on Netflix... everyone knows that's code for 'let's have sex.' Holy crap, I'm an idiot."

The cat purred before rubbing against the hoodie Hudson had left draped across the chair. She snatched it up. "Mr. Pibbles, no. You'll get hair all over it."

She hesitated before burying her face in the hoodie. It smelled delicious, and with a guilty look around, she pulled the hoodie on and zipped it up. She giggled to herself. It fell past her knees, and the arms were so long she couldn't see her hands. Lord, Hudson was a big man.

A very big man. How big do you think his penis is, Rosie? Super big, right?

She turned crimson. She shouldn't even think about

Hudson in any way other than as a friend. He didn't find her repulsive or anything, but he certainly wasn't attracted to her.

Still wearing his hoodie, she wandered into the living room and sat on the couch, staring blankly at the TV screen as Mr. Pibbles purred and rubbed against her legs.

CHAPTER 4

"Morning, Rosalie."

Rosalie smiled at Bria and paused at the reception desk. "Morning."

"How was the rest of your weekend? You left Ava and Bishop's new place without saying goodbye," Bria said.

"Oh, I had to help Lincoln with some car trouble."

"Lincoln?" Bria said. "You helped Lincoln?"

"She sure did." Lincoln's low purr from behind her sent shivers down her back. She couldn't stop the soft blush when he tugged on a lock of her hair. "You didn't text me back last night, Rosie-girl. I was worried."

She blushed again, ignoring how Bria rolled her eyes as she turned to face him. "It was late when I got your text, so I didn't want to wake you."

He smiled at her. "You text me whenever you want, gorgeous. Did you get things worked out with your car? I'm sorry I couldn't help."

"Oh, that's okay. I understand." She knew he could smell her lust for him, but she couldn't help it. God, he smelled good.

"You had car trouble too?" Bria asked.

"Yeah, flat tire on the way to the movies yesterday." Rosalie studied Lincoln's face. He hadn't shaved today, and she loved the blond stubble covering his face. She wondered how that stubble would feel brushing against her skin.

Why don't you ask Charlyn?

Reality dumped a bucket of cold water on her lust. Lincoln had been with another woman yesterday, yet she still couldn't stop mooning over him.

Lincoln's nostrils flared, and a slight frown crossed his face before stepping closer to her. "I brought you a coffee this morning."

"You did?"

"Of course. You're my favourite girl, right?"

"Right." Her face flushed, and a small smile crossed Lincoln's face before he turned to Bria. "Bria, did you get my email about the Harlow file?"

Bria nodded. "I did. Do you want to talk about it now?"

"If you have time?"

"I do. Oh, hey, Rosalie? Jace is looking for you."

"Thanks, Bria." Rosalie headed to her cubicle, nodding hello to Sam and Rhonda when she passed them. She dumped her purse and lunch at her desk, hung her jacket over her chair, and walked to Jace's office.

"Jace?" She knocked on the open door. "You wanted to see me?"

"I did. Come in and shut the door."

She did as he asked, sinking gracefully into the chair in front of his desk. The tall and lean tiger shifter smiled at her. "How was the rest of your weekend?"

"Good, thanks. You?"

"It was good. On Sunday afternoon, Bria and I ran some

errands and tried a new restaurant downtown with Kat and Ronin."

"Sounds like fun."

"It was. " Jace leaned back in his chair. "I wanted to talk to you about becoming an agent."

Her mouth dropped open, and she stared at him in stunned silence for a moment. "Bria told you."

He shook his head. "Not really. She just confirmed what I already knew."

"Listen, Jace, it isn't that I don't enjoy being your assistant. I do. I just -"

"Rosie, stop." Jace gave her a small grin. "I want you to become an agent."

"You do?"

"Yes. I think you'd be very good at it. I want to do whatever I can to help you achieve your goal."

She gave him a hesitant look. "But if I become an agent, I'll have to leave your company. You're not looking for any more agents."

"This isn't common knowledge yet, but Warren is retiring. Which means I'll be looking for a new agent."

Excitement sent her heart rate spiking. The only reason she hadn't started her schooling to be an agent was her sorrow at knowing she would have to stop working for Jace. But if she could still work for him...

She took a deep breath. "Does Warren have a specific retirement date? Because it'll take at least four to six months to do schooling, then I have to write the exam, and -"

"I know. Warren doesn't have an exact date, but even if he leaves in the next few months, we'll make it work, Rosie."

She couldn't stop the grin from spreading across her face. Jace gave her an identical grin. "Congratulations."

She laughed. "Don't congratulate me yet. I still have to

look into the schooling, make a plan, and figure out how I'll juggle working and going to school."

"It won't be easy, but if anyone can do it, you can. Listen, I know this week is busy for you because you're leaving on holiday, but when you return from vacation, schedule a meeting with me. We'll look at the education part together and determine what you need from me and the company to help you succeed. Okay?"

"Okay. Jace, thank you." She gave him a look of sincere gratitude. "You have no idea what this means to me."

"Happy to help, Rosie. I think you'll be a great agent. And you know what? Even if Warren weren't leaving, I'd find a way to keep you. The company would be lost without you."

She shrugged. "Not sure that's true, but I appreciate you saying it."

"It's true."

"Do you have any ideas for who might replace me as your assistant?" she asked.

Jace cocked his head at her. "Do you?"

"Bria," she said. "She's smart and fast, and she'd be great at it."

He nodded. "She would. But we'd have to work hard to talk her into it."

"Maybe," Rosalie said. "But you should seriously consider it."

"I will." Jace smiled at her. "Excited about your upcoming holiday? Going somewhere fun?"

"No, actually. Staying close to home."

"Oh. Well, it'll still be nice to have some time off. Did you know Lincoln's on holiday, too?"

"Is he?" She prayed that her face wouldn't betray her. "Good for him. Is he going out of town?"

"No, he's staying in the city." Jace had a weird look on his face.

"What's wrong?" she asked.

"Nothing." He checked his cell phone. "I should probably get going. I have a showing in an hour. Don't forget to send me a meeting request about the agent thing, okay?"

"Okay. Thanks again, Jace." She stood and, after a moment, held out her hand. Jace stood and shook it firmly.

"You'll be an amazing agent, Rosie. I know it."

"Thank you." She smiled happily at him and left his office. She grabbed her lunch from her desk and took a sip of the coffee that Lincoln had left for her. Her pulse was still pounding, and she couldn't stop from grinning. She was about to have her cake and eat it, too.

She took her lunch to the kitchen. She had just stuffed it into the fridge when she smelled Lincoln's aftershave. Her body tingled with awareness, and she turned to smile at him.

"You look like a kitty cat who's eaten the canary, Rosie-girl," Lincoln said.

She laughed. "Do I?"

"Yep." He stepped a little closer. "What's going on?"

She checked the doorway to the kitchen before saying, "I'm going to become an agent."

Lincoln gave her a look of surprise. "Really?"

"Yes. I've been thinking about it for a while now, and I'm taking the plunge."

"Oh. Well, good luck," Lincoln said as his phone buzzed. "It's a tough job, but I'm sure you'll be fine."

There was doubt in his voice and a bit of her good mood deflated. "You don't think I can do it?"

"What? No, I didn't say that." Lincoln was texting, and he looked up from his screen. "No, I'm sure you'll be just fine.

You're smart, and the only thing clients like better than a pretty agent is a smart one."

He just called you ugly!

He didn't, she snapped at her inner voice. He called her smart, and that was a compliment. Besides, she knew Lincoln thought she was pretty. Would he be so flirty if he wasn't?

He flirts with you because he knows you're hot for him, and he uses it to get what he wants from you.

Fine, maybe he did. But that was going to change. Lincoln found her attractive – God knows, he'd stared at her tits enough times for her to see that he wasn't completely immune to her looks – and as soon as she got her kink on and wowed him in bed, he'd be hers.

Why wait? You booked your vacation for the same time as his because you planned on seducing him, remember? Ask him out.

That was true. But she'd also thought she'd be further ahead in her plan to be an expert at kinky sex. She'd been so busy the last month she hadn't even had a chance to look for a shifter to help her. Heath had been her first chance. Somehow, she'd blown that in less than twenty minutes without even trying.

It's now or never, Rosie. Besides, you can fake being kinky. How hard can it be? Just tell him that you're up for whatever he is. It's just sex. For God's sake, you're not exactly a blushing virgin.

No, she wasn't, but vanilla sex with one guy didn't make her a kink master, either.

Just do it, Rosie! God. Be brave for once in your damn life.

Be brave.

Right.

"So, uh, I heard you were on holiday next week," she said.

Lincoln nodded without looking away from his screen. "I am. Two weeks."

"That's good. I am, too."

"Oh yeah? Nice. Where are you going?" His thumbs tap-tap-tapped.

"Staying here, actually. Jace mentioned you were staying in the city, too. Maybe we could get together? I'm a good cook. You could stop by my place for dinner, and we could talk about what it's like being an agent. What do you think?"

A smile crept across Lincoln's face as he stared at his screen. Tap, tap, tap, went his thumbs again.

After almost thirty seconds, she said, "Lincoln?"

He glanced up at her. "Sorry, what was that?"

"I was just saying that Jace mentioned you're also sticking around the city. Would you like to come by my place for dinner one night?"

"Oh, uh..."

The unease on his face made hers burn.

"To talk about being an agent," she said quickly. "I could use some tips and would like to learn more about what a day in the life of an agent is like. I'm, uh, a great cook."

Lincoln glanced at his watch before grabbing an apple from the fruit bowl on the counter. He gave her a vague smile and headed toward the door. "Sounds nice. But I'm not sure what my schedule is like yet. I'm meeting with some other friends and stuff during my holidays. Can I get back to you on it?"

"Sure. You've got my number."

"Sure do, Rosie-girl." He winked at her, bit into his apple, and left the kitchen.

She slumped against the counter, feeling awkward and stupid and...oh my God... did she just ask Lincoln out?

You did. And he turned you down flat.

No, she argued. *He said he would get back to me on it.*

You're not stupid, Rosie. Don't act like you are.

"Shit." She banged her fist against the counter as her face reddened and tears threatened. "You *are* stupid, Rosalie."

"You're far from stupid." Bria had entered the kitchen, coffee mug in hand. "Why would you think... Rosalie? What's wrong?"

"Nothing's wrong."

"Something's wrong." Bria touched her arm. "Please tell me."

Rosalie sighed. "I just asked Lincoln out, and he turned me down. I think."

"You think?"

"He said he'd get back to me on it."

"Oh."

"Yeah."

"Well, Lincoln is..."

"I know. But - and don't you dare say a word to anyone about this - I took my holidays because I knew Lincoln was taking his. He always takes holidays at this time of the year, and he always stays in the city. I planned to ask him out and to spend some time with him. But he blew me off. He said he had plans with friends and a pretty busy schedule."

She sighed and had to refrain from banging her fist on the counter again. "I'm such an idiot."

Bria frowned. "You're not. I don't think he lied when he said he had a busy schedule."

"How do you know?" Rosalie asked.

Bria lowered her voice. "Jace told me that every year at this time, there's a shifter's kink fest."

"What? I've never even heard of it."

"Me either. But it's been happening for the last fifteen years. It's held in Crossroads village."

"That's a shifters-only part of the city, right?"

"Yes and no," Bria said. "It's predominantly shifters who

live there, and all the stores and whatnot within Crossroads are shifter-owned, but humans aren't forbidden from living there or anything. It's just most of them don't."

"Right."

"Anyway, they hold a kink fest every year, and Lincoln attends it. Jace told me all about it. It's a ten-day event, and it has live bands, strip shows, a sex toy expo, public floggings and other, like, BDSM type of shows, as well as pole dancing competitions and that sort of thing. It's capped off with a big dance party that Jace says can get pretty raunchy. Like – public sex raunchy."

Rosalie knew her eyes were as wide as saucers, but she couldn't help it. "How does Jace know all of this?"

Bria grinned at her. "He hasn't been to the festival if that's what you're wondering. But he is Lincoln's best friend, and Lincoln isn't shy about sharing details."

"Oh. So, uh, are humans allowed to go to the kink fest?"

"It's shifters only until the last day, and then they open the doors to humans. They can also attend the dance party, but the festival charges them more."

Rosalie pulled absentmindedly on a piece of her curly hair. If she went to the dance party at the kink fest, Lincoln would realize she wasn't the naïve, innocent human he thought she was. Seducing him at the dance party would be the perfect opportunity to show him how kinky she could be.

Great plan, Rosie. Only you're not kinky. Remember?

Not yet, she wasn't. But she could be kinky by the time the last day of the festival rolled around. Maybe.

"When is the festival?" she asked Bria.

"Uh, the fifteenth to the twenty-fourth, I think Jace said. You can find information about it online," Bria said. "Why?"

"Just curious," Rosalie said.

"Rosie, you can't go to the kink fest," Bria said. "It's

shifters only. Besides, I don't think – I mean, I'm not sure that festival is the right place for someone as sweet as you."

"Maybe I don't want to be sweet anymore."

"Rosie -"

"I need to get back to my desk, Bria. It's almost eight-thirty, and I haven't done any work yet. I'll talk to you later."

Rosie hurried out of the kitchen, nearly vibrating with excitement.

This could work.

It had to work.

"You're always texting now, Rosalie. You're here but not really here." Her mother set the bowl of steaming potatoes on the table.

"I've been here for two hours, and it's the first time I've texted," Rosalie said.

"Who is it?"

"My friend, Maggie. We're having dinner tomorrow night."

"Maggie? I've never heard you mention a Maggie before. How do you know her?"

"I met her on Saturday while helping Ava and Bishop move. She's nice."

"How do you know that? You barely know her. And who are Ava and Bishop again? I swear, you suddenly think your Miss Popularity, don't you?" her mother said.

"Ava and Bishop are clients."

"Since when do you have to help clients move in? What kind of boss is this Shepherd guy?" Her mom set the chicken on the table with a disgruntled thump. "He's taking advantage of you, Rosie. He takes advantage of you all the time and _"

"No, he doesn't," Rosalie said. "He's a good boss. He had nothing to do with why I helped Ava and Bishop move. I'm just trying to make more friends, okay?"

"Why? Why do you need friends? You have me, and you have…"

"Exactly. I have you, and that's it."

Her mother's face deepened into a scowl. "What's wrong with me? I've given everything for you, Rosie. Everything."

"I know, Mom. I'm not saying there's anything wrong with you. I'm saying that it's good to have friends. I think we both need friends. Did you talk to Mrs. Nester about going to Bingo with her on the weekend?"

"No. I spent the weekend alone because my daughter decided that making new friends was more important than spending time with her mother."

She didn't want to feel guilty, but she did. She knew it was difficult for her mother to make friends and that she depended on Rosalie, but sometimes, she felt smothered by her mother's demands.

She decided to ignore her mother's comment. There was no point in trying to defend herself. It was a waste of energy. Her mother saw things in a different light than Rosalie ever would.

"The food smells really good." She helped herself to some chicken and potatoes before reaching for the steamed vegetables.

"Eat lots of vegetables, Rosie. Your pants are looking a little tight," her mother said. "You'll never get a boyfriend if you keep gaining weight."

"I'm not gaining weight. Besides, I thought you didn't

want me to have a boyfriend. You said he would take up too much of my time."

Her mother made a face before eating some potatoes. "Yes, well, I also want grandchildren before I die."

"So, guess what?" Rosalie decided another topic change was needed. "I'm getting my real estate license."

Her mother paused with a forkful of chicken in front of her face. "What?"

Rosalie ate a bite of steamed cauliflower. "I'm going back to school to become an agent."

"But you – your job. What about your job? You can't go to school and work simultaneously," her mother said.

"I can," Rosalie said. "The schooling can be done at night."

"Where will you get the money? It's expensive to go to school. You shouldn't be putting yourself into debt for a career where you aren't guaranteed a job afterward. You aren't doing this, Rosalie, and that's final."

Rosalie didn't mean to laugh, but it came busting out of her anyway. "Mom, I'm an adult. You don't get to tell me what I can and can't do anymore."

Her mother flushed before stabbing a piece of chicken with her fork. "I only want what's best for you. You're young, and you don't know how the world works. I do. But, that's fine. You don't want my advice. I won't give it anymore."

Oh, how Rosalie wished she could believe that.

"But," her mother pointed her fork at her, "when you're broke and can't make your mortgage and have to live with your mother again, know that you'll be following my rules while living under my roof."

"I'm not going to lose my house," Rosalie said. "I've been saving for school for over a year and don't have to go into debt. And Jace told me this morning that he wants to hire me as an agent when I finish school."

"Do you have that in writing?" her mother snapped.

"No, but I trust Jace. He won't screw me over."

"You can't trust anyone but family, Rosalie. How many times do I have to tell you that?"

Rosalie poked at the food on her plate, her appetite almost completely gone. "I told you about this because I thought you would be happy for me. This is a good thing for me."

Her mother drank iced tea before saying, "I only want what's best for you, Rosie."

"This is what's best for me."

"Is it?" Her mother cleared her throat. "Rosalie, are you sure you're…smart enough to become an agent?"

Ah, there it was. It had taken a while, but they'd finally gotten to the root of her mother's issue.

"I'm not dumb, Mom." She tried not to sound offended and failed.

"I never said you were." Her mother bristled. "But being an agent requires a lot of smarts, and you have never done great at school."

"I got all A's and B's."

"That was high school. High school doesn't count. Besides, there's a big difference between being a secretary and having a real career, Rosalie."

"Being a secretary is a career." Rosalie could feel the vein in her temple starting to throb. "A career that I've been very happy with."

"Then why change?"

"Because I want more. There's nothing wrong with that."

"It is if you're going to fail!"

"I won't fail."

"You don't know that."

Rosalie pushed her plate away. "I should go. It's getting late."

"No, Rosalie!" Her mother grabbed her hand. "Don't go. I'm sorry, okay? I'm just worried about you."

Rosalie sighed. "You don't need to worry. I'm fine, and becoming an agent is a good thing. All right?"

"If you say so." Her mother made her own heavy sigh before staring at her plate. "My appetite is ruined."

Don't apologize, Rosie. Don't apologize.

"I'm sorry, Mom."

"I know you are. You're a good girl, Rosie, and I love you, but I don't want you dreaming of things that you can never have. Do you understand? People like you and me - we have to be happy with what we have. Change and – and believing that something better is just around the corner is a very dangerous thing. Do you understand?"

"Sure, Mom."

"That's my good girl. Now," her mother picked up her fork, "did I tell you that I watched the weirdest show on TV the other night?"

CHAPTER 5

"Jesus, it's slow tonight." Judd leaned against the bar and stared at the cloth as Hudson swiped it over the gleaming surface.

It was just after seven, and there were three shifters in the whole place. A couple sat in one of the booths, but they had just finished their meal, and Tori had already brought them their cheque. A rabbit shifter was nursing a drink at the bar.

"I've never seen it this empty," Hudson said.

"Most shifters think the bar closed today for renovations." Porter had come out of his office, and he surveyed the empty room. "That's not a bad thing, actually. If I can get started on some of the renos tonight, I'll definitely be back open for the Friday night crowd. In fact," he walked over to the rabbit shifter and gave him a friendly slap on the back, "you sticking around for much longer, Benny?"

The rabbit shifter shook his head. "Nah. I gotta get home to the wife. It's baby-makin' night."

"Don't you already have six kits?" Porter said.

"Yep. Going for lucky number seven," Benny said with a grin before slapping some bills on the bar. "See you, Porter."

"Bye, Benny."

The couple followed Benny out the door, and Judd grinned when Porter shut off the open sign and locked the door. "You closin' early, Boss?"

"Yep. Might as well. Go home, you guys. I'll see everyone back here on Friday. Tori, can you come fifteen minutes early? I'll review the new cash register with you before your shift starts."

"Sure can, hon." the perky rabbit shifter said. She disappeared down the hall and into the staff room before reappearing only a few minutes later. Tennis shoes replaced her heels, and she had her jacket on. She stopped in front of Judd, and he leaned down so she could kiss him on the cheek. "See you handsome. Enjoy your days off."

"You too, gorgeous."

Judd slapped her on the ass, and Tori giggled before wiggling her nose at him. She headed toward the door, putting a little extra sway in her hips.

"You want me to walk you to your car, sweetie?" Judd asked.

"Nah, I'm good, hon. It's only seven. Bye, guys."

"You sure you don't need us to help with renovations?" Hudson asked as Porter stepped behind the bar.

"Yeah, we don't mind," Judd said. "Back in the day, Hudson and I worked construction for a couple of years."

"I appreciate that, but I've got my brothers coming in as well as Bishop and Ronin. We're good. Enjoy your two days off, and I'll see you Friday."

He grabbed the cash register drawer. "Hudson, I'll cash out for you. Judd, don't forget to punch out your timecard before you leave."

"Will do," Judd said. "Thanks again, man."

"You bet. Lock up behind you, okay, Hudson?"

Hudson nodded, and he and Judd headed to the small staff room. They both punched out and grabbed their stuff from the row of lockers on the left side of the room.

"What are you doing tonight?" Judd asked.

Hudson shrugged. "Nothin' planned."

"Let's have dinner. I know a good restaurant not too far from here. It's shifter friendly, so they have big booths. Even your giant ass could fit in one."

"Sure," Hudson replied.

"Cool. We'll take your truck and swing back to the bar on the way home so I can pick up my bike. Sound good?"

"Yep." Hudson followed the bear shifter out of the bar and locked the door.

"THANKS FOR HAVING DINNER WITH ME, ROSALIE."

"Thanks for inviting me." Rosalie smiled at Maggie. "I was really happy to get your text yesterday."

"I'm glad. I know you said you were open to hanging out, but I wasn't sure if this was too soon or not. Porter was teasing me last night, said I was acting as nervous as he was the first time he asked a girl out."

Rosie laughed. "You didn't have to be nervous. I like you, Maggie."

"I like you too," Maggie said. "I have a hard time making friends sometimes, and I'm awkward as shit, so…"

"Oh my God, me too," Rosalie said. "I always feel like I'm either coming on too strong or being too aloof. There's no happy medium with me."

Maggie grinned at her. "Welcome to the brain of Maggie. We should get along just fine."

Rosalie returned her smile before leaning back in the

booth. "My God, the hostess wasn't kidding when she said these booths were massive."

"I know," Maggie said. "Are you sure you don't mind sitting in a booth? They're specifically designed for shifters, which means they're giant. We can wait for a normal-sized table if you want."

"It's fine. The restaurant is super busy. We were lucky to get this booth," Rosalie said. "As it is, I'm pretty sure we'll have to wait about half an hour before the server even takes our order. This place seems crazy popular. Besides, I like sitting in a seat where my feet don't touch the floor. It makes me feel like a little kid again."

Maggie laughed and stared at her own dangling feet. "I thought I would have to ask the hostess to boost me into the booth. The good news is, with the table almost to our chins, there's no chance of spilling food on our boobs."

"Speak for yourself," Rosalie said. "I don't think I've gotten through a meal without some of it landing on my boobs since I started puberty."

Maggie eyed Rosalie's chest before staring at her smaller one. "I can only wish I had your boobs."

"Yeah, they're great until someone tries jogging without wearing a proper sports bra," Rosalie said.

Maggie laughed, and Rosalie eyed the restaurant as she sipped her glass of water. The restaurant was large and deco-rated in pale blues and greys. It featured modern art on the walls, and the large tables and booths were solid oak. The booths were padded in blue leather and were very comfort-able. Of course, she would have to sit forward on the very edge of the booth to eat, but still, they were comfortable. There were a wide variety of people – no shifters, she corrected herself, most of them were probably shifters – at the tables and booths.

"So, do you think we're the only humans here?" she asked.

Maggie shook her head. "Nope. Porter and I always come here, and he says it's usually about fifty/fifty for humans and shifters. It used to be just shifters, but I guess word got out about how amazing the food was, and humans started showing up."

"I wonder if that bugs the shifters." Rosalie eyed the other patrons. Some she was pretty certain were shifters, just based on sheer size, but others – she had no idea if they were human or shifters.

"Maybe some of them, I guess. Shifters are much more like humans than most people think, you know?" Maggie took a drink of water. "There are nice shifters, and there are asshole shifters - just like humans."

Their server, a harried-looking woman of about fifty, stopped beside their booth. She handed them both menus and took their drink order before leaving.

"So, did Heath call you?" Maggie asked.

"Uh, no, he didn't."

"That's so weird. He was totally into you on Saturday. Even Porter noticed. I can ask him why he hasn't called if you want?"

"Oh God, no. That's way too embarrassing. I must have said or done something to make him lose interest. Besides, it's fine. I've got a new plan anyway."

"New plan for what?" Maggie eyed her curiously.

Rosalie blushed. Was she really thinking about telling Maggie about her plan to seduce Lincoln?

Why not? If you can have sex with a stranger, why can't you tell someone about it?

Her inner voice had a point. Besides, she was dying to tell someone and didn't have anyone else to tell. She couldn't tell Bria. She liked the tiger shifter a lot, but she was dating

Rosalie's boss, and if Jace ever found out what she was going to do…she'd die.

She took a deep breath. Okay, she would tell Maggie, and if Maggie decided not to be her friend after, so be it.

"So, I want to tell you something, but first – I'm not crazy, okay? I know when someone prefaces a story with 'I'm not crazy,' it usually means they're crazy, but I'm not. I swear it. Just, maybe a little desperate and a lot…horny."

Maggie burst into laughter. "Noted. Go ahead and tell me."

Rosalie hesitated, and Maggie gave her a kind smile. "I'm not judgmental, Rosalie. I promise."

"Okay." Rosalie took another deep breath. "You know I'm in love with a lion shifter named Lincoln, right? Well, the only reason I'm not with him is that he's totally into kinky sex like most lion shifters are, and while I am not completely inexperienced in the bedroom, I'm not kinky at all. But I'm willing to learn, and if I do, I'm almost certain that Lincoln will be into me. Like, he flirts with me a lot – and yeah, some of it's just so that I'll pick up his dry cleaning or bring him a coffee or whatever – but it's not all that. There is an attraction between us. I can feel it."

She wiped her finger across the condensation on her glass. "He doesn't want to sleep with a woman who doesn't know how to be crazy in bed. I heard him say that himself. I know if I could just be different in the bedroom, be more adventurous and open to the idea of kink, that I would have a chance with Lincoln."

"Okay," Maggie said.

Rosalie hesitated. "I know it doesn't guarantee that Lincoln will date me, but I'll have a much better chance of winning him over if he knows I can keep up with him in the kinky bedroom behaviour department."

"It makes sense," Maggie said.

"Yeah?" Rosalie gave her a look of relief.

"I think so. I don't know a whole lot about lion shifters, but Mal's mate Willow knows a couple, and she says they're as far from vanilla as a person can get when it comes to sex."

"Has she, uh, been with them in bed?" Rosalie asked.

"Oh God, no," Maggie said. "She found out about their bedroom antics when… well, it's a long story how she found out, and kind of hard to believe, so let's just stick to your story. Okay?"

"Sure, okay. Anyway, after this week, I'm on vacation for two weeks, and Lincoln is also on holiday. I found out that Lincoln is attending the kink fest for shifters in the Crossroads village. It's not open to humans until the last day. It runs from the fifteenth to the twenty-fourth, which means once I start my holidays next week, I have almost two full weeks to learn to be kinky. Then, on the last day of the kink fest, I'll show up and seduce Lincoln."

"Okay," Maggie said slowly. "Learn to be kinky with who, though?"

"On Saturday, I thought maybe Heath, but that obviously won't work now. Plus, I don't have a lot of time to learn to do the things Lincoln is looking for in bed, so I can't waste my time with someone who may not be kinky. I'm not even certain Heath is kinky, right? And that's not exactly something you can just ask a person."

"That's true," Maggie said.

"What I need to do," Rosalie said, "is sleep with other lion shifters. We know that lion shifters are kinky – well, there are exceptions to the rule – but generally speaking, if I want to learn to be kinky *for* a lion shifter, what better way to learn than *with* a lion shifter? Right?"

"It would be the fastest way, I guess. But are you sure you

want to sleep with someone you don't even really know? Don't take this the wrong way because I am the same, but you don't strike me as the kind of girl to sleep with a guy she doesn't know."

"I'm not. But I'm changing that. Starting on Saturday night."

"What happens Saturday night?"

"I'm finding a lion shifter and banging him."

Maggie laughed before taking another drink of water. "Solid plan. Where are you finding this lion shifter?"

"I was thinking Bud's Bar. It's full of shifters."

"True," Maggie said. "But humans aren't always welcome there. Especially lone female humans."

"I'll be okay," Rosalie said. "I've been there before, and Hudson is there. He helped me once before when a shifter gave me a hard time at the bar."

"Still, I'm not sure it's a good idea for you to go alone. I'm not working Saturday night. I could go with you if you'd like?"

"Seriously? You'd do that?"

"Of course. Everyone needs a wingman – wait, wing-woman – right? I'll be yours. Plus, I'm there so much because of Porter, and I know a lot of the shifters. I don't know any specific lion ones, but I bet I could help you find one."

Rosalie smiled at her. "I'd appreciate that, Maggie. Thank you. And thank you for not thinking I'm super weird or…slutty."

Maggie laughed. "You're welcome. I'm just going to use the powder room. I'll be right back."

"IT'LL BE AN HOUR FOR A TABLE." JUDD GRIMACED. "YOU wanna go somewhere else?"

Hudson shrugged. "Doesn't matter to me. You decide."

"Yeah, maybe we'll try and – oh, hey, Maggie! Maggie, over here!"

Hudson watched as Porter's mate turned and smiled at them. She weaved her way through the crowd waiting for a table at the front of the restaurant. "Hi, Judd."

"Hello, gorgeous." Judd leaned down and kissed her cheek. "How are you?"

"Good. Did Porter close the bar early?"

"He did," Judd said with a grin.

"He mentioned he might if it was slow. Hi, Hudson."

"Hello." He nodded to Maggie.

"Waiting for a table, I assume?" Maggie said.

Judd nodded. "Yeah, it's busy as shit in here tonight. We're thinking we might go someplace else. It's a shame because I fuckin' love their steaks. Excuse my language."

"You should join us," Maggie said. "We have one of the big booths, so there's plenty of space."

"Yeah? You sure you wouldn't mind?" Judd said.

"Not at all," Maggie replied.

"What do you think, Hudson?" Judd turned to him.

Hudson hesitated. He had seen Maggie a lot at the bar, but he had never really talked to her. Spending dinner making small talk with a human he barely knew wasn't his idea of a good time.

"We shouldn't interrupt your dinner," Hudson said.

"I'm having dinner with Rosalie. I know she wouldn't mind if you guys joined us," Maggie said.

His polar bear made a happy growl at the mention of Rosalie's name. He was immediately even warmer than usual, and he had to fight the urge to adjust the front of his pants.

"Oh, that's okay," Judd said. "We'll find -"

"We'd be happy to join you. Thanks, Maggie," Hudson said quickly.

Judd stared up at him. Hudson ignored him as Maggie smiled. "That's great. Follow me."

They followed her to the booth. The server was at the table setting down drinks, and Maggie said, "Rosalie, look who I ran into. They're going to join us for dinner."

He couldn't tell from the look on Rosalie's face whether she was happy to see him. He *hoped* she was. He *wanted* her to be.

"If you don't mind," Judd said.

"Not at all." Rosalie's voice was welcoming. When it looked like Maggie was about to slide in next to her, Hudson pushed past the server and slid into the booth beside Rosalie before Maggie could. He was acting like an idiot, but he couldn't give up the chance to sit next to her. The booths were big, but he still took up a lot of the space. Rosalie's thigh pressed against his, and her hip brushed his.

She tried to move over a bit more but was thwarted by the wall. She gave him an apologetic look. "Sorry, Hudson."

"It's fine," he said gruffly.

Judd sniffed the air, and Hudson glared at his friend when a smile crossed his face. Judd winked at him before gesturing to Maggie. "After you, Maggie."

"Thanks." She slid into the booth, smiling at the server standing a little impatiently at the end of the table. "Sorry, we've added a couple more people."

"Yeah. Do you need more menus?" the server asked.

"No, we can share," Rosalie said.

"What do you guys want to drink?" The server gave Hudson and Judd another impatient look.

Hudson ordered a beer, as did Judd, and the server left.

Rosalie sipped at her drink before smiling at him. "So, are you off tonight?"

"Porter closed the bar early."

"Oh, that seems strange," she said.

"We're doing renovations tomorrow and Thursday," Maggie said. "We're hoping to be finished by Friday so we can open that night."

"If you're running behind, just call me and Hudson," Judd said. "We told Porter we can help."

"Thanks, Judd. We should be okay. Heath and Ellet are pitching in, and Kat said she could hold down the fort at the security firm, so Bishop, Ronin and Mal will help, too. But I'll call you if it looks like we're behind schedule. Now," Maggie flipped open the menu, "let's decide what we're having before our server returns. If we're not ready by the time she comes back with your drinks, pretty sure she's just going to abandon us."

Rosalie laughed, and the front of his jeans was suddenly too tight. Judd sniffed the air again before giving him a knowing grin. Hudson ignored him as Rosalie flipped open the menu on the table in front of them. "Here, we can look at it together. Okay?"

"Sure."

She bent her head, and he stared at how her dark hair gleamed in the light. She was wearing it down tonight and her dark curls looked silky soft. He wondered how it would feel to thread his fingers through them.

What would she do, he wondered, if he slid his hand into her hair and tugged her head back? If he pressed his mouth against hers, traced her full lips with his tongue? Would she accept his kiss? Would she make a sweet moan as her mouth opened under his? Would she press her soft body against his and beg him to make her his right there in the restaurant?

His polar bear growled excitedly, and he could feel his fangs dropping. A sharp kick to his shin made him jerk, and Rosalie looked up at him. "Hudson?" He could smell her alarm. "Are you okay?"

"Yeah, why?" He said hoarsely.

"You're, um, you're growing a beard."

He touched his jaw and, with intense effort, pushed his polar bear back. He stared across the table at Judd. His leg ached where the black bear had kicked him, but he was numbly grateful to his friend. He'd been about two seconds from trying to claim Rosalie right there in front of everyone. Christ.

Judd gave him a pointed look, and Hudson nodded subtly before staring at the menu. Rosalie's arm was touching his, and he hated the timid look she gave him before moving her arm away.

She glanced at Maggie and Judd, but they were studying the menu. She lowered her voice. "Sorry, Hudson."

"It's fine," he repeated. After a moment, he lifted his arm and laid it across the back of the booth. "It's my fault. I take up too much room."

"You don't," she said, lowering her voice. "I just know that you like your space. I don't want you to be uncomfortable."

"I'm not," he said. "Does this, uh, bother you? It gives us a bit more room if I do this." He stared at his arm. If he moved a little closer, she'd be tucked up against his body from shoulder to hip. People would look at them and assume she belonged to him.

That thought made him happier than it should have.

"No, not at all," she said. "Anyway, what are you having?"

"Not sure." He studied the menu. God, Rosalie always smelled so good. Like a combination of strawberries and... cookies, maybe?

Cookies? Now you're just embarrassing yourself.

"Have you eaten here before?" she asked.

"No, have you?" He leaned down, in the pretense of studying the menu, and inhaled the sweet scent of Rosalie's hair. Ah, that was where the strawberry smell came from. He inhaled again as Rosalie continued to study the menu.

"I haven't. The baby spinach salad with herbed chicken looks good. Maybe I'll try that. It has strawberries in it. I love strawberries," she said.

She glanced at the other side of the menu as he tried not to stare at her tits. It was almost impossible. She wore a green long-sleeved shirt with enough buttons undone to see a hint of cleavage. His hand curled around the back of the booth seat. Her skin looked delectably soft. Would she taste like strawberries?

She suddenly swept her hair up, fanning the back of her neck with her hand as she looked at the menu. "It's a bit warm in here."

He stared at the curve of her neck and the slight sheen covering her pale skin. He was sitting too close to her, and the heat of his body was overheating her. If he were a good guy, he'd at least move to the edge of the seat to give her some space, but he couldn't bring himself to move away from her. He so rarely allowed himself to be this close to her.

He resisted the urge to lean down and lick the long length of her throat. Instead, he said, "Sorry, that's my fault. I throw off a lot of heat."

She smiled at him. "It's fine. I hate being cold, so the heat is nice. If you were a heating blanket, I'd have you on top of me in a heartbeat."

Her face suddenly turned crimson. "Oh God, that was... I mean, that came out entirely wrong. I just meant..."

He bit back his smile as she flushed even more. "I knew what you meant."

"Right. Sorry. I didn't mean to make it…weird."

"You didn't." She hadn't. Of course, he thought about being on top of her fifty goddamn times a day, so it was nice that it was her turn to think about it.

Yeah, well, she doesn't think about you that way, so don't feel too smug about it. She's in love with that asshole lion shifter.

His polar bear snarled in anger, and he soothed it absently. It was better for him and Rosalie that she wasn't attracted to him. If he even thought for a minute that she lusted after him, he wouldn't be able to stop from seducing her.

Even knowing that it would put her in danger?

He grimaced inwardly. Maybe it would be fine. Maybe Corden had given up. It was over two years ago. Maybe he'd –

You killed his son. He'll never stop looking for you. Thinking you can stop looking over your shoulder, thinking you can have a life with Rosalie or anyone else, is insanity.

"Oh my God, they have seal!" Rosalie made a soft noise of excitement, and his groin tightened when she innocently touched his thigh under the table. "Hudson, look! Seal!"

Her excitement made him grin. "Guess I'm having seal."

"Can I try some of it?" Her hand was still resting on his thigh, and fucking hell, his cock was so hard it was going to bust through his jeans if she didn't move it soon.

"Uh, sure, yeah." Sweat was forming on his brow. He needed her to move her hand, but he couldn't push her hand away. If he touched her hand, he'd move it to his aching dick. "Uh, your hand, Rosalie…"

"Oh shit." She snatched her hand away and gave him a mortified look before saying in a low voice. "I am so sorry."

"It's okay."

"I got excited about the seal," she said, blushing again.

"I know. It's fine."

The server arrived with his and Judd's beer. They ordered their meals, and he drank half of his bottle in two large gulps. He needed to get control of himself before he did something really stupid. Why the fuck did he sit in the booth with her?

Rosalie was staring at her drink. Her cheeks were still pink, and he could smell her embarrassment. She felt bad about touching him, and Hudson hated that. But what fucking choice did he have?

"So," Maggie smiled at him, "how are you enjoying working at the bar, Hudson?"

"Really like it," he said.

He'd made a mistake by sitting in the booth with Rosalie, but he just had to get through the next hour or so, and everything would be fine.

He could do this.

"Thanks again for letting us sit with you," Judd said to Maggie.

"Of course." Maggie smiled at the bear shifter when he bent and pressed a kiss against her cheek. "Have a good night, Judd. See you Friday, okay?"

"You bet. Drive safe."

Maggie hugged Rosalie. "I'll see you Saturday. I'll text you about the time."

"Sounds good. Bye, Maggie."

"Bye, Rosalie. Wait, where did you park?"

"Just over there." Rosalie pointed to her truck parked across the lot.

Maggie frowned. "Judd, will you walk Rosalie to her truck? It's late and -"

"I'll do it," Hudson said.

"It's all right. I don't need -"

He scowled at Rosalie, and she shrugged. "Okay, fine."

Hudson turned to Judd. "I'll be right back."

"I'll be here." Judd gave him a shit-eating grin, and Hudson glared at him before moving to Rosalie.

Without speaking, they started across the lot. They stopped at her truck, and she unlocked it before giving him a quick darting glance. "Thanks for letting me try some of your seal."

"You're welcome. Did you like it?"

"Um, it was kind of rubbery."

He laughed. "Yeah, I know."

"Still, I guess I can say I've tried seal now, and how many humans can say that, right?"

"Right." He shoved his hands into his pockets so he wouldn't brush back the lock of hair curled against her cheek. "You okay to drive home? I can give you a ride and bring you here in the morning to pick up your truck before work."

If he gave Rosalie a ride home, she'd have to sit between him and Judd in the middle of the bench seat. She'd be pressed up tight against him, and he'd have a little longer to feel her soft curves.

"Oh no, I'm fine. I only had one drink. Besides, you have the day off. I'm sure you want to sleep in." There was an awkward silence, and then she blushed. "Oh, wait, you probably always sleep in because you work nights. Lord, I'm dumb."

"You're not," he said.

"Yeah, maybe," she said before sighing. "Anyway, good night, Hudson."

"Night, Rosalie."

He waited until she started the truck and drove away before trudging back to Judd. The bear shifter was leaning against Hudson's truck, a toothpick stuck in the corner of his mouth. He had no idea how the toothpick was even staying there, what with the giant grin on Judd's face.

"Shut up, Judd," he said before opening the door of his battered truck.

"What?" Judd asked innocently. He climbed into the passenger side as Hudson turned the key. The truck started with a wheeze and a groan, and he pumped the gas a little as Judd settled into the seat. "I'm not sayin' a word about your crush on the little human."

He didn't reply, but Judd kept going anyway. "I don't blame you. She's got a fucking great ass and those tits… you think she's a D or double D? I bet they're -"

Hudson growled so loudly that Judd gave him a startled look before growling in return. "What the fuck, Hudson?"

"Don't talk about her tits," Hudson snarled. "You're my friend, but you even look at her tits, and I'll tear your fucking eyeballs right out of your goddamn head. Got it?"

"Got it," Judd said. "Just calm down, big guy."

Hudson wrapped his hands around the steering wheel. He squeezed tightly as his polar bear snarled and growled. It wanted to be free. It wanted to rip out his friend's throat and drink from the spray of his blood.

The steering wheel creaked beneath his grip. Any minute now, it would simply crack in two. He took a deep breath as Judd, real fear in his voice, said, "Calm down, Hudson. I won't go near your woman. I promise. Just don't shift, buddy."

"She's mine." His voice was low, sounding gargled as he wavered on the brink of his shift. "Mine."

"Yeah, I know. Rosalie is yours. I won't touch her. I swear to fucking God, I won't go near her."

The sincerity in Judd's voice helped calm him, and he released the steering wheel. He ran his hands through his short hair, staring blindly out the windshield.

"Sorry, man," he said.

"That's okay. I didn't realize how bad you had it for Rosalie, that's all," Judd said. "Why aren't you claiming her?"

"She's not into me."

"You asked her out, and she turned you down? Because she seemed to like you just fine at dinner."

"We're just friends. She wants a lion shifter," Hudson said. Even just saying the words made his stomach contents curdle.

"Fucking lion shifters. She know what they're like?" Judd asked.

"She knows."

"Huh, she doesn't seem like the kinky kind to me."

"She's not." He put the truck in gear and drove out of the parking lot.

CHAPTER 6

"Ouch! Son of a motherf'n biscuit!" Rosalie let go of the heavy box. It slid off the tailgate of her truck and hit the pavement with a loud thud. She kicked the box, grunting when it sent pain darting up her foot. She shook her pinched finger, resisting the urge to scream true expletives at the sky above her before cautiously flexing the finger. It didn't seem to be broken, but holy hell, did it hurt. It was red and already swelling a little. A cold wind was blowing, and she was shivering despite her jacket. God, she hated being cold. Another storm was rolling in, and big, fat drops of cold rain were already starting to fall.

"You might have made a mistake, Rosalie," she muttered as she gazed at the pile of boxes in the truck bed. She had dropped by her mother's house after work. That was a definite mistake. Her mom was in a terrible mood, and after only an hour, Rosalie lied and said she needed to leave to pick up a closet organizer.

Sure, she needed a closet organizer, but the one she wanted was heavy and had a lot of parts that needed to be put together. She'd kept putting it off because she was completely hopeless when it came to doing shit like that, not because she was hoping that she might convince Lincoln to pop by during their mutual vacation time and help her put it together.

That was a total bust of an idea. Make that fantasy. She'd lain awake in bed more than a few nights, picturing Lincoln helping her build a closet organizer, then being overcome with lust and carrying her to her bed only a few convenient steps away.

She was so stupid sometimes. Thinking Lincoln would help her build a closet organizer was one of her more ridiculous ideas. He wasn't a 'build an organizer' kind of guy. He was more of a 'have sex while hanging off of a closet organizer' guy.

But, now that she'd told her mother she was buying one, she couldn't put it off any longer. After seeing one news story years ago about a break-in in the townhouse complex next to Rosalie's, her mother was convinced that Rosalie lived in a dangerous part of town and she rarely visited. But she also knew her mother, and it wouldn't be unlike her to drop by unexpectedly just to see the damn closet organizer.

She sighed and stared at the box on the ground. A very nice young man at the store had helped her load the heavier boxes into her truck, and she was kicking herself for not considering how she would get the boxes into the house. She was strong, but most of the boxes were large and heavy as shit.

She chewed on her bottom lip as more rain fell from the sky. Maybe she could drag the heavier boxes.

Call Hudson. He lives five minutes away, and he's Superman strong.

She couldn't call Hudson. Their friendship still felt in the early stages to her, and she didn't want to mess it up by using him as a pack mule. He probably got asked by people to lift heavy shit all the time. She wouldn't do that to him as well. Besides, it was almost seven, and he was working.

He isn't. The bar is closed tonight and tomorrow night for renovations. Remember? Call him.

No. She wouldn't. She was a strong, self-supporting woman who could figure out how to get some heavy boxes into her damn house.

How are you going to get them upstairs to the bedroom?

She'd worry about that later. Right now, she just needed to get them into the house before it really started raining.

She squatted and slid her fingers under one edge of the box.

"Lift with your legs, girl," she muttered before standing and heaving up one side of the box. Gripping the slippery box, she dragged it forward about a foot before it slipped out of her grip and fell on the ground, narrowly missing her foot.

"Goddammit!" She crouched and lifted the box again, staring grimly at her townhouse. The distance seemed like miles, and she shook her hair back when the wind whipped it into her face.

"You can do this, Rosalie. You're a strong woman who can move her own fargin' boxes," she puffed.

She dragged the box a few more inches. "You can do this, you've got this, you can do anything you put your mind... are you kidding me?"

She jumped back as the box slipped out of her grip again and crashed to the ground. Not caring that her neighbours were probably watching and enjoying the show, she kicked the box again.

"You stupid piece of -"

"Rosalie?"

She whipped around, staring in surprise at Hudson standing behind her.

"Hudson? What are you doing here?"

"Going for a walk."

"In the rain?"

He studied the sky before shrugging. "Wasn't raining when I started walking."

"Oh. Right." She cleared her throat as Hudson stared at the box at her feet.

"I bought a closet organizer," she said.

He didn't reply, and she pushed her hair out of her face again. "It's really heavy."

He bent and picked up the box like it weighed nothing. "I'll carry this into the house for you."

"Thank you so much." She hurried in front of him and unlocked the front door, scooping up Mr. Pibbles before he could dart out the front door.

He set it down in the hallway and gave her an expectant look.

"You can just put it in the living room," she said.

"It's for your living room?"

She blushed a little. "No, it's for my bedroom, but I don't want to make you carry it upstairs."

"I don't mind."

He lifted the box and carried it up the stairs. She followed him, trying not to stare at his ass, and quickly put Mr. Pibbles in the spare bedroom before leading Hudson to hers. Silently thanking God that she kept her bedroom neat and tidy, she opened the door.

"You can just set the box on the floor at the end of the bed," she said.

He set it down, and she smiled at him. "Thank you so much, Hudson."

"I'll get the rest of the boxes," he said.

"Oh no, you don't have to..." She followed him back downstairs and outside.

He pulled another box out of the truck bed, frowning a little. "These are heavy, Rosalie. You could have hurt yourself trying to carry them. You should have texted me."

She grabbed one of the smaller, lighter boxes, and they walked back into the townhouse. "I didn't want to bother you."

"It isn't a bother."

"I'm sure you're always asked to help with stuff like this." She followed him up the stairs again. Shit, he really did have an amazing ass.

He shrugged as he set the box next to the other. "Not that often."

Five minutes later, all the boxes were sitting on her bedroom floor. She smiled at Hudson. "Thank you so much. Really. It would have taken me forever to carry all the boxes myself."

"You're welcome."

They stood silently before he said, "I like your bedroom."

"Thanks." For the size of her townhome, her bedroom was large, with an attached bath, a walk-in closet, and a gas fireplace. "Does your townhouse have a large primary bedroom too?"

He shook his head. "No."

"My neighbour to the right has a bedroom the same size as mine, but the one on the left doesn't. Weird, huh?"

"Yeah." He glanced at her neatly made bed, and his cheeks reddened. She wondered if he was too warm. She kept her house cool, but he was a polar bear shifter.

"I should go." He turned and walked out of her bedroom.

She chased after him. "Hudson, wait."

He paused at the top of the stairs, and she said, "I know it's late, but I haven't eaten yet. Do you want to stay for dinner?"

"Sure," he said.

"Great. I'm just going to change out of my work clothes, and then I'll start dinner."

"Okay." He stayed where he was for a moment. "Who's helping you put the organizer together?"

"Oh, uh, I'm doing it myself."

He raised his eyebrows at her. "You can't do it by yourself, Rosalie."

"Why not?" She gave him an indignant look. "Because I'm a woman? Just because I'm female doesn't mean I can't build stuff, Hudson."

"It says right on the box that two people are required to build it," he said.

"Oh." Feeling stupid, she gave him an apologetic look. "Sorry."

"Can you build stuff?" he asked.

She shook her head. "Honestly? No. I suck at it."

He laughed, and a weird, warm flush infused her body. His laugh made her feel a little tingly in the pants if she was being completely truthful.

"You want some help building it?" he said.

"Yeah, if you don't mind?"

"I don't. I'll unpack the boxes while you make dinner and then we can start building it as soon as we eat. Okay?"

"Okay." She smiled happily at him, ignoring how her flush grew when he returned her smile.

"Hudson, are you sure you had enough to eat?" She gave him a worried look as she stood next to him in the closet. She'd made chicken wraps for dinner, and even though she stuffed them with chicken, rice, and vegetables, she was still concerned.

"Plenty," he said.

"Really? Because I could make you another wrap."

"I had four, Rosalie. I'm full, I promise. Hand me the drill."

She handed him the drill, and he attached the shelf. She picked up the next shelf, and he took it from her before eyeing the organizer. "I think I'll need you to hold this one in place while I screw it in."

"Sure."

He shuffled back a few steps and turned to her when she didn't move. "You'll have to stand in front of me, Rosalie."

"Right, of course." Feeling self-conscious and weird, she slid between his big body and the closet organizer. Her closet was spacious, but she wasn't small, and neither was Hudson. They'd been building the organizer together for the last two hours – well, he built it, she mostly just read the instructions to him and handed him screws and nails – and she'd been very careful to make sure to give him a wide personal bubble, even in the tight space of the closet.

He put the shelf in place, and she reached up and held it. A loud boom of thunder shook the organizer, and Mr. Pibbles, sitting in one of the empty boxes, hissed, jumped out of the box, and raced under the bed.

"The storm has gotten really bad," she said.

He nodded as more thunder drowned out the sound of her voice. The lights flickered and dimmed, and they both stared at the ceiling. After a moment, he said, "Ready?"

She nodded and clamped her mouth shut against the gasp that wanted to escape when Hudson leaned forward, and his crotch brushed against the top of her ass. His wide chest and hard abdomen pressed against her back, and she was pretty certain the sudden warmth in *her* crotch was not because Hudson threw off a lot of heat.

His warm breath blew tendrils of her hair into her face as he used the drill to attach the left side of the shelf. She stared straight ahead, trying desperately to ignore the feel of his hard body against hers.

She was not getting turned on. Nope, she absolutely was not. She was not so desperate for sex that just feeling a man's body against hers was making her horny.

Not just any man. Hudson. He's so big, Rosalie. Big and strong, and...c'mon, you're a little curious about how he is in the bedroom. Admit it.

Fine. Maybe she was a little curious. But what woman wouldn't be? She didn't often feel small and delicate, and standing next to Hudson made her feel that way. She wouldn't deny that she liked it. Hell, he could probably even pick her up.

Whoa, slow down there, Rosie. Hudson's strong, but you're almost six feet tall and carrying an extra forty pounds. He'd put his damn back out and then –

"Rosalie?"

She realized that Hudson had finished putting the shelf in, and she was still holding it like an idiot. She dropped her hands and turned around to face him. "Sorry."

He sniffed the air – oh God, could he smell her lust? – and said, "What were you thinking about?"

Desperate to distract him from knowing she was thinking dirty thoughts about him, she blurted out, "Just whether you could pick me up or not."

Shit!

"What?" He gave her a confused look as thunder boomed and the lights flickered again.

"Um, nothing."

She went to dart past him, pulling up short when he put one big arm on the organizer and penned her in. He studied her for a moment. "Explain."

Mortified and wishing she could just sink into the floor, she said, "Uh, it's just that, um, I'm a big girl, and so, uh, my previous boyfriend never, like, lifted me or anything, and I would watch romantic movies and the guy would lift the girl like it was no big deal, right? Only, like I said, girls my size, that never happens to us because we're too heavy. But you're big and strong, and I thought you probably could pick up someone even as heavy as me."

"You want me to... pick you up?" Hudson said slowly.

"I was just thinking you probably could. But then I was all, don't be stupid, Rosalie. He's strong, but he's not that strong, and -"

Rosalie, stop talking! Dear God, stop talking.

She pressed her lips together and stared up at Hudson. "I'm sorry. I don't know what's wrong with me."

He studied her for a few seconds more, and her eyes widened when his heavy arm circled her hips. "H-Hudson? What are you – oh my gosh!"

He lifted her with one arm, and she grabbed his shoulders as her feet left the ground.

"Holy crap. You're going to hurt yourself, Hudson."

"You're not heavy," he said.

She was pressed up against his body, her breasts smushed against his hard chest, the curve of her belly fitted against his flat abdomen. Her face was level with his for the first time since she met him. She studied him unblinkingly, her gaze wandering over his wide cheekbones, firm lips, and the blond stubble along his jaw that was only noticeable up close. She stared into his dark eyes framed with long, dark blond lashes. Man, he had pretty eyes. She always thought she preferred blue eyes, but there was something about the rich chocolate colour of Hudson's that made her feel warm and tingly.

Her gaze dropped to his mouth. He had a great smile. She saw it only slightly more than she heard his amazing laugh, but she loved it when he smiled.

Without thinking, she lifted her hand and brushed her fingertips across his jaw. The rough feel of his stubble brought goosebumps to her skin. He inhaled sharply, and she squeaked in surprise when he abruptly set her down and backed away.

"Hudson, I – I'm sorry. I shouldn't have touched you."

"It's fine." His voice was low and rough. "I just – don't do that again, okay?"

"I won't," she said as there was a huge crack of thunder. The lights went out, and they were plunged into darkness.

"Shit." She turned and fumbled her way toward the closet entrance. She tripped over the pile of empty boxes and went flying forward into the bedroom, landing with a painful thud on her hands and knees.

"Rosalie!" Hudson was suddenly behind her, his big hands hooking under her armpits, and for the second time in less than two minutes, he was picking her up again. He set her on her feet and turned her to face him as lightning flashed across the sky. It lit up the bedroom briefly, and Hudson's look of confusion and embarrassment made her shame grow.

"I'm sorry," she repeated. She yanked her phone out of her pocket and turned on the flashlight.

"Are you hurt?" he asked.

"No, I'm fine."

"Okay. I should go." He started toward the doorway.

"You don't have to leave," she said. "I'm sorry. I won't... I won't touch you like that again."

"No, it's not – it's late and without power, I can't finish the organizer, right?"

"Right." Even to herself, she sounded on the verge of tears, and he hesitated in the doorway.

"Maybe I could come back tomorrow night and finish it," he said.

"You don't have to," she said. "I'm sure I can figure it out from here. There isn't much left to do on it."

"I want to. What time will you be finished with dinner?"

"You could have dinner with me," she said.

He nodded. "Yeah, okay. Around five-thirty?"

"Sure. Can I at least drive you home? It's raining hard," she said.

"No, it's okay. I don't mind the rain, and it's only a five-minute walk. Bye, Rosalie."

"Bye, Hudson."

He left the room and she sank onto the bed before burying her hands in her face. What was wrong with her? She had made Hudson pick her up, and she touched him. He hated both touching her *and* being touched by her. Was it no wonder he left? She'd be surprised if he came back tomorrow night. Hell, she was pretty sure she'd just ruined their friendship.

Mr. Pibbles jumped up on the bed, and she stroked his soft fur as she blinked back the tears. "I'm an idiot, Mr. Pibbles."

CHAPTER 7

"It looks amazing, Hudson. Thank you so much."

He pushed in the last drawer of the organizer. "You're welcome. Thanks again for dinner."

"Of course." Rosalie sounded nervous and unsure, and even though he'd been here for almost two hours, she hadn't looked him in the eye once.

He picked up the drill and the extra screws as Rosalie backed out of the closet. He had fucked up yesterday. Fucked up big time.

He should never have picked her up like that, but after spending two hours in the tiny closet with her, his polar bear was going insane with its need to touch her. When she had started babbling about him picking her up, it had been the perfect excuse.

Yeah, well, you're damn fucking lucky she didn't feel your erection.

He was. Her soft curves pressed against his body, and the touch of her fingers against his face had made him sport a woody in five seconds flat. He'd set her down before she got a good feel of his wood, but it had been a very close fucking call.

Still, his reaction made her feel awful, and that made *him* feel awful. He had to fix this.

Maybe it's better if you don't. You're getting too close to her. You're using whatever excuse you can think of to be near her now. How many times did you fucking walk by her house last night before she finally came home? You're pathetic and being stupid about being around her. It's dangerous for her.

It was, but he was so damn tired of resisting her. He couldn't sleep with her. She would never want him the way she wanted that fucking lion shifter, but spending time with her at least kept his bear from going completely crazy.

He stepped into her bedroom, trying desperately not to stare at her bed. It was piled high with clothing from her closet, but how easy would it be to shove the clothes onto the floor, carry Rosalie to her bed and settle his body between her soft thighs?

Way too fucking easy.

"Hudson?" Rosalie took a deep breath. "I want to apologize again for yesterday. I don't know why I said or did what I did, and I realize it was incredibly inappropriate and made you very uncomfortable. I want to assure you that I won't ever do anything like that again. Okay?"

"I know," he said. "It isn't that big of a deal. I just felt like I was being inappropriate by picking you up, that's all."

"You weren't. I asked you to do it. I mean...sort of."

She sighed and rubbed at her temples. "Anyway, can we just forget what happened last night?"

"Yes."

"Okay, good."

There was a moment of silence before she said, "So, it's

only seven. Did you, uh, want to watch a movie? I could make some popcorn."

He should go home. He should go home and masturbate in the goddamn shower to thoughts of Rosalie like he'd been doing for the last three weeks straight. Instead, he said, "Sure. I'd like that."

"Really?" There was a mixture of surprise and relief on her face.

"Yes."

"Okay, great. I'll start the popcorn, and you can pick the movie." She smiled at him, and his heart skipped an actual goddamn beat. Fuck, he was in deep trouble.

"WHAT DID YOU THINK OF THE MOVIE?"

Rosalie smiled at him. "For a Tom Cruise movie, it wasn't half bad."

"You don't like Tom Cruise?"

"Eh, he's okay."

Hudson grinned and set the empty popcorn bowl on the coffee table. He was sitting on Rosalie's couch next to her. Another stupid idea, but determined to make her feel better, he had insisted they both sit on the sofa when Rosalie had hesitantly moved toward the uncomfortable looking armchair.

"So, I was wondering something."

"What's that?" Hudson stretched his long legs out and tried to ignore the feel of Rosalie's thigh brushing against his.

"Does it hurt when you shift?"

He shook his head. "Nah, mostly it just…tingles."

"How do you shift?" she asked.

"What do you mean?"

"Like, do you say a magic phrase or…"

He laughed. "No. I just call for my bear, and then I shift."

"Oh."

"It's kind of hard to explain."

"Yeah, I imagine it is. You think of your bear as separate from you, right?"

"He *is* separate from me," Hudson said.

"Do you talk to him?"

"We communicate. He talks to me, and I hear it as words, but it's not words. I know that doesn't make sense, but I'm not sure how to explain it. I definitely know when he's happy or angry or…hungry. He's hungry a lot."

She smiled at him. "I bet. Do you ever shift without meaning to?"

He shrugged. "It depends on the situation. If my emotions get the better of me, it can be harder to control my bear."

"So, if you're really sad or something?" she asked.

"More like angry or afraid."

"I doubt you're ever afraid," she said.

"Sometimes I shift while I'm sleeping."

"That would be awkward if you fell asleep on a plane or something."

"I have to be sleeping pretty deep and be fairly relaxed to shift in my sleep," he said.

"Oh. It seriously doesn't hurt when you shift?"

"Nope."

"Weird. It looks like it hurts," Rosalie said.

"You've watched a shift before?"

"Sort of. I watched some YouTube videos." She took a deep breath. "Will you shift and let me watch?"

He turned to study her, and she flushed and looked down at her lap. She brushed some stray Mr. Pibbles' hair from her jeans.

"Why do you want to see me shift?"

"Like I said, I've never seen a shifter change into their animal form in real life, only on YouTube," she said.

He didn't reply, and she gave him a chastised look. "Oh God, is it rude to ask you to shift? I'm sorry. I was just curious about it. I didn't mean to offend, though."

"You didn't," he said. "I've just never had a human ask to watch me shift before."

"I really didn't mean to offend you," she said.

"You didn't," he repeated. "It's just…"

"What?"

"I'm usually naked when I shift."

Her soft mouth rounded into the perfect 'o', and her gaze skittered over his chest as red covered the apples of her cheeks. "Oh God, I forgot about that."

There was silence, and then she said, "I could stand at a distance and hold up a towel in front of your, uh, private parts."

A grin crossed his face, and she gave him a soft slap on the thigh. "Stop laughing at me. It was just an idea. I really want to see you shift."

"All right."

"All right, what?" she said.

"Grab the towel."

"Are you serious?" Her look of unabashed glee made his grin widen.

"Yes."

She jumped off the couch and he heard her run into the guest bathroom before returning with a hand towel. He eyed it and the size of her small living room before shaking his head. "Not big enough."

"What do you mean?"

He pointed at the towel before gesturing to the living

room. "The distance you have to stand back from me – that towel won't be big enough to cover it."

"Cover it... oh. *Oh!*" She studied the towel in her hand, and he was weirdly amused when her flush brightened. "Um, congratulations."

He laughed. "Yeah, thanks."

"Seriously though, it's not big enough?" She glanced at the hand towel and then gave him a doubtful look.

He just shook his head, and she chewed on her bottom lip as her gaze settled on his crotch. Fuck, if she didn't look away in the next three seconds, he was going to get a hard-on. She snapped her gaze to the fireplace as if she'd read his mind. "Okay, I'll be right back."

When she returned from upstairs, he had already removed his socks and shirt. She stared at his naked chest for the briefest of seconds before hurrying to the far side of the living room. She held up the larger towel and said, "Okay, ready."

He studied her silently. She was bright red, and he couldn't quite decipher her expression. "You sure you want to do this? Your face is really red."

"Yes," she said. "I'm just, uh... I'm sure. If you're still okay with it. I can't, uh, see anything below the waist and above the knees, I promise."

He unbuttoned his jeans and thought briefly about telling Rosalie not to peek before deciding against it. He could already smell her embarrassment and didn't want to embarrass her further by teasing her. Besides, she wasn't the kind of girl who peeked.

He shoved his jeans and underwear down and stepped out of them before kicking them to the side. "Ready?"

She nodded, and he closed his eyes. He would never have imagined that he would shift purely for a human's curiosity, but he couldn't resist anything Rosalie asked of him. Besides, it weirdly didn't bother him that she wanted to see it. Her curiosity was just that…curiosity, and he liked that she was interested in his shifting ability.

He called for his bear. His bear surged forward immediately, eager to show his mate how strong and powerful he was and how easily he would protect her and their future cubs.

DON'T YOU DARE PEEK, ROSALIE. DON'T YOU DARE.

As Hudson closed his eyes and his body swelled, she held tight to the towel. She wouldn't look, she wouldn't let the towel dip, no matter how curious she suddenly was about Hudson's penis.

Besides, he was probably totally exaggerating. Sure, he was a big guy, and that meant his penis was probably pretty big, but it wasn't *that* big. It couldn't be. Could it?

The towel dipped just a little in her hand.

Rosalie! Don't you dare peek. Don't you –

She peeked.

As the towel dropped down just enough, she stared wide-eyed at what was – in fact – an incredibly large penis. The largest penis – in fact – that she had ever seen.

Holy forking shirtballs. He wasn't exaggerating.

Rosalie! Stop it, you pervert!

She tore her gaze from the giant penis and straight up into the warm dark brown of Hudson's eyes. They locked gazes for a moment.

He knew.

He knew she looked.

He knew that *she* knew that *he* knew she looked.

Before she could die of complete and utter shame, his eyes closed again, and she watched in fascination as his body swelled to an almost impossible size and thick white fur sprouted out of his skin. She heard his bones cracking, he made a low growl, she blinked, and suddenly, a polar bear stood in her living room.

"Holy shit," she whispered.

Standing on all fours, he stretched slightly before making a low chuffing noise. Rosalie dropped the towel and approached him slowly. She couldn't get over his sheer size. Hudson, in his human form, was an imposing figure. As a polar bear...

She moved even closer. His dark eyes studied her unblinkingly, and he made another low chuff.

"Holy crap," she said. "You're so big. You have to weigh at least a thousand pounds."

She cocked her head and studied him. He was about five feet tall, just on all fours and maybe eight feet long from head to butt.

"Can I touch you?" she asked.

He made a snorting noise, and hoping that was a yes, she reached out with a trembling hand and touched the fur on his shoulder. It was incredibly thick, and she stroked it lightly. He lowered his big, shaggy head, and she made a squeak of surprise when he nudged her hip with his snout. She patted his neck tentatively, and when he leaned his head against her hip, she hesitated for only a moment before digging her fingers into his thick fur and scratching.

She was rewarded with a contented snort, and he twisted his head back and forth. She scratched all around the back of his neck before leaning over him and scratching along his back. He chuffed happily, a low growl spilling from his throat.

She laughed and scratched as much of his big back as she could reach. She could have stood there and scratched and petted him for the rest of the night, but a loud hissing made them turn toward the doorway.

Mr. Pibbles stood in the doorway and hissed again, his back arching and a low yowl rising from his throat. All his fur was standing on end, and he hissed for a third time before turning and racing out of the living room.

"Mr. Pibbles, it's okay." Rosalie smiled at the big polar bear. "I think you scared the crap out of Mr. Pibbles. I'll be right back."

She left the room and called for Mr. Pibbles. He wasn't in the kitchen, so she searched the guest bedroom before checking her bedroom. He was sitting on her bed, staring balefully at her, and she made a soft, soothing sound before sitting next to him. "It's okay, Mr. Pibbles. It was just Hudson. He didn't mean to scare you, Pib-Pib. You're okay."

Mr. Pibbles meowed before standing and rubbing up against her. She petted him again, smiling when he purred loudly.

"Is he okay?"

She glanced at the doorway. Hudson was standing in the doorway, fully dressed.

"Yeah, he's fine. He was just a little scared. It's not every day I have a polar bear in my living room."

To her surprise, he smiled and sat beside her on the bed. Mr. Pibbles made a loud chirp of excitement and bounced across her lap to stand on Hudson's big thigh. He kneaded happily, headbutting Hudson's chest as the big man petted him roughly.

"Well, at least he isn't afraid of you when you're in your human form," she said.

"Nope."

She sat silently for a moment, trying her best not to look at Hudson's denim-covered crotch. Shit, why did she have to peek. She'd never get the image of his giant penis out of her head.

Do you want to, though? Damn, girl. He's packing some serious dick.

Yes, he was. She should be apologizing for looking, but she was too mortified by her behaviour. How would she even begin to apologize for staring at his penis when she had said not a minute earlier that she wouldn't?

She couldn't. And if Hudson didn't bring it up, she sure as hell wasn't going to bring it up.

"What did you think?" he asked.

She stared blankly at him. Was he really asking her what she thought of his penis? Should she tell him what she thought? Because somehow it didn't seem polite to be all, "Your penis is amazing, sir, and I am suddenly very curious as to how it would feel inside of my vagina."

"Uh, it was, um… it was…"

"Shit, I scared you," he said.

Scared? He thought she was scared of his dick? Maybe she *should* have been scared of the sheer size of his penis, but fear wasn't making an appearance. Horniness? Now that was screaming front and center, and holy God, what was wrong with her? She needed to stop thinking about Hudson's damn penis before he smelled her lust for him.

"I'm sorry. When I growled, it wasn't because I was angry or -"

"What? No, I know." Shit, he wasn't talking about his penis.

Rosalie! Stop thinking about his penis!

"It didn't scare me at all, Hudson. I swear." She reached to pat his arm before stopping herself and tucking her hands into her armpits. "It was very cool. Thank you for doing that for me."

"You sure?" He sounded uncharacteristically shy and nervous, and her urge to touch him heightened. She clenched her hands into fists.

"Positive. I was surprised at how big you were. How much do you weigh in your polar bear form?"

"About twelve hundred pounds, I think. Don't know for sure."

"Holy crap. That's wild. Your fur is really thick."

He nodded, and she gave him a tentative smile. "You like having your back scratched, huh?"

"My bear does," he said.

"Right."

"I do, too, though."

She laughed, and he gave her a cute grin. "I'm impressed that you weren't too afraid to touch me."

She smiled at him. "How often does one get the chance to touch a polar bear, you know? Hey, could you understand me when I spoke to you?"

He nodded. "Yes. I'm still in there, and my bear and I understand you. Shifters are different from animals. Different but the same."

"That makes perfect sense," she said teasingly.

He just smiled again at her and petted Mr. Pibbles. The cat was rubbing against him like crazy, and, oh hey, was that jealousy again? Nice. She was jealous over her damn cat touching Hudson. God, she really did need to get laid.

Maybe you should talk to Hudson about teaching you to be kinky.

She almost snorted out loud. Even if Hudson were kinky, which she had no idea if he was or not, he would never agree to it, and it was stupid of her to even consider it. She was just on a high from seeing his beautiful penis.

She needed to remember that he wasn't the least bit attracted to her, and if she even hinted that she wanted to have sex with him, she'd lose his friendship in a heartbeat. The thought of not being his friend anymore made her burgeoning lust disappear just like that.

She sighed and stared morosely at her hands. What was wrong with her? Why was she attracted to men who would never be attracted to her?

Hudson suddenly set Mr. Pibbles on the floor before standing. "It's getting late. I should go."

"It's not that late." She checked her alarm clock. "It's only nine-thirty. We could watch some more TV if you -"

"Nah, I should get going. You have to work in the morning, and I have to be back at the bar tomorrow night. See you, Rosalie."

"Okay, well, thank you again." She followed him out of the bedroom and down the stairs. He slipped his boots on and opened the front door.

"Are we still on for a movie on Sunday?" she asked.

"Yes. I'll text you Sunday morning."

"Right, okay. Good night, Hudson."

"Night, Rosalie."

CHAPTER 8

"Rosalie, you look amazing!" Maggie was waiting for her in the parking lot of Bud's Bar.

"Are you sure?" Rosalie tugged self-consciously at the top of her dress. "It's a little more low-cut than I normally wear, but my boobs are my best asset so..."

"They look fantastic." Maggie eyed her breasts before sweeping her gaze down the rest of her. "That colour looks lovely on you."

"Thank you." She had bought the dress this morning. It was a dark purple, empire waist maxi dress with a scoop neckline that showed off a generous amount of cleavage thanks to her push-up bra. Her heels were short but still brought her height to six feet. She towered over Maggie, and a wave of self-consciousness washed over her.

What she wouldn't give to be short and dainty and feminine like Maggie.

"What's wrong? You're looking a little pale," Maggie said.

"Nothing. I just feel really... tall and big," she said.

"I'd kill for your height," Maggie said. "You look beautiful,

Rosalie. That dress is super flattering, and your hair looks incredible. Did you straighten it?"

She nodded. She'd hit the salon after dress shopping and gotten a blowout. She loved how sleek and straight her hair looked, and she smoothed it down before giving Maggie a hesitant look. "Is my make-up too much? I'm wearing way more than I usually wear."

"Nope, it looks good. *You* look good. The lion shifter won't know what hit him," Maggie said.

"If one even shows up tonight," Rosalie said. "If I can't find a lion shifter, what's the next kinkiest shifter, do you know?"

Maggie laughed. "I have no idea. But there's a lion shifter already in there."

"Seriously? How do you know?"

"I came a bit early and saw him. I confirmed with Judd, and he's definitely a lion shifter."

"Is he...attractive?"

"Yep. He's tall with a good body, beautiful blue eyes, and short blond hair. He's been hitting on women left and right, though, so we need to get in there before he leaves with someone else. Are you ready?"

"I think so." Rosalie took a deep breath and followed Maggie into the bar.

———

HUDSON POURED ANOTHER BEER AND ADDED IT TO THE THREE already sitting on the tray. Tori lifted the tray, the muscles in her slender arms bulging, and gave him a cheerful smile. "Thanks, Hudson."

He grunted out a reply and nodded to the cheetah shifter waving at him from the far end of the long, curved bar. Last night had been insanely busy, and tonight was shaping up to be the same way. It felt like every damn shifter in the city was stopping by to see the renovations done to the bar.

He poured the cheetah's bourbon and took his money, tossing the tip into the jar below the bar before ringing the drink through the cash register. Porter was mixing a margarita, and he grinned at Hudson.

"You doing okay, man?"

"Yeah. Thanks for helping out. I know you got paperwork and shit to do."

Porter shook his head. "It can wait. If this keeps up, though, I'll have to hire another bartender."

"I can come in tomorrow night if you need me to," Hudson said.

"Nah," Porter held up his hand when a rat shifter, her nose twitching wildly, leaned over the bar and tried to get his attention. "One second, ma'am."

He turned the blender on and raised his voice to be heard over the noise. "Tomorrow's your day off, and I'm not gonna make you come in to work."

Hudson shrugged. "I don't mind."

"It'll be fine, but I appreciate the offer."

Hudson stared at the crowd of shifters in the bar. "Well, if you change your mind, just let me…"

"Hudson, what's wrong?" Porter followed his gaze to Maggie and Rosalie and then growled softly. "Do not stare at my mate."

"I'm not," Hudson bit out.

Porter relaxed and sniffed the air. "You like Rosalie, huh?"

Hudson's hand clenched around the beer glass, and Porter clapped him on the back.

"You're going to break that glass. Ease up, would you? I just bought those."

He set the glass down but didn't take his eyes off Rosalie. He couldn't. He leaned forward, using the bar to hide his immediate erection. He could barely breathe, and his polar bear was struck silent for once.

He couldn't blame it. Rosalie looked beautiful. Her usual curly hair was straight and hung down her back in a sleek curtain of soft silkiness. And that dress… he stared hungrily at her tits, at all that unfamiliar pale skin that was begging to be touched and kissed and licked.

Normally, her clothing style was more modest, but this dress clung to her breasts and dipped so low in the front he swore he could see the edge of her bra. A myriad of emotions flowed through him. He wanted to cross the room, pick up Rosalie and carry her somewhere quiet and private where he could have a nice long look and taste of her delectable tits. Another part of him wanted to storm across the room and demand she cover up before other shifters saw what belonged to him.

His polar bear growled. Rosalie and Maggie were walking to an empty table, and every fucking male shifter in the goddamn bar was staring at his woman. The growl escaped his throat when a coyote shifter stared at her tits before touching a lock of her hair as she walked by. Rosalie didn't notice, but Hudson's urge to kill the coyote was over-whelming in its intensity.

Rip his throat out for touching what's ours, his polar bear snarled.

An excellent idea. He'd kill the coyote for touching her, and everyone in the bar would know that she belonged to him. He braced his hand on the bar, about to leap over it, when Porter's hand wrapped around his upper arm.

"Hudson? You all right?"

Only the tiniest shred of his self-control remained. He

pulled his arm out of Porter's grip, but instead of killing the coyote shifter, he turned and braced his hands on the counter behind them. He stared at the rows of liquor bottles gleaming under the lights as he took breath after breath. His polar bear snarled and growled at him, but he ignored it grimly.

"Hudson?"

"Sorry," he rasped. "I'm fine."

"You sure?" Porter gave him a skeptical look. "You're about to shift, man."

"I'm not."

"Maybe you should take a break."

"I don't need one. I'm fine."

"You sure?" Porter asked again.

"Yeah."

"Hey, Porter?" Tori's high-pitched voice grated on Hudson's shredded nerves.

"What is it, Tori?" Porter glanced at the rabbit shifter.

"I need one of whatever the lion shifter is drinking." Tori pointed to the lion shifter standing at the bar's end. He was flirting with a long-limbed tiger shifter who was staring at him with a mixture of amusement and annoyance.

"You don't know what he wants?" Porter said.

"Oh, like, he didn't actually order it," Tori said. "That human girl with Maggie wants me to, like, send him a drink. I think she's, like, totally into him."

"Yeah, okay. Hold on," Porter said.

"Um, is Hudson totally shifting right now?" Tori said.

The roar of his heartbeat in his ears drowned out the sound of Tori's voice. She wasn't wrong. The minute he'd heard her say Rosalie was buying the lion shifter a drink, his polar bear had rushed forward. He held onto the counter's edge like a lifeline as his heartbeat thumped and thudded, and the beard on his face grew thicker. His fangs were out, and the back of his t-shirt ripped with a low purring sound as his body swelled.

Hudson, stop. If you shift, you'll lose your job. Take a breath. Just one breath.

He sucked in air like a man drowning. It helped a little, and he sucked in another breath and then a third. His body returned to normal size, and his bear retreated. It was furious with him, but it retreated.

"You gonna shift on me, or do you have control?"

He turned his head and stared down at his boss. "I have control. Sorry."

Porter studied him for a moment before nodding. "Your shirt's ripped. Go grab a new one from the staff room."

Hudson nodded, and Porter gave him one final scrutiny before walking away.

"Here he comes. Rosalie, are you listening?"

"Hmm...what?" Rosalie continued to stare at Hudson. The big polar bear shifter was standing at the bar, but he hadn't looked her way once. She was considering going up to say hello when Maggie had spoken.

"I said the lion shifter is on his way over," Maggie said.

"Right. Okay, good." She gave Hudson another anxious look. He looked even grumpier than usual, and even from across the bar, she could see the tension in his shoulders and neck. Something was wrong, and she was worried about him. "There's something wrong with Hudson, I'm just going to check and make sure he's -"

"Rosalie!" Maggie's hand clamped down on her arm when she started to stand. "Sit down."

She sat, staring blankly at Maggie. Maggie gave her a pointed look as a low purr drifted into Rosalie's right ear.

"Thank you for the drink, darlin'."

The lion shifter eased his big body into the chair beside her. His gaze lingered on her chest, and she had to fight the urge to tug up the front of her dress a little.

"What's your name, beautiful?" He smiled at her, revealing perfect white teeth. His light blue eyes drifted down her entire body and back up to her tits before finally settling on her face.

"Uh, Rosalie."

"Rosalie. Pretty name for a pretty girl. I'm Koren."

He held his hand out, and she shook it. She blushed a little when he lifted her hand to his mouth and kissed her knuckles.

"It's nice to meet you, Koren."

"You as well, pretty Rosalie."

She swallowed heavily as Koren continued to hold her hand, his thumb rubbing over the pulse in her wrist. He was incredibly handsome, and she waited for her lust to kick in.

C'mon, Rosalie. Be attracted to him.

Yeah, that would help.

She smiled again at the lion shifter. "This is my friend Maggie."

"Hello, Maggie." Koren didn't take his gaze off Rosalie's face. "It's nice to meet you."

"You as well," she said.

Koren studied Rosalie's hair before reaching out and brushing a strand back over her shoulder. "So, I know that your lovely friend Maggie is mated to the wolf shifter who owns this place, but you," he squeezed Rosalie's hand, "are not mated. Is that right?"

"How did you know she was mated to Porter?" Rosalie asked.

"He can smell Porter's scent on me," Maggie said.

Koren grinned at her. "That I can."

"Actually," Maggie said, "if you wouldn't mind keeping Rosalie company, Koren, I need to speak with Porter."

"It would be my pleasure," Koren said.

Rosalie glanced at Hudson again as Maggie squeezed her arm and left. He was pouring a beer, and the mixture of anger and – was that worry? – on his face, ratcheted up her anxiety. What was wrong with him? Did he get some bad news? Was he not feeling well?

"Rosalie?"

She forced her attention back to Koren. "Uh, sorry. What were you saying?"

"I asked why you bought me a drink."

"Well, I, um," her gaze drifted back to Hudson. Shit, he looked upset. Maybe she should forget trying to seduce the lion shifter and find out what was wrong with him.

Rosalie, no! You need to do this. Don't chicken out now, you pansy!

Her inner voice was right. If she wanted to learn to be kinky, she needed to focus and get her head in the game. So what if she wasn't attracted to Koren immediately? She'd talk to him for a bit, have a drink or two, and no doubt she'd start to find him hot. Besides, did she have to be completely attracted to him to sleep with him? No, she didn't.

She made herself focus on the lion shifter still holding her hand. "I bought you a drink because you looked thirsty."

His laugh reminded her of the low throaty purr of a big cat. "Did I?"

"Yes." She turned her hand until she could link fingers

with him and gave him her most confident smile. "Are you sure you don't mind hanging out with me tonight, Koren?"

"Not at all. I am, however, waiting for my brother Keegan. He may join us for... drinks if you're open to that." His smile was full of dark promise.

"Is he a lion shifter as well?"

"He is," Koren said. "He'll be very happy to meet you, I'm certain. He's always had a thing for," his gaze drifted over her body again, "beautiful women with gorgeous curves. Of course, I might be guilty of feeling the same way. Your body is stunning, Rosalie."

"Oh, um, thank you. You have a nice body, too." She took a sip of her drink to ease her dry throat. Already, she was feeling a little overwhelmed by his flirting. No doubt he would be happy to teach her how to be kinky.

And his brother, too, apparently.

Her cheeks flushed. Oh God, was she really going to have sex with two lion shifters tonight? The thought made her a little afraid rather than turned on.

Keep it together, Rosie. You can do this.

Yes, she could. She had to. Still, it wouldn't hurt to slow it down just a bit and ease into the whole 'hey, do you want to have kinky sex with me' thing. She cleared her throat and gave Koren another smile. "So, what do you do for a living?"

"You okay, buddy?" Judd leaned against the bar.

"Fine." Hudson twisted off the cap to a beer bottle and handed it to the deer shifter. She gave him a nervous smile of thanks and handed him some cash before disappearing into the crowd.

"You sure?"

"Why wouldn't I be?"

"Because a lion shifter is hitting on your woman."

"She's not my woman." He kept his gaze on the bar. If he even looked at Rosalie and saw the lion shifter touching her, he'd rip him apart. He was holding on to his self-control by the thinnest of threads.

His hand clenched around the bar rag when he caught a whiff of the lion's scent. He looked up just in time to see the asshole walk down the hallway toward the bathroom. He chanced a glance at Rosalie. She was sitting by herself at the table and staring at him. She gave him a nervous smile and a little wave.

He gave her a short nod, and the smile on her face disappeared. When she mouthed, "What's wrong?" he immediately looked away.

"I can kick the lion shifter out," Judd said. "Make up some excuse and give him the boot so you don't have to watch him keep touching her."

Fresh new anger rushed through Hudson. He glared at Judd. "He's touching her?"

"Uh," Judd shook his head quickly, "probably not. I mean, I don't know. I didn't get a good look at them and -"

Hudson threw the rag into the sink. "Porter? Can I take a five-minute break?"

Porter nodded from the other end of the bar. "Yeah, take your full fifteen."

"Thanks."

"Hudson, don't do anything stupid. Okay?" Judd grabbed his arm.

"Let go of me," Hudson said.

"Just don't do something dumb to that lion shifter," Judd said.

"I just want to talk to him," Hudson said in a low voice.

His fangs dropped, and he bared them at Judd. "Let go of me. I won't ask again."

"Well, shit." Judd released him.

Hudson stepped out from behind the bar and headed down the hallway. The lion shifter was coming out of the bathroom. Surprisingly, the hallway was empty, and Hudson stopped in the middle of it, blocking the lion's path.

The lion cocked his head and looked him up and down. "Excuse me, please."

"Stay away from the human."

The shifter's gaze turned cool, and he gave him an insolent look. "Does she belong to you, polar bear? Because I can't smell even a whiff of your scent on her. Besides, since when do polar bears fuck humans?"

Hudson growled at him, and the lion shifter made a low hiss in return.

"Do not touch her again, lion shifter, or I'll tear you apart."

"She came on to me," the shifter said. "If she's your woman, you'd best get a handle on her before she decides fucking a lion shifter is more fun than fucking a polar bear with anger issues."

Hudson snarled and grabbed the lion shifter by the throat. He slammed him up against the wall and glared at the impudent little prick. "Don't look at her, don't touch her, don't even get within a foot of her, or I'll -"

"Hudson? Hudson, what are you doing? Let him go!" Rosalie hurried forward and grabbed his arm. She yanked on it, her eyes wide and frightened looking. "Hudson, stop."

He released the lion and stepped back, breathing harshly as the lion shifter coughed and then dragged in a breath of air.

"Koren? Are you okay?" When Rosalie tried to get close to

the lion, Hudson growled and wrapped his arm around her waist. He pulled her up against his body as she made a startled noise and stared up at him. "Hudson, what is wrong with you?"

"Don't touch him."

"I...what?"

Koren straightened his shirt and pushed away from the wall. He rubbed at his throat before giving Rosalie a thin smile. He walked away, and when Rosalie tried to follow him back into the bar, Hudson tightened his grip on her waist.

"Koren, wait!" Rosalie called. She yanked on Hudson's arm before glaring up at him. "Hey, let go of me."

He released her but grabbed her hand before she could follow the lion shifter. "Rosalie, come with me."

"What? Where?"

He held her hand tightly as two female raccoon shifters, giggling and swaying drunkenly, wandered into the hallway.

"Oh wow, you're totally the biggest dude I've ever seen. I think I wanna climb you like a tree," the one on the left slurred out and then hiccupped.

Completely ignoring the drunk raccoon shifters, Hudson tugged Rosalie into Porter's office and slammed the door shut behind them.

PORTER'S OFFICE WAS SMALL. ROSALIE BACKED UP UNTIL HER butt hit the edge of his desk. She glared at Hudson when he slammed the door shut and gave her an angry look.

"What's your problem, Hudson?"

"My problem? You're out there trying to pick up a goddamn lion shifter, and you want to know what my problem is?"

"Koren is nice and -"

"You don't know anything about him, Rosalie."

"Do you?"

"No, but that's not the point. He could be dangerous."

"Or he could be a perfectly normal guy who wants to sleep with me."

Hudson's face turned red, and he growled deep in his chest. "You're going to sleep with him?"

"Yes, probably. I think. I mean, if you didn't scare him off, then yeah, yeah, I'm going to sleep with him."

His scowl was so deep she could practically climb into it. "No, you're not. You are not taking that lion shifter home."

Her mouth dropped open. "I'm an adult, and you don't get to tell me what to do. If I want to sleep with a lion shifter, I will, and you can't stop me."

He growled again, and she glared at him. "Growl all you want. I'm not afraid of you."

"I thought you were in love with that idiot Lincoln," he said. "I thought you wanted to fuck him."

Now, it was her turn to go red. "Stop being crude."

"It's the truth, isn't it?"

"Yes, but you don't have to be so, so -"

"If you're in love with the stupid lion, then why are you going to fuck a different stupid lion?"

Her temper flared. "For practice, okay? Lincoln likes kink, and I have two weeks to learn and practice some sex stuff before I ask him out."

"Two weeks to practice," he repeated.

"Yes." She tugged at the top of her dress. "I don't have much experience, and I need to change that if I'm going to seduce Lincoln so…"

"How many shifters are you planning on sleeping with?"

"Not that it's any of your business, but as many as it takes to learn to do what Lincoln wants in bed," she said, "and before you start slut shaming me, there's nothing wrong with a woman having multiple sex partners if that's what she -"

"No."

"No, what? Why are you growing a beard?" Her eyes widened as the shoulder seams of his t-shirt ripped. "Are you shifting? Stop shifting!"

He took a deep breath, and she watched in fascination as his body slowly returned to normal size and the beard faded from his jaw.

"You're not sleeping with other shifters," Hudson said.

"Uh, yeah, I am," she said.

"No."

"Stop saying no! I need to learn how to be kinky and -"

"I'll teach you."

"If I even want to have a chance at winning over Lincoln, I have to stop being so shy in bed and start... what did you say?" She stared at the giant bear shifter.

"I'll teach you how to be kinky in bed."

She gaped at him and then burst into laughter. "Good one, Hudson. Seriously, that was funny. But, if you don't mind, I need to see if Koren -"

"I'm not joking, Rosalie." Hudson stepped toward her.

Her laughter died out. "You are. Of course, you are."

"I'm not."

"But you're not attracted to me. You hate it when I touch you. You won't even be able to..."

He stepped even closer. Even with her heels making her six feet, she still had to stare up at him as he rested his big hands on the desk on either side of her. "Won't even be able to what?"

"Get it up." Her voice came out in a high squeak that didn't sound remotely like her usual voice.

"Are you saying I'm impotent?"

"What? No, no, I'm not saying that." She couldn't seem to look away from his gaze. "I'm saying you're not attracted to me, so you're not going to…"

Her voice ended in another of those weird little squeaks when he traced one thick finger over her collarbone.

"H-Hudson, what are you doing?"

He bent his head and sniffed her neck. "A shifter would have to be blind or stupid not to be attracted to you, little human. Do you think I'm stupid?"

"No, but… you don't like to be touched by me," Rosalie whispered.

He gave a lock of her hair a gentle tug before bending his head again. This time, he licked her collarbone and every muscle deep in her lower belly clenched. She was suddenly finding it hard to breathe, and her nipples were hard points against the fabric of her bra.

Oh God, was she getting wet?

She was getting wet.

For Hudson.

Desperate to regain control, she lied through her teeth. "I'm not attracted to you."

He laughed, that warm, deep laugh that she heard so rarely. It had the same effect it always did. Butterflies swarmed to life in her stomach, and goosebumps rose on her arms.

"There you go, trying to lie again, little human."

"I'm not lying. I'm not -"

His lips pressed against hers as one heavy arm curled around her waist. He drew her up against him, and she grabbed his arms, sinking her fingers into his hard flesh. Dear God, was he – was that his erection pressing against her belly?

He sucked on her bottom lip before pressing soft kisses against her mouth. He teased and coaxed, licking the seam of her lips with the tip of his tongue as his big hand rubbed her lower back through her shirt. He was being so damn gentle. Until now, she would never have believed this type of gentleness could exist in Hudson.

"Open your mouth, sweet Rosie." His low voice saying her nickname sent fresh arousal through her. She opened her mouth immediately.

He growled his approval and licked her upper lip before sucking on it. He traced her bottom lip with his tongue before kissing his way to her ear. He sucked on her earlobe, and her heart banged against her ribcage. She was growing increasingly distracted by the low pleading for a kiss. Who the hell was sounding so desperate? So needy?

"Shh, little Rosie." Hudson's breath tickled her ear. "I'll give you what you need."

Holy shit. *She* was the one pleading.

Another low moan slipped out. "Hudson, please kiss me."

He nipped her bottom lip, and she moaned happily when he slipped his tongue into her mouth. He angled his mouth over hers, his hand threading through her hair and cupping the back of her skull to hold her steady as he tasted her. She rubbed her tongue against his, slid her arms around his waist, and shoved her hands up the back of his shirt. His skin was deliciously hot against her fingertips. She pressed herself up against that hard length digging into her belly.

He kissed her repeatedly. Kissed her until she was weak and trembling and fuzzy-headed. There was a gentleness in each brush of his mouth against hers, but she could sense the hunger beneath it. Like he was holding back, maybe. Like he was afraid he would hurt her or scare her.

"I want more," she breathed against his mouth. She

reached for his big hand where it rested against her hip, and tried to tug it to her breast. "More, Hudson."

She was frantic for his touch. She wanted to see what was under that gentleness. She wanted to make him lose control.

"Not here, Rosie."

"Yes!" If she hadn't been so damn horny, she might have been embarrassed by the whine in her voice. "Hudson!"

He kissed her again, but she couldn't pry his hand away from her hip no matter how hard she tried. She stood on her tiptoes and rubbed her aching pussy directly against his erection. It brought a low groan from his throat, and excitement rushed through her. His hand tightened on her hip, and she rubbed against him again.

"Please." She licked his mouth, and his low growl sent a wave of lust through her. She licked his mouth again and scratched her nails across his lower back. "Please."

His second growl was louder. Hungrier. He kissed her hard just as the door to Porter's office opened.

"Hudson, are you... shit."

Hudson pulled away from her, and she staggered back against the desk. She stared wide-eyed at Judd standing in the doorway.

"You can't do this in here, man. Porter's a good guy, but he'll fire you for fucking a human in his office," Judd said.

"We weren't, he wasn't..." Rosalie touched her swollen mouth as Hudson made a sound of frustration.

The three of them stood in silence before Rosalie straightened her back. "I have to go."

"Rosalie, don't let the lion shifter touch you," Hudson said.

She turned to him, ready to let loose with a barrage of indignant and well-deserved retorts about how he didn't have the right to tell her who she could or couldn't touch.

The look of intensity on his face shut her mouth with a snap. She nodded mutely.

"Promise me," he said.

"I promise," she whispered before pushing past Judd and walking rapidly down the hallway and back into the bar. She needed to find Maggie and get the hell out of there before Koren tried to touch her. If Hudson saw Koren touching her, he'd kill him. She was sure of it.

Don't be stupid, Rosalie. Hudson wouldn't kill a guy just for touching you. God, you really think you're all that, don't you?

She almost laughed when she saw Koren. Her fear had been for nothing. The lion shifter was back standing at the bar, already flirting with another woman.

"Rosalie? What the hell is going on?" Maggie was suddenly standing next to her, and Rosalie grabbed her hand.

"I want to leave. Please, can we leave?"

Maggie studied her face. "Your mouth is swollen. Oh my God, did Koren hurt you? Did he -"

"No, no, nothing like that," Rosalie said. "Something's happened, and I need to talk – can we go somewhere more private?"

"Of course." Maggie squeezed her hand, and Rosalie followed her out of the bar.

CHAPTER 9

"You're shaking, Rosalie." Maggie gave her a look of concern.

"Just feeling a little chilled." She sipped at her coffee before glancing around the coffee shop. It was about half-full, but Maggie had snagged them a table in a quiet corner. "So, this is where you work, huh?"

Maggie nodded. "Tell me what happened back at the bar, honey."

Rosalie sighed. "I kissed Hudson."

Maggie's mouth dropped open. "You kissed Hudson? Polar bear shifter Hudson?"

"Yeah."

"When? Why? How? I mean, I know how, but… why?" Maggie asked. "I thought you guys were just friends."

"We are just friends. I mean, I think we are… shit, I don't know." Rosalie wrapped her cold fingers around her coffee cup. "Koren went to use the men's room. Hudson went down the hallway after him, and I – I don't know, but I just had this bad feeling, you know? I was right. When I got to the hallway, Hudson had Koren up against the wall and was choking him."

"What? Why?"

"I don't know. I told Hudson to let him go, and he did, but when I tried to leave with Koren, he wouldn't let me. He said I needed to stay away from him and couldn't touch him."

Maggie frowned. "That's weird."

"No, what's weird is that I made out with Hudson in Porter's office!" Her voice was rising, and a guy in a knitted cap reading an iPad glanced at them.

Rosalie took a deep breath and another sip of coffee. "Hudson and I went into Porter's office, and he was mad that I was hitting on Koren. He kept asking why I even wanted to sleep with him and acting like he was in charge of me, and I finally just lost my temper and told him the truth."

"Uh oh," Maggie said.

"Yeah, only slightly humiliating," Rosalie said. "Only, Hudson didn't... I mean, he outright told me I wasn't allowed to sleep with other shifters to learn how to be kinky. When I told him it wasn't his decision to make and that I'd sleep with any shifter I wanted, he said he'd teach me to be kinky in bed."

"Oh." Maggie sat back in her chair. "I was not expecting that."

"Me either," Rosalie said. "He doesn't even like to be touched by me... ever."

Maggie raised her eyebrows, and Rosalie said, "It's true. Normally, he practically flinches if I get close to or touch him. But tonight, he..."

"He what?"

"He had an erection," Rosalie whispered. "When he said he'd teach me, I thought it was a joke. Only, he-he licked me, and then he pulled me up against him, and I could feel his... and then he started kissing me."

"And then what?" Maggie asked when she didn't say anything else.

"Then I kind of lost my mind," Rosalie said. "He's a really good kisser."

She stared at her coffee. She knew she sounded stupid, but she was utterly and completely disarmed by what had just happened with Hudson. She touched her lips. They were still slightly swollen, and she could feel her cheeks heating up. She'd begged Hudson to kiss her, had tried to make him touch her tits, *and* rubbed up against him like a cat in heat.

"Oh my God," she groaned and dropped her head into her hands.

"What's wrong?" Maggie asked.

"What's wrong?" Rosalie raised her head and gave Maggie a look of disbelief. "I kissed Hudson. I kissed him, and I tried to make him touch me, and then I rubbed myself up against his dick like a-a whore."

"Wait, I thought Hudson kissed you."

"He did, but I... I tried to take it further, right there in Porter's office, Maggie. If Judd hadn't interrupted, I probably would have started begging Hudson to bang me."

She closed her eyes and concentrated on pushing air in and out of her lungs in long, slow breaths. Her heart was pumping too fast, adrenaline was shooting through her veins, and she felt like she was on the edge of hyperventilating.

"Better?" Maggie asked after a few minutes.

Rosalie nodded and opened her eyes. "Sorry. I'm kind of freaking out here."

"It's okay. But, Rosalie, *why* are you freaking out? The way

I see it, this is a good thing. You and Hudson are friends, right?"

"Yeah."

"So, why not let him teach you to be kinky? It's better than just sleeping with some random shifter. Honestly, I was never really comfortable with you sleeping with guys you didn't know, but I wanted to be supportive, and, well, you're an adult, so you can make your own choices. But still... I'd feel a lot better if you were learning to get your kink on with someone you know."

"Maggie, I can't have sex with Hudson."

"Why not?"

"Because it's Hudson! Because he hates it when I touch him. Because he's not attracted to me."

"Yeah, I think tonight established that he is attracted to you." Maggie glanced around before lowering her voice. "Most guys don't get a full-on erection just from licking a woman, Rosalie."

Rosalie blushed furiously. "Maybe it was just some weird random blip. Like, he was acting strange before I even talked to him. Maybe something else had happened, and it just made him..."

"Start kissing you?" Maggie shook her head. "I don't think so."

"It could be," Rosalie insisted. "Maggie, you don't know Hudson the way I do. This is just so weird of him. Why would he kiss me? Why would he offer to teach me to be kinky? This isn't him."

"You haven't known him for that long," Maggie said, "and didn't you tell me before that you just started to talk more? Maybe he's been attracted to you all along, and you just didn't know it."

"Nope," Rosalie said immediately. "He wasn't – isn't –

attracted to me. I guarantee you he's already regretting what happened in Porter's office. He just had a moment of insanity, and I'll be lucky if he even talks to me after this. In fact -"

Her cell phone buzzed, and she pulled it out of her pocket, her eyes widening. "Shit."

"What?"

"Hudson just texted me."

"What did he say?"

Rosalie swallowed heavily. "That we-we'd have our first lesson tomorrow night, and I'm to meet him at his place at seven."

"Huh," Maggie sipped delicately at her coffee before smiling at Rosalie. "Guess it's not quite a moment of insanity, after all."

Rosalie didn't reply. She was texting furiously, and when she was finished, Maggie said, "What did you text back?"

"That we needed to talk, and he could come by my place tomorrow afternoon."

Her phone buzzed, and Maggie grinned. "Well?"

"He just said okay," Rosalie replied.

"That's good. You can discuss ground rules and find out if Hudson is even kinky. I mean, no point in having him teach you how to be naughty in bed if his idea of kink is, I dunno... doggie style sex or something."

Rosalie blushed furiously. "Maggie!"

"What?"

"I'm not doing this with Hudson. I can't do this with him."

"Why not?"

"I told you!"

"Tell me the real reason," Maggie said.

Rosalie stared at her for a moment before her shoulders slumped. "Fine, you want the truth? I don't have many friends. In fact, I have two friends – you and Hudson – and I don't want to lose him as a friend. *And* I'm still not convinced that he's just not high on something, and tomorrow, when he's back to normal, he'll freak out."

Maggie shrugged. "I don't think Hudson is the type to do drugs. But your point about not losing him as a friend is valid, so I understand. Still, when you talk to him tomorrow, and he's still interested in helping, you should seriously consider it. Hudson knows you're in love with Lincoln, right?"

"Yes."

"So, for him, it's probably just about getting to have sex without any strings attached."

Rosalie flinched, and Maggie frowned. "Does that bother you? I thought that's what you were looking for."

"It is," she said. "It doesn't bother me, it just… I didn't think Hudson was the kind of guy who was into casual sex."

"I'm not judging him," she said hastily when Maggie didn't reply. "I'm not. I mean, I'm looking for the same thing, right? So, I'm not judging him. I just don't want to lose his friendship."

"So, tell him that. Be very clear about it, and if either of you think you can't remain friends for any reason, you don't do it."

Rosalie hesitated. Maybe this would work. She needed someone to teach her, so why couldn't it be Hudson? Truthfully, she'd never felt very comfortable at the idea of sleeping with shifters she didn't even know. She would never sleep with a random guy if it weren't for how badly she wanted to be with Lincoln.

Rosalie, it's Hudson. He isn't attracted to you. You're trying to decide on something that will never happen. Relax, would you? Tomorrow, you'll get a text from Hudson explaining that he was drunk or high or something, and you'll return to how it was with him.

"Rosalie?"

She smiled at Maggie. "You know what? It doesn't even matter. Tomorrow, when whatever he's on wears off, he'll either have forgotten about what happened, or he'll apologize, and we'll move on."

Maggie cocked her head at her. "Okay, if that's what you want to believe, I'll go with that. So, it's not that late. Do you want to go to another club and find a lion shifter?"

Rosalie shook her head. "Uh, no, I don't think so. I'm pretty tired, and it's been a weird night. I'm on vacation now, so I'll try again at the shifter bar tomorrow night. Hudson doesn't work Sundays, so I won't have to worry that he'll get weird again."

"I'm working tomorrow night," Maggie said.

Rosalie smiled at her. "I'll be fine by myself."

Maggie frowned. "I'll ask Porter to make sure that any shifter you talk to is a good guy, okay?"

Rosalie blushed. "I don't want him to know what I'm doing."

"I won't tell him. I'll just let him know that you're going to be there and ask him to tell you if a shifter you're talking to is a… wanker."

Rosalie smiled a little. "Okay, thank you, Maggie."

"You're welcome, honey. Just be careful tomorrow night. All right?"

"I will."

"And for God's sake, text me and let me know what happens with Hudson tomorrow. I'll be on pins and needles waiting."

HUDSON KNOCKED ON ROSALIE'S DOOR AT PROMPTLY TWO o'clock. He didn't get nervous, but if his father were here, he'd take one look at Hudson and announce that he was as anxious as a long-tailed cat in a room full of rocking chairs.

His father would be right.

His back was sweating, his legs felt weirdly weak, and the sandwiches he'd eaten for lunch were threatening to come back up. If Rosalie didn't agree to this, his polar bear would lose its fucking mind. He'd have no choice but to pack up and haul ass out of the city.

No! His polar bear nearly howled with rage. *I will not leave my mate.*

She's not your mate. Stop saying that.

She's mine. She's mine, and I'll kill anyone who touches her.

He clenched his hands into fists. His polar bear might think Rosalie was his mate, but it was wrong. He couldn't make Rosalie his mate.

Then why are you going to have sex with her?

Because there was no way in hell, he was letting some other fucking shifter touch her. If Rosalie were insistent on learning how to be kinky for that goddamn lion shifter, then he would be the one to teach her. Letting her sleep with some random shifter she didn't know was not happening.

You're putting her in danger.

No, he wasn't. In fact, this was his way to get what he wanted without putting Rosalie in danger. He could finally sleep with her, finally know what she tasted like, how she looked when she had his cock in her, and not have to worry that she would want more.

He'd been wrong about her not being attracted to him. He'd realized that the moment he'd licked her. Her arousal had been strong and instant. If Judd hadn't walked in on them, Hudson would have given in to her demands and fucked her right there. He'd been almost as giddy as a teenager when he'd smelled her lust.

Still, just because she was attracted to him didn't mean she loved him. She was in love with the lion shifter, which was a good thing. She wouldn't ask Hudson for anything more than a few sex lessons, and he wouldn't have to worry about her falling for him.

Corden wanted revenge for the death of his son, and he wouldn't hesitate to use Rosalie as leverage, but that would only work if Corden thought Hudson cared for her. If he wanted to keep Rosalie safe, he could never have a relationship with her, but a few meaningless nights of sex were fine.

What about when you're done? When she decides she's learned enough from you, takes all her new knowledge, and seduces the lion shifter, what then?

She's my mate, his polar bear snarled immediately. *She's mine, and no one else can have her.*

The door opened, and he tuned out his polar bear's insistent growls. When Rosalie was finished with him, he'd leave the city and start over again. Simple as that.

"What are you doing here?" she asked.

She was wearing jeans and a t-shirt that hugged her breasts. He tried not to stare at her chest. Hell, why hadn't he at least touched her breasts last night? She'd wanted him to, and if she didn't agree to this, he'd never get the chance to touch them.

He wiped his sweaty palms on his denim-clad thighs. "You told me to come over this afternoon to talk."

"I know, but I..."

"What?"

"I didn't think you would."

He frowned. "Why wouldn't I?"

149

"I don't ..." she glanced around the neighbourhood before stepping back. "Come in."

He shut the door behind him and followed her into the kitchen. He sat in his usual seat and petted the cat when it jumped into his lap. Rosalie was standing by the counter and chewing on her bottom lip, and she jumped when the tea kettle whistled on the stove.

She shut off the burner, and he stood when he saw her hand trembling. "Rosalie, sit down. I'll make the tea."

"I hate tea. I was going to have some honey and lemon in hot water." She pointed to the jar of lemon-flavoured honey sitting next to her mug.

"Sit down. I'll make it."

She sat, and he grabbed another mug and poured hot water in both before adding a few teaspoons of honey to each mug. He stirred them and then brought the mugs to the table, setting one in front of her.

He sat down, and she took a sip before smiling faintly at him. "It's good. Thank you."

"Are you all right, Rosalie?"

He heard the click in her throat when she swallowed. "Yes, I... do you remember what happened last night?"

He frowned at her. "Of course, I remember. Why?"

"I thought maybe you were drunk or high on something."

"Why would you think that?"

She stared at him. "Because we kissed, Hudson."

"We did," he said.

"We need to talk about this," she said.

"You're right. Are you on birth control?"

She gave him a blank look. "Am I on..."

"Birth control," he repeated.

"Yes, why?"

"I don't like wearing condoms. I'm infection free. I'll show you my medical records if you'd like."

Her mouth dropped open. "Hudson, this isn't... I mean, whether or not you're STI free is not what I want to talk about."

"What do you want to talk about?"

"What do I want to... oh my God, what is going on with you? We kissed last night. You told me you'd have sex with me...what do you think I want to talk about?"

He took a deep breath. He needed to get this right. He needed to say exactly the right thing to convince Rosalie that she should use him for goddamn sex practice instead of some other random shifter.

"Why did you kiss me?" She asked suddenly. "You're not even attracted to me, for God's sake."

"I am," he said. "I'm attracted to you, Rosalie, but I'm not looking for a relationship, so I never acted on it. Not to mention that you're in love with a lion shifter, so it would have made me a real dog to tell you that I wanted you."

She stared into her mug. "You seriously are attracted to me."

"Yes."

"Why don't you want to be in a relationship?" She lifted her head to study him.

"Polar bears are loners," he said. "It's not unusual for my kind to never marry or have a family."

"Oh."

"But it doesn't mean that I want to live the life of a monk," he said. "Which is why I'm volunteering to help you. We both get what we want, right? You learn some new skills, and I get laid."

She flinched a little, but he didn't apologize for his blunt-

ELIZABETH KELLY

ness. Maybe if he told himself repeatedly it was just about the sex, he'd start to believe it.

"C'mon, Rosalie," he made his voice light, "this is perfect for both of us. You know it is."

"Are you even kinky?" She blushed furiously but kept his gaze. "I know how to have sex. What I want to know is how to have kinky sex."

"That won't be a problem," he said. "I can teach you everything you want to know."

"How do I know that for sure?" she said.

He grinned at her. "You'll just have to trust me, little human."

She chewed again at her lip. "Are you sure you don't want to be in a relationship? Because if you do want a relationship, then what I'm doing is just using you, and that makes me feel awful."

"I'm positive," he lied. "This is exactly what I want, Rosalie."

She studied him for over a minute before finally saying, "I don't want it to ruin our friendship. Being your friend is very important to me, Hudson."

"It won't," he said. "We both know exactly what this is and what to expect. It won't ruin our friendship. Look, it's because I'm your friend that I want to do this for you. The thought of you sleeping with random shifters that you know nothing about worries me. I want you to be safe, and you'll be safe with me."

"Have you slept with a human before?" she asked.

"No, but I know how to be gentle, Rosalie. I won't hurt you."

"I know that." She scowled at him before sighing. "Listen, I appreciate your willingness to help, but, uh, I'm just not attracted enough to you to -"

"That's bullshit. You're attracted to me," Hudson said.

She glared at him and stood up. She crossed to the counter and stared out the window. "I didn't say I wasn't attracted to you. I said I wasn't attracted to you *enough* to sleep with you."

He stood and moved to where she was standing, resting his hands on the counter on either side of her. She stiffened and kept her back to him when he let his body brush against her. He inhaled the scent of her hair, resisting the urge to nuzzle her neck.

"You think I didn't see you checking out my dick when I shifted, Rosalie? You liked what you saw, didn't you? How many times have you wondered whether your little pussy could take all of it? How many times have you pictured being under me, your legs spread around my hips, watching as I slide my dick into your tight pussy?"

"Hudson," she moaned.

He was already fully erect, and he pressed his dick against her ass, making a low sound of appreciation when she ground against him. "I'll go slow, sweet Rosie. I'll give you every inch of my dick until you're full, until the only thing you can feel is how good it is to have my cock inside of you."

He gave in to temptation and nuzzled the soft skin of her throat. "I can smell how wet you are for me. Just like I could smell your wetness last night."

Her cheeks were a bright red, and he pressed a kiss against the line of her jaw. "Turn around."

She turned to face him. He pushed one thick thigh between hers, forcing her to straddle it. He rubbed it against her pussy, smiling in satisfaction when she moaned again and gripped the counter behind her. Her hips arched, and she gave him a hazy look of need.

He leaned down until his mouth was just above hers. He

ELIZABETH KELLY

was playing dirty pool, using Rosalie's lust for him to convince her to say yes, but he didn't care. Now that he knew she wanted him, if she didn't let him into her bed, he'd go crazy.

"Say yes, little Rosie," he breathed against her mouth. "Let me show you how good I can make you feel."

"Yes," she whispered and pressed her mouth against his.

Her tongue licked at his lips, and he parted them so she could slide it into his mouth. He sucked on it until she ground her pussy against his thigh. His erection was huge, and he pressed it against her hip.

"Can you feel how much I want you?" He nipped at her bottom lip.

"I want you too," she moaned. "Let's go upstairs and -"

He felt the vibration of her cell phone against his dick before they heard it ring. She groaned, and he pulled back a little so she could yank it from her pocket. She studied the screen. "It's my mom. I'm sorry, I have to take it, or she'll keep calling."

He nodded and stepped back, staring at her flushed cheeks. He wanted to cup her breasts but instead shoved his hands into his pockets as she answered her phone.

"Mom? Hey, can I call you later? This is a bad time, and... what? Okay, calm down. It's just a plugged sink. Leave it for tonight, and in the morning, call a plumber and..."

She closed her eyes and rubbed at her temples. "Now isn't a good time for me to come over, and I don't know a thing about plumbing. Just use the bathroom sink for tonight and in the morning... no, I don't... yes, I know Mrs. Nester's daughter comes over every Sunday, but I spent most of yesterday with you and..."

Hudson frowned when Rosalie sighed. "Yeah, okay. I'll be right over."

154

She hit the end button and gave him an apologetic look. "I have to go over to my mother's for a bit. Her kitchen sink is plugged, and she's freaking out and wants me to try to fix it."

"I can go with you and look at it," he said.

"Oh God, no."

From the look on her face, you'd think he'd said he would fix her mother's sink while butt naked.

"It's no big deal," he said. "I'm pretty handy with stuff like that and -"

"No," she said. "I can handle it."

He nodded, trying to ignore the hurt he felt. So what if Rosalie didn't want her mother to meet him? They were friends, not dating, for God's sake.

As if she'd read his mind, Rosalie said, "It isn't you. My mother is difficult, and if I brought a guy over, she'd freak out and ask a bunch of questions and... trust me, you don't want to meet her."

"Yeah, okay." He sounded cranky and put out, and he made himself smile at her. "So, you'll come by my place around seven?"

"Um, yeah, that should work. I should be done at my mom's by then. Are you sure you want to do this, Hudson?" she asked.

"Positive. See you later, Rosalie."

"Bye, Hudson."

He left before she could change her mind. He tried to control his excitement and trepidation as he headed back to his townhouse. Everything would be fine. This wasn't putting Rosalie in danger. He would sleep with her a few times, and then she'd start dating the lion shifter, and he'd leave. He'd never see her again, and with time, his bear would forget all about her.

Like hell, I will. I'm not leaving my mate.

He broke into a jog and ignored his bear's angry growl.

CHAPTER 10

R*osie, are you really going to do this?*
She pulled her jacket around her tighter and walked down the sidewalk to Hudson's complex. Considering Hudson's townhouse was only a five-minute walk from hers, she had left her car at home. She'd also hoped the fresh air and brisk walk would help her pounding head.

She hadn't really slept last night, and the lack of sleep, combined with four hours of dealing with her mother, had given her one skull thumper of a headache. She couldn't fix the sink, which had stressed and upset her mom, and Rosalie had stayed longer than she'd wanted to just to calm her down. She'd found a few numbers for plumbers and written them down for her mother to call in the morning.

If you were a good daughter, you'd go over there tomorrow and call them for her.

She winced. She hadn't told her mother she was on holiday. If she had, her mother would have called every day, insisting Rosalie spend time with her and that she needed her for every little thing.

She loved her mother, but the thought of spending two

weeks at her mother's beck and call made her shudder. Besides, she'd been planning to seduce Lincoln, which would have been impossible if her mother knew she was on vacation.

So, now you're going to seduce Hudson instead? You're an awful person, Rosalie. What kind of woman is in love with one man but will fuck another?

He's fine with it, she argued. *Hudson wants this. He wants to get laid, remember?*

Well, I guess if you're fine with acting like a whore, then it's all good.

She rubbed at her temples as she walked slowly toward Hudson's home. Fuck, now her inner voice was sounding remarkably like her mother.

Not that it wasn't wrong. She had a feeling that a big part of her apprehension about doing this was how it made her look. More accurately – the way it made her look to Hudson.

So then don't do it! You can change your mind, Rosalie.

She could. Except she didn't want to. Wrong or right, she was attracted to Hudson, and she wanted to know what it was like to have sex with him. Under all her worry and anxiety that she was making the wrong choice, a big part of her couldn't stop thinking about that kiss in Porter's office.

What about this afternoon? You liked it when he talked dirty to you. Admit it.

She blushed, and the extra rush of blood made her head ache even more. Yeah, maybe she did like it. She'd had zero idea that Hudson even thought things like that, let alone would say them to her, and even her usual shame at knowing he could smell her lust for him was a little muted.

Wet. He said he could smell how wet you were for him.

Standing at the edge of the sidewalk leading up to Hudson's home, she paused, trying to control the crazy beat of her heart. Was she seriously going to do this? She'd always considered herself a nice girl, but nice girls didn't sleep with other men when they were in love with someone else.

She was on the edge of bolting when the door to Hudson's place opened, and he stepped out onto the front step. "Hey, Rosalie."

"Uh, hi." She stayed where she was, and he gave her a small smile.

"Come in, okay?"

She chewed on her bottom lip before nodding and walking the few steps to his house. She followed him inside and removed her shoes and jacket. He hung the coat in the closet as she smoothed her t-shirt nervously.

"Sorry, I'm a little late," she said. "I was at my mom's place longer than I thought, and I wanted to shower before I came over, so…"

She stared at the floor. She was late because she couldn't decide what to wear after her shower. Did she dress sexy? Did she wear something that showed a little cleavage? Her head had been hurting too much to make a proper decision. It felt weird and almost wrong to be dressing up for Hudson. It wasn't that kind of relationship. It was just sex.

She'd stripped off her dress and kicked the stupidly high heels she had bought on a whim and never worn into the corner. She'd finally settled on a matching bra and panty set, throwing her usual t-shirt and jeans over them.

"That's fine," Hudson said. "Did you get things sorted out at your mom's?"

"I couldn't fix the sink, but I found a few plumbers for her to call in the morning." She continued to stare at her feet.

"You're on vacation this week, right?"

"The next two weeks, actually," she said.

"Right. Are you going to your mom's in the morning?"

She shook her head, grimacing when it made pain dance across her forehead. "No, I didn't tell my mom I'm on holiday."

He didn't reply, and she folded her arms over her torso. "I know how that makes me sound, but if I tell her I'm on vacation, she'll expect me to spend all my time with her."

"Rosalie, look at me."

She could feel Hudson's gaze on the top of her head. Suddenly near tears, she made herself look at him and smile. "So, you got my medical records that I emailed, right? I assume you did because I got your email with your records and -"

"Rosie, shh."

She pressed her lips together as Hudson slipped his arm around her waist. "You're pale. Did you eat?"

She shook her head. "No, but I'm not hungry."

"You should eat."

"I can't," she whispered as a tear slipped down her cheek.

He wiped it away with his thumb before stepping back and opening the closet. "Come on, I'll walk you home."

"What? I thought we were going to… I mean, why?"

He smiled at her, but she could see the disappointment in his eyes. "Because you don't really want this, Rosalie."

She shook her head and refused to take her jacket when he held it out to her. "No, I do. I want this."

He studied her, and she wiped at the tears collecting in her eyelashes. "I'm just a little tired, and it's been a stressful day, and I have a really bad stupid headache. But I want this, Hudson, okay? Please don't make me leave."

"Okay." He took her hand and led her down the hallway. His townhouse had the same floor plan as hers, and she hesitated when he tugged her into the living room.

"Aren't we going to go to your bedroom?"

"In a little bit." The living room was sparsely decorated with a big leather sectional, a floor lamp, a television, and a coffee table. A few generic art pieces were placed on the walls, and a couple of mason jars with fake flowers were set on the fireplace mantel.

"This is nice," she said.

He shrugged. "It's not my stuff. I'm renting it furnished."

"Oh."

He sat down on the couch and pulled her down beside him. He put his arm around her and pressed on her head until she rested her cheek on his wide chest. It felt supremely weird to be sitting this close to him. She was tense, and her mind screamed at her to scoot down the couch and give Hudson his space.

"Hudson, I..."

"Shh, just relax, Rosie." His fingers kneaded the tense muscles in the back of her neck, and that was all it took. She tucked her feet under her, closed her eyes, and curled into Hudson like a contented kitten.

"God, that feels good," she groaned as his fingers pressed and kneaded and flexed. He found a knotted muscle in the middle of her upper back and massaged it out as she snuggled closer and yawned.

"Hudson?"

"Yeah?"

"Do you think I'm awful for being attracted to you when I... like someone else?" She couldn't bring herself to say either the word love or Lincoln.

"No." His hand rubbed the back of her neck again.

"Do you mean that?" She put her arm around his waist and rubbed her cheek against the soft material of his t-shirt. God, he was warm. The chill she'd felt since getting out of her shower was almost completely gone.

"Yes."

"I'm not a slut, I swear." Her head was still pounding, but the ache grew distant and unimportant as she drifted toward sleep.

"I know you're not," he said.

"Do you," her sentence was broken by a huge yawn, "promise?"

"I promise. Shh, little Rosie. Get some rest."

"I am a little tired," she sighed. "I'll just close my eyes for a few minutes, okay?"

"Yes." His fingers continued to rub and caress. "Sleep, honey."

"OH SHIT!" SHE SAT UP WITH A START, BLINKING OWLISHLY AT Hudson in the dark. "What time is it?"

He checked his phone. "Just before ten."

"I slept for three hours? Why did you let me sleep so long?"

"You were tired. How's your head?"

"My head?' She gave him a blank look before remembering. "Good. My headache is gone."

"That's good." He smiled at her and clicked on the lamp before straightening and stretching his back and arms. His back cracked, and he grimaced a little before saying, "Are you hungry?"

She just stared at him. "Is your back okay?"

"Yeah. A little stiff from sitting."

"I'm sorry. You should have woken me."

"It's fine. Are you hungry?"

She shook her head. She hadn't eaten much today but didn't have an appetite. She felt slightly disoriented from her nap, and the supreme weirdness at being in Hudson's personal space had returned with a vengeance.

She slid down the couch, putting some space between them before clearing her throat nervously. "Uh, I guess I should go now."

"Why?" He asked.

"Well, it's late and -"

"You don't have to work tomorrow, and neither do I," he said.

"Right." She cleared her throat again.

"Are you sure you don't want to eat something? I have fruit and -"

"I can't eat," she said. "Please, I just…"

He gave her an encouraging look. "What, little human?"

"I'm nervous," she blurted out. "And I have to pee like crazy, and I think I might have drooled on you while I was sleeping and I… I'm nervous."

He grinned at her before standing and holding out his hand. "C'mon."

She took his hand, and he pulled her up off the couch and led her to the guest bathroom. "Use the bathroom, and I'll get us some water to take upstairs, okay?"

"Yeah, okay."

She ducked into the bathroom, closing and locking the door before using the toilet. She washed her hands and stared critically at herself in the mirror. Her curls on the right side of her head were a little flat and mashed down from resting on Hudson, and she tried to fluff them before taking a deep breath.

"You've got this, Rosalie. You're about to sleep with Hudson, no big deal. It's just Hudson, the biggest man you've ever met with the biggest dick you've ever seen. Nothing to worry about."

Her soft laugh was a little jagged. She gripped the sink and took a few deep breaths. She'd been so preoccupied with whether she *should* sleep with Hudson that she hadn't thought about *how* she would sleep with Hudson.

But now that it was time, she kept seeing Hudson's penis in her head. The length and thickness and... oh boy, what was she doing?

It wasn't even erect when you saw it, Rosie! Think about how big it'll be when it is!

Her inner voice sounded positively giddy.

"It'll be fine," she murmured to her reflection. "If it's too big for me to take, I'll just tell him, and he'll stop."

Yep. Easy-peasy! You got this, champ! Now, get out there and ride that bear shifter's giant penis like you mean it!

"Rosie?" Hudson's knock made her let out a soft squeal of surprise. "You okay?"

"Yes." She opened the door and stepped into the hallway, her nervous smile fading at the look on his face. "What's wrong?"

"You're still pale, and," he inhaled, "I can smell your fear."

"It's not fear," she said, "just, uh, nerves."

She took a bottle of water from him and drank a few swallows. "Ready?"

"Yes." He took her hand again, and she followed him up the stairs to his bedroom. He opened the door and ushered her inside. The bedroom wasn't as big as hers, although it had a primary bathroom attached to it as well, and the only thing in the room was a king-sized bed and a small nightstand with a lamp on it squeezed in between the bed and the wall.

"Is that the footboard to the bed?" She pointed at a piece of wood leaning against the far wall as he placed both bottles of water on the nightstand.

He nodded. "Yeah. My feet hang over the bed, so I took it off."

She stared up at him when he joined her. "How tall are you, anyway?"

"I'm 7'2". How tall are you?"

"Just shy of six feet," she said. "Can you order a custom-made bed that's longer?"

"Yeah, but it wouldn't fit in the room."

"Right." She smiled nervously at him and clasped her hands together. "So, should we get started?"

"You're still afraid," he said.

"I'm not."

He scowled at her, and the familiarity of his scowl relaxed her a little. "I'm a shifter, Rosalie. I can smell your fear, remember?"

"I'm nervous," she said. "But you would be, too, if you were about to take on a dick the size of yours."

His scowl turned into a grin. She poked him in his flat abdomen. "It's not funny."

"It kind of is," he said.

"What's funny about my vagina being wrecked, Hudson?"

This time he laughed out loud, and her traitorous vagina went all tingly. "Rosie, I won't wreck it."

"You might," she said. "I haven't had sex in a long time, and the last guy I slept with had an average-sized dick." She was trying for funny, but even she could hear the anxiety in her voice.

The smile faded from his face, and he put his arm around her waist, drawing her up against him. "Rosie, I won't hurt you. I'll be slow and gentle."

"Will you stop if it's too painful?"

"Yes," he replied, "but I promise it won't hurt."

"It's gonna hurt a little," she said. "That can't be helped."

"It won't," he insisted. "Let me show you that it won't."

"Okay." She placed her hands tentatively on his wide chest. "Let's do this. Show me how to be kinky, Hudson."

He hesitated. "I'll show you how to be kinky, but tonight, I think we should stick to vanilla sex."

"I know how to have vanilla sex," she said. "I've done nothing but vanilla sex. I want to get my kink on, remember?"

"Yes, but I still think we should start with vanilla."

She thought about the size of his dick and nodded. "Yeah, maybe you're right. I'm not entirely sure I can take your dick just in plain old missionary style, so it's probably good to hold off on the kinky, uh, reverse cowgirl sex."

Her *A Human's Guide to Sex With a Lion Shifter* book had a whole chapter dedicated to sex positions. The reverse cowgirl was noted as a lion shifter's favourite, and she was anxious to perfect it.

His grin was back, and she said, "What? That's a kinky position, right?"

"Kinkier than missionary," he said.

Her forehead creased, but before she could ask him what positions were considered kinky, he bent his head and nuzzled her neck. Immediately, her brain flipped to barely functioning mode, and she arched into his big body. His low growl of approval made her hot and tingly all over, and she clutched at his arms when he licked her neck.

"You smell good, little human."

"Th-thank you," she whispered. Already, she could feel Hudson's erection pressing against her stomach, and it hardened further when she stood on her tiptoes and pressed a kiss against his throat.

His hand threaded through her hair and cupped the back of her skull. She could feel the strength and power in his hand, but her nervousness was gone. One touch, one lick, from Hudson and she was ridiculously turned on.

He bent his head and licked her bottom lip. She moaned and opened her mouth. Like before, he teased her lips with soft nips and licks until she was squeezing his arms and panting.

"Hudson, more," she demanded.

He finally kissed her, angling his mouth over hers and sliding his tongue in to taste and explore. She sucked on his tongue, her nerve endings sizzling when he groaned in response. She had no idea how long they kissed, but when he tugged on the hem of her shirt, she lifted her arms without a lick of shame.

He pulled her shirt over her head, another low growl of appreciation spilling from his throat when he stared at her breasts. "This is pretty." Hudson touched the strap of her pale pink bra.

"Thank you." She pulled on his shirt, anxious to see his naked chest again. He stripped off his shirt, and she bit at her bottom lip. "Can I touch you?"

"Yes."

She ran her hands over his flat abdomen, tracing the hard muscles before gliding her fingers up his chest. He had a light layer of blond hair covering it, and she liked its roughness against her skin. The tip of her finger grazed across one flat nipple, and when he groaned, she leaned in and licked it experimentally.

"Jesus, Rosie." His hot breath stirred her hair, and she grabbed at his broad shoulders when he suddenly picked her up. He carried her to the bed and dropped her on it before reaching for the button on her jeans. He unbuttoned and unzipped them before dragging them down her body.

She grabbed the waistband of her panties before they

could follow her jeans down her legs, not quite ready to show Hudson all of the business.

He tossed her jeans on the floor and shed his own as she stared wide-eyed at the way his boxer briefs tented at the crotch, her nervousness popping back up like a Jack-in-the-Box. Hudson paused with his hands at the waistband and sniffed the air. Keeping his underwear on, he stretched out on the bed beside her.

"You okay?" he asked.

"Yes. I'm sorry."

His kiss was surprisingly sweet. "Don't be. We can go as slow as you want."

"Thanks." She touched his chest again, running her fingers to his collarbone and then over one wide shoulder. "Your body is incredible."

"So is yours." He ran his hand down over her arm, and she tried not to feel self-conscious when he rested his hand on the curve of her belly. "Your skin is so soft."

He trailed his fingers over her midsection, smiling when goosebumps prickled her skin. He traced along the band of her bra and then lightly circled the outline of her hard nipple through the silk.

She moaned and arched a little as he traced her other nipple through her bra. She wished he would just take the damn thing off and touch her properly. She was starting to feel weirdly warm and squirmy inside, and she moved on the bed a bit, crying out when Hudson bent his head and kissed her nipple.

"Hudson!"

"What's wrong, little Rosie?" His smile teased and tempted.

"I'm still wearing my stupid bra. That's what's wrong."

He laughed and tugged her onto her side. "Let me help you with that."

She expected him to fumble at the clasp, his fingers weren't built to be nimble, but he easily flicked it open. She stared at him as she relaxed on her back again.

"What?"

"You're surprisingly good at undoing bras."

He laughed again. "I told you I wasn't a monk, little human."

A weird and unpleasant tingle went through her belly. After a moment, she recognized it as jealousy. Shit, she was not jealous of the women that Hudson had slept with before her. Was she?

Her bra straps sliding down her arms snapped her attention back to the man above her. He tugged off her bra completely and tossed it over the side of the bed. She watched his face as he stared at her breasts for almost a minute.

"Hudson?" she whispered. "Are they okay?"

Oh, sweet mother of Mary, did she really just ask Hudson if her tits were okay?

He glanced up at her, and her breath caught in her throat at the intense need on his face. "Hudson?"

"They're perfect," he growled.

She cried out when he bent his head and sucked one rose-coloured nipple into his mouth. He sucked hard, his fingers tugging and pulling on the other one as she arched beneath him and pulled at his short hair.

"Oh my God!" She cried out when he nipped at one pale globe before licking between her breasts. When he sucked her other nipple into his mouth and gave it the same careful treatment, she couldn't help but rub herself against him.

He pushed one thick thigh between hers, and she

wrapped her legs around it and rocked her pussy against the hard length of it. His cock was pressing against her hip, but when she reached down to touch it, he caught her hand and kissed the palm of it.

"No, little Rosie."

"I want to touch you," she whispered.

He groaned and pressed a kiss between her breasts again. "I know, but I can't...you've got me so fucking hot, I don't trust myself not to just come in your hand."

She stared wide-eyed at him as a tingle of pride and self-satisfaction went through her. She'd done this to Hudson. She'd made him so hot for her that he was on the brink of losing control. Before she could give him a smug grin, he bent his head and teased her nipples with his tongue and teeth again, and the tingle of pride was immediately buried under a tidal wave of pure lust.

She rubbed her pussy against his hard thigh again before taking his hand and trying to push it between her legs. He lifted his head and smiled at her, his big hand resting on her belly. "Be patient, sweet Rosie."

"No," she scowled at him, "touch me, Hudson."

"I am touching you." He traced the waistband of her panties.

"Hudson!" She gave him a threatening look, and his grin widened as he made circles on her thigh with his fingers.

"Yes, Rosie?"

She scratched across his lower back with her nails before lifting her head and nipping his broad chest. He groaned, and his hand moved between her thighs to cup her pussy through her panties.

He touched the damp material, and she squirmed against his hand. "Hudson, please!"

"Your panties are wet, Rosie."

She blushed, and he licked one hard nipple. "Very wet. Your sweet pussy is so needy, isn't it?"

He sucked on her nipple as he lightly rubbed the wet silk. She dug her nails into his warm back. "Please, Hudson. I want it."

"Want what?" He nipped her neck. "Tell me what you want, honey."

"I want you to touch me. Really touch me." She gave him a look of frustration, and he licked her mouth again before sliding his hand into her panties. She spread her legs wide, moaning softly when he touched the soft curls at the top of her mound.

She couldn't read the look on his face as he continued to touch her curls. She gave him a self-conscious look. "I, um, I don't generally wax it bare, but if that's what you like, I could maybe -"

"No," he growled as he stared at her. "Don't you dare. You leave your sweet pussy just like this, little human. Do you understand?"

"Yes, Hudson," she whispered immediately, a little taken back by the intensity of his gaze.

He seemed mollified by her quick response, and she squeaked when he gave her curls a gentle tug. He grinned, and she moaned again when his rough fingers moved to the wet lips of her pussy.

"So wet for me," he said.

She wanted to be embarrassed, but the look of satisfaction on Hudson's face wiped it away. When the pad of one finger brushed against her clit, she cried out and arched against him.

"More! Hudson, more!"

"Yes, little Rosie."

To her immense relief, he rubbed her clit with firm

circular strokes. The fiery ache grew, and she writhed against his touch as he brought her to the edge of her climax. When he stopped touching her, she wanted to scream in frustration, and she had to stop herself from clawing at his back like a wildcat.

"Hudson!"

"Shh," he whispered.

"I want to come! Please!" There was no room for shame in her begging. She was too consumed by need.

"Soon." One thick finger probed and then slipped inside of her. She cried out again, clenching around him, and he made a low groan before rubbing his cock against her hip. "Fuck, Rosie."

"Hudson," she moaned. She rocked against his finger. Just having it inside of her helped ease the ache a little, but she needed more. She needed his cock. "Please, I want you to fuck me."

She squeezed his waist and gave him a pleading look. "Please, will you fuck me now?"

"Soon, honey." His thumb brushed against her clit, and she moaned happily. "I want you to come for me first, okay?"

"Yeah, okay, sure," she panted. "I have no problem with that."

His low chuckle made her blush but didn't stop her hips from rising and falling. He rubbed her clit again, and she clutched at his waist, her eyes widening. Fuck, it felt so good. She rocked harder against him, her breath coming out fast and hot. The pleasure grew and grew. Hudson's touch was the only thing that mattered, the only thing she needed.

When Hudson bent his head and sucked on her aching nipple, the pleasure crested and burst. She shouted his name, her hips arching and her body shuddering wildly as she climaxed. She squeezed his waist and collapsed against the bed, sucking in oxygen in harsh gasps as Hudson nuzzled her neck.

"That's my good girl, sweet Rosie. Are you ready to be fucked?"

She nodded, still gasping for breath. She raised her hips when Hudson tugged on her panties. He pulled them off her legs and feet and dropped them over the side of the bed before removing his boxer briefs.

She stared at his dick, a small trickle of apprehension winding through the pleasure still shuddering across her body.

"I won't hurt you, little Rosie," Hudson said.

"I know," she said as he started to lie on his back. "What are you doing?"

"You should be on top," he said.

"I don't want to be."

He studied her, and she tugged on his arm. "I don't want to be on top this time, Hudson."

"Are you sure? You can control the pace better, decide how much you take if you're on top."

"I want you on top," she said. She did. She really did. Probably stupid, considering the size of Hudson and his dick. Once he was on top of her and between her thighs, she would lose any control of the situation. He could fuck her as gentle or hard as he wanted.

Excitement threaded through her at that thought – lord, maybe she was kinky – and she tugged on his arm again. "Please, Hudson. Unless," she gave him a shy look, "you don't like missionary or…"

"I like it," his voice was hoarse. "I just want to make sure you're okay with it."

"I am. I want it this way for our first time," she repeated.

He continued to hesitate, but she could see the excitement

and the need on his face. He wanted to be on top, she realized. He wanted it very much but, for whatever reason, was reluctant.

Feeling sexy and powerful, she cupped her breast and ran her thumb over her nipple. "Please, Hudson. I want you between my legs. I want you on top of me and...fucking me."

Her attempt at sexy talk sounded mostly silly to her, but Hudson apparently was digging it. He growled, and a gold-coloured beard mixed with white appeared on his face.

There was no hesitation in his big body when he pulled her legs apart roughly and knelt between them. He pulled her down the bed until her feet were almost hanging off the end of it and rubbed her thigh before he gripped the base of his cock. She stared wide-eyed at it. The head was a dark red and slick with precum, and both apprehension and need went through her when he pressed the head against her opening.

"Wider, sweet Rosie," he rasped.

She spread her legs as wide as they could go, and he growled his approval before propping himself up on his hands above her. "Look at me, honey."

Their height difference meant she had to tilt her head up to see him, but she didn't mind. She realized suddenly that if she were the height of most women, they wouldn't have been able even to attempt missionary. For once in her life, her height worked for her rather than against her.

She lifted her gaze to his face, staring obediently into his dark brown eyes as he pushed the head of his cock into her. She gripped his arms, but he stopped almost immediately.

"Good?" He asked.

She nodded, and he pushed a little further. To her surprise, there wasn't even a flicker of pain. She could feel his thickness stretching her walls as he retreated and then pushed again. There was need and desire etched into his face, but he took his time, giving her a little more of his cock with every gentle thrust.

She was starting to feel almost impossibly full and squeezed his arms again. She had to have taken all of him by now. There was no way she hadn't. He stopped and studied her carefully. "Too much?"

"No, I don't – I just feel really full."

"You're doing so well," he praised. "Just a little more."

She blinked at him. "You're kidding me."

He shook his head before smiling at her. "Can you be my good girl and take all of my cock, Rosie?"

She moved a little under him, liking how his breath hissed between his teeth. "Jesus, honey, stop moving."

"I'm just trying to…" She wiggled again and then hooked one long leg around his hip, resting her foot on the back of his calf. "I'm good."

He pushed into her and then groaned. "Fuck, you feel so good."

"Hudson," she moaned. She was trapped beneath his big body and loved every minute of it.

She squeezed her leg around him, and he groaned again. "That's my good girl, honey."

"Is that all of it?" She asked.

He nodded, and she was inordinately pleased with herself.

He stared down at her, and when he began to move in and out of her with slow, gentle thrusts, she met each of them eagerly. "Oh God, that's good," she whispered.

He moved faster, and she admired his self-control as their bodies rocked against one another. "So tight," he gritted out.

She gripped his waist, meeting each of his thrusts with enthusiasm as his beard grew thick. He was moving hard and fast now, each stroke bouncing her on the bed as he stared at her breasts.

"Touch your nipples," he suddenly demanded.

She reached between them and cupped her breasts, pulling and pinching her nipples as he fucked her. The feel of his big body on hers, the way her thighs were forced wide around him, was turning her on, and she gasped as the pleasure grew in her belly.

His gaze was hot and fierce as he stared at her tits, and he growled when she gave one nipple a hard pinch.

"Good, honey. Now your clit. Rub your clit while I fuck you," he said.

She'd never touched herself in front of someone before, but she reached between their bodies without any hesitation. She rubbed at her clit with her right hand, crying out when it sparked fresh pleasure in her belly, and pulled at her nipples with her left.

"Good, baby. So good," he groaned. "Can you take it harder?"

"Yes," she gasped. "Please, Hudson, fuck me harder."

He muttered a curse, and she rubbed furiously at her clit when he increased the pace. The feel of his thick cock sliding in and out of her, the pressure on her clit was too much, and her orgasm washed over her in a hard, fast rush that brought sparks of light behind her tightly-closed eyelids.

Hudson moaned, the intensity of his thrusts grew, and then he stiffened above her, sliding in deep and staying there. Warm wetness gushed into her pussy, and he rocked back and forth, the cords in his neck standing out as they rode out their orgasms together.

When she collapsed on the bed below him, he pulled out of her and laid down on his back next to her. He stared at the ceiling, his big chest rising and falling heavily as she gave him a tentative look.

"Was it okay for you?"

"Yes." His voice was still hoarse. "Did I hurt you, little human?"

"No. It was good. Really, really good. Amazing good."

He smiled a little and pressed a kiss against her bare shoulder. "For me, too."

He rested one big hand on her thigh and rubbed it before yawning widely. She could feel wetness sliding down her thighs, and she sat up. His hand tightened on her leg. "Where are you going?"

"Just to the bathroom."

"Okay." He yawned again, his eyelids drifting shut.

She walked to the primary bathroom, glad that Hudson had his eyes closed and couldn't see how much she jiggled. She shut the door and flicked on the light before using the toilet. She washed her hands and stared at herself in the bathroom mirror.

"You just had sex with Hudson," she whispered.

Even her whisper seemed too loud, and she blushed before rubbing at her thighs. She was starting to feel a little self-conscious and wondered if she was supposed to leave now or climb back into bed.

Just go back out there and climb into the bed. It's dark and late, and Hudson wants you to stay the night.

She didn't know if he did, but her inner voice had a point about it being dark and late. This was only sex between them, but Hudson was a good guy. He wouldn't kick her out now. She turned off the light and left the bathroom, stopping beside the bed. The bedside lamp was still on, and she had no problem seeing Hudson.

He was sprawled on his stomach in the middle of the bed,

all four limbs spread wide and his head taking up both pillows. He was snoring softly, and she could tell by the even rhythm of his breathing that he was sleeping deeply. There was no way she could fit onto the bed without waking him and asking him to move over.

So, wake him up.

She reached for his shoulder before hesitating. Maybe this was Hudson telling her she wasn't welcome to stay the night. She chewed on her bottom lip as she stared at his tanned back.

Oh, for heaven's sake, girl. Just wake him up.

She backed away from the bed. Nope, she couldn't. Better to just quietly leave than wake him up and risk humiliation when it became more than obvious that he wanted her to leave. It would take her less than five minutes to walk home, and her neighbourhood would be safe, even at this time of night. She dressed quietly before glancing at the big polar bear shifter one last time.

She wanted to slide into bed with him and snuggle up to all that warmth, but if he didn't want her there, he didn't want her there. They weren't in a relationship, it was just sex, so staying the night was a stupid idea anyway. She'd go home and get a good night's sleep in her bed, then text Hudson in the morning.

CHAPTER 11

Rosalie wiped away the condensation from the mirror and stared at herself. The bathroom was warm and steamy from her shower, and she studied her face and wet hair. She looked the same, so why did she feel so different?

Because you just had sex with Hudson, and it was amazing?

She sighed and hung up her towel before flicking off the light and leaving the bathroom. She grabbed her robe from the closet and slipped into it, tying the belt securely around her waist. She glanced at her bed. She was tired but also incredibly wired. She'd never fall asleep, and there was no point in trying. She'd have some lemon-infused honey in hot water, and it would help calm her down.

Are we going to talk about how unbelievably good Hudson is at sex?

She ignored her inner voice as she walked down the stairs, Mr. Pibbles weaving around her feet. Okay, so maybe the sex was the best of her life, but that didn't mean Hudson was some sort of sex god.

Like hell, it doesn't. Hudson had you begging, Rosie. Begging!

Her face flushed hot, and she filled the teakettle with

water before setting it on the stove and turning on the burner. She might have begged just a little, which was incredibly humiliating now that she thought about it, but it still didn't mean that Hudson was a god in the bedroom.

She didn't have a lot of experience. For all she knew, Hudson could be average in bed and –

There is nothing average about Hudson in bed, girl. You know it, and I know it.

She grabbed a mug from the cupboard and spooned a few teaspoons of the honey into it. She had to stop thinking about sex with Hudson, or she'd never get to sleep. God, she hoped he'd enjoyed himself, hoped that he wanted to keep teaching her how to be kinky.

Now that she'd had a taste of him, she wanted more.

A lot more.

The teakettle started to whistle, and she turned off the burner before pouring hot water into her mug. Mr. Pibbles jumped up on the counter, and she pushed him away from the mug.

"That's hot, Mr. Pibbles. You don't want -"

The loud knock on her front door made her heartbeat triple. She stared wide-eyed at the cat, who jumped from the counter and strutted out of the kitchen toward the front door. Her heart still banging away, she crept after him and paused a few feet from the door.

"Rosalie, let me in."

Her mouth dropped open, and she hurried forward to unlock and open the door. She stared in stunned silence at Hudson, clutching the neckline of her robe, as he glared at her from the front step.

"You left."

"I -"

"You walked home by yourself in the middle of the night.

Do you know how dangerous that is, Rosalie?" He brushed by her, and she shut the door and locked it. He was already halfway down the hall, and she followed him into the kitchen.

"It took me five minutes to walk home."

"I don't care." His voice was a low growl. He ignored how Mr. Pibbles brushed up against his legs as he folded his arms across his chest and scowled at her.

"Eleven thirty isn't the middle of the night." She glanced at the clock on the microwave. "Twelve forty-five is the middle of the damn night."

He ignored her pointed look. "You are not to walk anywhere at night by yourself. Do you understand? Ever. Why did you leave?"

"Because I – because we hadn't talked about me spending the night, and when I came back from the bathroom, you were sleeping and taking up the whole damn bed. I assumed that was your subtle way of telling me to leave."

He snorted in displeasure. "I'm a big guy, Rosie. I take up most of the bed. You should have woken me up and told me to move over."

"Well, now I'll know for…"

"Know for what?"

"Nothing, never mind."

He glared at her. "Tell me."

She shrugged. "I was going to say for next time, but that seems a little presumptuous since I have no idea if you're even still interested in teaching me to be, uh, kinky. I'm sure you've figured out that I don't have very much experience in sex in general, and I don't even know if you enjoyed the sex tonight or if I was terrible or -"

He pulled her into his arms and kissed her hard on the mouth. Warmth flooded through her, and despite having two orgasms not three hours earlier, she was immediately and undeniably horny. She pressed up against him, gasping when he squeezed her ass with one hard hand.

"I want to fuck you again, right now, little Rosie," he murmured against her mouth. "Do you want to be fucked?"

"Yes, please," she moaned.

He picked her up and carried her out of the kitchen, up the stairs and into her bedroom. Instead of carrying her to the bed, he stopped in front of the full-length mirror in the corner of her bedroom. He set her on her feet, facing the mirror, before crossing the room to grab the high-heeled shoes she had rejected earlier.

"Hudson? What -"

"Put these on." He set the shoes on the floor in front of her. A little bewildered, she stepped into them as Hudson moved behind her. The heels made the top of her head brush against his chin and made her ass fit snugly against his hardening dick.

He pressed a kiss against the side of her neck as his hands reached for the belt on her robe.

"Hudson, wait." She tried to stop him from untying her robe.

He gave her a sharp nip to her throat, and she jerked against him as he licked the sting away. He untied the belt and quickly pulled off her robe, letting it pool on the floor at her feet. She immediately closed her eyes as embarrassment flooded through her. She wanted to cover herself with her arms, but as if he sensed it, Hudson's big hands were already wrapping around her wrists and holding her arms down.

"Open your eyes, Rosie."

"I don't want to," she whispered.

He licked the side of her neck before sucking on her earlobe. "I want you to."

"Please…"

"Open your eyes." His voice demanded obedience.

She opened her eyes and glanced briefly at her naked body in the mirror before staring at Hudson's face. Her breath caught in her throat at the look of lust in his gaze. Her core tightened in response, liquid flooding her pussy in a frantic bid to ready herself for his cock.

"So beautiful." His voice was a low growl. "So soft and warm."

He lifted her arms and hooked her hands behind his thick neck. "Keep your arms up."

She did as he asked, watching as he cupped both her breasts in his big hands.

"Beautiful," he repeated as he stared at their reflections. Rosalie arched her back, her ass rubbing against his denim covered erection, when he tugged on her nipples. They hardened into tight buds and he played with them until they were swollen and throbbing.

"Hudson, please," Rosalie moaned. She stared at him in the mirror, and he smiled at her.

"Look at yourself, Rosie."

"No," she whispered.

"Yes." He pinched her nipple, and she cried out, her hands clenching around his neck. "Look and see what I see."

She stared at her body in the mirror, watching mesmerized as Hudson's hands squeezed her breasts.

"Gorgeous full breasts with pretty pink nipples." His thumbs brushed across her nipples, making her tremble. "So sensitive. You like it when I suck on them, don't you, Rosie?"

"Yes," she whispered.

His left hand cupped her hip, and his right hand brushed over the swell of her stomach. "Soft skin, hips that fit perfectly in my hands. He squeezed her hip before running his hand over her thigh. "Long legs that look so fucking good wrapped around my waist."

She moaned and rubbed her ass against his dick as he petted her thigh. "Spread your legs, sweet Rosie."

She spread her legs apart, watching breathlessly in the mirror as his big hand circled closer and closer to her pussy. He kissed her throat again, and she dug her fingers into his neck when he stroked her inner thigh.

"The prettiest, tightest pussy I've ever fucked." His voice was a low rasp against her ear.

"Oh please," she whispered. She was so wet she could see moisture on her inner thighs, but her embarrassment was buried under a desperate need for Hudson.

"Please, what?" He traced tiny circles on her inner thigh.

"Please fuck me."

"Soon. Show me your pretty, pink clit, little Rosie."

"W-what?" She blinked at him in the mirror.

He took her right hand and kissed the palm of it before guiding it down to her pussy. "Spread your wet pussy lips and show me your clit."

"I can't," she whispered.

"You can." He stepped away from her, and she heard him strip off his shirt and unzip his jeans before he pushed them down his legs. He stepped out of them, kicked them aside, and stepped close again. He spread her ass cheeks apart and nestled his dick between them, rocking against her with a gentle rhythm as he held her hip.

"Show me right now, or I won't fuck you, Rosie."

"Hudson, you're being mean."

God, could she sound any whinier?

He laughed, and fresh liquid dripped out of her pussy. She had to be the only woman in history who got wet from a man's laugh.

"Show me your clit, and I'll give you what you want."

Her fingers trembling, she reached down and parted the lips of her pussy. Her clit was wet and swollen, and she moaned when Hudson kissed the curve of her jaw. "I love your perfect pink clit, honey. Are you ready for my dick?"

"Yes." The eagerness in her voice was shamefully obvious.

"Good." He pulled her legs further apart as she glanced around his broad body at the bed.

"Hudson, are we – oh my God!"

Hudson's arm locked around her waist. Thanks to the heels she wore, all he needed was a slight bend of his knees and a twist of his hips, and he pushed into her. She cried out as he filled her, her walls stretching around him. He curved one heavy arm under her left thigh and lifted it, spreading her legs wide. He pushed forward relentlessly, and she was helpless to look away from the mirror. She watched his thick cock sliding further in, watched her pussy spread around his massive width as he held her in a strong grip. He didn't stop until his entire cock was sheathed, and she moaned and panted as her body adjusted to being impaled on Hudson's dick.

He waited patiently, stroking her hip and kneading her thigh as she clutched at his arm and stared at where they were connected.

"Okay?" He kissed the top of her shoulder.

"Full," she moaned.

"I know." He rubbed her hip. "You're such a good girl to take all of my cock."

"Please," she whispered, "I need…. please."

"What do you need?" He kissed her shoulder again.

"I need you to touch me, fuck me," she pleaded. She wiggled against him, and his harsh groan brought goose-bumps to her skin. "Please, Hudson."

His hand tightened under her knee, pulling her left leg a little further back. He smiled at her in the mirror and began a slow, rhythmic thrusting pattern. She couldn't look away from the mirror. Couldn't stop watching his dick sliding in and out of her hot core. He was making low groans into her ear with every thrust, and his big hand moved from her waist to cup her breast as he moved a little harder and faster. She rocked against him, still watching in utter fascination as her pussy took every inch of his cock.

He was shiny and slick with her wetness, but she wasn't embarrassed by the wet sucking sounds her pussy made with each of his thrusts. Hudson liked how wet she got, liked the way her pussy took his cock like it was meant for her.

She cried out, both hands digging into his meaty forearm when he dropped his hand to her pussy and rubbed her clit. She arched into his touch as he fucked her, letting her head fall back on his broad shoulder and staring wide-eyed at his rough fingers rubbing her swollen clit.

He was moving faster now, taking her with hard, quick strokes that made her curvy body shudder all over.

"Oh God," she moaned, "oh, that feels so good."

Hudson growled into her ear before nipping her earlobe. Her cries of excitement grew progressively louder as he rubbed and stroked her clit with a roughness that rapidly brought her to the edge.

He growled again, louder and more urgent, and when he brushed his lips against her cheek, she could feel the growth of his beard. It sent fresh excitement through her. The beard was a sign that he was losing control, and, right or wrong, she loved that her body made him lose control.

"Do you know how beautiful you look right now, little Rosie?" His hot breath washed over her, and she stared at his face in the mirror. He smiled, revealing his straight white teeth and – her pussy tightened around him – his fangs.

He groaned when she squeezed around him and gave her a hard pump of his cock. He tugged on her clit. "Your sweet pussy is so pretty when it's full of my cock. Don't you think?"

"Yes," she whispered.

"Very pretty. And wet and hot and so fucking tight..." Hudson's voice grew lower, and another shudder of desire went through her.

"Come for me, little Rosie. I want to see how pretty you look when you're coming on my cock."

He circled her clit and then rubbed it with hard strokes. She moaned, her body arching again. He lowered his mouth to the base of her neck, and the sudden sharp pain, combined with the pleasure of his touch against her clit, sent her orgasm roaring through her. She screamed his name, her nails digging into his skin as she shook and shuddered against him. He held her tightly, keeping her upright as he fucked her through her orgasm.

His growl of pleasure became a low roar as he thrust hard and then came deep inside of her. He held her close, pumping in and out of her as she shuddered her way through the last of her orgasm.

He was trembling behind her, and he pressed a kiss against her shoulder before pulling out of her. He released her leg, and she immediately kicked off her heels. Her legs were shaking so hard she was certain she'd fall over if she kept wearing her shoes. She could feel some of his come starting to drip out of her, but before she could be embarrassed, he'd picked her up and carried her to her bed. It was a queen-sized bed and much too small for Hudson. He tucked her under the covers and climbed in beside her, bending his legs so they didn't hang off the end of the bed. He held her against his big body, her sensitive nipples rubbing against the rough hair on his chest made her shiver. When she tried to squirm free, he shook his head and cupped her ass in a tight grip.

"No, Rosie. Stay right here."

"I should go and clean up," she protested. "I have your, uh…"

"My what?"

She could feel her cheeks turning bright red. "Your, uh, cum is, um…"

He gave her a wicked grin. "Is your sweet little pussy full of my cum, Rosie?"

She poked him in the side. "Don't be crude."

He nuzzled her cheek. "I like knowing my cum is inside of you."

"Technically, it's starting to drip down my thigh which is why I need to clean up."

He laughed so hard the bed shook. She couldn't help but giggle – God, she loved his laugh – and he kissed the tip of her nose. "Now who's being crude?"

"I really should go and clean up," she said before yawning.

"Later." He bent his head and licked her throat.

It was rather nice to be tucked against Hudson's warm body. She was tired from her orgasm, and the way he licked the base of her throat was almost soothing. It was stinging for some reason, and his tongue eased the pain.

"Why are you licking me?" she asked sleepily.

He stopped and pressed her head against his chest. "Go to sleep now, sweet Rosie."

"Yeah, okay. Night, Hudson."

"Night, Rosie."

ROSALIE SIGHED AND SNUGGLED CLOSER TO THE HEAT radiating from her right. She rubbed her face against the thick fur, smiling a little as she slowly woke. She couldn't quite remember when she decided to buy a fur blanket for the bed, but it was the right decision. It was toasty warm and oh so soft. The blanket made a low snoring noise, and her eyes flew open. She stared blankly at the white fur two inches from her face.

"What the hell?" she said.

She tried to scoot back on the bed, squeaking an expletive and grabbing the thick fur before her when she nearly fell off the bed. Normally, she slept in the middle of the bed but was lying on the edge this time.

Not surprising, considering the rest of her bed was taken up by a twelve-hundred-pound polar bear.

She probably should have been terrified, but instead, she could hardly hold in the giggles. She had a polar bear sleeping in her bed. *A polar bear.*

Hudson snored again, and she carefully propped herself up on one elbow. Half of the bear's big body was nearly on the floor, with one front and one back paw resting on the floor. She had no idea how he hadn't just rolled off the bed.

She touched his fur again, smiling slightly at how soft it was. The heat radiating from him was incredible, she was starting to sweat a little, and she ran her hand down his thick side before studying the large paw resting on the pillow beside his head. The claws at the end were thick and razor sharp, and a trickle of unease ran down her spine.

She knew Hudson would never hurt her on purpose, but if he woke up and was disoriented... she could end up dead.

Yep. Time to get out of the bed, Rosie.

Very good idea. Before she could slide out of the bed, the

polar bear's eyes blinked open. He stared at her, and she could see the confusion in them.

"Hudson, it's me. It's Rosalie," she said quickly. "You're in my bed."

He lifted his head and moved his big body just a little, and that was all it took. Her bedframe snapped like a chicken bone, and the mattress dropped to the floor. The headboard and footboard hit the floor with a loud bang, and the headboard landed on top of Hudson.

He pushed it off with an angry roar, and it toppled to the floor with a splintering crash. Rosalie shrieked as she fell against the giant polar bear. Hudson growled, and Rosalie tried to scramble away before he accidentally took her head off with one swipe of his paw.

Warm, thick fur turned to hard, hot flesh, and Hudson's arms wrapped around her squirming body. "Rosie, stop. It's me. It's okay."

She slumped against him, resting her cheek on his chest.

"Are you okay?" He sat up before sitting her up. He cupped her face, staring anxiously at her.

"My bed broke," she said stupidly.

"Rosie, are you all right? Did I hurt you?"

She shook her head. "You didn't hurt me. Are you okay? The headboard landed on you."

"I'm fine." He brushed her hair back from her face. "Are you sure you're okay?"

"Yes." Feeling a little self-conscious about her nudity, she climbed off the bed and skirted around the broken pieces of bed frame that littered the floor. She grabbed her robe, putting it on quickly as Hudson stood and yanked on his jeans.

They studied the broken bed, and he gave her a look ripe with embarrassment. "I'm so sorry."

"It's fine." She hated the look of shame on his face. "It's no big deal, Hudson. It was, uh, an older bed."

A complete lie – she had just bought the bed this year – but there was no way in hell she was telling him that.

"I don't know what happened," he said. "I don't…"

"You shifted into your polar bear while we were sleeping," she replied.

He stared blankly at her for a moment. "I don't, I mean – that's not what normally happens. I'm sorry for scaring you."

"You didn't scare me," she said. "I was just worried that you might be a little disoriented when you woke up and think I was, I dunno, a seal or something."

She grinned at him, but his solemn look of shame didn't change. He ran his hand through his hair. "I can't believe I did that. I'll buy you a new bed."

She shook her head. "You don't have to do that."

"Of course I do." He gave her an agitated look. "I'm buying you a new bed, Rosalie."

"Hudson, please don't feel bad, okay? It was an accident."

"Yeah," he muttered before grabbing his shirt. "Listen, I have to go, but leave this mess. I'll come back later and clean it up."

"Hudson, I -"

"Just leave it, Rosalie," he snapped.

"Okay, fine," she snapped back.

He scowled at her. "Bye."

"Bye."

He hesitated and then stomped out of the bedroom. Rosalie sighed and stared at her broken bed before grabbing her phone off the nightstand. Her eyes widened. Holy crap, it was almost noon, and there were about a dozen progressively more worried sounding texts from Maggie.

Before she could text her, her phone vibrated in her hand.

She hit the answer button. "Hi, Maggie. No, no, I'm fine. I'm sorry, I had my phone on silent. No, I didn't go to another bar last night... I didn't sleep with a random shifter last night, but I did, uh, have sex with Hudson. Listen, are you free for lunch or coffee or something?"

She nodded and poked at the broken bedframe with her foot. "Yes, that would be great. Are you sure? Okay, I'll be there in about half an hour. Thanks, Maggie."

"Wait, so he actually," Maggie glanced around the coffee shop and lowered her voice, "broke your bed?"

Rosalie sipped at her coffee. "Yes. He's nearly twelve hundred pounds in his polar bear form."

"Holy crap." Maggie sat back in her chair. "Were you scared?"

"Not really. A little nervous that he would be disoriented when he woke, but he wasn't. He shifted almost immediately to his human form." Rosalie sighed. "He felt so bad, Maggie... it made *me* feel bad. He was embarrassed and insisted that he was buying me a new bed. I couldn't talk him out of it."

"Well, he did break your old one," Maggie grinned. "So, how was it?"

"The bed breaking? Loud and unexpected."

Maggie laughed. "The sex, you dork. How was the sex with Hudson?"

"Incredible. I think Hudson might have some serious skills in the bedroom."

"Nice," Maggie said. "What kind of kinky stuff did he show you?"

Rosalie blushed, and Maggie gave her a look of chagrin. "I'm sorry. That's really personal. Forget I asked."

"No, it's okay. I'm glad to have a friend to talk to about this," Rosalie said. "I'll share details, but if it's too much, let me know, okay?"

"I will," Maggie said with a small grin. "And if I start sounding too weirdly interested, you let me know."

"Deal." Rosalie laughed. "We didn't have kinky sex the first time. Hudson said it would be best to have vanilla sex first, so that's what we did."

"Good idea," Maggie said. "Just jumping straight into the kink would probably be super awkward. So, the vanilla sex was incredible, huh?"

"Yes. I mean, I've only slept with one other guy besides Hudson, but the sex wasn't... well, it wasn't awful, but it wasn't anything like sex with Hudson. He's really good at, uh, making me come. Like, amazingly good."

"Well, that's important," Maggie said.

"It wasn't just that, though," Rosalie said. "Before last night, I always thought that I liked sex, you know? It was fun and pleasant and a nice way to pass the time when you were bored but with Hudson? I was..."

"You were what?" Maggie asked.

Rosalie could feel the heat blooming in her cheeks, but she forged ahead. "He had me begging him to make me orgasm, Maggie. Begging. I don't even know what happened to me, but I feel like I went a little crazy. The way he touched me, the things he did and said... in the moment, I honestly felt like I would have died if I hadn't climaxed. That's weird, right?"

Maggie shrugged. "Well, it's not like I have much experience, but I've felt that way more than once with Porter. So, if it's weird, then we're both weird."

"I just never thought that I would feel that way about sex," Rosalie said.

"You know that lion shifters like lots of sex, right?" Maggie said.

"Yeah, why?"

"Well, I know you want to be in a relationship with Lincoln, and I guess I'm just worried that you'll be overwhelmed by how much he wants it. They want sex a lot."

"I know," Rosalie said. "Trust me, I've done my research. Besides, now that I know what sex can be like with someone who is, uh, good at it, I'm more than happy to give Lincoln as much sex as he wants."

"What if Lincoln isn't good at it?" Maggie asked.

"He will be. He's a lion shifter. It's all they do, remember?" Rosalie said.

Maggie shrugged. "I don't think it's all about whether a person is good at sex or not. You have to have a connection with the person, too. Honestly, I think that's what good sex is really all about."

"I do have a connection with Lincoln." Rosalie could hear the irritation in her voice. "I've known him for over two years, and we're friends – *good* friends."

"Okay," Maggie said. "I'm sorry, I didn't mean to overstep."

"You didn't," Rosalie said. "I shouldn't have snapped like that."

"It's fine."

Rosalie stared at her coffee. She hated how sensitive she was about her relationship with Lincoln. She needed to keep that sensitivity under wraps if she didn't want to ruin her budding friendship with Maggie.

Maybe you wouldn't be so sensitive about it if you truly believed that you were friends with Lincoln. You know as well as I do that he's just using you, Rosalie. Always has and always will.

She blocked out her inner voice viciously. It wasn't true.

Lincoln cared about her, and as soon as she proved to him that she wasn't uptight in bed, he'd be all over her.

"You okay?" Maggie asked.

"Fine," Rosalie said. "Anyway, it was a bit awkward after because I used the bathroom, and when I came back, Hudson was sleeping and taking up the entire bed. I went home because I thought that was a hint for me to leave, but he woke up and came to my house. We had sex again, and it was, uh, just as good as the first time and kind of kinky, too."

"Ooh, do tell." Maggie rested her elbows on the table and leaned forward.

"We had sex in front of the mirror. Hudson made me watch as we did it, and it was surprisingly hot."

Her face was bright red, but to her immense relief, Maggie just nodded. "Porter and I recorded ourselves having sex once. I was hesitant to watch it after, but like you said, it was pretty damn hot. I wanted to bang Porter again just watching me bang him."

Rosalie giggled, and Maggie wiggled her eyebrows at her. "What? It's true."

"Hey, has Porter ever, um, bitten you during sex?"

Maggie went still. "Did Hudson bite you?"

Rosalie nodded and pulled aside the collar of her t-shirt. Maggie studied the bite mark surrounded by a small purple bruise at the base of her neck. "Hudson bit you during sex?"

"Yes. Just a nip, really – but I bruise easily. I didn't mind. In fact, I liked it. I just wondered if it's a polar bear thing or a shifter thing. You know?"

Maggie was giving her a careful look, and Rosalie frowned. "What?"

"Porter has bitten me once," Maggie said. "But wolf shifters bite to claim their mate."

"To what now?" Rosalie asked.

"When a wolf shifter bites the woman they're sleeping with, it marks them forever as their mate. I have a scar on the back of my shoulder from where Porter bit me."

Rosalie's mouth dropped open. "You're kidding me."

"I'm not. It's why that lion shifter could smell Porter's scent on me so easily. I don't know exactly how it works, but Porter bit me, and now I'll smell like him to other shifters for the rest of my life. It's a wolf's way of keeping other shifters away from their mates."

Rosalie stared wide-eyed at her. "Did Porter ask you if he could bite you?"

Maggie nodded. "Yes. It's really bad if a wolf shifter bites a woman without her permission. Once they've bitten her, they're mated for life. He'll never love another woman."

"But it's only a wolf shifter thing, right?" Rosalie was starting to feel a little lightheaded. "Polar bear shifters don't bite to claim their mate. Do they?" She ran her fingers over the bite mark.

"I don't know," Maggie said. "Hold on."

She grabbed her phone as Rosalie sat back in her chair before sniffing her arm. Before her shower, she smelled like Hudson but now she just smelled like her body wash.

I don't think the smells-like-his-scent thing works that way, idiot.

A surge of adrenaline made her jittery, and she stared blankly at Maggie as the smaller woman scrolled through her phone. What if Hudson had claimed her? What if she belonged to him now? What if she smelled like him forever, no matter how often she showered? She'd never get Lincoln to fall in love with her if she smelled like a polar bear.

Oh well. Guess you belong to Hudson now.

She traced her fingers over the bite mark again as her pulse thumped and thudded. But it wasn't panic or dismay making her blood roar in her ears. It was – shit – it was excitement and a little bit of breathless anticipation.

Would it be that bad belonging to Hudson? Would it be so awful to have him in her bed every night? To be under his big body, hear the low and intoxicating rasp of his voice as he fucked her over and over?

Her pelvis throbbed, and she shifted against the hard chair. Maybe not that bad, she decided. She could think of worse things than banging Hudson every night.

Let's find him and bang him right now.

That wasn't a bad idea. Her nipples were hardening in her bra at just the thought. They couldn't go to her place with her bed broken, but she could text Hudson and ask him if she could drop by.

She'd just grabbed her phone from her purse when Maggie said, "Well, I don't see anything definitive from Googling, but I could text Porter and ask him."

Rosalie stared at her. "Ask Porter what?"

Maggie gave her an odd look. "If polar bears bite to claim their mate."

"Oh right. Uh, that's okay. I'll ask Hudson."

"They probably don't," Maggie said. "And honestly, it does look like just a nip, and Porter's was a full-on bite. You know?"

"Yes, I'm sure it doesn't mean anything," Rosalie said.

But what if it does, Rosie? You could belong to Hudson now and not even know it.

Another weird buzz of excitement went through her, and she shifted on the chair again.

"You okay, Rosalie?" Maggie asked.

"What? Uh, yeah, I'm fine."

"Don't be worried." Maggie squeezed her hand reassuringly. "From what I just read online, most polar bear shifters rarely even talk with humans, let alone have sex with them. I doubt a polar bear would claim a human as a mate. And even if they did, Hudson said this was just sex, right?"

"Right."

"So, he wouldn't claim you without your permission."

"No, he wouldn't." Her little rush of excitement was fading. Maggie was right. Hudson wanted sex only, and even if he did want a relationship, he'd never claim her as his mate without asking her first.

"You sure you're okay, Rosalie? You look upset."

"I'm not," she replied.

"Okay." Maggie gave her a doubtful look. "So, you guys had sex, went to sleep, he shifted to his polar bear form and broke your bed, and now what?"

"I'm not really sure. Keep having sex with him, I assume. We seem pretty compatible, so I'm hoping that he's still into teaching me to be kinky. Although, if he keeps shifting into his polar bear form and breaking my bed, it'll get super expensive for him."

Maggie laughed. "I've seen Porter in his wolf form many times, but he's never shifted when sleeping."

"Hudson says he has to be relaxed and sleeping deeply to shift in his sleep," Rosalie said. "I'm actually sort of flattered that he was relaxed enough to shift in my bed."

"It is kind of sweet in a weird, this is my life with a shifter, kind of way." Maggie glanced at her watch. "Okay, I hate to cut this short, but my lunch break is almost over, and I know Simone has a few errands to run on her lunch break. I'd better get back to work."

"Thank you so much for using your lunch break to listen to me," Rosalie said. "I really appreciate it."

"Any time." Maggie smiled at her. "I mean that. Just text me whenever you need to talk, okay?"

"Okay," Rosalie said. She watched as Maggie headed back toward the counter before staring out the window and sipping her coffee. She would stop and pick up a few groceries and then head home. She hadn't heard from Hudson yet and wondered if she should text him before dismissing the idea. She wasn't in a relationship with him. It was just sex, and she would be smart to remember that.

CHAPTER 12

Rosalie had just finished putting the groceries away when the doorbell rang. She headed toward the front door, Mr. Pibbles trailing behind her.

She opened the door and smiled at the big polar bear. "Hi, Hudson."

"Hey, Rosie. Can we come in?"

She stared at the grizzly shifter standing just behind Hudson. "Uh, sure. Hi, Bishop."

"Hello." He stepped aside and ushered the curvy, redheaded woman behind him into the house. "Go ahead, Ava."

"Thanks, honey." Ava held Lila in her arms. "Hi, Rosalie. Do you mind if I feed Lila while the guys work?"

"No, I don't mind," Rosalie said. "Did you want to use the spare bedroom or...?"

"Kitchen is fine," Ava said cheerfully. "As long as you're good with that?"

"I am."

Hudson slipped past her in the hallway, and Bishop kissed Ava's forehead before following Hudson. She watched in disbelief as the big grizzly shifter crouched and held his fingers to Mr. Pibbles. The cat sniffed his fingers before rubbing up against his legs. Bishop petted him gently, smiling a little when the cat purred.

"What's your cat's name?" he asked.

"Mr. Pibbles."

"Hey, Mr. Pibbles." Bishop petted him again before straightening and turning to Hudson. "We can throw the old bed into the back of my truck. I'll take it to the dump."

"You sure?" Hudson asked.

"Yeah."

"Okay. Bedroom's this way." Hudson and Bishop walked up the stairs, and Rosalie stared at Ava.

"What's wrong?" Ava asked.

"I have no idea what's happening," Rosalie said.

Ava grinned at her and jiggled Lila when she fussed. "Hudson asked Bishop to help with the bed. I came along because I was going stir-crazy in the house with the wee muffin here, and I thought it would be nice to get to know you a little better."

"Come into the kitchen," Rosalie said.

Ava followed her to the kitchen and sat down in the chair. She unbuttoned her shirt as Rosalie said, "Can I get you something to drink? Tea or water or coffee?"

"Tea would be lovely," Ava said. Lila latched on and made small grunts of happiness as she drank. Ava smiled down at her, stroking her fine red hair. "Thank you, Rosalie."

"You're welcome." She found the box of tea pods at the back of the cupboard and popped one into the coffee machine. As the tea poured into the mug, she looked up in time to see Bishop and Hudson walk by the doorway, both carrying large pieces of the broken bed frame.

She set the tea in front of Ava as Mr. Pibbles jumped on the table and sniffed at Lila's hair.

"Mr. Pibbles, get down," Rosalie said.

"It's fine," Ava replied. "We have a cat at home. Bishop loves cats."

Rosalie sank into the chair across from her. "Hudson likes them too."

Ava laughed and rubbed Mr. Pibbles head with one hand. "I find it hilarious that such big men love cats. Bishop is ridiculous about Princess. She has him wrapped around her furry little paw."

Hudson and Bishop walked by again, this time carrying the box springs. Rosalie gave Ava a confused look. "Hudson asked Bishop to help get rid of the broken bed?"

"Technically, he asked him to help him carry in the new bed. I guess it's one of those custom ones, but Hudson wasn't sure he could get it upstairs alone."

Rosalie didn't reply, and Ava took a sip of her tea. "Bishop broke my bed when we were first dating, too. He felt terrible about it."

"Hudson feels bad, but it was an accident. He doesn't have to feel bad." Rosalie said.

"I told Bishop the same thing. I think it's just one of those things that's bound to happen when you date a bear shifter." Ava laughed. "Then one day, before you know it, every piece of furniture in your house is built for the weight of a bear. Our couch is about the size of two couches, I swear."

Rosalie laughed, and Lila turned her head at the sound. She stared at Rosalie before latching on again.

"Trust me, you're going to love the new bed. Bishop has a custom bed and, oh my God," Ava grinned at her, "it's magnificent. Large enough that there's enough space for both Bishop and me, even with his giant body. I love cuddling, but I also like having space to sleep. You know?"

"I do," Rosalie said.

"So, how long have you and Hudson been dating?" Ava asked.

Rosalie hesitated before saying, "Not very long."

"Cool. You ever dated a shifter before?"

"No," Rosalie said. "Just humans."

"Bishop was the first shifter I dated as well," Ava said.

"Is Lila a bear shifter?" Rosalie asked.

"No, she's human like I am." Ava lifted Lila to her shoulder and patted her back. The baby burped, and Ava kissed her head. "Good job, sweetie. Rosalie, would you mind holding her while I use the bathroom?"

"Not at all." Rosalie took the baby eagerly when Ava handed her over. "The bathroom is just down the hall."

"Thanks." Ava left the kitchen, and Lila stared at Rosalie.

"Hi, sweetie," Rosalie said. She laughed when the baby broke into a wide grin, showing off her gums. "Oh my goodness, you're just the cutest baby ever. Yes, you are. So sweet and adorable. Look at those chubby cheeks."

She nuzzled the baby's cheeks, and Lila's smile grew. There was a noise to their left, and Rosalie and the baby turned to see Hudson standing just outside the doorway. He held the broken headboard in his hands and stared at them, and Rosalie gave him a tentative smile. "Everything okay?"

"You like cubs?" he said.

"Sorry, I - what?"

He cleared his throat. "I mean, you like babies?"

"I do," she said. "I want at least two."

His gaze drifted to her belly before returning to her face. Heat blossomed in her pelvis. The look on his face made her suddenly certain that he very much wanted to put a baby in her belly.

Yes, please.

She flushed bright red. Holy shit, she was being an idiot. Hudson absolutely did not want her to be knocked up with his baby – *cub, he wants you to have his cub* – and she was reading something in his face that wasn't there.

Feeling stupid and awkward, she said, "You didn't have to buy me a new bed."

"I wanted to." He walked away without saying anything else, and Rosalie stared at Lila.

"I'm an idiot, baby girl," she said.

Lila stared solemnly at her before breaking into another wide smile.

Rosalie laughed and kissed her soft cheek. "Thanks, baby."

"OH MY GOD." ROSALIE STARED AT THE BED IN STUNNED disbelief.

Ava and Bishop had just left, and after saying goodbye and thanking Bishop for helping, she climbed the stairs to see Hudson finishing making the bed. He had bought green sheets and a green and white duvet cover that perfectly matched the green on her walls.

The size of the bed was massive, and while it fit in her bedroom, it certainly took up way more space than the old one. The cost of the bed, sheets, and duvet must have cost a fortune. "Hudson, you - you shouldn't have done this."

"I broke your bed," he said.

"Yeah, but... this had to have cost so much money. You could have just bought another queen-sized bed."

"I don't fit in a queen-size bed."

"I know, but…"

"But what?"

"I would have been okay just going to your place for, um, sex. You didn't have to spend a boatload of cash on a custom-made bed."

He just shrugged. "Your place is nicer than mine, plus I figured you wouldn't want Mr. Pibbles being alone every night while you were at my house."

"You bought the custom bed because of Mr. Pibbles," she said.

He rolled his eyes. "No. I bought it because I broke your bed. It's no big deal, Rosalie. I knew your bedroom was bigger, and the custom-sized bed would fit, so I bought it."

"But to spend all that money when in two weeks, we'll be…"

The words died in her mouth. She didn't want to say, 'We'll be over,' for some weird reason. Not that she thought she was in a relationship with Hudson, but it felt rude to bring up the fact that he was only teaching her to be kinky for the man she was in love with.

"It's fine," he snapped. "Just drop it, okay? I wanted to do it, so I did it."

"All right," she said. "Don't be cranky about it."

"I'm not."

"You are." She hesitated and then decided she might as well tell him. He was already cranky. "I told Ava we were dating."

He stared at her across the room, and she chewed on her bottom lip. "I'm sorry. I know I shouldn't have done that, but in my defense, the words 'I'm dating Hudson' didn't come out of my mouth. Ava just assumed we were, and I didn't correct her."

He stayed silent, and she gave him an uneasy look. "I

really am sorry. I didn't want a stranger to know that we're only having sex so you can teach me to be kinky. But that's no excuse for lying about it. I can call her right now and tell her the truth. I'm sure Maggie has her number or can find it for me." She fumbled her phone out of her pocket as Hudson shook his head.

"It's fine," he said.

"Are you sure?"

"Yeah."

"Okay. Well, um, thank you again for buying me the bed. It looks comfortable."

He grinned, and the awkward moment passed. She crossed the room and hoisted herself up to sit on the bed. Hudson sat down beside her. His feet touched the floor, but hers dangled like a little kid's.

"It's almost dinner. Would you like to stay and eat with me?"

He nodded, watching as she ran her hand over the sheets. "These are so soft. Thank you, Hudson."

He rested one big hand on her thigh when she started to slide off the bed. Warmth drenched her belly, and her mouth went dry as she stared at him. She was beginning to recognize the look on his face, and her desire for him immediately kicked in.

He studied her mouth and then her breasts as his hand stroked her thigh almost lazily. "Rosie?"

"Yeah?" Her voice was barely above a whisper.

"What do you say we break in your new bed and then eat dinner?"

"I think that's a good idea," she said.

"Me too." He leaned down and kissed her. She clung to his thick arms, returning his kiss with an embarrassing amount of enthusiasm.

When she was flushed and panting, he broke the kiss and pulled her t-shirt over her head. He reached for her bra, and she gave him a startled look when he made a sound that was remarkably close to a whimper.

"Hudson? What's wrong?"

"I hurt you." He stared at the bruise at the base of her neck.

She touched it. "It's fine. I bruise easily."

"I was too rough. I shouldn't have bit you. I'm sorry." The shame was back in his eyes, and she immediately crowded close to him, rubbing his big body and shaking her head emphatically.

"No, I liked it. I liked it a lot, Hudson. You didn't really bite me. It was more of a nip, right? I swear I bruise easily, that's all. Okay?"

"I won't bite you again," he said.

"You can, I don't mind," she replied.

He shook his head, a stubborn look crossing his face. "No, little human. No more biting."

She gave him a saucy look. "What if I want to bite you?"

He laughed. "You're allowed to bite."

"I don't mind if you bite me," she repeated. "I swear."

He just shook his head, and she sighed. "Fine. Hey, um, Maggie told me once that wolf shifters bite during sex to claim their mate. Polar bears don't... I mean, they don't bite to, uh..."

Oh, Lord, she sounded like a complete moron.

"It was just a bite, little human. Nothing more," Hudson said. He didn't sound like he thought she was stupid, but she felt stupid anyway.

"I'm sorry. That was a dumb thing to ask. I know you only want sex, and you're not going to, uh, claim me or something, but I don't know much about shifters, and I just wanted to..."

"It's fine," he said.

"Okay." Anxious to make him forget how awkward and weird she was, she unclasped her bra and took it off. Hudson's gaze immediately dropped to her tits, and her nipples hardened.

He growled in approval before cupping one in his big hand. "Christ, I love your tits."

She blushed but didn't object when he pushed her onto her back and stripped off his shirt before leaning over her. "They're fucking gorgeous. Did you know that?"

"Thank you, I – oh God!"

He had licked the tip of one nipple, and she immediately arched up. He growled again and cupped her right breast, squeezing it gently as he teased her nipple with his thumb. He bent his head and licked around her left nipple before pressing soft kisses along the underside of her breast.

She tangled her fingers in his short hair as he kissed between her breasts and then sucked on her nipple. She moaned and arched again, moving one hand to his shoulder and gripping tightly. He kissed his way across her collarbone before licking at the bite mark at the base of her throat.

He lifted his head, and she cupped his face when he stared down at her. "I'm sorry, sweet Rosie."

"It's fine," she said again. "Hudson, I liked it when you bit me. It made my, um, orgasm more intense."

Dark light flared in his eyes, and she gasped into his mouth when he kissed her hard. He rolled onto his back, bringing her with him. He was so big that she didn't worry about crushing him. She laid on top of him, straddling one thick thigh and rubbing her pussy against it as they kissed repeatedly. He threaded his hand through her hair, holding her steady while they kissed.

"You're a really good kisser," she said breathlessly.

"So are you." He kissed the line of her jaw and then sucked on her earlobe.

She moaned and then reached down, cupping the thick length of him through his jeans. He groaned into her ear, and she rubbed him firmly as he skimmed his hands down her body and squeezed her ass.

"Hudson?"

"Yeah?"

"Can I be on top this time?"

"Yes," he groaned when she gave him a gentle squeeze.

"I want to, um, try reverse cowgirl. Is that okay?"

"Whatever you want, honey." Now, it was his turn to arch into her hand. She sucked on his bottom lip before giving it a light nip.

He growled, and she grinned when the beard appeared on his jaw. She kissed the rough hair and then kissed his throat as he squeezed and kneaded her ass again.

"We should probably finish getting undressed," she said.

"Fuck, yes."

She laughed when he tipped her off of him onto the bed. He stood, and she had barely gotten her jeans unbuttoned and unzipped when Hudson, now naked, grabbed the waistband of her jeans and yanked them down her legs. They dragged her panties with them, and he dropped both on the floor before pulling her socks off.

"How did you get undressed so fast?" she asked.

He just grinned at her and stretched out on the bed. It was long enough that his feet didn't even come close to the end of the bed. He patted his flat stomach. "Hop on, cowgirl."

She giggled and was about to straddle him when he held her hip, preventing her from moving. "Wait, little human."

She frowned at him. "I don't want to wait."

He shook his head. "I'm so fucking horny, I wasn't thinking straight. You need to come first, baby. You need to be nice and wet before you -"

"I'm already wet." Feeling a little bold, she took Hudson's hand and slipped it between her thighs. "See?"

His rough fingers rubbed across her pussy, and she moaned when he probed between her lips and caressed her clit.

"Told you." She was a little breathless, and she moaned again when he continued to rub her clit.

"So wet," he said. "But I want you to ride my fingers first."

"Hudson, I can't just…"

"You can," he said. "Put my fingers inside your tight pussy, little human."

She bit at her bottom lip before sliding her hand between her legs on top of Hudson's. Feeling a little self-conscious, she guided his fingers toward her tight opening. She pressed them against her, and Hudson said, "Look at me, sweet Rosie."

She stared at him obediently, and he smiled at her. "Don't look away, baby."

He slid two of his fingers inside of her. She made a low sound of need, staring into his dark eyes when he didn't move them.

"Hudson, please."

"Move your hips, honey."

She did what he asked, rocking her hips back and forth over his fingers. It felt incredible, and she spread her legs a bit wider and braced her hands on his flat stomach before riding his fingers hard. She cried out when he added a third finger, staring wide-eyed at him as he made a soothing sound.

"That's my girl. Keep going, honey."

She moved harder and faster, staring intently at Hudson as she did. He didn't break her gaze, keeping his eyes on her face as she reached for her release. She was on the very edge when he abruptly pulled his fingers out of her pussy.

"No!" Her nails dug into his abdomen, but he didn't flinch, just grinned at her.

She glared at him. "You're the worst."

His grin turned into a laugh, and he patted his stomach. "Now you can hop on."

Too turned on to feel any awkwardness, she straddled him backwards. She braced one hand on his thick thigh as his hands cupped her waist and helped to lift her. She gripped his cock, liking the sound of his harsh gasp, and helped guide it into her pussy.

"Oh God," she moaned. "Fuck, you're so thick."

She took him little by little, Hudson helping her rise up and down on his cock until she finally took all of it. He raised his legs and braced his feet on the bed, and she gripped his knees for support before making a few experimental thrusts. His hands gripped her ass, and he squeezed roughly as she rode him.

She stared at the wall, wishing she could see Hudson's face. She thought about looking over her shoulder, but that felt weird and awkward. She bit her lip and continued to ride him. She hated this position, she decided, hated not being able to see Hudson's face and how he looked at her with lust and need.

She tried to move faster, suddenly anxious to get it over with so she could turn around and see Hudson again. Why did lion shifters even like having sex this way? There was no intimacy to it, no shared looks of mutual desire. Without being able to look at Hudson, he became just a warm body to fuck, something to use to slake her need.

Bingo, her inner voice whispered. *That's why lion shifters like this position. They don't have to look at the woman's face or pretend they care for her when they don't. This is what it'll be like, Rosie. No intimacy, no love. Just fucking. Is that what you want?*

Hudson's big hands suddenly cupped her hips, forcing her to a stop. "Rosie, what's wrong?"

HUDSON GRIPPED ROSALIE'S HIPS, MAKING HER STOP MOVING. Although she was still riding him enthusiastically, the strong scent of her desire was fading. "Rosie, what's wrong?"

"Nothing." She stared at the wall. "Nothing's wrong."

"Little human," he said, "be truthful."

She perched on top of him, her soft, curvy body stiff and tense. He rubbed her lower back. "Tell me, honey."

"I don't like this position." She gave him a glance over her shoulder. "I'm sorry. Can I... would it be okay if I turned around?"

"Yes," he said immediately.

Her body sagged with relief, and she braced one hand on his abdomen before staring at him over her shoulder. "Are you sure?"

"I'm sure." He helped her climb off him, and she gave him a shy look as she knelt on the bed beside him.

"I'm sorry."

"Don't be. You can fuck me however you want."

Her face broke out into a smile – God, she was gorgeous when she smiled – and she threw one leg over his hips. "Thank you."

Her pussy rubbed against his aching cock, and he gritted his teeth when she carefully slid her tight wet heat over him. Fuck, he was in goddamn heaven. He'd never been in a pussy as tight as Rosalie's, and while he had no idea how she took all of him, he wasn't complaining.

Rosie was staring at him intently. "Oh, this is so much better," she breathed happily.

He reached up and cupped her glorious tits. "Much," he agreed.

She smiled and arched into his hands, riding his dick with slow, almost lazy thrusts of her body. He was glad she'd turned around. Not that the sight of Rosie's ass wasn't amazing, but he liked staring at her sweet face, liked watching the need wash across it.

She moaned and ground herself against his cock, making him growl with need. Fuck, being with Rosie was everything he'd dreamed it would be, and he couldn't stop thinking about her soft body, her low cries, and the way she looked when she was stuffed full of his dick. Ever since they'd had sex, he'd been walking around with a permanent half-woody. The only thing that eased it was Rosalie's tight pussy.

She rode him a little harder, biting her full bottom lip in concentration as she bounced up and down. She was starting to lose her inhibition and shyness, and he gave one nipple a little tweak, making her cry out. His gaze dropped to the bite on her neck, and he growled his disapproval to his polar bear. His bear had surged forward and given Rosalie the love bite, anxious to mark her in some way so that other shifters would stay away from her.

It felt no shame over what it had done to his mate, but Hudson hated that he had bruised her. She was fragile, and he needed to remember that. But it was so hard to maintain control when he was fucking her. She was so wet and tight...

"Hudson?' Rosalie traced her soft hands over his chest.

He raised his gaze to her face, and she smiled at him before touching the bite mark. "It didn't hurt, honey. I liked it."

His bear made a happy little growl when she called him 'honey.' He wanted to roll his eyes at it but was just as pleased. He gripped her hips and thrust upward, meeting each of her strokes.

"Oh, oh, that's so nice," she moaned.

"Rub your clit, honey," he demanded.

She reached down without any hesitation and rubbed at her perfect clit. Hudson waited until her body was tensing, until she was almost about to come, before he took her wrist and pulled her hand away.

She glared at him and slapped his wide chest with her free hand. "Hudson, no!"

He grinned at her and grabbed her other wrist, pinning her hands against his chest before increasing the intensity of his thrusts. She forgot about her anger with him and bounced on his cock, her soft coos of excitement making him even harder.

He kept her hands pinned with one hand and reached for her clit with the other. Her eyes widened, and she rubbed herself frantically against his fingers as he drove in and out of her. Her fingers dug into his chest, her thighs clamped around his waist, and she came with a soft cry of excitement.

Her pussy gripped him hard, squeezing his cock as her orgasm washed over her. He groaned her name and released her hands, grabbing her hips with both hands so he could hold her steady as he pumped in and out of her.

She leaned over him, her full breasts brushing his chest and her hands gripping his shoulders. Her soft, dark hair fell around them like a curtain, and he stared into her eyes as he

ELIZABETH KELLY

moved harder. Faster. His cock was swelling, and his balls tightened. When she pressed a soft, open-mouth kiss against his lips, he made a hoarse shout and climaxed deep inside of her.

She ground against him, keeping her gaze locked on his face as he came and came and came some more. She took every bit of his seed deep into her soft, supple body. When she tried to slide off of him, he wrapped his arms around her and pressed her against his body. She rested her head on his chest, and he stroked her bare back from her shoulder blades to her hips.

She made a contented sound and snuggled into him. He was softening, but he kept her where she was, enjoying the soft weight of his mate on top of him. God, her skin was so smooth, and she smelled so good. He loved that he could smell his scent on her now. It would keep her safe and protect her from other shifters when he wasn't around. No other male would even dare to go near her when they smelled the scent of a polar bear on her.

Humans will, his polar bear growled. *They're stupid and can't smell our scent.*

His arms tightened around Rosalie, and she poked him lightly. "Too tight, Hudson."

He loosened his hold on her. "Sorry."

"That's okay." She stroked her tiny hands over his chest. "That was really good. Thank you."

He kissed the top of her head. "You're welcome."

She laughed and then raised her head when his stomach growled. "You're hungry."

"A little," he admitted.

"C'mon," she kissed his chest, "let's go downstairs, and I'll make you something to eat."

HUDSON STROKED ROSALIE'S SOFT HAIR. AFTER DINNER – SHE had made some kind of delicious chicken thing, and holy hell, both he and his polar bear loved that his mate could cook – there had been a bit of awkwardness. He knew he should leave, but he'd stood in the kitchen like an idiot until Rosalie invited him to watch TV with her.

She was still concerned about intruding on his personal space. He could see it in how she kept her distance from him while they were in the kitchen and how she tried to sit as far away from him on the couch as she could. Her little squeak of surprise when he'd reached over and pulled her against him was admittedly adorable.

He didn't like people in his personal space, and he didn't like to be touched, but that didn't include Rosalie. He couldn't get enough of touching her. He wanted her soft body pressed up against him, wanted to be allowed to touch her whenever he wanted.

She was a little stiff at first, but in less than half an hour, she was curled against him with her head resting on his shoulder. Rosalie started yawning repeatedly in the last hour and fell asleep almost fifteen minutes earlier. He kissed the top of her head before pushing her back gently. She cracked open one eye and stared blearily at him.

"Hudson? What time is it?"

"Late." He stood and lifted her into his arms.

She giggled sleepily and wrapped her arms around his neck before burrowing her face into his throat. "You make me feel tiny and cute."

"You are tiny and cute."

She snorted, and he grinned to himself. Even her snorts were adorable. He carried her up the stairs and into the bedroom. He set her on the bed, and she gave him another sleepy look. "Thank you, Hudson."

"You're welcome, baby." He pulled back the covers, and she curled up on her side. She wore a thin shirt and sleep shorts, and he studied the curve of her ass before pulling up the covers. He touched her soft hair again before heading toward the door.

He wanted to stay. He wanted to climb into her bed and feel her soft curves against his body all night.

Not going to happen. You broke her bed, remember? Plus, you shifted into your goddamn polar bear while you were sleeping. She won't let you sleep in the same bed as her ever again.

His polar bear whined unhappily. He tried to ignore it. He didn't want to leave either, but there was nothing he could do –

"Hudson?"

He turned in the doorway, studying her sweet face in the darkness. "Yeah?"

"You could stay."

His heart repeated that stupid skip-a-beat thing, and his polar bear roared happily.

"If you wanted to stay. You don't have to, but this bed is probably more comfortable than yours and… anyway, you're welcome to stay the night, but don't feel obligated to stay." Her voice was thin with uncertainty.

He was stripping off his t-shirt and shucking his jeans while she was talking. He slipped into the bed beside her, and she made a startled sound before smiling at him.

"Hi there."

"Hey." He reached out and wrapped his arm around her waist, pulling her across the bed and into his arms.

She giggled again and slipped her arm around him to rub

his back. "It's like having a body-sized hot water bottle in my bed."

He nuzzled her neck. "If you get too warm, just push me away."

She yawned and rested her head on his chest. "Do you want to have sex again?"

He did, and the evidence of how much he did was pushing prominently against her hip, but he could smell her weariness. Besides, he'd taken her three times in the last twenty-four hours, and despite how easily her pussy took his cock, she had to be a little sore.

"Go to sleep, little Rosie," he said.

"You sure?" Her voice was lowering as she drifted toward sleep.

"Yes."

"Okay. Night, honey."

Another stupid and pointless tingle of excitement at the endearment. He pushed it aside and kissed the top of her head. "Goodnight, Rosie."

CHAPTER 13

R osalie slid down in the tub of hot water until just her head was sticking out. She closed her eyes and tried not to think about the fact that she had woken up this morning with a naked Hudson in her bed.

Waking to find herself all tangled up with Hudson's big, warm body pleased her more than it should have. It also made her horny as hell. She'd been sorely tempted to wake him up and ask if she could ride him like a pony again. But it was early, and she was sure Hudson would want to sleep in. She might be on vacation, but he had to work tonight.

She'd carefully slid out from his warm embrace and used the bathroom before brushing her teeth. She'd fed Mr. Pibbles and drank her morning coffee, checking Facebook as she sat on the couch with Mr. Pibbles in her lap, purring and kneading.

She decided to forego her usual morning shower for a bath because, as much as she hated to admit it, her lady parts were feeling a little tender.

With the size of Hudson's dick, you're lucky you aren't completely wrecked down there.

Her inner voice made a good point. Still, now that she'd had it three times, she wanted more. Was it possible to become addicted to a person's penis?

What if Lincoln isn't as big? Can you be satisfied with Lincoln's average-sized penis after Hudson's?

Her face turned scarlet. Lincoln probably had a big dick too. He was a big guy and –

It won't be as big as Hudson's.

No, it wouldn't be. She knew that without a doubt. Still, it wasn't that big of a deal. Size didn't matter, right?

Her inner voice remained stubbornly quiet. She closed her eyes, and immediately, an image of naked Hudson popped into her head. God, he really did have an amazing body. He was so strong and hard and...

Her pussy throbbed, and she sat up abruptly, splashing water over the side of the tub and onto the floor. Why was she denying herself what she wanted? Hudson was in her bed. He was hers for the taking, and dammit...she was going to take. Tender lady bits be damned.

She dried off haphazardly and then wrapped the towel around her body. She opened the door to the bedroom, her heart sinking when she saw the empty bed. Before she could feel sorry for herself, she heard the toilet flush in the guest bathroom. A few minutes later, a naked Hudson walked into her bedroom.

He stared at her, and she tugged self-consciously at the top of the towel. "Hey."

When he didn't reply, she crossed her arms over her torso. "What's wrong?"

Hudson stared mutely at Rosalie. She was saying something, but he couldn't concentrate on that. Not when she was standing in front of him, wearing nothing but a towel. Her hair was piled on top of her head in a messy bun, and he could see small drops of water sliding down the smooth slope of her shoulders.

As he watched, one slid from the hollow of her throat and down between her breasts to disappear beneath the towel. He wanted to follow its path. He wanted to rip that stupid towel right off of her, put her on her hands and knees, and fuck her hard and rough.

His pulse was hammering, his blood was roaring, and his dick was stiffening. He walked toward her, and her eyes widened when he made a low growl.

"Hudson?" she said.

"I want to fuck you, pretty little human," he growled.

Her gaze dropped to his cock – it was fully erect now and standing proudly out from his body – and heat rose up her neck. He could smell her immediate arousal, and he grinned at her.

"I can smell your wet pussy."

Shame mixed in with the scent of her lust. He reached out and traced the edge of the towel along her chest. "Why are you embarrassed?"

She stared at the floor. "It's just kind of humiliating that you can smell how much I want you."

He stepped even closer, pinning her body back against the wall. He leaned down and buried his face in the crook of her neck, inhaling deeply. "It isn't," he murmured into her ear. "I like smelling it."

She stared up at him, and he nodded. "It's true. It makes me so fucking hard to smell your lust, sweet Rosie."

He took her hand and wrapped her long fingers around

his dick, groaning when she stroked him a bit tentatively. "Do you see what you do to me?"

"Yes," she whispered.

"I like how your body reacts when I'm near you," he said. "I like knowing that your nipples get hard and your pussy goes wet when you see me."

"That, um, that doesn't happen." She gave him a flustered look, but her soft hand was still sliding up and down his aching dick.

"No?" He grinned at her, letting her see how his fangs had dropped.

Her gaze fell to his mouth, and fresh arousal filled the air, but she shook her head defiantly. "No."

His polar bear growled and surged forward enough to make him bend his head and give his mate a sharp nip on her shoulder for lying to him. She gasped and arched a little, her hand tightening on his dick until it made him groan with need. He licked the bite, cleaning away the small trickle of her blood as she pumped him rapidly.

"Lying to me will only get you in trouble, little human," he said.

She gave him another defiant look, and Christ, did that get his motor running. He tugged on the towel. "Show me your hard nipples and wet pussy."

The blush moved from her face down her neck and into her chest. She released his dick and held onto the towel when he tugged on it again. "Hudson, I…"

"Show me, little Rosie."

She stared up at him and slowly untucked the towel before dropping it. It pooled on the floor, and he stared at her pale body in the soft glow of sunlight through the window. She was so fucking beautiful. That someone as beautiful as her would want someone like him was a damn miracle.

He took a deep breath and cupped her breast, running his thumb over her nipple. "See? Hard for me."

She pressed her lips together and looked away, but her soft hands clenched onto his biceps when he trailed one hand down the curve of her belly to her mound. "Spread your legs, Rosie."

She shook her head, and he gave her another hard nip to her shoulder. She cried out, the smell of her lust deepening, and it took everything in him not to lift her and bury his cock deep inside of her.

"Do what I tell you, little human," he said before licking away the fresh drop of blood. "Spread your legs."

She spread them apart, and he reached between them to cup her pussy. She was dripping wet, and he growled in satisfaction before showing her his fingers. "Wet for me."

"Please fuck me," she suddenly whispered. "Please, Hudson. I need you to fuck me."

He lifted her and carried her the few steps to the bed. He placed her on her back, and she spread her legs wide, her hands cupping her breasts as she gave him a desperate look of need.

Ignoring her pleading look, he stretched out on his stomach between her thighs and lifted her legs until her feet were braced on the bed. He curled his big hands around the back of her thighs, easily keeping her legs spread open when she tried to close them.

"Hudson, what are you – holy fuck!"

Her voice became a high-pitched squeal. He grinned up at her and licked her pussy again, letting his tongue brush over the protruding bud of her swollen clit. She tasted delicious, and he licked her a third time before glancing at her. She was cupping both of her breasts, and she arched her back, silently pleading for more.

Her eyes popped open when he didn't move, and she glared at him. "Don't stop!"

He nibbled on the inside of her thigh, letting the tips of his fangs press against her soft flesh before he rubbed the rough hair of his beard over her skin. He licked the crease of her thigh and kissed her soft curls.

She made a sound of frustration, and one hand came down to push on his head. "Hudson! Don't tease!"

He kissed her wet pussy lips and then licked her clean with long slow strokes, deliberately avoiding her clit. She moaned and panted and tried to grind her pussy into his face, her hand tugging on his head in an effort to move his mouth where she wanted it.

After nearly five minutes, her entire body was shuddering, and she was almost whining with need.

"Hudson!" Her usual low voice was shrill with frustration. "Please!"

He licked her clit. Once, twice, three times, before stopping. Her moans of happiness turned to groans of dismay.

"Oh please, honey," she whispered.

His cock twitched, and he wanted nothing more than to make his mate come all over his face. Instead, he blew lightly on her wet lips before raising his head. "Rosalie, look at me."

"Please," she moaned. "I need to come, Hudson."

"I know, baby. Look at me."

She opened her eyes and gave him a dazed look of hunger. He rubbed his beard across her soft curls before kissing them. "Will you lie to your mate again?"

"No," she said immediately. "No, I won't lie to you ever again. I promise. You make me wet all the time. All the time, I swear! Just make me come. Okay? Please?"

"Good mate," he said and buried his face in her pussy.

She arched her hips up against his mouth. He licked her clit and then sucked hard on it. She screamed his name again, her fingers digging into his scalp as she came against his mouth. Wetness covered his lips, and he licked her clean again, reveling in the sweet fresh scent and taste of his mate as she climaxed.

When her curvy body finally collapsed against the bed, he straightened to his knees. He lifted her left leg and braced the back of her thigh against his chest before sliding one hand under her ass and lifting her lower body. He lined up his cock against her pussy and slid into her slick heat with one hard push.

She moaned and let her other leg drop open as her hands clenched into the sheets. Hudson kissed her calf and held tight to her leg as he thrust in and out of her. Her pussy clung to every inch of his dick, her muscles still contracting and releasing around him with glorious pressure. He moved harder and faster, worried he was hurting her but unable to stop.

He wasn't going to last long. Hell, he was lucky he hadn't come all over the sheets while he was eating her out. He moaned her name. She opened her eyes, staring hazily at him as he stared at her delectable tits. When she gave him a slow smile and cupped her breasts, he muttered a curse, his hand tightened on her ass, and he came in a rush of pleasure that made his entire body shudder wildly.

He drove in deep, filling up her sweet pussy with his come as they stared at each other. When he was finally empty, he kissed her calf again before pulling out and collapsing on his back next to her on the bed. He was panting for breath, and she gave him a cute smile before patting him weakly on the chest.

"That was a good one, huh?"

"Fuck, yes," he said.

She giggled and didn't object when he pulled the covers around them. "For me, too."

"Good." He pressed a kiss against her forehead when she curled up against him and slung one soft thigh over his legs. "Are you hungry?"

"Nap now, eat later," he said.

She laughed and kissed his chest. "Yeah, okay. Thank you, Hudson."

"You're welcome, my m -"

He cut himself off abruptly, his slowing heartbeat racing again as he stared at the ceiling. Fuck, he had almost called Rosalie his mate.

So what? You called her mate when you were eating her out.

His heart stopped in his chest before clanking back to life. Holy shit, he'd called Rosalie his mate. What the fuck was wrong with him?

You bit her, too.

His polar bear made a smug growl of satisfaction, but he sat up abruptly, making Rosalie jerk all over before sitting up next to him. "Hudson? What's wrong?"

"I bit you again." He stared at her shoulder where he could see not one, but two goddamn bites on her shoulder. "Fuck, I bit you twice."

He could tell they were small bites and not very deep, but it didn't stop the dismay from settling in his chest like a heavy weight. "I'm sorry."

She shrugged and pushed on his chest until he was lying down again. "I told you I don't mind if you bite me, Hudson."

"I made you bleed." He curled his arm around her and rubbed her hip anxiously.

"It's fine," she said. "I'm not bothered by it, and you shouldn't be either. Now, are we napping or not?"

She kissed his chest and snuggled up against him. He stroked her smooth hip, wondering what excuse he could come up with for calling her his mate. She didn't know much about shifters. Maybe he could sell the whole 'mate' thing as something that all shifters said to the women they were sleeping with. It was just a pet name like 'sweetheart' or 'honey.'

Idiot. She's not going to believe that, but it doesn't matter. She was so turned on it didn't even register with her that you called her mate. Just relax, for fuck's sake.

He slumped against the bed, his heartbeat finally slowing down. Rosalie hadn't said anything about the mate thing, and she wasn't acting freaked out, so his inner voice was probably right. She probably hadn't even heard him.

Still, in the future, he needed to be very careful when he was fucking her. If she even suspected that he was in love with her, she'd walk away and not look back. She might be attracted to him but wasn't in love with him. She loved the lion shifter, and that wasn't going to change.

Once he'd taught Rosalie how to be kinky, she'd end it with him, and he'd never be with her again. His arm tightened around her, and she made a sleepy murmur of protest. He relaxed his grip on her and stroked her smooth hip again.

So, you take a few weeks to teach her to be kinky. You can drag this out. It's already been two days, and it's only been vanilla sex so far. She hasn't asked for a lesson in kink, and you don't need to give her one until she does. Who knows, if you distract her enough with the vanilla sex, it might take months to teach her how to be kinky. And by then, she might be over the lion shifter and...

He snorted inwardly. And what? Be into him? That wasn't going to happen. Rosalie had been in love with the lion for a long time. She wouldn't fall out of love with him just because she was sleeping with Hudson. That wasn't how love worked. Besides, he couldn't forget that being with her would put her in terrible danger if Corden ever found him again. It was better that she was only using him. Better that he would move on the moment she finished with him.

Thinking of Corden made him think of Samuel, and sorrow flooded through him. Rosalie snuggled closer and kissed his chest again as if she sensed it. "You okay?"

"Yeah," he said. "I'm good."

He closed his eyes and tried not to think of Samuel as he listened to Rosalie's soft and even breathing.

HE WAS DREAMING. HE KNEW HE WAS DREAMING, AND HE wanted desperately to wake up. Instead, he followed the path of Samuel's scent through the woods. His breath steamed out in front of him, and the fresh snow that had fallen this morning gave way beneath his boots with a satisfying crunch. Winter in Northern Alberta was no joke. After the snowfall, the skies had cleared, and the temperature had plummeted to a ball-shrinking minus twenty-seven degrees Celsius.

Not that the cold bothered him. He only needed a light jacket to stay warm, even in his human form. He continued moving deeper into the woods. The logging company he and Samuel worked for had yet to invade this section of the forest. All around him, trees towered high into the air, frost covering their dense trunks.

He raised his head and sniffed the air again. His bear growled at the new, thick, unpleasant scent of blood.

His pulse picked up, and his body swelled. He pushed his

bear down with grim determination and barely concealed panic. Samuel had gone missing for a few days before and had been fine. When your best friend had a heroin addiction, you had to be prepared that they'd disappear from time to time.

But his disappearance felt different this time. Felt... wrong. Maybe it was because Samuel's heroin addiction had gotten worse in the last six months, or maybe it was because Samuel was spending too much time with John.

The scent of blood grew thicker, filling his mouth with its cloying, metallic smell. There was no mistaking that it belonged to Samuel. The panic rose again, his heart hammered in his chest, and his breathing laboured. He broke into a run, his feet pounding through the snow and his nose twitching as he followed the trail.

It led him to an abandoned cabin. The wood was grey and rotting and the door hung on by a single rusty hinge. He ran up the decaying steps of the small porch, the wood splintering beneath his heavy weight, and pulled open the front door, freeing it from its tenuous grip on the frame. He tossed the heavy door aside like it weighed no more than a brittle, dried leaf and ran into the cabin.

He staggered to a stop, his breath released on a harsh moan as he stared wide-eyed at his best friend.

Wake up! Wake up! Wake up!

"Samuel." He didn't recognize the sound of his own voice. It was too faint, too...small, to be him.

He stumbled forward on the wooden blocks that had become his legs and fell to his knees in front of the chair. Samuel's big body had been lashed to it with ropes, bungee cords, and duct tape. His big head drooped forward to his chest, and, his hand trembling, Hudson reached for him.

Don't. Don't look. Wake up, wake up, wake up!

He lifted Samuel's head, a low whine escaping when he saw the damage. The shifter's nose was broken and canted to the left, his right eye was a swollen bulge of flesh and blood, and blood poured from his mouth. A flash of white caught his eye, and he looked down at Samuel's lap, staring numbly at the objects littered across Samuel's pants.

Teeth. They were Samuel's teeth.

Another whimper, this one louder and filled with sorrow and despair. Hudson jerked when Samuel made a small groan at the sound, and his left eyelid fluttered up.

"Samuel! Samuel, stay still."

"Hudson?" The bear shifter moaned before coughing. He spit out blood and more teeth, and Hudson gave him a horrified look as Samuel tried to smile.

"Fucked up, Hudson."

"You'll be okay, buddy. I'm going to untie you and get you to the hospital."

"Too late," Samuel wheezed. "Too busted up."

"Your healing will kick in and -"

"No healing. Too much even for me." Samuel coughed again before crying out. "Dying."

"You're not dying," Hudson said. He raised his hand, the nails turning to sharp claws, and cut through the rope, tape, and bungee cord. Samuel fell forward into his arms, and Hudson sat on the floor with a harsh thump, cradling Samuel. "You're going to be just fine. Stay awake, Samuel. Do you hear me? Stay awake."

"Hudson." Samuel's voice was weak and thin. "Too late."

"It isn't," he growled fiercely. "Don't be a dickhead, Samuel."

Samuel grinned, and Hudson winced at the jagged, broken teeth sticking out from his gums. "Always was a dickhead."

"Yeah, you were." Hudson gripped Samuel's head. "But you're not going to die. Do you hear me?"

"Sorry, man. Was supposed to deliver it for him, but I kept it. Shouldn't have, but I needed it. Sorry for fucking up so bad," Samuel whispered.

"It's okay. We'll fix it together. You and me." Hudson rested his forehead against Samuel's. "Just keep breathing, Samuel."

"Too late," Samuel whispered again. "Love you, dickhead."

Tears streaming down his face, Hudson squeezed the back of Samuel's skull. "I love you too."

Wake up. Oh God. Please. Wake up.

Samuel's breath hitched once, twice, and...silence. Hudson whined softly, staring into his friend's empty gaze before kissing Samuel's forehead. He closed his eyes, tears slipping from his closed eyelids to splash against Samuel's face.

His bear was growling a warning as new scents drifted to him, but he ignored it. What did it matter? Samuel was dead.

"Ain't that sweet. Always thought you two were gay for each other."

His big body jerked, and he opened his eyes to stare silently at the five shifters in the cabin. One of them was smoking a cigarette, and he dropped it on the floor, grinding it out beneath his heel and grinning at Hudson.

"He had it comin', man. He stole from me, and when you steal from me -"

Hudson's growl made him stop and cock his head. "You ain't seriously thinkin' you can take on me and my boys, are you?"

"John," the shifter to his left gave him a nervous look, "we should go."

"Shut up, Paul," John said dismissively. He stared at his

blood-smeared hands before sticking his thumbs through his belt loops. He studied Hudson as the big man placed Samuel's body gently on the floor and stood. "I'm going to do you a favour, Hudson, just cause my old man likes you so… god… damn… much. I'm going to let you walk out of here."

Hudson growled again, his big hands tightening into fists. His polar bear was so close to the surface. It wanted to tear apart the five bear shifters in front of him. It wanted – *needed* – to take its revenge. It wanted blood. His mouth watered in anticipation.

He held his bear back with the last thread of his self-control as John cocked one heavy eyebrow at him. "You hear me, asshole? You can walk away right now. Or, you can end up in a shallow grave like your friend."

"He's a polar bear," the one named Paul said.

"So fucking what?" John snarled and bared heavy fangs at him. "You're a fucking bear too, or have you forgotten that?"

Wake up. Please wake up.

Paul shook his head, and John growled again before turning back to Hudson. "What do you say, asshole? You gonna do the smart thing, or will you be just as stupid as old Samuel here and -"

His tenuous control over his bear shattered when the shifter said Samuel's name. His bear surged forward, and his clothes shredded around him as he shifted.

"Kill him," John said.

Hudson lifted his head and roared as his bear took control, and the world turned black.

Hudson? Wake up. Please, honey, wake up. Wake up, honey…

"Please," John whispered. "Please, I'm sorry."

His polar bear retreated, and Hudson, his naked body covered in warm blood, stared at the man he had shoved up against the wall with one tight fist around his throat. Blood oozed out between his fingers, and he spared a glance around the cabin.

The other four shifters lay sprawled on the floor, their bodies gory messes of blood and brains and fur and fractured bone. The cabin was filling with blood, the red pool rising rapidly past Hudson's knees and up his thighs. He turned his attention back to the shifter in his grip and bared his fangs at the dying shifter.

Wake up, Hudson.

He stared with dreamlike detachment at the loops of intestines that swung back and forth from the gaping hole in John's abdomen. The river of blood was rising, swallowing the hanging intestines with insidious speed.

"My father," John choked out. "If you kill me, he'll never stop hunting you. He'll kill you, man, he'll…"

Hudson leaned close, his hand moving from John's throat to grip his sweaty hair. He stared into John's eyes at the reflection of the blood and gore-covered man he could see in their depths.

"He can try," he said.

His fangs lengthened, and he buried his face into the bear shifter's throat. John's shrill scream cut off as Hudson tore open his throat with a roar. Warm blood sprayed across his face, and he drank it eagerly, rejoicing in the taste of his enemy's blood before dropping the dead bear shifter. The river of blood was chest high now, and he lifted his head and roared again, a primal scream of rage and despair.

"Hudson? Please wake up."

He whirled and stared wide-eyed at Rosalie. She stood in the middle of the cabin, her curvy body clad in a long white gown. The river of blood parted around her, like Moses parting the Red Sea, and she gave him a pleading look.

"Please wake up. You're scaring me."

A tidal wave of blood rose behind her, towering to the ceiling of the cabin, and he made a sharp roar of fear and lunged for her. The blood surrounding him had turned thick as quicksand, and he tried to wade through it, his muscles straining and the cords in his neck standing out.

"Rosalie!" he screamed as the wave of blood hovered above her. "My mate! Take my hand! Rosalie!"

He reached for her as the wave of blood washed over her, drenching, drowning, dragging her under. He screamed again and again as her sweet face disappeared beneath the sea of red.

"Hudson! Hudson, wake up! RIGHT NOW!"

A stinging slap across his face made him jerk, and he woke with a gasping, shuddering bellow of surprise and fear. He scrambled back in the bed, slamming the back of his head into the heavy headboard so hard that he saw stars.

"Hudson!" Rosalie was sitting beside him in the bed, and he stared wide-eyed at her before yanking her into his lap. He touched her face and head, and she patted his chest soothingly. Both of them were shaking, and when he threw his arms around her waist and buried his face in her neck, she comforted him like she would a small child. Rocking his big body back and forth and stroking his hair as she murmured meaningless words of comfort.

When he had finally stopped shaking, she leaned back a little and stared at his face. "Are you okay?"

"Yeah. Bad dream."

"I'll say." She looked pale and sick to her stomach.

"Did I hurt you?" He was suddenly terrified, but she shook her head and grabbed his hands when he ran them over her body.

"No, you didn't hurt me. You were just – you sounded scared, and I've never heard you sound like that before."

"Sorry."

"It's okay. I slapped you on the face to wake you up. I'm sorry I did that, but I didn't know what else to do." She touched his cheek and pressed a kiss against his throat. "Who's Samuel?"

He stiffened beneath her. "What are you talking about?"

"You kept saying Samuel's name in your sleep. Is he a friend or -"

"He's no one."

She frowned. "Obviously, he isn't *no one*. You were saying his name repeatedly in your sleep."

"Let it go, Rosalie." He could hear the impatience in his voice, but he wouldn't tell Rosalie about Samuel. He couldn't. It was better and safer that she didn't know anything about him.

"Hudson, I'm worried about you. He means something to you, and you had a terrible dream about him. Why don't you tell me about it? You'll feel better, I promise. It helps to talk about it."

"There's nothing to talk about." He lifted her off his lap and slid out of the bed, grabbing his jeans and yanking them on as she gave him a hurt look.

"I'm just trying to help. I don't -"

"And I said, let it go." He glared at her.

"Fine. I won't ask you anything ever again."

"Good," he snapped.

Her face was bright red, and she looked both pissed off and ready to cry. Hudson yanked his t-shirt over his head and shoved his arms into it. "I gotta go."

"Fine," she said. "If you're gonna be such a jerk, I don't want you here anyway."

He growled at her, more hurt than angry by her comment, but she crossed her arms over her chest and gave him another scowl. "I'm not afraid of you, Mr. Jerkface Growlypants."

He grabbed his phone and headed toward the bedroom door. "I have to go."

"I heard you the first time."

He huffed out another growl that sounded embarrassingly like a whine before stomping out of the bedroom.

CHAPTER 14

"Rosalie! You're not listening to a word I say and haven't been since you got here. What is wrong with you?"

"Sorry, Mom." Rosalie gave her mother a faint smile. "Just a long day."

"Well, you need to put it behind you when you're here with me. It's rude to be so preoccupied and distant when visiting someone," her mother said. "You haven't even complimented me on my new haircut."

"It looks really good," Rosalie said.

Her mother sniffed before staring at the TV screen. *Wheel of Fortune* was playing, and she made a face. "That man is a shifter. I can tell. He has very ratlike features. Ever since they started letting those filthy animals onto the show, it's become a joke. I'm surprised Mr. Sajak even agreed to it. He stands so close to the contestants, one of them could rip his head off before he knew it."

"They wouldn't do that, Mom. Shifters aren't that much different from humans."

"How would you know?" her mother snapped.

"I work for one, remember?"

"I do, and I have to tell you, I've never trusted that Shepherd guy. He's hinky, Rosalie. He's hinky, and you can't see it because he's a smooth talker."

Rosalie stared numbly at the television. "Jace is a good guy."

"Is he, though? You know, one time when I dropped by your office, he was a little too friendly. Going on and on about how amazing you were and how the office would be lost without you. He acted like you ran the whole place instead of just being a secretary. And I swear I could smell meat on his breath. I bet he eats raw meat every night. He probably has all sorts of worms and other diseases coursing through his body. You know, I saw on the news the other night that..."

Rosalie stared blankly at the television as she drowned out her mother's voice. It wasn't anything she hadn't heard before, and for one brief moment of insanity, she considered telling her mother that she was banging a shifter. Maybe it would shock her into silence, and they could finish watching *Wheel of Fortune* in peace.

She would have laughed at the thought of telling her mother about Hudson if she hadn't been so miserable. Knowing her daughter was sleeping with a shifter wouldn't just shock her mother into silence. It would give her a damn stroke.

She glanced at the clock on the wall above the television. Almost seven. Hudson would be at work by now. Before their fight, she was going to ask him if he wanted to come by once his shift was over, but now....

She sighed and blinked back the hot tears. Crying over her fight with Hudson wouldn't help. She had fucked up with him, and the only thing she could do was apologize and hope he still wanted to teach her some kink.

He won't, Rosalie. He was mad when he left. You just had to keep pushing him to talk, didn't you? What's that old saying? Don't poke the bear. Well, you poked him all right, and now he'll never sleep with you again. Hell, he'll probably never talk to you again.

Panic made her pulse thud heavily. The thought of not sleeping with Hudson was dismaying, but the idea of never speaking to him again? That made her sick to her stomach.

Fuck, she was so stupid. Did she really think she could sleep with Hudson and not ruin their friendship? Why did she –

"*Rosalie!*"

She twitched and stared at her mother. "Sorry, what?"

"You haven't heard a word I said, have you? What is going on with you? First, you hardly eat a bite of supper – I worked hard on that casserole, you know – and now you won't grunt out two words, and you're ignoring me. Maybe you should go if you won't pay attention to me."

Rosalie stared at her mother. That was it. She could fix things with Hudson. She just needed a peace offering. She stood up and grabbed her jacket from the back of the chair. "You're right. I should go, Mom."

Her mother gave her a startled look. "What?"

"I said you're right. I'm in a terrible mood and shouldn't take it out on you. I'm going to go." She bent and kissed her mother's cheek. "I love you."

"Well, are you... I mean, will I see you tomorrow?"

She shook her head. "I can't come by tomorrow night, but I'll text you. Love you, bye!"

She stood outside of Bud's Bar, holding a plastic container full of lasagna.

Just go inside, Rosalie.

Right. Go inside. All by herself. Into a bar that's primarily for paranormals.

You've been in there before. Besides, it'll take you five minutes to hand the food to Hudson, apologize, and invite him back to your place after he's finished work. Just walk through that door and do it.

She took a deep breath, grabbed the handle and yanked the door open. She walked into the bar and slowed to a stop. The place was surprisingly busy for a Tuesday night. A few of the shifters closest to her were giving her curious looks. She ignored them and stared at the bar. Hudson wasn't behind it, and her fledgling courage failed immediately.

She backed up, making a sharp cry of surprise when she ran into something warm and hard.

"Watch where you're going, for God's sake."

She whipped around, staring at the irate shifter behind her. He was about her height and had a thick dark beard and angry black eyes. He glanced at his companion, a smaller man with buck teeth and a wisp of a mustache. "Humans. You know, I ain't so happy about the fact that this place is just letting in humans left and right. Remember when it used to be a paranormal-only bar? Why the fuck is the new owner messing with that?"

His companion shrugged, and the shifter turned back to Rosalie. He eyed her up and down, and she swallowed heavily when a new light shone in his eyes. He gave her a hard grin. "You ain't bad lookin' for a human. You lookin' for a shifter to fuck, baby? Is that it? Is that why you're -"

"Eddie, don't," his companion said.

Eddie scowled at him, and the companion sniffed at

Rosalie before jerking his head toward the bar. "She smells like him. You really wanna fuckin' mess with *his* woman?"

Eddie stared at Rosalie before leaning forward and inhaling deeply. He immediately backed up a few steps before glancing at the bar. "Excuse me, ma'am. Didn't mean to upset you. Have a good night."

He and the smaller man walked away. She stared at the lasagna container in her hand as her heart thudded and thumped. She was okay. She was fine. A woman walked by her with the lithe grace of a large cat and sniffed at Rosalie before glancing at the bar.

Rosalie followed her gaze, but there was still no sign of Hudson. Before she could turn and run out of the bar, a familiar voice said. "Rosalie? Hey, how's it going?"

She looked up, relief coursing through her. "Hi, Judd. Good. How are you?"

He studied her, a line creasing between his eyebrows. "You're pale. You okay?"

"Uh, yes. I'm fine. I was looking for Hudson. I thought he was working tonight, but he isn't here."

"He's here. He's grabbing a keg from the back – there he is now."

She looked toward the bar, lust immediately licking along her veins. Hudson walled out of the back hallway, one arm balancing a keg on his broad shoulder. God, he was so strong. She studied the flatness of his belly and the thickness of his thighs through his jeans as another wave of lust rolled through her.

Judd grinned at her. "Before Hudson came along, it took three of us to move a keg from the back to under the bar. I think Porter will give him a raise just based on him moving the kegs by himself."

She smiled uncertainly, her horniness taking a back seat

to the anxiety that had made a sudden and unwelcome return.

"That smells good." Judd pointed to the container in her hands. "Lasagna?"

"Yes. I made it for Hudson for dinner." Oh God, she sounded so stupid.

"Nice. Here, I'll walk you up to the bar," Judd said.

"Oh, uh, that's okay. Maybe you could give it to him? I know he's busy and -"

Judd shook his head. "Nah, he won't mind if you say a quick hello. C'mon."

He placed a hand near but not quite touching her lower back and started forward, leaving her no choice but to walk with him. Porter was moving the empty keg out of its place under the long, smooth bar. Hudson replaced it with the full one, and Porter connected it. Hudson heaved the empty keg up to his shoulder before heading toward the back hallway.

"Yo, Hudson. Rosalie's here," Judd said.

Hudson froze at the entrance to the hallway. He turned around slowly, and Rosalie gave him a small wave. "Hi."

"Hey," he grunted. "Be right back."

He turned and walked into the hallway. Judd smiled at her and patted a bar stool. "Have a seat, Rosalie."

"Thanks." She slid onto the bar stool, setting the lasagna container down as Porter stopped in front of her.

"Hey, Rosalie. How's it…"

He stopped and inhaled deeply. Rosalie blushed furiously as Porter grinned. "How's it going?"

"Good. How are you?"

"Good. You're here to see Hudson, huh?"

"I brought him dinner," she said stupidly.

"Nice. Can I get you something to drink?"

"A glass of wine, please."

"Red or white?"

"White. Thanks, Porter."

He brought her the glass and shook his head when she reached for the purse. "On the house."

"Thank you, that's very nice of you."

"You're welcome." He moved to the other end of the bar.

Rosalie sipped at the wine. It helped ease her dry throat. She took a deep breath, glancing to the left at the sound of raucous laughter. The two women sitting at the end of the bar screamed laughter again. They looked familiar to her, and after a moment, she placed them. They were the two drunk women who had wandered down the hallway the night Hudson said he would help her.

They were raccoon shifters. She'd worked with Betty long enough to recognize a raccoon shifter when she saw one. The prettiest one took a long drink of her beer and smoothed down her dark hair before nudging her friend. Rosalie followed their gazes. Hudson had returned. He walked behind the bar, and Rosalie bristled when the pretty raccoon shifter grabbed his arm as he walked past her.

He stopped, and Rosalie could feel another bite of jealousy when the woman traced her long painted nails up and down his forearm. She couldn't hear what they were saying, but her stomach was in a tight knot, and she could almost feel her chest going blotchy from anger. The woman crooked her finger, and Hudson leaned down so she could whisper in his ear.

He shook his head and straightened, tugging his arm free. The raccoon shifter pouted at him, and he shook his head again before continuing toward Rosalie. He stopped in front of her. "Hey."

"Hi, Hudson."

He didn't say anything else, and she took another swallow

245

of wine to calm her nerves. What was she doing? Was she really trying to get back into Hudson's good graces with food? She was an idiot.

"What are you doing here?" Hudson asked.

"I brought you lasagna," she said.

His gaze dropped to the container sitting on the bar. "You made me lasagna?"

"I, well, it was in my freezer. I mean, I made it, just not tonight. I cooked it a few weeks ago and froze it for nights when I was working late and didn't feel like cooking. I heated it before I left, so it's not, like, frozen or anything. Anyway, I should go. I'm sorry about earlier. I shouldn't have _"

"Hudson?" Porter was back, and he gave them both a cheerful grin. "If you want to take your dinner break a bit early so you can spend it with Rosalie, go ahead."

There was silence. Rosalie wanted to sink into the floor. Porter stared at Hudson. "Hudson?"

"Yeah, okay." Hudson grabbed the container of lasagna. "Follow me."

She slid off the bar stool and followed him to a booth in the corner near the hallway. It was twice the size of the other booths in the bar, and the table had a "staff only" sign on it. Hudson sat down and picked up a napkin-wrapped fork and knife from off the table. Rosalie slid into the booth across from him with her glass of wine.

Hudson snorted irritably, and Rosalie looked up to see Tori bouncing toward them, a beer in hand. "Hey, guys. You on your break, big guy?"

"Yes," he said.

"Nice. Those two sexy ladies over there asked me to give this to you." She set the beer on the table before wiggling her nose at Rosalie. "Hi again. You're…Rose, right?"

"Rosalie," she said.

"Yeah, right. You're Lincoln's friend. I haven't seen him in the bar for, like, days now. Is everything okay with him?"

"He's on vacation," Rosalie said.

"Oh, nice. Good for him." Tori paused, her pert little nose wriggling in the air before she squealed. "Oh my God, are you and Hudson, like, totally dating?"

Rosalie turned bright red. Hudson glared at Tori. "None of your business."

She rolled her eyes. "Don't be so grumpy. It's not like we can't tell. She stinks to high heaven."

She smiled at Rosalie. "No offense, hon. I'm just not into polar bears."

Rosalie stared at her as Hudson growled under his breath. Tori giggled and pushed on his broad shoulder. "Don't be upset with me, big guy. It's not like you wanna bang me anyway."

She winked at him and walked away, the sway of her small hips catching the attention of several shifters.

There was an awkward silence, and Rosalie cleared her throat. "So, the bar looks good. They did a good job with the renovations."

"Yeah." Hudson stared at the container of lasagna.

"Hudson?"

He finally looked at her, and she gave him a small, apologetic smile. "I'm very sorry about earlier. It was none of my business, and I shouldn't have pushed you to talk about it. Also, I shouldn't have called you a jerkface growlypants. That was very immature and – are you smiling? Why are you smiling?"

Hudson's grin widened. "Just never thought I'd be called jerkface growlypants."

She sighed. "I promise I have a higher maturity level than

a twelve-year-old. I was just angry, and I'm not great with witty comebacks. Anyway, I am sorry. I brought you the lasagna as a peace offering."

"I'm sorry too," Hudson said. "I shouldn't have gotten angry with you."

"No, you had every right to be angry and I -"

"I didn't," he said. "You were trying to be nice, and I was a...jerkface growlypants."

She smiled at him, and the tension in his shoulders seemed to ease a little. He hesitated and then said, "Samuel was my best friend. He died a few years ago."

"I'm very sorry for your loss." She reached across the table and squeezed his hand, surprised when he linked their fingers.

"Thanks." He stared at their clasped hands for a moment before releasing her and peeling off the lid of the container. "This smells good."

"You should probably heat it for a few minutes," Rosalie said.

He placed his napkin on his lap and took a large bite of lasagna. He chewed and swallowed before grinning at her. "Nah, it's still warm and delicious."

"Good."

He dug in with obvious enthusiasm, and she watched him eat for a few minutes before saying, "Hey, Hudson?"

"Yeah?" He hadn't touched the beer the raccoon shifters had sent him, and she stared at the amber-coloured liquid.

"Do I smell like you to other shifters?"

His face went red, and he stabbed at the lasagna. "Yeah."

"I thought you said that the bite was just a bite. That it wasn't a claiming thing like with wolves," she said.

Shit, could he hear the weird excitement in her voice?

"It's not permanent," he said. "You smell like me because we've been…"

"Oh, right," she said. 'So, if we stopped, uh, having sex, I wouldn't smell like you anymore?"

"It would take a few days for my scent to wear off, but yeah, eventually, you wouldn't carry my scent."

She sniffed her arm, and he grinned at her. "Only other shifters can smell it, Rosie."

She blushed and lowered her arm. "Well, it explains why that guy backed off."

He tensed, dropping the forkful of lasagna back into the container. "What guy?"

"Hmm?" Rosalie was staring at the two raccoon shifters sitting at the bar and still staring at Hudson. Maybe she should walk by them a couple of times and let them smell Hudson's scent on her.

"Rosalie," Hudson's voice was a low growl, "what guy?"

Still preoccupied with the raccoon shifters, Rosalie said, "When I first came in, this guy was kind of angry with me, and then he got a little crude, but -"

Hudson's growl was louder and angrier. Rosalie tore her gaze from the raccoon shifters and gave him a startled look. "Hey, what's wrong?"

"Who's the guy?" Hudson snarled. "Point him out to me, little human."

She stared at the beard on his face, at the tips of his fangs and shook her head. "No."

"Do as I say, Rosalie."

She shook her head again. "Nope, no way. Not when you're all… growly and weirdly angry."

"Did he touch you?" Hudson asked.

"No. He was just crude, but then he sniffed me, and he must have smelled you because he apologized and left."

Hudson was still growling and staring around the bar. She grabbed his hand and squeezed it. "Hudson, look at me."

She squeezed his hand until he finally looked at her. "It was no big deal. I shouldn't have brought it up. I didn't understand what he and his friend were talking about, but now I do. Relax, okay?"

He leaned forward, the intensity in his gaze making her feel oddly turned on. "If any shifter touches you, you tell me immediately. Do you understand, Rosie?"

"Yes," she said. "I will, Hudson."

That seemed to calm him, and he leaned back and picked up his fork again. He ate lasagna as if he hadn't almost just freaked out and shifted. Rosalie took another drink of wine. Man, she'd never really understand shifters.

"How was the rest of your day?" Hudson asked.

"Fine. I did some research about getting my real estate license. I already know most of it, but I want to have a proposal for Jace when I return to work about how I'll balance schooling and work. He's already said he'll work with my school schedule, but I want to be prepared for my meeting with him."

"When are you going to start?" Hudson asked.

"Probably next year. There's a course starting mid-January. It seems like forever, but it's the end of September, so that's only three months. After that, I went to my mom's house for dinner and a visit."

"Did she get her sink fixed?"

"Yeah. A plumber came out yesterday and fixed it. How's work going?"

"Busy." Hudson finished the lasagna and placed the lid on the container before wiping his mouth. "That was really good. Thanks, Rosalie."

"You're welcome. So, it's been busy, huh? Lots of, uh, people in tonight?"

"For a Tuesday night, yeah."

"Good, good… what did that raccoon shifter say to you?" she asked, then blushed.

He glanced at the two shifters. They were staring at him, and the one winked at him. He looked back at Rosalie. "How do you know they're raccoon shifters?"

"I work with one," she said. "I recognized the nervous energy and dark circles under the eyes."

He laughed. "Yeah, they're one of the easier shifters to pick out."

"So… what did she say? I saw her whispering in your ear."

Rosalie! Cool it. You're not dating, for God's sake.

"She asked me to go for drinks after my shift."

Her face went hot and then cold and then hot again. Through numb lips, she said, "Oh. Are you?"

"No."

"You can," she said. "I mean, we're not dating, so if there's someone you're interested in…"

Rosalie! What are you doing? Shut up!

She ignored her inner voice. As much as she hated the thought of Hudson hooking up with the pretty raccoon shifter, she would feel terrible if he had a chance at a relationship and didn't take it because of her. He was her friend, and she wanted good things for him, even if the thought of Hudson in the raccoon shifter's bed made her want to barf.

It almost looked like hurt in his eyes when he said, "You want me to go out with her?"

"What? No! But we're friends, and I want the best for you. If you're attracted to the raccoon shifter, then I don't want… that is, I wouldn't want to -"

"I'm not going to go out with someone else while we're... together," he said.

Relief swooped through her.

He didn't say he wasn't attracted to her.

She grabbed her wine glass and drank the rest of it in two large gulps. It was fine. No big deal. In two weeks, she'd be with Lincoln, the man she loved, and she'd be happy – no *delighted* – if Hudson started dating that trampy little raccoon.

"What's wrong?"

"Nothing," she said.

"You're angry."

"I'm not angry," she said.

"I can smell your anger, Rosalie."

She sighed and lied through her teeth. "I was just thinking of something my mother said earlier about shifters. She's racist about shifters, and it pisses me off."

"You can't choose family," he said.

"Yeah, I know." She smiled at him, trying to work up her nerve to ask him to come over after work. Before she could, he glanced over at the bar.

"I should get back. My break is almost over."

"Oh, right. Of course."

She slid out of the booth and grabbed her purse and the empty container, staring in confusion at Hudson when he stood beside her. "What?"

"I'll walk you to your truck."

"It's only nine," she said, "It's perfectly safe."

"I'll walk you," he repeated.

"Thank you." She walked toward the door, acutely aware of Hudson's hand resting against the small of her back, of the brush of his body against hers. He walked her out of the bar and across the parking lot to her truck. She'd gotten a decent spot close to the bar but still liked that he walked her out. Apparently, chivalry was a turn-on for her.

She unlocked her truck and, before she could lose her nerve, said, "Do you want to come over after work?"

"It'll be late," he said. "After one."

"I don't mind. I'm on holiday, remember?"

"Are you sure?" He gave her a searching look, and she nodded before digging into her purse.

"Here, this is a spare key to my place."

He hesitated, and she gave him an encouraging smile. "I might be in bed and don't want to leave the house unlocked."

He frowned. "If you're in bed, I shouldn't -"

"I want you to come over. Really. Wake me up if I'm sleeping, okay?" She pressed the key into his hand. "I mean it, Hudson."

"Okay." He pocketed the key and shoved his hands into his pockets while she tossed her purse and the empty lasagna container into the passenger seat.

When she turned to face him, he said, "Thanks again for the food. It was delicious."

"You're welcome."

Was she really hoping he would kiss her goodbye? They weren't in a relationship so why the hell would he? Still, disappointment swirled in her belly when he started to edge away.

"I'll see you later," he said gruffly.

"Yeah, okay. I'll…"

Jealousy suddenly flared. That damn raccoon shifter was standing outside of the bar. She was staring at them, a cigarette burning between her fingers. She studied Hudson's big body with blatant appreciation, and when she had the audacity to give Rosalie a smug little smile, Rosalie's jealousy flamed into a burning torch.

She pressed her body against Hudson, stood on her tiptoes, hooked her hands around the back of his thick neck and tugged. He bent and then made a startled noise when she mashed her mouth against his.

She might have taken him by surprise, but in five seconds flat, he was taking control of the kiss. His big hands slipped around her body, and he cupped her ass as he angled his mouth over hers. His tongue traced the seam of her lips, and she opened immediately. He made a low growl before sliding his tongue deep into her mouth. She sucked hard on it, and he squeezed her ass in a possessive way that made her whole body hot.

He kissed her repeatedly, not with his usual gentleness but in a hard and demanding manner that made her ache to have him inside of her. Maybe she could lure him into the truck for a quickie. Show that slutty little raccoon shifter that Hudson belonged to her.

Rosalie!

She tuned out her shocked inner voice and reached for the front of Hudson's pants. She wanted him. She *needed* him.

"Stop, little human." Hudson's big hand covered hers.

She whined in disappointment. "I want it."

Jesus, she could almost feel the pout on her face.

He grinned and pressed a quick kiss against her swollen mouth. "You can have it later."

"I want it now," she said tartly.

His grin turned to a laugh, and he nuzzled her neck affectionately. "Later. Go home, little Rosie. I'll be there soon."

"Promise?" she said.

"Yes." He turned her and boosted her into the truck. She leaned out and gave him another slow kiss before peeking around his broad body. The raccoon shifter was still smoking her cigarette, but there was a clear look of disappointment on her face.

Rosalie gave the raccoon her own smug smile, and Hudson said, "Who are you smiling at?"

"No one." She pressed another quick kiss against his mouth. "See you later, Hudson."

"Bye, Rosie."

SHE WAS SLEEPING WHEN HE SLIPPED INTO HER BEDROOM, MR. Pibbles weaving around his legs and meowing at him.

"Shh, Pib," he said, quickly petting the cat before stripping off his clothes. He laid them neatly over the chair in the corner and slid into the bed next to Rosalie. The cat jumped up on the bed, purring and meowing, and when he head-butted Rosalie's face, she made a snorting sound and rolled to face Hudson.

He slid closer and put his big arm around her waist, drawing her up against him. She slung her arm around him and kissed his chest before muttering, "Time is it?"

"It's late," he said in a low voice.

She didn't open her eyes, but she kissed his chest again. "Tired."

"I know, honey. Go to sleep."

"Stay, 'kay?"

"Yes." He kissed the top of her head and closed his eyes. The soft, warm curves of his mate, her rhythmic breathing, and the low purr of the cat as he sat on Hudson's hip calmed him. His fear of having another nightmare disappeared, and he drifted.

CHAPTER 15

"Tell me why you're nervous, little human."

"I'm not," Rosalie lied.

Hudson stared at her from across the kitchen table, and she rolled her eyes. "Can I just say that I kind of hate that you can smell my emotions?"

Hudson just shrugged before finishing off the last of his sandwich. "Can't help it."

"I know." She pushed at the raw carrots on her plate before crunching one down. "Are you still hungry?"

"I'm good. Thank you for lunch."

"You're welcome. You can take some more of the lasagna to work tonight if you want?"

"Sure. Thanks. Why are you nervous?" he asked.

This time, she poked at her sandwich. This morning, she'd woken a little after ten, surprised to feel Hudson's warm body pressed against hers and his big hand cupping her breast. She'd assumed when he got home, he would wake her for sex.

She'd snuggled with him for a bit, enjoying how nice it was to not wake up alone in her bed, before Mr. Pibbles' 'feed me now, human' stare and her need to pee made her slide out from his grip and hop off the bed.

She'd made breakfast, tidied the kitchen, and surfed the internet until Hudson came downstairs just before noon. He'd apologized for sleeping so long, but it hadn't bothered her. She liked having Hudson in her house but also enjoyed her alone time.

"Is it something I did to make you nervous?" Hudson asked.

"What? Of course not." Rosalie pushed her plate away. "I was just wondering about when we were going to start having kinky sex."

Hudson didn't reply, and she froze and gave him a look of dismay. "Not that the sex isn't good! It is – it's fantastic! It's the best sex I've ever had. It's just... I wanted to try some kink."

"I know," he said. "What do you want to try first?"

She took a deep breath, her nerves a tangled, jangled, mangled mess, and made herself say it. "I thought maybe, um... a spanking?"

"Me or you?" Hudson asked.

"What?"

"Do you want me to be the spanker or the spankee?" He reached across the table, snagged one of her carrot sticks and bit off a piece.

"Oh, I... would you seriously let me spank you?"

"Yes."

She stared dumbfounded at him. Never in a million years would she have thought that Hudson liked to be spanked.

She cleared her throat and said, "I didn't realize you liked to be spanked."

He shrugged. "It's not my kink, but I said I'd teach you, so if it's yours..."

"I want you to spank me," she said quickly. Her cheeks flamed traitorously red, and she stared at her half-eaten sandwich.

"No."

Her head shot up. "No?"

"No."

She frowned at him. "But you said you would teach me to be kinky."

"And I will. But I won't spank you."

Frustration edged out her nervousness. Lions liked spanking women. It had specifically said so in her book, and she wanted to try it with Hudson before committing to it with Lincoln.

Why is that? Is it because you don't trust Lincoln will stop if you don't like it?

She was starting to get damn irritated with her inner voice. It didn't seem afraid to point out everything she didn't want to hear. Lincoln would stop if she asked him to. It was just that the idea of being spanked didn't do anything but make her feel anxious.

She'd watched a few porn videos of women being spanked, and it hadn't done a thing for her – other than make her cringe. But maybe it was one of those things you had to experience to enjoy.

"I want you to spank me," she said.

He grinned, and her scowl deepened as he said, "I know you do, little human."

"So, you'll do it?"

"No." He ate the rest of her carrot stick and leaned back in his chair, his expression serene.

"But you said I could spank you."

"I meant it," he replied.

"But you won't spank me?"

"Nope."

She stood and paced the kitchen, throwing angry death stares at him. "That makes no sense, Hudson. And – and you know what? You can't just renege on a promise like that. That's a shitty thing to do."

"I'm not," Hudson said. "I'll teach you to be kinky. It just won't involve spanking."

She crossed her arms and gave him another furious look. "Fine. Maybe I'll find someone else to spank me."

He was up and out of his chair way faster than should have been possible for a man his size. His big hands cupped her hips, and he picked her up and sat her on the counter. They were face-to-face now, and he made a low growl before dipping his head and giving her a light nip on the base of her throat.

"I will not spank you, little human, and you're not letting anyone else spank you either."

"What is with you and this no spanking thing anyway?"

"I won't do anything that hurts you, sweet Rosie." This time, he licked her throat, and she wasn't sure what turned her on more - his statement or the throat licking.

"I have three bite marks from you," she pointed out.

"That's different." He pushed aside her t-shirt and licked the closest bite mark.

"It isn't." Her damn back arched like it had a mind of its own when he cupped her breast.

"It is." He ran his thumb back and forth over her nipple until it hardened. "Like my scent, the bite marks will protect you from other shifters when I'm not around to keep you safe."

"I don't need protecting." Her hands wrapped around his big biceps and squeezed when he licked her throat again.

"You do, little Rosie," he said. "The world is a dangerous

place. When shifters smell my scent and see my bite marks, they'll know you're mine."

Being told she was Hudson's sent a weird but undeniable wave of lust through her. Hudson sniffed the air before grinning at her. She blushed furiously and said, "You promised to teach me to be kinky."

"I did." He lifted her into his arms and carried her out of the kitchen and up the stairs. When they reached her bedroom, he set her on her feet and disappeared into her closet. When he returned, she stared at the two scarves in his hand. "Wh-what are those for?"

He set them on the bed before reaching out and hooking one big finger through the belt loop of her jeans. He tugged her closer, step by step, as she stared up at him.

"Hudson, what are the scarves for?"

"You'll see, sweet Rosie." He tugged her shirt over her head and unclasped her bra, giving her tits an appreciative look before he unbuttoned her jeans. He tugged them and her panties down to her feet, and she stepped out of them. She resisted the urge to suck in her stomach. Hudson found her attractive - the bulge in his jeans made it more than obvious.

She reached out and palmed the bulge. He sucked in a breath and quickly stripped off his t-shirt before shoving his jeans down his thick thighs. She stared at his cock, and her mouth watered in anticipation.

Mine, she thought greedily before wrapping her hand around his thickness. She stroked him, and he made a low growl of pleasure before cupping both her breasts. She ran her thumb over the wide head and through the drop of precum that had gathered there. When she sucked the liquid off her thumb, Hudson's face twisted, and he pulled her up against him. He rubbed his dick against her soft skin, and she stared up at him.

"I want to taste you, Hudson."

"Fuck." His fangs dropped, and his big hands tightened around her hips before he shook his head. "Not this time, honey."

"Why not?" she asked.

"I have something else in mind."

"But you've gone down on me. I want to return the favour."

He cupped her face, his thumb rubbing across her bottom lip. "You will, baby. Just not this time."

Before she could pout, he turned her around and reached for one of the scarves on the bed. He folded it into a long strip and kissed the back of her shoulder. "Give me a safe word, Rosie."

Her breath eased out of her in a shuddering exhale. Just the phrase 'safe word' made her pulse race and anxiety brew in her belly.

Hudson kissed her shoulder again. "I'm not going to do anything that hurts or you don't like, honey."

She twisted her neck to stare up at him. "I know."

He pressed a quick kiss against her mouth, and she said, "Apple."

She waited for him to tease her about her choice of safe word, but he just nodded. "If you want me to stop, say apple, and I'll stop. All right, baby?"

"All right," she whispered.

"Close your eyes."

She closed her eyes, trying to breathe through her anxiety when Hudson placed the scarf over her eyes and tied it behind her head. Her breath puffed out of her in little gasps, and she jerked when Hudson slipped his arm around her waist.

"Relax, honey," he murmured before leading her a couple of steps to the bed. He helped her onto the bed and pressed on her back. "Lie on your back."

She did what he asked, trying not to feel self-conscious. Not being able to see Hudson was freaking her out just the tiniest bit. What if he didn't find her as attractive as he said? What if right now he was staring at the way her stomach stuck out and her thighs touched or –

"You're so beautiful, sweet Rosie." Hudson's low growl washed over her, and the sincerity in his voice washed away all of her doubts.

"Thank you." She cupped her breasts and parted her thighs enticingly. "I want you, Hudson."

"I want you too."

She felt the bed dip under his weight and his hands wrapped around her wrists. He tugged until her hands were held out in front of her, and she froze, her head turning back and forth a little when she felt him wrap the second scarf around her wrists. "What are you doing?"

He kissed the palm of her hand. "Do you trust me?"

"Yes."

He tightened the scarf around her wrists and raised her hands above her head. She tilted her head to see, but it was a useless gesture with the blindfold on. It didn't matter anyway. He was tying her to the headboard. She didn't need to see to know that.

Anxiety and lust warred within her. Lust won when Hudson finished tying her to the headboard and trailed one finger down her chest and between her breasts before circling her belly button almost lazily.

"Comfortable?"

She tugged on her restraints, both turned on and alarmed when she realized that she was truly trapped. "Um, yes."

"Good."

She cried out when his warm mouth closed around her nipple and sucked. She arched and twisted, crying out again when his fingers tugged on her other nipple. He released her nipple, and she waited in the darkness in breathless anticipation for his next touch. His tongue licked down her ribs, and she squealed and moaned, her thighs clenching together.

"Hudson, please!" she begged. "Fuck me."

His warm laugh against her ribs made goosebumps prickle to life on her skin. "I've only just started, little Rosie."

"Please!"

"Patience," he said.

Her hips arched when his fingers traced around her belly button again. When he tugged on her dark curls, she immediately let her legs fall apart, moaning in disappointment when he trailed his fingers back up her body and teased her nipple instead.

His warm mouth and wet tongue tasted and licked across her upper body, leaving no spot untouched. She twisted beneath his skillful mouth, the only sound her harsh panting and breathless cries of need. The blood roared in her ears, a rhythmic whoosh that almost drowned out the sound of her begging.

When he sucked on her nipple again, she cried his name and twisted her body toward him, trying to wrap her legs around his thick thigh. If she didn't find some release for the ache in her pussy, she'd go mad.

He pushed her onto her back again and pinned her there with one heavy hand on her abdomen. She turned her face toward him and scowled, yanking futilely at her bonds. "Untie me, Hudson."

He laughed. "No, little human."

"Yes! Untie me right now so I can…"

"So, you can, what?"

"Tie you up and fuck you!" Her voice was shrill with need, but she wasn't the least bit ashamed.

"You can tie me up next time," he said.

"Hudson, no! Let me go right now!" she said.

He paused. "Honey, you remember that you say your safe word if you want this to stop, right?"

She scowled impatiently. "Yes, I know. I don't *want* to say my safe word. I want you to untie me so that I can fuck you."

He just laughed again, and her protest died on her lips when she felt *his* lips press against the curls at the top of her pussy.

"Do that again," she demanded.

He did as she asked, kissing her curls again before she felt his big body settle between her legs. His wide shoulder nudged her thighs apart, and she spread her legs wide and lifted her hips in silent appeal.

When he didn't do anything, she yanked at her bonds before kicking his thigh with one foot. "Hudson! Be nice!"

"I am being nice, Rosie."

"No, you're not! You're not being nice at all. You're being – oh, oh God!"

She arched again at the unexpected warmth of Hudson's tongue licking her pussy from her tight entrance to her throbbing clit. He didn't linger on her clit, and she made a whine of disappointment when he kissed her inner thigh.

He nibbled on her inner thighs, licking and nipping at them with his sharp fangs. Blind and restrained, she could only wait helplessly for each touch, each taste, each torment. His warm tongue licked down her thigh to her kneecap, and he kissed the top of her knee before kissing his way back up the top of her thigh.

"Oh my God!" She cried out. "Please, Hudson! Please!"

Her entire body tensed as she waited in the darkness to see if he would give her what she wanted. His tongue slid across her clit, and she immediately arched into his mouth, her arms straining at her bonds. When he sucked on her clit, she came in a roaring rush that sent bright lights flashing across the darkness. She came and then came again, her body writhing under Hudson's mouth and tongue as he licked her clit repeatedly.

When she finally collapsed against the bed, her limbs trembling with exertion and her pulse pounding in her eardrums, she barely felt Hudson moving on the bed. His big hands grasped her hips, and he lifted and turned her onto her stomach in one smooth motion. The scarf twisted and tightened around her wrists as he lifted her to her knees.

"Spread your legs." Hudson's voice was hoarse.

Feeling a little vulnerable and exposed, she kept her legs closed. "Hudson, I – oh!"

He'd slapped her on her ass, and he spanked her other cheek when she still didn't move. "Spread your legs, Rosie. Now."

She spread them apart, and Hudson pushed his big body between them before pressing his big hand on her back and pushing her upper body to the bed. "Wider."

She opened them wide until the strain in her thighs matched the strain in her arms, and Hudson made a growl of approval before caressing her ass. "So fucking beautiful, little human."

His dick pushed at her entrance, pushed and then slid in, and she cried his name as he filled her. She tried to wiggle forward, but his hands clamped down on her hips and held her still as he pushed forward relentlessly.

"No, Rosie, be my good girl," he growled.

She stopped wiggling and arched her back in supplication. Hudson made another low growl of approval and ran one hand down her back. "Good."

"Hudson," she moaned into the darkness, "it's too much."

He retreated until just the head of his cock was in her, and she took a deep breath. "I can't take all of you like this."

"Yes, you can." He pushed forward again, his hands refusing to let her wiggle away from his invasion. "Relax, honey."

"It's too much," she gasped out. "Too – oh god, ohhhh...."

One hand had slipped under her to rub at her clit, and she pressed against his rough fingers as he thrust and retreated until she felt his pelvis resting against her ass.

He kneaded her ass with one hand, his other hand slipping from her clit to her abdomen to lift until she raised her upper body. He kept one hand on her stomach, helping to support her weight as he rubbed her lower back with his other hand. "Good girl, honey."

"All of it?" She panted, her head twisting back and forth behind the darkness of the blindfold.

"Yes. You feel so good, baby. So fucking wet and tight."

She was stuffed to the brim with cock, her pussy stretched to the limit, but holy hell, did it feel good when he pushed in and out of her. His thickness brushed against her inner walls, and she rocked her hips, meeting each of his strokes as he pushed in and out.

He was making low growls and groans of pleasure as he took her repeatedly. She stiffened when he tilted her hips up, and the head of his cock pressed against a lightning bolt of a spot in her pussy.

"Fuck!" She shrieked, not caring if her neighbours could hear her.

Hudson growled again and thrust harder and faster, holding her still as he hit her g-spot with every stroke. She screamed his name, her entire body shaking and shivering as pleasure so intense she never even imagined it could exist exploded through her.

Hudson roared her name. He pushed deep and stayed there, her pussy squeezing around his cock with every pulse of her orgasm. Fresh wetness flooded her pussy, and Hudson rocked back and forth, both of them panting and moaning until he pulled out of her, and she collapsed on her stomach.

Before she could even ask, Hudson had untied her hands and pulled the blindfold off. She kept her eyes closed, her body still shaking with pleasure as Hudson turned her on her side. He rubbed her arms with his warm hands, massaging away the pins and needles as she tried to control her runaway heartbeat.

After about five minutes, he kissed her forehead. "Okay?"

She opened her eyes and stared silently at him.

He rubbed her arms again and gave her a worried look. "Honey, are you okay?"

"I think I just had a g-spot orgasm," she whispered.

He grinned at her, and she touched the full beard still on his face. "I didn't… I mean, I've never… that was really good."

He laughed, his fangs flashing in the light, and she gave him an embarrassed look. "I mean, it was amazing. Sorry, my brain is still recovering from the most intense orgasm of my life."

"You're welcome," he said.

She started laughing, and he pulled her into his embrace, nuzzling her throat and pressing kisses against her shoulder. She kissed his thick neck and rubbed his back. "Was it good for you?"

"Really good, little human."

She poked him in the back, and he laughed and gave her a playful nip. "It was incredible. Did you like being tied up and blindfolded?"

She considered his question for a moment before nodding. "Yes."

"Good." He pulled her even closer and nuzzled her throat again, licking at the healing bite marks.

"You spanked me," she said.

"A couple of slaps isn't really a spanking."

"Says the guy who didn't get his ass slapped."

He laughed and kissed her throat. "Did you like it?"

She hesitated, and he lifted his head and stared at her. "Did you?"

"I didn't hate it," she said.

"But?"

"But I don't think spanking is for me. I mean, I know it wasn't actually spanking, but I think it was enough for me to know it's not a kink for me."

He just nodded, and she pressed her face against his chest. She should be worried about her newfound discovery. If she didn't like being spanked, then –

She cut the thought off before it started. She didn't want to think about being with someone else. Not when she was in Hudson's arms, and not when he'd just given her the best damn orgasm of her life.

"You okay?" Hudson's voice rumbled from his chest, and she nodded and snuggled closer.

"I'm good. Thank you, Hudson. It was amazing."

"For me too, sweet Rosie."

CHAPTER 16

"Hey, Rosie?"

"Hmm?" She stirred the stew bubbling on the stove before turning the burner to low and placing the lid on it. "Do you want two containers of stew to take to work or just one?"

"Two, please. I'm sorry about this morning."

She turned to face Hudson. He was sitting at the table, her iPad in front of him, and Mr. Pibbles sitting on his lap.

"You don't have to apologize, Hudson. I don't care if you shift to your polar bear form while we're sleeping. Besides, it was a good way to test if the bed was worth its cost, right?" She smiled at him, and he grinned at her before studying her iPad again.

She turned to the counter and flipped through the recipe book, idly wondering if she had enough time to make homemade biscuits to send along with the stew. One thing she'd learned about Hudson was how much he enjoyed eating. She'd gone grocery shopping again yesterday after he went through the veggies and fruit that usually lasted her an entire week in just a day and a half.

It was Friday afternoon, and Hudson had joined her at her place every night this week after he had finished work. She'd been sleeping both nights – as hard as she tried, she wasn't a night owl – and he hadn't woken her, just climbed into bed with her. He was in his polar bear form again when she woke this morning.

She rubbed her thighs absentmindedly as she turned the page on the recipe book. She was a little grateful he didn't wake her. They had so much sex during the day before he went to work she wasn't sure she could handle another round when he got home.

She grinned to herself. Not that she would say no if he did wake her up. Sex with Hudson was delightfully addictive. He was incredible at making her climax, and he was all about giving her pleasure.

She paused in the middle of turning a page. She still hadn't even given him a blow job. It wasn't that she didn't want to give him one, but once they were in bed, he had this way of making it all about her that was both sweet and exhilarating. But maybe he thought she was a selfish lover.

Her stomach twisted. Maybe Hudson wasn't enjoying sex with her as much as she was enjoying it with him.

He is. Would he spend all day with you if he didn't? He goes home to grab a change of clothes, and that's it. What you need to be concerned about is that you're not even being remotely kinky with him. You have one week left before you go to that kink dance party and seduce Lincoln, and the only kinky thing you've tried is being tied up.

She closed the recipe book and chewed on her bottom lip. She did need to be kinkier. Time was rapidly running out, but more problematic was how her entire body recoiled when she thought about going to the dance party.

Is it the thought of the dance party or the thought of seducing Lincoln that's making you feel sick?

She ignored her inner voice. She loved Lincoln. She wanted to be with him. She wanted to marry him and have lion babies with him.

Do you, though?

"Rosie?"

She turned and smiled at Hudson. "Sorry, just all up in my head."

He was studying her and hating that he could read – well, smell – her emotion so well, she said, "I think it's time for another kink lesson, don't you?"

He was silent for a long moment before he nodded. "Sure. What do you want to try this time?"

She didn't know what to tell him. She had the book she bought, *So You Want to be Kinky*, but the thought of bringing it out and casually perusing it with Hudson made her cheeks burn. Why the hell couldn't she remember what she'd read?

Because you didn't read it. You made it as far as suggestion number five –nipple clamps – and noped right out of reading the rest. Remember?

Shit. That was right. She had read about nipple clamps and then made the fatal error of googling images of them. She'd closed the browser in about thirty seconds flat, shocked and a little horrified by what she'd seen. The book had gone to the bottom of her nightstand drawer, and she hadn't opened it since.

"Rosie?"

"Not nipple clamps," she blurted out and then gave him an appalled look. "Oh God. Did I just say the words 'nipple clamps' to you?"

He laughed. "Yeah. C'mere, honey."

She crossed toward him as he set the cat on the floor and pulled her into his lap instead. He put his arms around her and rubbed her hip. "What did you want to try?"

"Honestly, I'm not sure what there is. I mean... I don't know..."

God, why did she have to sound like such a naïve idiot all the time?

Hudson kissed her upper chest before grabbing her iPad off the table. She rested her head on his shoulder, watching as he used one finger to type into Google. He scanned through the results and then picked a link. The page loaded, and she read the list's title out loud, trying not to feel embarrassed.

"Thirty Sex Ideas to Try With Your Partner." She cleared her throat and read through the list. Oh, super... nipple clamps were number ten. Why did so many kinky things have to involve pain? She vetoed the hot wax, the nipple clamps, and the flogging almost immediately. She didn't like pain and didn't understand why it turned some people on. The two light butt slaps Hudson had given her, while not a total turn-off, had solidified her views on how she felt about having painful things done to her during sex.

She was a little embarrassed that she didn't know what some terms meant. As the silence dragged on, she began to feel awkward and weird that she couldn't find one she wanted to try. Her discomfort growing, she decided to pick one that seemed relatively innocuous.

"How about pegging?" she said.

Hudson raised an eyebrow at her, a look of surprise crossing his craggy features. "That's a strong no."

"Why not?" she asked.

"Do you know what pegging is?" he said.

"Of course."

He sniffed the air, and she sighed. "Fine, no, I don't know exactly what it is. It involves a vibrator or dildo, right?"

"Pegging is when a person wears a strap-on dildo and fucks..." he stopped and cleared his throat, "penetrates their partner anally."

Her mouth dropped open, and she stared at Hudson silently before bursting into giggles. She laughed until tears ran down her face, until her stomach ached, and she couldn't breathe. Every time she started to get some semblance of control, she would stare at Hudson's calm and unruffled expression, and the laughter would start all over again.

"Oh my God," she wheezed. "Oh God, I can't... I can't even picture doing that to you."

"Good. Because you're not," Hudson said. "I'll teach you a lot of things, but how to peg isn't one of them."

She laughed again, resting her head on his shoulder and wiping at her streaming eyes. "Oh man, I'm sorry, Hudson. That's the last time I suggest something without being completely clear on what it is."

"Good idea, little human."

She giggled a final time and straightened on his lap. "Anal sex is considered kinky, right?"

"Some people think it is, yes."

"Have you had anal sex with a woman before?"

He nodded, and she chewed at her bottom lip. "Okay, well, let's do that then."

He studied her for a moment. "Do you want to have anal sex, Rosalie?"

"I want to learn to be kinky," she said. "Anal sex is kinky."

"Yes, but do you actually *want* my dick in your ass?" Whether it was the bluntness of his words or the honest curiosity in his tone, she couldn't help but tell him the truth.

"No. Not really."

"Then we don't do it. Find something else."

She thought about arguing but already knew Hudson well enough to know that he wouldn't budge on his decision.

She scanned the list again, feeling hopeless and stupid when none appealed to her.

Face it, girl. You're just not kinky. Never will be.

She was! She could be! She thought fiercely. She just needed to be brave and remember why she was doing this.

"Public sex," she said. "I want to have sex in a public place."

"Okay," he said. "Any particular spot come to mind?"

She shook her head before giving him a shy look. "Do you have any ideas?"

He shrugged. "A public bathroom is the most cliché, I suppose."

Her nose wrinkled. "They're not very clean. I guess I could bring some disinfectant spray in my purse."

He laughed. "Nothing sexier than a woman with disinfectant spray in her purse."

She poked him in the side. "Quiet, you. You can't blame me for wanting to protect my lady bits from gross things."

He laughed again and kissed her neck. "Fair enough. Maybe we could have sex in the bathroom at the theatre."

She gave him a horrified look. "There are always a ton of kids at the theatre. What if they heard us?"

"You'd just have to be very quiet." He licked her collarbone, and the familiar beat of lust started up in her belly.

"I think we've established that I'm not very good at being quiet when we're having sex," she moaned when his hand cupped her breast.

"You are rather loud when I make you come all over my face. Any complaints from the neighbours yet?" He asked.

She blushed and shook her head. "No, but I expect they'll give me a written notice at the next condo board meeting."

He grinned at her and rested his hand on her thigh as he stared at the list again. "So, we can try public sex, but it isn't something we can do right this very minute. What about the dom/sub thing?"

"Um…" Shit, it was the first time that he had made a suggestion for kink, and she hated that she was going to shoot it down. "I'm sorry, but I'm just not into pain."

He rubbed her thigh. "A dom/sub relationship doesn't have to be about pain."

"Doesn't it?" She could hear the doubt in her voice. "I thought the dom told the sub what to do, and if they didn't do it, they would be punished with a spanking or a flogging or something like that."

"Not all punishment has to be spankings and floggings. Besides," he gave her a devilish grin, "do what your dom tells you, and there won't be any punishment."

"Are you – are you a dom?" she asked.

He shrugged. "I like being in control in the bedroom."

Yes, she supposed she already knew that. She hadn't been with him for all that long, but there were signs if she looked for them. The bites he gave her when she didn't obey him fast enough, the way he took charge when they had sex. Even when she was on top and riding him, there was no doubt that he was the one in control.

She took a deep breath. "Okay, we can try that then."

He studied her for a few moments, then cupped her breast again. He kneaded it gently and kissed her neck before sucking on her earlobe. "I like your dress. It's pretty."

"Thank you." If she didn't get off his lap soon, she'd be leaving a wet mark on his jeans, and he'd discover that she wasn't wearing panties.

Tart.

Maybe, but after her shower this morning, there had been something freeing and a little naughty about going without panties. Not that she'd been planning on seducing Hudson in her kitchen, but now that she was sitting on his lap and she could feel the thick hardness of his cock against her ass…

She ground against his erection, and he groaned before squeezing her knee and then pushing on her leg. "Open."

She spread her legs for him immediately, and he slipped his hand under her dress to stroke her inner thighs. "You should wear a dress more often, little Rosie," he said. "I like how easily I can…"

His fingers made contact with her bare pussy, and she would have giggled at the look of surprise on his face if she wasn't already feeling a little desperate for him.

"No panties?" He raised his eyebrows at her.

"Thought I'd try something different," she said. "You like?"

"Very much," he growled as he stroked her wet pussy lips with the tips of his fingers. "But," he gripped the back of her neck with his other hand and tilted her head back so he could nip her throat, "you don't leave the house without wearing panties."

"You're not the – oh god, oh that feels so good - boss of me." He'd slid one thick finger deep into her pussy, and she squirmed on his lap as he added another finger.

He fucked her slowly with his fingers as he stared at her. "Your pussy is for me and only me, Rosie. The only time you go without panties is at home with me. Understand?"

"I do what I want," she whispered unconvincingly. If this was what a dom/sub relationship was about, she was definitely down for it. She was soaking wet and already close to coming just from Hudson's fingers.

The bite at the base of her throat had healed completely over the last few days, and she cried out when Hudson bent his head and gave her a new bite mark. She cried out at the sharp but deliciously sweet pain, and her pussy squeezed around his fingers. He groaned and rubbed his dick against her ass as he licked away the trace of blood.

When he pulled his fingers out of her warmth, she gasped in disappointment and grabbed his arm. "Hudson, no."

He rubbed her clit with the tips of his fingers. "Will you wear panties when you leave the house?"

"Probably."

He gave her clit a soft pinch that, shamefully, almost made her come right there and then.

"Rosie," he said.

She grinned at him and then bit at her bottom lip when he rubbed her clit again. Fuck, she was so damn close...just a little bit more...

"No!" She gave him a look of frustration when he stopped touching her.

"Your pussy is only for me, sweet Rosie. Say it." He stroked her wet pussy lips as she squirmed on his lap.

"Touch me, please," she begged.

He smiled at her and pressed a kiss against her mouth. "Say it, little Rosie."

"Hudson!" She tried to move his hand by yanking on his wrist, but she couldn't budge it.

He nipped her throat, and she moaned again before whispering, "It's only for you."

He gave her clit a quick rub. "What's only for me?"

"My pussy."

"That's right." He kissed her throat before pulling his hand out from under her dress. She watched with blank surprise as he pulled his shirt off and folded it into a square before dropping it on the floor between his feet.

She reached out and traced one of his flat nipples. He groaned and caught her hand, kissing the palm of it before stroking her hip. "On your knees, Rosie."

"But I -" she gave him a confused look, "I said it. Isn't this the part where you make me come?"

He grinned at her. "But you required a lot of prompting to say it, didn't you, honey?"

"Yeah, but I... Hudson, I want to come."

"I know you do, but you have to wait."

"I don't want to wait," she pouted.

"Then, be a good girl next time and do what I say. On your knees."

He tugged her off his lap and then pushed lightly on her shoulders. A little bewildered, she knelt on his folded-up shirt and stared at him. "Hudson, what are you – oh.... oh!"

Her face turned bright red as she suddenly realized this was her punishment and why he had her on her knees. As Hudson smiled at her and unbuttoned his jeans, she wished that just once, she could be a sexy, confident goddess who didn't go red at the idea of giving a man a blow job.

"I'm not an expert at this or anything," she said as he reached into his pants and tugged his – oh sweet, merciful heaven – very erect cock out. Hudson groaned when she licked her bottom lip.

She gave him a nervous smile. "I'll give it my all, but I just want you to know that I've only done this a few times before and, again, the guy had, like, an average size dick, so, I mean, I'm not sure that I can even get my mouth -"

"Rosie." Hudson's big hand cupped the back of her neck, mercifully making her stop her stupid babbling. "No more talking, honey."

His hand tugged, guiding her forward. "Suck."

She slid her mouth around the wide head of his cock and sucked a bit tentatively. He groaned, his hand tightening on the back of her neck, and she sucked harder.

"Good girl," he whispered. He gathered her hair in a loose ponytail and cupped the back of her skull with his other hand. "Take more."

She did what he asked, taking as much of him into her mouth as she could. She ran her tongue up and down his smooth, hard flesh before tracing the ridge. His low groans and the way he studied her as she sucked, made her pussy ache, and her nipples harden. She pressed her thighs together and leaned forward, sucking hard and bobbing her head up and down his cock.

She could feel wetness sliding down her inner thighs, and she was a little surprised at how much she was getting into this. She hadn't expected that giving Hudson a blowjob would be a turn-on. It certainly hadn't done much for her in the past.

But the way Hudson watched her every move, the way he held her hair and guided her head back and forth over his cock, and the words of praise he kept muttering made her almost embarrassingly eager to please him.

She wanted to be good at this. She wanted to make Hudson lose control the way he made her lose control. She sucked harder and faster, gripping the base of his cock with one hand and stroking back and forth as she licked and sucked.

"Good, baby. So good," he groaned. His hand tightened in her hair, and she stared up at him as she sucked.

"Good," he repeated. More wetness dripped from her pussy, and she gave him a pleading look. She wanted to please him, but she also wanted – *needed* – to be fucked.

He pushed on the back of her skull, forcing her to take more, watching her lips spread wide around his length. The head of his cock touched the back of her throat, and she moaned around him.

He shuddered, his hand tightening in her hair before he tugged her off of his cock. He studied her red and swollen mouth before rasping, "Stand up."

She stood immediately, and when he patted his lap, she straddled him without hesitation. He lifted her dress around her waist, bunching it in one hand at her back and touched her wet pussy with the other hand.

She made an eager cry, and he smiled at her before gripping the base of his dick. "Do you want this, little human?"

"Yes," she said. "So much."

Without waiting for his reply, she lowered her body and pressed her wet entrance against the head of his dick. The head slipped in easily, and they both groaned as she settled her body onto his lap, her tight pussy taking every inch of his cock.

"Ohhh," she breathed, bracing her hands on his shoulders. She could just touch the floor with her tiptoes, and she bounced up and down, smiling when he groaned loudly and slipped his arm around her waist.

"Hang on, sweet Rosie," he growled.

She had just enough time to wrap her arms around his neck before he was thrusting hard in and out of her wet pussy. She clung to him, moaning his name as he fucked her. He made a low growl of approval when she slipped her hand between them.

"That's right. Rub your clit until you come on my dick."

His hot words set her nerve endings ablaze, and she rubbed frantically at her clit as he plunged in and out. She flung her head back and cried his name as she came, her body shaking with pleasure. His big hands tightened on her hips, and he ground his pelvis against hers as a thick beard grew on his face. He came with a harsh roar, and she rocked against him, her pussy milking his thick cock.

She collapsed against his wide chest, listening to his harsh breath and the rapid beat of his heart as he thrust lightly into her body twice more. She settled on his thighs, liking how he made no effort to move her off of him as he softened inside of her.

"Hey, Hudson?"

"Yeah?"

"I think you might be on to something with this dom/sub thing."

"I'm glad you enjoyed it, honey." He kissed her temple.

"Hmm," she replied. "it's good with us. Isn't it?"

"Yes," he answered. "It is, little Rosie."

"ROSALIE! OVER HERE!"

Standing uncertainly just inside the entrance of Bud's Bar, Rosalie turned toward the sound of Maggie's voice. Maggie was sitting in a booth near the bar and waved at Rosalie.

Rosalie walked toward her, smiling happily at her friend. She removed her jacket and set it on the seat before sliding into the booth. "Hi, Maggie."

"Hey, how are you?" Maggie replied.

"I'm good." Rosalie glanced at Hudson. He was staring at her, and she smiled and waved at him, secretly delighted when he returned her smile.

"You look good," Maggie was eyeing her critically, "you look...different."

"What do you mean?" Rosalie pulled self-consciously at her shirt.

"I don't know, just... different." Maggie's gaze fell to the bite at the base of her throat. "That bite mark still hasn't healed?"

"Oh," Rosalie touched the bite, "no, this is new."

Maggie grinned at her. "Hudson's a biter, huh?"

"No, not really. I mean, I don't think he is. It's just sometimes he..."

"Sometimes he what?"

"Nothing." She suddenly realized how weird it would sound if she said Hudson gave her little bites if she didn't agree that she belonged to him. "I'm sorry I'm a little late. Have you been waiting long?"

"Nope. Just got here myself. My shift at the coffee shop ran late," Maggie replied. "Thank God it's Friday, and I have the weekend off. It's been a crazy week. How was your day?"

Rosalie glanced at Hudson again. He was pouring a beer, and she stared at how his t-shirt hugged his abdomen before looking away. Somehow, telling Maggie she'd given Hudson a blowjob in the kitchen and then rode him like a pony seemed crude.

"Rosalie?" Maggie asked.

"I gave Hudson a blowjob in the kitchen and then rode him like a pony."

Shit.

Maggie laughed and held out her fist. "Nice."

She fist-bumped Maggie, her cheeks hot and a silly grin on her face. "Sorry, that was way too much information."

"I don't mind," Maggie said. "Hey, did you notice how all the shifters got out of your way quickly when you walked through the bar?"

Rosalie shook her head. "I... no, not really. Did they?"

"Yep, like you had the plague or something."

"It's because she smells like Hudson." Porter slipped into the booth next to Maggie and kissed her. "Hello, darlin'. How was your day?"

"Good. How was yours?"

"Better now that you're here." He winked at her, and Maggie laughed before taking his hand.

"Always the charmer. So, the shifters are staying away from Rosalie because of Hudson?"

Porter nodded. "Not many shifters are stupid enough to mess with a polar bear's woman. Hudson will rip off their heads if they even touch her."

"No, he wouldn't," Rosalie said. "He's not like that."

"Trust me. He is," Porter said. "All polar bear shifters are like that, even the females. Both males and females get real touchy about their mates being around other shifters."

"Rosalie isn't Hudson's mate. They're just... dating." Maggie glanced at Rosalie.

Porter shrugged. "Doesn't matter. His scent is strong on her. I can smell it across the bar. Most shifters will believe she's his mate. Anyway, I'm not going to interrupt your girls' night out. I just wanted to say hi. I might be a bit late tonight. It's been busy all night, and I think it'll get busier."

"All right. Wake me when you get home," Maggie said.

"Will do, darlin'." Porter gave her another kiss that lasted a little longer than the first. When he pulled away, Maggie was a bit flushed, and she gave him a shy smile that made his grin widen.

He stood and nodded to Rosalie. "Good to see you, Rosalie."

As he walked away, Maggie stared appreciatively at his ass before smiling at Rosalie. "So, everyone in this bar thinks you're Hudson's mate. Does that bother you?"

"No." Rosalie tried to sound casual. "Hudson and I know the truth, so it's fine. And he said his scent will fade once we stop having sex, so… it's no big deal."

"Right." Maggie smiled at Tori when the rabbit shifter placed menus on the table.

"Hi, sexy ladies. What can I get you to drink?" she asked.

"I'll have a glass of wine. Thank you, Tori," Maggie said.

"Me as well, please," Rosalie said.

"Sure, hon. You guys going to have something to eat? Maybe share an appetizer?"

"We'll share the spinach dip. Sound good, Rosalie?" Maggie asked.

Rosalie nodded, and Tori moved on.

"So, how's the kinky sex going?" Maggie lowered her voice and leaned forward.

"Good. We, um, that is, Hudson, tied me up and blindfolded me the other night. I liked it."

"That's great. What else have you done?" Maggie asked.

"Oh, um," Rosalie cleared her throat, "well, I asked him to spank me, but he refused."

"He did?"

"Yeah. Hudson said he wouldn't do anything that would hurt me. Which, you'd be surprised at how many kinky sex ideas that eliminates."

"Yeah, I can imagine," Maggie said. "But it's sweet that he refuses to do anything that might hurt you."

"It is," Rosalie said.

"But not helpful for what you're trying to accomplish. What else have you done kink wise?"

Rosalie traced the bite mark on her throat. "We tried the dom/sub thing."

"Oh." Maggie gave her a doubtful look. "Doesn't that involve pain?"

"That's what I thought, but Hudson said it didn't have to. He was the one who suggested it, and once he said he wouldn't, like, spank me or flog me or something for punishment, I agreed to try it."

"Did you like it?"

Rosalie nodded. "Yes. Quite a bit, actually. I mean, it didn't feel super kinky or anything. It was mostly just Hudson, um, asking me to say or do certain things, and when I didn't, his punishment was a little bite and then having to give him the blowjob before he'd let me have an orgasm."

"Wait," Maggie said. "So, you're not into pain, but," she eyed the bite mark on Rosie's throat, "he keeps biting you, and you let him do that?"

"It's not that painful."

"He breaks the skin, it's painful."

"Fine, it's painful," Rosalie said. "But the thing is, even before we deliberately tried the dom/sub thing, it was obvious that he likes to be in charge, you know? He does the biting thing when I won't tell him I belong to him."

She hesitated before blurting out the rest. "I deliberately don't say it at first because I like it when Hudson gets possessive, and I like it when he bites me."

"Okay," Maggie said.

"Okay? That's it?" Rosalie said.

Maggie laughed. "What else do you want me to say?"

"I… well, I don't know."

"You found a kink you like. That's a good start," Maggie said. "What else have you tried?"

"That's it, really," Rosalie said.

Maggie blinked at her. "Oh. Well, do you think maybe with Hudson's refusal to do certain things, you should consider finding someone else to teach you some stuff?"

"No," Rosalie said quickly. "No, I'm sure we can find some

other kinky stuff to do. We were, uh, just getting to know each other's likes and dislikes first, you know?"

"Sure. But you've only got a week until that party at the kink fest, right? And if you smell as strongly of Hudson as Porter says you do, then you should probably stop having sex with him by, like, Monday or Tuesday. Otherwise, Lincoln will smell him on you and not go near you. So, that's not a whole lot of time to -"

"It's fine," Rosalie said. "We'll probably amp up the kink this weekend."

"Here's the thing," Maggie said. "Maybe this isn't any of my business, but I've been doing some Googling on lion shifters, and from what I can tell – a dom/sub kink isn't their thing. They seem to be into S&M a lot, but it doesn't seem that many of them are interested in being a dom. So, while it's great that you like it, Lincoln might not be willing to do that particular kink."

Tori returned with their drinks and gave them a quick smile before walking away. Rosalie sipped at her wine as awkward silence descended.

"Rosalie, I -"

"It's me," she said. "I'm the problem."

"What do you mean?" Maggie asked.

"I don't think I'm all that kinky," Rosalie said. "I mean, I'm trying, but I'm not sure that I..."

She sighed and sipped at her wine again. "We looked over a list of some kinky things to try, and I couldn't find a single one that I was even interested in. I finally said public sex because I had to say something, you know? I'm glad Hudson refuses to do anything that might hurt me because I don't want to try it."

Maggie gave her a worried look. "It's fine if you're limited in what you like in kink, Rosalie, but if you want to be with Lincoln, then -"

"I know," Rosalie buried her face in her hands. "Believe me, I know."

"Do you even want to be with Lincoln anymore?" Maggie asked.

"Of course I do. I love him, I just..."

"Just what?"

"I don't know," Rosalie lifted her head and stared at Maggie. "Hudson is sweet and kind and amazing in bed - incredible in bed - but he's made it clear that he's only in this for the sex. Plus, I'm in love with Lincoln, right? And if I'm not, what kind of person does it make me to be so madly in love with someone and then forget about them because someone else is in my bed?"

"Rosalie -"

"It makes me awful. That's what it makes me," Rosalie said.

"You're not awful," Maggie said. "I think you're not certain you're in love with Lincoln, and that's not surprising. You were never more than friends with him, right? Sometimes, what you think is love just isn't. You know?"

"Maybe," Rosalie said. "But I'm an idiot if I try to have something with Hudson. The only reason he's even sleeping with me is because he's looking to get laid without commitment."

"Well, isn't that why you picked Hudson? He's basically like Lincoln and -"

"They're nothing alike," Rosalie said. Even she could hear the irritation in her voice. She sighed. "Sorry. It's just that Hudson isn't anything like Lincoln. He's sweet, funny, supportive, and he... he's just really great."

"So why are you going after Lincoln instead of Hudson?"

Maggie asked. "Because, no offense, but the only things I've heard you say about Lincoln is that he's super good looking and a flirt."

"I don't know," Rosalie groaned. "I feel like I don't know *anything* anymore. Like, I was so sure that I was in love with Lincoln, and now I can't stop thinking about Hudson. But I don't know if it's because I'm sleeping with him and he's good at sex, or if it's because of something more or -"

"Rosalie?"

She glanced up to see her boss standing next to their table. Shit, had he heard what she said about sleeping with Hudson?

Uh, Rosalie? Jace is a shifter. He can smell Hudson all over you.

Her inner voice made a good point. She smiled at her boss. "Hey, Jace. How are you?"

"Good. Just stopped in after work to grab a bite to eat."

Bria joined them and smiled at Rosalie. "Hey, Rosalie. Are you enjoying your vacation?"

"I am, thanks," Rosalie said.

"Glad to hear it." Bria turned to Jace. "I just did a quick tour of the place, and all the booths and tables are full. How hungry are you? Do you want to wait for a table or go somewhere else?"

"You can sit with us." Rosalie glanced at Maggie who nodded and slid over in her seat.

"You don't want to hang out with your boss on vacation," Jace said.

Rosalie laughed and patted the seat next to her. "I don't mind."

"All right." He started to sit down, glancing at Bria when she took his arm.

"I should probably sit beside her," Bria said.

Jace glanced over at the bar. Hudson stood at the end of

the bar closest to them. He had a bottle of whiskey in one hand and a glass in the other but was completely ignoring the shifter sitting in front of him and waiting for the drink. Instead, he was scowling at Jace, his big hand squeezing around the bottle.

"He knows I'm with you," Jace gave Bria a teasing grin, "and maybe I feel like living life on the edge tonight."

"Yeah, well, I prefer you with all four limbs, and the way Hudson is looking at you, he's gonna rip 'em all off if you sit next to Rosalie," Bria said. "Sit beside Maggie."

"Don't be silly. Hudson won't hurt you," Rosalie said.

"Oh really? Because he currently looks like he's trying to kill me with his stare alone," Jace said with a grin before sitting next to Maggie. "So, you're dating Hudson now, huh?"

Rosalie blushed and nodded as Bria sat down next to her. "Uh, yes."

"Good for you, Rosie." Jace studied a menu as Rosalie handed a menu to Bria.

Bria took the menu and opened it before lowering her voice. "You and Hudson?"

Rosalie gave her a small shrug and waited for Bria to ask why she was suddenly over Lincoln. Instead of asking about Lincoln, Bria studied her for a few moments before smiling. "You look really happy."

Rosalie blinked at her. "Oh, um, thanks. Yeah, I am."

"Good. I'm glad. The four of us will have to go on a double date sometime."

"Um, I'll talk to Hudson. He's not really social."

"Most polar bears aren't," Bria said. "I've never even heard of one dating a human before, but I'm not surprised he couldn't resist you. You're awesome."

As Bria studied the menu, Rosalie glanced at Hudson. He was staring at her, and her whole body reacted to the possessive heat in his gaze. It practically screamed 'mine,' and another soft tremor went through her body when he gave her a brief but wicked grin before walking to the far end of the bar.

Jesus, she was making damn sure she was awake when Hudson got home tonight. She was suddenly and undeniably horny for him. She made herself look away from his amazing ass and stare at the menu instead.

No doubt both Bria and Jace could smell her lust for Hudson. To her surprise, there was no surge of embarrassment. So she was feeling all tingly for her man. No big deal. It was to be expected.

He's not your man, Rosalie.

She swallowed down the disappointment that surged through her. God, what was wrong with her? Now she wanted another man who wasn't interested in anything but sex. She was hopeless.

"HEY, HUDSON? TAKE YOUR FIFTEEN, BIG GUY," PORTER SAID.

Hudson nodded and immediately headed toward the back hall. It was perfect timing for his break. Rosalie had just left her friends to use the bathroom. He would intercept her before she joined her friends again, take her into the small supply room, and fulfill her fantasy of public sex.

Are you sure you're doing this for her? Or are you doing it because you want your scent on her again? You want to make it clear to every shifter in this bar that she belongs to you.

He shook off his inner voice. He was doing this because Rosalie wanted it. Not because of some macho misguided effort to ensure that every part of her milky soft skin carried his scent. She already smelled like him.

Not enough, his polar bear sulked.

He ignored it. Rosalie was practically swimming in his scent, but it would never be enough for his polar bear.

She's ours, the bear growled.

Knock it off, he growled back. *And don't think I haven't noticed how you keep trying to force me to make Rosalie say she's my mate. It's never going to happen. I won't make her say that.*

His polar bear's answering growl was decidedly smug. *You will.*

Sadly, it was a possibility. The last two times he'd had sex with Rosalie, he'd come stupidly close to trying to get her to say she was his mate. It didn't help that every time he said or did anything even remotely possessive, there was a noticeable increase in her lust for him.

Listen to me, he tried to reason with his bear. *Even if I make Rosalie say she's our mate while we're fucking, it doesn't mean she's our mate. Do you understand?*

She's ours.

He sighed and leaned against the wall. It was pointless to argue with his bear. He'd just have to make sure the damn thing didn't take over at some point, or he'd start spouting off to Rosalie about being his mate. She'd freak out for certain, and he'd never see her again.

In a week, you'll never see her again, anyway.

The thought – one he'd been steadily ignoring as each day ticked by - brought on a dismaying sense of panic. Before it could settle too deeply, the door to the ladies' room opened. Rosalie appeared in the hallway, and fuck, he loved the way she smiled when she saw him, loved the intoxicating scent of happiness and lust that always covered her when he got close.

"Hi," she said.

"Hey." He held out his hand, and she took it without hesitation. He led her the few short steps to the door marked 'employees only' before quickly looking up and down the hallway. It was empty, and he opened the door and pulled her inside the room, shutting it firmly behind them.

"Hudson? What are you doing?"

He flicked the light on, and she studied the small room. Large closet was more apt of a description, and she grabbed at his shoulders when he lifted her and pressed her back against the door, holding her in place with his body.

"Legs around my waist, little human."

She did what he asked, hooking her feet in the small of his back. Her look of confusion turned to surprise when he rubbed his erection against her core.

"Hudson?" she whispered.

He kissed her, coaxing her mouth open with small nips and licks. She moaned into his mouth, and he cupped her breast, squeezing it gently through her bra and shirt as their tongues tasted and teased. When he went to flick open the button on her jeans, she reached down and pressed her hand over his, stopping him.

"What are you doing?" she whispered.

"Public sex," he kissed her soft throat, "and it's not even in a gross bathroom."

She giggled, and he grinned at her before kissing her again. "We've only got fifteen minutes, but I can do a lot to you in fifteen minutes."

He stroked his hand along her thigh before kneading her ass. She returned his kisses, but he pulled back after only a few minutes. "What's wrong?"

"Nothing," she said.

"I want the truth, little Rosie."

She sighed. "You'll think I'm an idiot or, even worse, a tease."

"I won't," he said.

"I know I said I wanted to try public sex but," she hesitated, "but this is where you work, and if we get caught, you'll be fired, and I'd feel terrible, and my boss is here, and if I go back to the booth after fucking you, he's going to know, and I don't want him to think bad about me."

She ran out of breath and gave him a miserable look as she sucked in another big gulp of oxygen. "I'm sorry."

"It's fine."

"Is it?" she asked. "Or are you just saying it's fine when it isn't?"

He grinned and gave her a quick kiss. "I mean it. I was doing this for you, little human." He kissed her again, making this one long and slow as he ground his erection against her pussy again. "My preference when fucking you is to have plenty of time to," he nipped at her earlobe and squeezed her breast again, "kiss and lick every inch of your amazing body before I bury my dick in your perfect pussy."

She moaned, and her lust was back in full force for him. He kissed the tip of her nose before setting her on her feet. She stared up at him. "Maybe it wouldn't be that bad to have a quickie just for... reasons."

"Nope. Now you have to wait until I'm finished work to get all of this." He lifted his shirt just enough to show her his flat abdomen, and she gave him a cute pout.

"You don't play fair."

"I don't." He kissed her again.

"Will you wake me if I'm asleep when you get home?" she asked.

Christ, he liked hearing her refer to her place as his home a little too much.

"Yes," he said.

"Do you promise? You haven't woken me up at all this week."

"I will tonight." He squeezed her ass a final time before opening the door and peering into the hallway. "All clear. Go back to your friends, little Rosie. I'll see you," he paused, "at home later."

"Okay." She stood on her tiptoes, and he bent so she could give him a soft kiss. "Bye, Hudson."

CHAPTER 17

Hudson stripped off his clothes and slipped into the bed. Rosalie was sound asleep in the middle of the bed. He spooned her, his hand cupping one heavy breast as he pressed a kiss against the silky skin of her back.

She'd had a bath before bed, and her skin was fragrant with the scent of vanilla. He smiled a little. Even the body wash she used wasn't enough to mask his scent. He kissed her skin again as his cock stiffened against her ass.

Normally, she slept in shorts and a t-shirt, but tonight, she was completely naked. Any guilt about waking her disappeared, and Hudson palmed her breast, squeezing it lightly as she made a soft sighing moan and pressed her ass against his dick.

He wondered if he could convince her to always sleep nude. Waking up to Rosalie's naked body every morning was his idea of heaven.

Yeah, well, in a week, you'll never wake up with her again, so there's no point in –

"Hudson?" Rosalie said sleepily.

"Hi, honey."

"Hi." She arched her back when he gave her nipple a light pinch.

He kissed her neck as she reached behind her and rubbed his hip before muttering, "How's work?"

"Fine. Did you have fun with Maggie?" He teased her nipple with his thumb and forefinger.

"Hmm, yeah."

God, she was adorable when she was a combination of sleepy and turned on. He slid his hand down to her curvy thigh. "Open."

She spread her legs immediately, and he cupped her pussy as he kissed the top of her shoulder. "That's my good girl."

"I like being your good girl." Her eyes were still closed, and her yawn turned into a low moan when he rubbed her clit.

"I like it too, baby." He circled her clit with his rough fingers, feeling a smug sort of satisfaction at how quickly she got wet for him.

She was still mostly asleep, but she rocked her hips against his fingers, making soft and sexy moans. A thick beard sprouted on his face, and his fangs dropped. His deep voice lowered an octave, and he growled, "You're my good mate, sweet Rosie. Say it."

"I'm your good mate," she said, her voice slow and dreamy.

He rubbed her clit more firmly. "Again."

"I'm your – mmm…" she arched into his hand, her eyelids flickering up briefly before closing again, "good mate."

He rubbed his beard across the back of her shoulder and nipped her soft skin with his fangs. "That's right. My mate. No one else's."

"No one else's," she repeated languidly. "Only yours."

"Does my mate want to be fucked?"

"Hmm, yes," Rosalie said with a soft sigh, widening her legs even more.

He lifted her leg up and over his hip before moving his body down a bit and guiding his cock to her wet entrance. She pushed back against him, moaning quietly as he slid deep inside of her. When he was fully sheathed, he cupped her pussy again, resting the tips of his fingers against her clit while he waited for her to adjust to his size.

"Good, my mate?" he asked after a few moments.

"Yes," she moaned. "Fuck me."

He didn't move, holding her still with his hand on her hip when she tried to move.

"Hudson, fuck me." Her sleepy pout was ridiculously endearing.

He waited patiently. His mate was clever. She would figure it out.

She tried to move again, making a low sound of frustration in the back of her throat. His polar bear growled happily when she squeezed her tight pussy around his dick and moaned, "Fuck me, my mate."

He rewarded her with slow and gentle thrusts. She met each of his thrusts, her body soft and pliant against his. He closed his eyes and concentrated on how good his mate felt, how wet her pussy was, the low sounds of her moans and the way her body shuddered when he lightly rubbed her clit. He kept the same slow pace, thrusting and retreating as she rocked her pelvis and matched his languid tempo stroke for stroke. He continued to rub her clit as her soft cries grew louder and her pussy grew wetter. He was close himself, the hot, wet grip of his mate's pussy making his balls tighten and the base of his spine tingle.

When his mate cried out and arched against him, her body trembling as her orgasm washed over her, he moaned her name and thrust deep. Her pussy squeezed around him, pulling his seed deep into her body as he came. He buried his face in her back, his hand tightening around her pussy as he held her flush against him.

When he finally came down from his high, he slid his hand from his mate's pussy to her breast. He cupped it, her nipple a hard pearl against his palm, before kissing her naked back and raising his head. He was still deep inside of her, and he rested his head on the pillow behind hers.

"My mate?" he whispered.

"Hmm?" She was already almost asleep again.

"I lo -" He shoved his polar bear down and shut his mouth with a snap, his heart pounding as his bear roared angrily and tried to surge forward again.

He held it back grimly as Rosalie made a sleepy sound. "What?"

"Nothing," he said. "Go to sleep, sweet Rosie."

She made another happy and drowsy sigh. "Good night, my mate."

His hand squeezed her breast compulsively as his bear finally retreated with a contented growl. "Good night, little mate."

"YOU HAVE NO IDEA HOW AWFUL IT IS TO BE AFRAID IN YOUR own home, Rosalie."

"Hmm," Rosalie stared at the television, barely hearing her mother's voice. She kept thinking about last night with Hudson.

She'd been asleep when he came home from work and she'd mostly woken up when he'd started touching her.

They'd had sex, and she'd gone back to sleep almost immediately.

Are you sure you had sex, Rosie?

Yes, they'd had sex when Hudson got home from work. She knew that for certain. But she must have been half asleep because something didn't make sense.

You're my good mate, sweet Rosie.

She almost swiveled in her chair to look behind her, so clearly did she hear Hudson's deep voice.

You dreamed it, Rosie. He didn't say that to you.

She sighed and rubbed at her forehead. Her inner voice was right. She'd had sex with Hudson while half-asleep and dreaming. He hadn't said anything like that to her, and she knew it because she'd asked him about it just before he left for work.

Not that she had asked him specifically about the mate thing. She couldn't seem to say the words – Hudson, did you call me your mate last night and make me say I was your mate before you would fuck me – but she had awkwardly admitted to being half asleep before asking if they'd talked during sex. He'd given her a strange look. A look that was confusion mixed in with…

Guilt, Rosie. He looked guilty.

She rubbed her forehead again as if she could rub her inner voice right out of her head. Why would Hudson look guilty? She'd been imagining it, that was all. He had shaken his head in denial of her question, and feeling dumb, she'd quickly changed the subject.

So, she'd had sex with Hudson and dreamed that he called her his mate. Was it all that surprising when there'd been more than once during sex that he made her say she was his? No, it wasn't.

"Rosalie!"

She jumped in the recliner and gave her mother a guilty look. "Sorry, Mom."

"What is going on with you lately?" her mother asked. "You've barely come by this week to see me. You didn't come over today until after five, and now you completely ignore me."

"I'm not," Rosalie said. "I have a lot on my mind right now, that's all."

"Well, what about me, Rosalie? I'm terrified." Her mother crossed her arms over her torso and stared at the front door. "I think you should call a locksmith for me and get a second lock on the door."

"Mom," Rosalie said, "you're not in any danger."

"A shifter moved in next door, and you think I'm not in danger?" Her mother glared at her.

Rosalie took a deep breath and held it briefly before releasing it slowly. "Mrs. Nester was outside when I got here. I chatted with her for a few minutes, and she told me the new neighbour is a rabbit shifter. He's not dangerous, Mom. I promise. Even if he were a tiger or bear shifter, you still wouldn't be in danger."

"You're not worried about me being here alone, are you?" Her mother's voice was full of hurt. "You don't care about me."

"Stop it," Rosalie said. "You know I love you and that I care about you. But you're not -"

"If you cared about me, you'd ask me to live with you." Her mother leaned forward. "I'm getting old, Rosie, and money is tight. If I lived with you, we could spend more time together, and I wouldn't be so lonely."

Something close to panic raced through Rosalie. Trying to keep her voice neutral, she said, "I'm a little too old to live with my mother again. Besides, you love this house."

"It's expensive living on my own."

"You have a very good pension, savings in the bank, the house is paid for, and inexpensive hobbies. You're not penniless, Mom."

Her mother sniffed loudly as a few tears slid down her cheeks. "I also have a daughter who refuses to spend time with her mother, who thinks she can just abandon the mother who sacrificed everything for her, who raised her and took care of her and made sure she had everything she wanted."

"I'm not abandoning you, Mom." Guilt was creeping in, and she made herself smile cheerfully at her mother. "I love you so much and appreciate everything you've done. It's just that living together doesn't work for me right now. I need my space and quiet time, especially when I start school for my real estate license."

Her mother blinked in surprise. "Are you still on about that? I thought you'd decided it wasn't a good idea for someone like you."

"No," Rosalie forced another smile. "I never said that."

Her mother frowned. "I remember a specific conversation about it."

"I'm doing it, Mom. Now, Mrs. Nester said she dropped by yesterday for tea, and you had a lovely visit. I'm glad you're becoming friends."

Her mother sniffed. "It was okay. She had cat hair on her clothing, which made me all stuffed up."

Rosalie sighed and discreetly checked her watch. Only two more hours until her mother's bedtime. She could do this.

"DID YOU LIKE THE MOVIE?" HUDSON GLANCED AT HER AS HE turned down the street toward her complex.

"It wasn't bad for a shoot 'em up action flick," she grinned.

He laughed and reached across to squeeze her thigh. "Thanks for going to that one. I know you weren't really into it."

"It was better than I thought it was going to be." She smiled at him, a little flicker of pleasure going through her when he left his hand resting on her thigh. At the movies this afternoon, she'd left the usual empty seat between them. To her surprise, when Hudson came into the theatre with their popcorn and drinks, he flipped the armrest up and sat beside her.

He hadn't put his arm around her or held her hand or anything, but she'd decided that sitting right next to Hudson in the theatre made the Sunday afternoon matinee about a thousand times better.

Hope you enjoyed it while it lasted. By next Sunday, you'll be just friends again, and it'll return to how it was. Do you think Hudson will still go with you to the movies if you're with Lincoln? He hates Lincoln for some reason, and there's no way he will hang out with you once you start smelling like a lion.

She shoved that thought out of her head with lightning speed. Even the thought of smelling like anyone other than Hudson made her feel weird and uncomfortable. She belonged to Hudson. It was his scent and only his scent that should be on her.

You're my good mate, sweet Rosie.

She jerked all over, and Hudson rubbed her thigh as he pulled into the complex. "You okay?"

"Yeah, just...um, yeah."

He parked in front of her townhouse but kept the truck idling.

"You're not coming in?" She asked, then berated herself for sounding so needy. It was Hudson's day off, but that didn't mean he was required to spend the entire day with her.

"Just gonna go home and grab a change of clothes," he replied. "I'll park my truck at my place and walk back."

"You should just bring enough clothes and toiletries over for the week," she said. "I can make a spot in the closet for them. Then you don't have to return to your place every day."

His entire body stiffened, and he gave her a cautious look that made her instantly regret what she'd said. "This is just a casual thing, Rosalie."

"I know," she said hurriedly.

"Do you? Because you just asked me to move in."

Her face flushed bright red. "No, I didn't. I was trying to make things easier for you, that's all."

"I'm not interested in dating you. I made that clear. This isn't anything but sex," he said.

Her embarrassment turned to anger. Hudson was acting like she was an idiot. "I'm aware of that. I was being nice, Hudson. A woman can be nice to you without it meaning she's demanding a relationship or something."

He still gave her that guarded look, and she glared at him. "Stop looking at me like that. I'm not asking you to move in with me, for God's sake."

"Maybe I should do my own thing tonight," he said.

"Maybe you should."

"I'll text you tomorrow."

"Fine." She grabbed her purse and opened the truck door. She slid out, slammed the door shut, and then walked to her townhouse. She fumbled for her keys, blinking back tears, before opening the door and stepping inside.

She shut the door and leaned against it, listening to

Hudson's truck roaring out of the complex. She stared miserably at Mr. Pibbles as the hot tears slid down her cheeks. "Stupid polar bear shifter. He's a jerk, Pib."

The cat meowed and rubbed against her legs, and she wiped away the tears before petting the cat. "I guess this confirms that I was dreaming the 'you're my mate' thing. It doesn't matter, right? You're the only one I need anyway, Mr. Pibbles. C'mon, you can keep me company while I have a hot bath and forget all about dumb Hudson and his stupid freak out over me just trying to be nice."

HUDSON SHIFTED THE SIX PACK OF BEER TO HIS OTHER HAND, stuck the package of cookies under his arm, and dug the key out of his pocket. He hesitated, shoved it back into his pocket, and knocked on the door instead.

Three hours. He'd made it three hours before his polar bear's whining, whimpering, and carrying on had sent him straight back to Rosalie.

Are you sure it's just your polar bear?

Yes, it was just his fucking polar bear. It was stupid, and refused to acknowledge that come Friday, his little infatuation with Rosalie would have to end anyway.

She's our mate! his polar bear roared.

No, she isn't! And I swear to fucking God, if you try to make me tell her I love her again, I'll kick your furry ass all the way back to goddamn Canada.

His polar bear snarled in fury, and Hudson shoved it down as Rosalie's voice drifted through the closed door. "What do you want?"

"Can I come in, Rosalie?"

"Why? You're doing your own thing tonight, remember?"

He sighed. "Let me in so we can talk."

There was silence, and he held up the beer and the cookies. "I brought beer and cookies."

The door unlocked, and she swung it open. His bear growled happily at the sight of her, even when she scowled at him. "I wasn't asking you to move in with me."

"I know," he said. "I overreacted, and I'm sorry."

She pushed Mr. Pibbles back with her foot before scooping him up and turning around. He stared at her ass in her tight yoga pants as she said, "Come in."

He stepped into the house, removing his boots and jacket before following her into the kitchen. He set the beer and the cookies on the table as she put the cat on the floor and sat down. She must have just gotten out of the bath, her skin was flush with warmth, and her hair was piled on top of her head in a messy bun.

He swallowed heavily when his gaze dipped to her chest. She was wearing a tank top and was clearly braless, and he studied the outline of her nipples.

"Up here," she said.

He raised his gaze to her face and gave her a sheepish smile. "Sorry."

He could smell her anger with him, but underneath that anger was lust and Christ, did he want to pick her up, carry her to the bed and eat her sweet pussy until she was screaming his name.

Instead, he opened a can of beer and handed it to her before opening one for himself. She took a long drink and helped herself to a cookie as Mr. Pibbles jumped on the table. He sniffed at her open can of beer before sauntering across the table to Hudson. He petted the cat roughly, smiling a little at its loud purr.

"I'm sorry," he said again. "I was a dick."

She sighed and poked at the half-eaten cookie. "I'm embarrassed that you think I was trying to make this more than it is. You were very clear about what you wanted, and I do understand what this is."

"I know you do," he said. "I overreacted."

She gave him a weirdly apprehensive look. "If you want this to be finished now rather than Friday, you can tell me that. I won't be offended. You don't have to keep having sex with me if you're tired of -"

"I don't want to stop," he said quickly. "Unless you want to stop?"

"No," she replied.

She fidgeted in her chair, looking sad and near tears, and he couldn't stand it any longer. He leaned over and pulled her chair across the floor to him before plucking her out of it and putting her on his lap. He wrapped his arms around her waist and kissed her upper chest.

"I'm sorry, Rosalie."

She rested her forehead against his. "I'm sorry, too."

"You have nothing to be sorry about. I was being an idiot."

"You weren't," she said.

He rubbed her back, and she kissed his thick neck. "Did you eat dinner?"

"No, I wasn't hungry."

She straightened and gave him a small smile. "Do you want to have dinner with me?"

"Yes," he said. "I also want to stay the night with you if that's okay."

"It is," she said.

He kissed her briefly. "Thank you. After dinner, we can take another look at the kink list and -"

"I don't want to," she said. "Can we just have vanilla sex tonight?"

"We can do whatever you want."

"I want to have dinner with you, maybe watch a little television, and then take you upstairs and ride you until I come."

Her face flushed red, but she stared steadily at him. He loved that his shy little mate was learning to be bold with him.

He kissed her upper chest again. "Add in pussy eating, and you have yourself a deal, little human."

"I'll agree to those terms." She gave him a cheeky smile and he patted her ass when she slid off his lap. "Come on, you can put those muscles to good use and peel the potatoes while I start the steaks."

ROSALIE WASN'T SURE WHAT WOKE HER UP – IF IT WAS THE needle-sharp claws of Mr. Pibbles as he launched himself from his spot on her hip or the weird high-pitched whine. She opened her eyes, staring blearily at the alarm clock. Almost noon. Shit, they had slept in even later than normal.

The whining noise continued and she turned her head to stare at Hudson. He was in his polar bear form and sprawled on his stomach. One heavy, claw-tipped paw actually rested on her thigh, but she didn't feel any anxiety over it. Much like Mr. Pibbles, she'd grown used to seeing Hudson as a polar bear and she knew without a doubt that he'd never hurt her – whether he was in his polar bear form or human form.

She rubbed her hand across the thick fur of the paw. When Hudson made a snoring sound and turned his shaggy head away, she realized the whine wasn't coming from him. Frowning, she pushed his paw off of her and sat up.

Her eyes widened, and she threw back the covers, staring

at the woman standing in the doorway of her bedroom. "Mom? What are you doing here?"

Her mother's face was the colour of old cheese, and the whining noise intensified when she sucked in a breath. She was staring slack-jawed at Hudson and her entire body was trembling.

"Shit." Rosalie slid out of bed. "Mom, it's okay. Don't panic. It's not -"

Her mother drew in another deep breath and let out a shrill scream that sent Mr. Pibbles, who'd been sniffing at her legs, bolting out of the room.

"Mom! Stop!" Rosalie shouted as Hudson woke with a loud snarl. He half-fell, half-jumped off the bed, the floor shaking when he landed on it with a loud thump. Her mother screamed again, and Hudson growled loudly, baring his fangs at her.

Rosalie ran toward her mother, grabbing her by the arms and swinging her around to face her. "Mom, stop screaming! It's fine."

Her mother clutched at her, giving her a look of pure panic. "Run, Rosalie, run! He'll kill us both!"

She tried to drag her out of the room, but Rosalie dug her heels in. "Mom, stop! He won't hurt us."

Her mother threw another terrified look over Rosalie's shoulder. Her mouth dropped open and she whispered, "Oh my God."

Rosalie turned to look at Hudson. He had shifted to his human form, and he stared at Rosalie's mother as she whispered, "He's n-naked."

Rosalie put her arm around her mother's waist and led her out of the bedroom. "Come downstairs with me, Mom. Come on."

She helped her mother down the stairs and into the

kitchen. She sat her in a chair and squeezed her mother's cold hands. "What are you doing here?"

"I went to your office. You've been so distant this last week, I thought we could have lunch together. But, the girl at the front said you were on vacation. So, I came here and when you didn't answer the door, I let myself in. I thought you'd been hurt or kidnapped. Why else would my own daughter not tell me that she was on vacation?"

"Mom, I didn't mean -"

Her mother pulled her hands free. Some of the colour had returned to her face and she gave Rosalie an accusatory look. "What have you done, Rosalie?"

"His name is -"

"You- you're sleeping with an animal. You're a dirty, *dirty* girl, Rosalie. You should be ashamed."

"Hudson isn't an animal. He's a polar bear shifter."

"He's a freak!" her mother snapped. "He's a filthy animal, and you let him touch you. You let him into your bed!"

Her mother's gaze flickered to the left, her face paled, and Rosalie turned to see Hudson, wearing jeans and a t-shirt, standing just outside of the kitchen doorway. It was obvious from the look on his face that he'd heard what her mother said. Her heart sank, and she tried to smile at him as he handed over her robe.

She was wearing just her sleep shorts and tank top, and the house was cool. She slipped into the robe, appreciating his thoughtfulness despite the shit that was currently going down. "Thank you."

"You're welcome," he said. He cleared his throat and ducked into the kitchen, holding his hand out. "I'm Hudson."

His mother shrank back, and she made a low moan of fear before closing her eyes. "Get away from me, don't-don't kill me."

ELIZABETH KELLY

Rosalie wanted to roll her eyes at her mother's theatrics. She knew her mother well enough to know that her real terror had passed. "Stop it, Mom. Hudson won't hurt you. Hudson, this is my mother Beverly."

"Nice to meet you," Hudson said.

Beverly crossed her arms over her torso and looked away. "You almost gave me a heart attack, Rosalie. I almost died because you lied to me."

A tiny flame of anger flickered to life in Rosalie's belly. She turned to Hudson. "Could you give us a few minutes?"

He nodded. "I'll head home and -"

"No," Rosalie said. "We have plans today and that hasn't changed." They didn't have any specific plans, but she'd be damned if she'd let her mother drive Hudson away. "If you don't mind waiting upstairs for a little bit though, I'd appreciate it."

"Yeah, okay." Hudson turned and left the kitchen.

Rosalie's mother released her breath in a shuddering sigh. "He's a monster, Rosalie. A monster, and you're letting him -"

"Enough!" Rosalie had never used such a harsh tone with her mother before and her mother shrank back, real anxiety flickering in her eyes.

"I'm your mother. You can't speak that way to me."

"You're my mother, and I love you, and I respect you, but you're going to do the same for me and listen quietly for the next five minutes."

"I don't know what is happening with you. You – you're having sex with a shifter, and you - you have a cat! A cat! What are you thinking?" She glared at Mr. Pibbles as he sauntered into the kitchen.

"Listen quietly, Mom. Or I swear, I'll never talk to you again."

She was bluffing, but her mother's eyes widened, and she shut her mouth abruptly.

Rosalie took a deep breath. "Hudson is not a monster or an animal. He is a polar bear shifter, a bartender and," she hesitated only briefly, "my boyfriend. He is also smart and sweet and the best guy I know. He cares for me, and I know he looks scary, but he isn't. I promise you."

"He's dangerous, Rosalie. Shifters can't be trusted. Everyone knows that! He's going to get you hurt and -"

"Mom!" Rosalie glared at her. "Being with Hudson keeps me safe."

"What are you talking about?"

"When I go somewhere, when I walk down the street, shifters avoid me. They get out of *my* way. Do you know why? Because I have Hudson's scent on my skin, and there isn't a shifter alive who is stupid enough to hurt a polar bear's mate."

She took her hands and squeezed them tightly. "Hudson keeps me safe, Mom. I care about him deeply, and I'm happy when I'm with him."

A crocodile tear slid down her mother's cheek. "I don't approve."

Rosalie lifted her mom's hands to her mouth and kissed her knuckles. "I don't need your approval."

More tears and her mother made a low sobbing sound before whispering, "You're breaking my heart. How could you do this to me?"

Rosalie squeezed her mother's hands again and waited patiently. After a couple of minutes, her mother gave her a wide-eyed look of sorrow that couldn't quite hide the glimmer of slyness in its depths. "I can't watch my only child ruin her life by dating a shifter. I won't watch. You have to choose between me and that – that polar bear, Rosalie."

"I choose him," Rosalie said without hesitation.

Her mother's mouth dropped open, and Rosalie released her hands. Guilt was flooding through her, but she shoved it aside ruthlessly. Her mother was bluffing, she was sure of it, but she still felt sick to her stomach. She didn't want to lose her mother, but she wouldn't give up Hudson. She *couldn't* give him up.

"What did you say?" her mother whispered.

"I love you, Mom," Rosalie said, "but I won't let you dictate how I live my life. If you can't deal with that and want to cut off communication, it makes me sad, but I won't tell you how to live *your* life either. If you change your mind, just call me, okay? Drive home safe."

She stepped away and her mother lunged to her feet and grabbed Rosalie's hand. "Rosie, no!"

Rosalie smiled at her mother. "I won't choose you over him."

"I know. It was wrong of me to ask you to do that. I just need time to process this. I don't want to lose you, okay?"

"Okay." She hugged her mother. "I love you, and I'm sorry I didn't tell you about Hudson or Mr. Pibbles earlier. I shouldn't have kept either a secret from you."

"I love you too, Rosalie," her mother said as Rosalie guided her toward the front door. "You know that, right?"

"I know."

"Are you coming over this week?"

"Honestly? Probably not. But I will text you and I'll come by on Saturday. Okay?"

Her mother sighed. "Okay. Maybe I'll ask Mrs. Nester to take me to Bingo with her on Wednesday night."

"That's a great idea." Rosalie opened the door and hugged her mother again. "Bye, Mom."

"Bye, Rosalie."

She waited on the front step until her mother got in her car. She waved goodbye and stepped inside as her mother drove away. She shut the door and stared at Mr. Pibbles who was sitting in the doorway to the living room. "Holy shit, Pib-Pib, did you see what I just did?"

The cat lifted his back leg and lazily licked his ass. Rosalie laughed and hugged herself before whispering, "I stood up for myself. I didn't let her guilt me into doing what she wanted."

I'll say. Too bad most of the stuff you told her about Hudson was a lie.

She frowned. It wasn't a lie. Hudson was sweet and smart, and he kept her safe. She did care about him, and this was the first time in a long time that she could honestly say she was happy.

That's great, Rosie. Glad you're so happy...but you remember that Hudson isn't looking for anything but sex, right?

Yeah, she remembered. They'd just fought about it yesterday, for God's sake. Still, she didn't regret anything she had said to her mother. She wanted to be with Hudson and as long as she kept it casual, as long as she followed his rules, she could probably drag this 'teach me to be kinky' thing out for months.

Uh, Rosie? Are you forgetting about someone? What about Lincoln?

She closed her eyes. Fuck, what about Lincoln? Did she still want to seduce him? Did she still even love him?

"No," she said. "I mean... maybe?" She buried her face in her hands. "Shit, I don't fucking know."

"Don't know what?"

She lifted her head and smiled at Hudson, standing at the base of the stairs. "Hey there."

"Hi. I heard your mom leaving. Everything okay with her?"

She shrugged. "It will be. She's still in a bit of shock I think."

"I'm sorry about what happened."

"It isn't your fault."

"Maybe. But meeting your mom first as a polar bear and then butt naked wasn't my finest moment."

She stared at him before bursting into wild out-of-control laughter. She knew it was partly the stress of the situation, but she couldn't stop giggling as Hudson stared solemnly at her.

"Oh God," she gasped out, "oh God, my mom has seen your penis."

He winced. "Don't remind me."

She snorted more laughter and when a smile cracked his face, she walked to him and threw her arms around his waist. "Just so you know, I do not approve of you showing off your penis to other women, and that includes my mother."

"Please stop talking about my penis and your mother in the same sentence," Hudson said.

She laughed and palmed his crotch before giving him a saucy smile. "This is mine. Say it."

He picked her up, and she wrapped her legs around his waist as he turned and headed up the stairs. "Yours, little human."

She nipped his neck and then kissed the stubble on his jawline. "That's right it is. Now take me to the bedroom and fuck me. If you give me another g-spot orgasm, I'll make you pancakes afterward."

He growled and reached down to squeeze her ass. "Sex and pancakes? Best fucking day off ever."

She pressed a kiss against his mouth. "Agreed."

CHAPTER 18

"So," Maggie blew on her coffee before taking a sip, "tomorrow is the big day. How are you feeling about it?"

Rosalie picked at the piece of banana bread sitting in front of her. "I'm not going to the kink dance party thing."

"What? Why not?"

"I still smell like Hudson."

"It's Thursday. If you stopped sleeping with Hudson by the end of the weekend, then it should..." Maggie's eyes widened, "You're still sleeping with Hudson."

"I didn't want - I mean, Monday was his day off and there was this whole thing with my mother and I was upset, and I didn't want to be alone, you know? Then Tuesday I forgot to ask him for my key back before he went to work. He crawled into bed with me that night after work like he always does, and I couldn't just kick him out at one in the morning."

Maggie stared silently at her, and Rosalie gave her a defensive look. "I still don't know enough kinky stuff anyway. Hudson still has to teach me some more things."

"What did he teach you this week?" Maggie asked.

Rosalie stared blankly at her, trying desperately to think of something, anything.

"You just had regular sex all week, didn't you?" Maggie said.

"Maybe."

"Do you think you want to be with Hudson, not Lincoln?" Maggie asked.

"I love Lincoln," Rosalie replied.

"Do you, though?"

"Fuck!" Rosalie ran her hands through her hair. "I don't even know. I thought I did, but now…"

She sighed and stared morosely at her coffee. "It doesn't matter anyway. I think Hudson is finished with me."

"What do you mean?" Maggie asked.

"He's really grumpy."

"Porter says Hudson's always grumpy," Maggie replied.

Rosalie smiled a little. "Not with me, at least not lately. But the last few days, his mood has just gotten worse and worse. This morning he barely said two words and he left around two. Normally he stays with me until he leaves for work."

"Did you talk to him about what's wrong?"

"I tried, but he changes the subject or…distracts me."

Hudson distracted her all right. She hadn't thought it would be possible, but they'd had even more sex this week than last. In fact, they'd spent almost all of their time in bed this week. Hudson even woke her up when he got home each night for a quick but intense bout of sex.

They hadn't spoken once about more kink lessons, and while she still enjoyed their lovemaking, it almost felt like Hudson grew more distant with each round of sex they had.

"Rosalie?" Maggie squeezed her hand. "You okay?"

Suddenly near tears, Rosalie whispered, "He left the key

on the table today. After lunch, he took me to bed and afterward I fell asleep. When I woke up, he was gone and the house key I gave him was sitting on the table."

Now the tears did fall, and Maggie handed her a napkin. "I'm sorry, honey."

"Screw this." Rosalie straightened and dabbed at the tears on her face. "I'm done feeling sorry for myself. Hudson gave the key back because he thought I wanted this to be over by Friday. All I have to do is tell him I want more lessons and things will go back to normal."

"Normal?" Maggie said.

"You know what I mean," Rosalie replied. "Anyway, I'll make Hudson a nice dinner and take it to him tonight at work. I'll ask him for another few weeks of kink lessons and give him back the key."

"What if he doesn't want to?" Maggie asked delicately. "Hudson isn't looking for a relationship, right?"

"This isn't a relationship," Rosalie said. "Nothing has changed, I just want a few more lessons, that's all."

"Are you sure?" Maggie said. "Because I feel like maybe you're becoming infatuated with a guy who isn't looking for the same things you are."

"I'm not," Rosalie said. "I know what Hudson wants, and I also know that it's not me, at least not in the typical relationship sense. I'm fine with what he can give me. Besides, it's mutually beneficial to both of us, right? Hudson gets as much casual sex as he wants, and I gain a bunch of experience to use to seduce Lincoln."

"Rosalie, I -"

She stood up abruptly and gave Maggie a strained smile. "I have to go. I need to stop at the grocery store and pick up a few things to make Hudson's dinner. I'll talk to you later, Maggie. Okay?"

Maggie gave her a troubled look but nodded. "Yeah, okay. Bye, Rosalie."

"WELL, IF IT ISN'T MY FAVOURITE GIRL." THE LOW PURR drifted down the aisle of the grocery store.

Rosalie turned with the package of pasta in her hand. "Lincoln?"

"Hello, Rosie-girl." Holding a basket piled high with meat, Lincoln ambled down the aisle toward her. "How's my favourite -"

He stopped abruptly and inhaled before a look of surprise crossed his face. He stared at her for a moment then cleared his throat. "How's my favourite girl doing?"

"Good. How is your vacation?" She studied his handsome face. He actually looked a little tired and worn out with dark circles under his eyes, and his face looked a bit thin.

Probably all the sex he's been having at the kink fest. No time to sleep or eat.

Probably. She waited for the jealousy to wash over her, but she was curiously unaffected by the thought of Lincoln banging a bunch of women. Two weeks ago, the jealousy would have been eating her up inside.

"It's been good. Busy." He looked her up and down, his gaze lingering on her tits before he smiled at her. "You look...different."

"Do I?" She put the pasta in her basket and checked her watch. She needed to leave if she wanted to get the spaghetti made in time for Hudson's dinner break.

"Yes. You look beautiful today, Rosie-girl."

"Thank you." His compliment didn't bring its usual flush of pleasure to her.

He inhaled again before moving close. "So, what's new? Are you enjoying your time off?"

"I am. Not much is new. Just grabbing a few groceries."

He was standing beside her now, and he gave her a flirty little grin as he stared at the ingredients in her basket. "Looks like you're making some pasta."

"I am." She checked her watch again.

"Hey," Lincoln traced his fingers down her forearm. "I've missed seeing your gorgeous face while I've been on vacation. You still want to get together and chat about being an agent? I'm busy tonight and tomorrow night, but my Saturday night is free. You could drop by my place, we could have a few drinks and I can tell you anything and everything you want to know. What do you say, sweetheart?"

"Are you asking me out on a date?" she said.

"I guess I am, Rosie-girl."

She stared at him. Lincoln, the man she'd been in love with for two years was asking her out. Her dream was coming true in a goddamn grocery store. What she'd wanted was finally happening and she... she couldn't care less.

Holy shit. She couldn't care less.

She didn't want Lincoln. She wanted Hudson.

Grumpy, quiet, possessive, and oh so sweet, Hudson.

"Rosie?"

A smile broke out across her face. "You're kidding me, right?"

Lincoln shook his head. "No. I've been thinking a lot about you lately and -"

"Bullshit," she said. "You don't think about me at all, unless it's whether or not you can get me to pick up your dry-cleaning, or do your work for you at the office, or drive you to a party when your car breaks down so you can fuck another girl."

"Rosalie, I -"

"No, don't bother. You've been using my crush on you to your advantage for the last two years and you know what? That's okay. Because I'm a big girl and I let you take advantage of me. But not anymore, Lincoln."

"Then let me take you to dinner to apologize," Lincoln said as he took her hand. "Saturday night, we can -"

"Seriously? Are you telling me that all this time, all I had to do to make you want me was to blow you off?" She couldn't stop her laughter.

He gave her a cocky little grin. "I like it when lovely ladies like you play hard to get."

She snorted more laughter. "I'm not playing hard to get. I'm just not interested."

He raised her hand to his mouth and kissed her knuckles. "Maybe I can change your mind."

"I know you can smell him on me, Lincoln. What do you think he'll do to you if he smells your scent on me?" Rosalie said softly.

Lincoln dropped her hand and took a step back. "You don't seem like the type to fall for a bartender, Rosalie."

"How would you know? You don't know anything about me."

The smile fell from his face, and she patted his arm. "It was really good to see you, Lincoln. Enjoy the rest of your vacation. I'll see you at the office on Monday."

She walked away without looking back, as a wave of giddiness washed over her. Holy shit, she really didn't love Lincoln. Why she thought she did...she'd never know. But did it really matter? No, she decided, it didn't. She knew now with one hundred percent certainty, what she wanted.

Hudson.

She hurried toward the register, eager to get home and make dinner for him.

Uh, Rosie? Are you forgetting something? Hudson doesn't want you. At least, not the same way you want him.

Her steps slowed, and she took a deep breath. Okay, so maybe he didn't. But that didn't mean she couldn't change his mind over the next couple of months. She'd win him over with amazing sex and a really good meal plan.

She laughed inwardly – it was probably the dorkiest plan ever for winning a man's heart, but Hudson loved sex and food, it would work.

Rosie, you're just exchanging Lincoln for Hudson. You know that, don't you? You're going from one man who will never want you, to another.

No, she wasn't. Lincoln and Hudson were nothing alike, and it was stupid of her to think she'd ever get someone like Lincoln to fall for her. Hudson liked her, she knew he did, he just needed more time to get used to the idea of dating her.

"JESUS CHRIST, HUDSON, WHAT THE HELL IS GOING ON WITH you tonight?" Judd asked. "Your goddamn grandmother die or something? You're an even bigger asshole than usual."

Hudson glared at Judd. "Nothing's wrong."

"Well, ain't that the biggest load of bullshit I ever heard," Judd said cheerfully. "I don't know what the fuck you're so miserable about. I haven't had sex in like a month, but I know you've been gettin' it on the regular from that curvy little human. She's practically swimming in your scent."

"I'm busy, Judd," Hudson growled as he poured a beer and handed it to the tiger shifter waiting impatiently. "Three bucks."

The tiger handed him a five and walked away. Hudson rang it through the register and threw the tip into the tip jar under the bar.

"Seriously, what is going on?" Judd said. "You'd think a shifter with a woman as hot as -"

"It's over," Hudson snapped. "Me and Rosalie are done, and I don't want to fucking talk about it."

"You sure you're done?" Judd said.

"Why the fuck wouldn't I be?" He growled as he swiped at the top of the already-gleaming bar with a rag.

"Because your little human just walked into the bar and she's headed right for you."

Hudson's head jerked up and he stared in shock at Rosalie. His polar bear's roar of happiness was so loud that he winced. Fuck, she looked good. She was wearing his favourite dress, her long curly hair cascaded down her back, and her lips were painted a bright red. He had a vision of those red lips sliding down his cock and pressed his lower body against the bar to hide his immediate erection.

"Hello, Rosalie." Judd grinned at her when she joined them. He glanced at the container in her hand. "Bringing my boy Hudson his dinner?"

"Hi, Judd. Um, yes." Rosalie gave Hudson a nervous smile. "Hi, Hudson."

"Hey." He told himself not to read anything into it. Rosalie was a nice girl. She was probably bringing him dinner because she had made too much or something.

Too bad he couldn't get his fucking polar bear to calm down. It was practically dancing a goddamn jig at the sight of her. He didn't know what was worse to deal with – it's unabashed excitement over seeing Rosie, or the over-whelming despair and depression it had been in since the moment he left Rosalie's house this afternoon.

"Do you have a minute?" She asked.

"I can't take my dinner break yet," he said.

"I know. I only need a minute."

"Yeah, okay." He headed to the end of the bar where there was no one sitting on the stools. Rosalie sat down and placed the container in front of him.

"It's spaghetti," she said. "I wanted to make biscuits for you, but I, uh, ran out of time."

"That's okay," he replied. "You didn't have to bring me dinner."

"I wanted to." She gave him a searching look. "You left without saying goodbye."

He stared at the container of pasta before mumbling, "Sorry."

Rosalie's long fingers placed the house key on top of the container. He glanced up at her, and she smiled at him. "You forgot this at home."

"We were done," he said. His polar bear reared up and growled at him as the smile dropped from Rosalie's face.

"I was thinking," she said tentatively, "that maybe we could extend the kink lessons for a few weeks longer. I don't feel like I've learned everything I, um, can from you."

Tell her no. You can't keep doing this. If Corden finds you, he'll —

"There is some more stuff I could teach you," he said.

Her smile returned, and happiness flooded through him. She picked up the key and held it out to him. "You'll need this."

He took it from her, stuffing it into his pocket as she gave him a sweet look of affection.

"You look really pretty," he said. "I'm sorry I was being such a dick the last couple of days."

"You can make it up to me tonight," she said with a pert

grin. She hesitated and then took his hand. He linked their fingers together, and she squeezed his hand. "So, I'll see you at home?"

"Yes." He kept a hold of her hand when she tried to slide off the stool. "If you don't mind waiting around for an hour or so, I'll be taking my dinner break and you could join me."

"Sure," she said happily. "I don't mind waiting."

"All right. I'll bring you a glass of wine, okay?"

"Okay. Thanks, Hudson."

ROSALIE DRANK THE LAST OF HER WINE AND SET THE EMPTY glass on the bar. Another fifteen minutes or so and Hudson would be on his dinner break. She studied him as he mixed a drink for an incredibly tall and thin shifter. God, Hudson was handsome. She couldn't wait until he got home tonight. She'd drink five cups of coffee if she had to, just to make sure she was awake. She had plans to blow his socks off with the sex tonight. In the morning she'd ply him with French toast and bacon and be well on her way with Operation 'Make Hudson Want to Date Her'.

"I told you, asshole! They're gonna win the cup this year, and that's the fucking truth."

She glanced over at the group of shifters who were crowded around a table just a few feet from her. They were young, early twenties maybe, and based on the natural grace of their big, lean bodies, she guessed they were a group of cat shifters. Tori had brought them pitcher after pitcher of beer in the last forty minutes or so, and their good-natured arguing over some sort of sporting event had gradually gotten more heated.

She slid off the stool and smoothed down her dress. She

would use the washroom and check her hair before Hudson started his break. As she started toward the bathroom, the two cat shifters stood and glared at each other.

"You're a fucking idiot, Terry!" the larger one snarled. "They'll never win the goddamn cup, and you know it."

"Shut the hell up," Terry said before baring his fangs and hissing at him. "You're just fucking upset because your team didn't even make the goddamn semi-finals. Not that I'm fucking surprised by that. Your team couldn't throw their way out of a wet paper bag if they -"

"You fucking dickhead!"

As Rosalie skirted by their table, the larger shifter reached out and shoved Terry in the chest. Terry staggered back, and Rosalie cried out when his heavy body smashed into hers. It knocked her on her ass, and she made another sharp cry when the back of her head hit the bar. She crumpled to the floor, her ears ringing and bright lights flashing in her vision.

Above her, the two shifters were swelling in size. They growled at each other as black and orange fur began to sprout from Terry's skin. Faintly, she heard Hudson shout her name as Judd grabbed the larger shifter.

"Hey, knock it off, ya dickweeds. Or I'll kick – fuck me! You son of a bitch!" The larger shifter had turned and sliced Judd's chest open with a quick flick of his nails. Judd roared with anger and pain as Rosalie struggled to her feet.

Judd, blood soaking into the front of his t-shirt, grabbed the larger shifter and threw him to the ground. He made another roar of anger that sent Terry skittering back and directly into Rosalie again.

This time, she caught herself on the bar as the tiger shifter turned and hissed at her. He raised his hand, and the nails became sharp claws as more fur sprouted across his face. "Stupid human bitch! You'd better watch where you're going, or I'll fucking slice you open from -"

"Hudson, no!" Rosalie shouted as the giant polar bear lumbered into view behind Terry.

He ignored her, his roar of anger making the glasses vibrate on the table as one massive paw smashed into Terry's side. The tiger shifter went flying, his big body landing on one of the tables. It collapsed under his weight as beer bottles shattered on the floor, sending the cloying scent of hops into the air, and Terry groaned in pain. Rosalie could see blood dripping down the tiger shifter's ribs as Hudson growled and dropped to all fours before striding toward him.

"Hudson, get back." Judd, still in his human form, stepped in front of the polar bear, blocking him from the terrified tiger shifter lying on the floor. "He didn't mean to hurt your woman. Go on, I'll take care of this. C'mon, man, don't be - shit!"

Judd, moving way faster than a man his size should have been able to, dove to the left as Hudson stood and swiped at him with one paw. It just missed his head, and Judd glared at him from the floor.

"Goddammit, Hudson! You asshole, knock it off!"

Hudson bared his teeth at him before turning his gaze to the tiger shifter. Terry had staggered to his feet and he licked his lips nervously before holding out his hands. "Please, man. I didn't know she was your woman. I didn't mean to hurt her, I swear."

Hudson snarled again before rising up on his back feet. He towered over the frightened shifter and raised one paw. Terry's moan of fear trailed off when Rosalie stepped in front of him.

She stared up at Hudson and shook her head. "Hudson, no."

He snarled and bared his fangs, saliva dripping off their very pointed ends as he stared at the tiger shifter over her head.

She stepped toward him as Judd shouted, "Rosalie, get away from him! He's not thinking straight!"

She shook her head again. Despite his anger, despite the blood that was splattered on his thick fur and coating his claws, she wasn't afraid. Hudson would never hurt her.

She reached up, ignoring the frightened gasps of the shifters around them, and pressed her hand against the thick fur that covered his chest. "Hudson, look at me, honey."

The bear growled again. Rosalie could feel it reverberating through her hand and down her arm, and she rubbed her hand through the thick white fur.

"Look at me," she demanded.

His gaze dropped to her, and she smiled up at him. "Don't do this, honey. Please."

He studied her for a long moment before he shivered all over. Thick fur turned to warm, hard flesh, and she smiled at him when he was fully human again. He picked up her hand from where it rested against his chest and pressed a tender kiss against the palm.

"My mate," his voice was low, "are you all right?"

"Yes," she said. "I'm all right, honey."

"Well, fuck me sideways. Ain't this just fucking great."

They both turned at the sound of Judd's voice. He was looking at his chest and he winced and touched the bleeding gashes before studying the utterly silent crowd of people staring at Hudson and Rosalie. Judd shook his head as Porter came out of the back hallway and joined them.

"What the hell just happened?" He peered at Judd's bleeding chest. "Jesus, Judd, are you all right?"

"I'll live," Judd growled.

Porter stared at the bleeding tiger shifter and at the naked Hudson before running a hand through his hair. "Will someone please tell me what the fuck is going on?"

"HUDSON, I'M FINE," ROSALIE SAID.

Hudson ignored her and carried her up the stairs to her bedroom. He set her on the bed with infinite gentleness, and she gave him a look that was half amusement and half exasperation. "The ER doctor said I was fine. I don't even have a concussion."

He knelt in front of her and removed her shoes.

"Hudson, sit down." She patted the bed next to her and he finally sat beside her. She took his big hand. "Did you text Judd?"

"He's fine," he grunted. "Fully healed."

She sighed with relief. "Good. What about the tiger shifter?"

"Healed. He told Porter he wasn't going to press charges."

More relief flooded through her. "Thank God."

They lapsed into silence, and she gave him a small smile. "It was nice of Porter to let you leave early to take me to the hospital."

"Yeah."

He didn't say anything else, and she hated the uncomfortable silence. "Hudson, are you upset with me?"

"What?" He gave her a look of bafflement. "Of course not. Why would you think that?"

"Because you're acting so weird and -"

"I'm sorry," he said. "I'm sorry for scaring you and for growling at you and... but when I saw you fall, I thought you were really hurt and I..."

"You didn't scare me." She squeezed his hand. "Not even when you growled. I knew you wouldn't hurt me, Hudson."

"I wouldn't," he whispered. "I swear to God, Rosalie. I would never hurt you."

"I know." She stroked his light hair and pressed a kiss against his shoulder. "Are you hungry? You never did get to eat dinner."

He cupped her face and kissed her on the mouth. "I'm not hungry."

"In that case." She reached for the bottom of his shirt, but he put his hands on hers.

"Rosalie, wait."

"Don't you want me?" she asked.

"You know I do, but maybe you should rest."

"I'm fine. Just a small bump on the head." She tugged his shirt over his head and dropped it to the floor before running her hands over his broad chest. He inhaled sharply, and she smiled to herself before hopping off the bed.

She stood in front of him and said, "Take off your jeans, Hudson."

He stripped them and his briefs off in record time, leaving them on the floor by the bed. He sat back down on the side of the bed, one big hand rubbing his growing erection as he stared at her body. She turned around. "Unzip me, please."

He unzipped her dress, and she shivered delicately when he pressed kisses along her exposed spine. She let the dress slide to the floor and didn't object when Hudson pulled her into his lap.

She ground her ass against his erection as he quickly unclasped her bra and raked it down her arms. He tossed it aside and she leaned back against him, bracing her hands on his heavy thighs as he cupped her breasts and kissed her neck.

"You smell so good, little human," he said.

She arched her back, moaning and crying out with pleasure as she watched him play with her tits until her nipples were swollen and aching. He pinched the right one, growling with satisfaction when she cried out with pleasure.

"So beautiful," he growled again.

She jerked with surprise when he tore her panties from her body as easily as if they were made of paper. He dropped them on the floor and rubbed her thighs. "Open."

She spread her legs apart, letting them dangle on the outside of his thighs. He spread his legs, exposing all of her pussy to him, and she clutched at his forearm when he rubbed her clit.

"Please, Hudson," she moaned as he circled her clit.

He pressed against her core, making a small grunt of surprise when his finger slipped into her easily. "So wet already, honey."

"I need you," she said.

"Do you want me to fuck you?" He slid his finger into the last knuckle and pressed against the front wall of her pussy.

She cried out, her entire body trembling. Her cry of need turned to frustration when Hudson slid his finger out of her pussy and resumed his lazy circling of her clit. "Hudson, no!"

"Does my good girl want to be fucked?"

"Yes," she moaned.

He weaved one hand into her long hair and tugged her head back so he could nip her throat. His other hand cupped her pussy, his rough fingers tapping gently on her wet entrance. "Whose pussy is this?"

"Yours," she said immediately. "It's your pussy."

"Only mine," he said.

"Only yours," she whispered.

"That's my good girl." He squeezed her pussy and then patted her thigh. "Turn around, good girl."

She slid off his lap and turned around before climbing eagerly into his lap. She straddled his hips, rubbing her wet pussy back and forth over his thick cock. The head bumped against her clit, and she moaned and rocked against it. Fuck, she could come like this. In fact, she was going to come with just another stroke or two...

She pouted, and smacked Hudson's back in frustration when his hands cupped her hips and stopped her from moving. "I was going to come."

His low laugh made her pussy drip. "Not until I say you can."

He reached between them and gripped the base of his dick before pressing it against her. She wiggled eagerly into place, crying out a little when the head slipped into her. She pressed up against him, feeling her walls stretch around his thickness as he cupped her ass and carefully eased her down over his cock.

When they were completely joined, he leaned back and stared at her pussy before rubbing her clit with the ball of his thumb.

"Oh God," she moaned and rocked against him again.

He made a low growl as his other hand rubbed her lower back. "Don't come yet, little human."

"I want to," she said.

"I know." He hooked his arm around her hips and held her tight as he thrust in and out of her. "But I want you to wait. Are you my good girl?"

She cupped his face, studying the lovely chocolate shade of his eyes and rubbing her fingers against the stubble on his jaw. "I'm your good mate," she whispered.

Lust flared in his eyes, and his arm squeezed her tight before he thrust hard and deep. "Good mate," he growled.

She closed her eyes, letting her head fall back as she rode Hudson. He cupped her breast and placed hot nips and kisses against her upper chest as she squeezed her pussy around him and met every stroke of his cock.

"Look at me, my mate," Hudson demanded.

She opened her eyes and stared at him as he took one hand and linked their fingers.

He kissed her deeply, sliding his tongue into her mouth before sucking on her bottom lip. "My mate," he breathed against her mouth.

"Your mate," she whispered.

He groaned and rubbed her clit, kissing her again and swallowing her cries of pleasure as she came on his cock. She squeezed around him as he released her mouth and groaned with desire.

She cupped his face, grinding her body against his as they stared at each other. When he came, his big body shuddering and twitching beneath hers, he moaned her name. She held him tightly, studying his face intently as he found his pleasure in her body.

He collapsed on his back, bringing her with him, and she rested her head on his chest, smiling at the sound of his heartbeat beneath her ear.

"My mate," he said again, the sound vibrating from his chest.

"Yes," she murmured. "Yours."

CHAPTER 19

"You're such a good boy for letting Mama sleep in," Rosalie cooed to Mr. Pibbles. She poured his food into the dish and petted the purring cat before leaving him to eat. She made herself a cup of coffee, added a generous splash of milk, and then sat down with her phone.

Before she could check her texts, the phone rang in her hand. She hit the answer button. "Hi, Maggie."

"Hey, are you okay?"

"Yeah, I'm fine. Did Porter tell you what happened?"

"He did. Apparently, Hudson freaked the heck out last night and almost killed a tiger shifter," Maggie said.

Rosalie sipped at her coffee. "That's a bit of an exaggeration. He just got upset and shifted, but he wasn't going to kill the guy or anything."

"I saw the video, Rosalie. If you hadn't stepped in between them, he would have killed him."

"Video?" Rosalie set her cup on the table. "What video?"

"Shit, you haven't seen it yet?"

"I just got up. After we returned from the hospital last night, Hudson and I went straight to bed. He's still sleeping."

Maggie laughed. "Girl, you've gone viral."

"What are you talking about?" Rosalie said.

"Someone recorded what happened last night with their phone and uploaded it to YouTube. It already has three hundred thousand views. Hell, there's even a meme going around Facebook."

"You're kidding me," Rosalie said.

"I'm not. You might even be trending on Twitter. Hashtag Beauty tames the Beast," Maggie said with a giggle.

"I – what? Beauty tames the Beast?"

Maggie laughed again. "Hang up the phone and Google 'polar bear shifter freak out' or 'Beauty tames the Beast.' You'll find it."

"Okay, um, bye, Maggie."

Feeling a little like she'd been hit by a train, Rosalie Googled the words "Beauty tames the Beast' and then clicked the YouTube link that immediately popped up. She watched the video silently, paying no attention to Mr. Pibbles when he weaved around her leg.

"Oh my God," she whispered when it ended. She immediately hit play again and watched it a second time. The person had started recording just as Judd was telling Hudson to stop. She stared wide-eyed at the giant polar bear, sweat breaking out on her temples when he tried to attack Judd. Her hands clenched around her phone when she stepped into view.

She looked incredibly small and fragile standing in front of Hudson in his polar bear form, and she could hear the audible gasps on the video when she stepped toward him and placed her hand on his fur-covered chest. He shifted to his human form, and the way he kissed the palm of her hand so tenderly made her pulse go skipping into overdrive.

The video ended, and she read some of the comments,

her face turning bright red and hot. Some of them were crude – *did you see how much blurring they had to do to hide his dick?* Some of them were horribly racist – *all fucking shifters should be shot on sight. I'd fucking hang his head on my trophy wall where it belongs,* but the majority of the comments focused on how she'd convinced Hudson to shift to his human form. She read comment after comment, her eyes nearly bugging out of her head.

"Beauty tames the Beast!"

"What the hell? That bitch's got nuts of goddamn steel!'

"I'm a coyote shifter. She can tame me anytime she wants. Anyone know her name? I need a woman like that in my life and my bed."

"I gotta find this woman. I think I'm in love. I'll be her beast."

"Who knew a hot chick could tame the savage beast?"

"Is this 4 real? How the fuck she get that bear 2 calm down?"

"That giant bear loves his woman. She about to get some 2nite!"

She sat back with a thud, staring at Mr. Pibbles when he jumped on the table. After a moment, she checked Facebook. She didn't have many friends, but Sam, the squirrel shifter from work, had already tagged her in a post with a "Holy shit, it's you, Rosalie!" comment.

The post was a still shot of the video turned into a meme. It had already been shared thousands of times, and this time, she didn't bother to scroll through the long list of comments.

'How a Beauty Tames a Beast" was written in bold, dark red letters across the image. It was the moment when Hudson kissed her hand, and she stared at their images – at the way he looked at her as he kissed her palm and the way she looked at him – for a long time.

"Mr. Pibbles," she finally whispered. "He called me his mate last night. He called me his mate, and he almost killed a man for knocking me down. I – I think he loves me."

Mr. Pibbles sat on his haunches, his green eyes studying her as she whispered, "He loves me and… and I love him."

She sat up straight. "I love him, Pib-Pib. I freaking love him. He's my…mate."

A rush of happiness made her nearly light-headed. She loved Hudson.

There was no uncertainty, no second-guessing. For a moment, she could have smacked herself in the head. How had she ever thought that what she'd felt for Lincoln was love… she was a damn idiot.

Hudson was still sleeping, but she didn't care. She was waking him up and telling him exactly how much she loved him.

***

HE HEARD HER RUNNING UP THE STAIRS. HE HAD ALREADY dressed and stood at the window, staring at the cloudy sky. A war had been going on within him for the last ten minutes. Last night, he called her his mate, and there was no pretending he hadn't. She would remember this time. She wouldn't chalk it up to a dream. He had called her his mate at the bar and in bed.

You have to end it, Hudson. You have to before she starts to feel real emotion for you, not just lust.

It's too late, his polar bear growled. *She is our mate, she loves us.*

Maybe she didn't. Maybe she only called him her mate

because she knew he liked it when she did. She was in love with the lion shifter. She wanted him, not Hudson.

She was supposed to be with the lion shifter last night, remember? She chose you. End it, Hudson! End it before she dies.

We'll protect her! His bear growled. *We'll keep her safe.*

Like we kept Samuel safe?

His polar bear made a low whimper and retreated as the door to the bedroom opened. He smelled her sweet scent and heard the excited rush of her breathing as she crossed the room. She put her arms around him and kissed the middle of his back.

"Hi," she said.

"Hey, how are you feeling?"

"Perfectly fine."

She was nearly vibrating against him, and he turned around to face her. She beamed at him, and his heart sank when she gave him a shy smile. "How do you feel, my mate?"

Nausea made his stomach churn, and he said, "Don't call me that."

The smile dropped from her face, and she stepped away, folding her arms over her torso with a familiar gesture of anxiety. "I – you were fine with it last night."

"That was a mistake," he said. "This is just a casual thing, remember?"

Two spots of red appeared high on her cheeks, and he both admired and hated her bravery when she said, "No, it isn't. Maybe it started that way, but it isn't anymore. I love you, Hudson. And I think you love me too."

His polar bear tried to surge forward and force him to tell her she was right. He fought it back grimly, his entire body shaking with the effort. Concern etched into Rosalie's face, and she reached out for him. "Hudson? What's wrong?"

He stumbled back and shook his head. "You love the lion shifter, not me."

"No," she said. "I don't. I only thought I loved Lincoln, but now that I've been with you, I know that -"

"So, you were in love with the lion, but you fuck me a few times, and now suddenly I'm the one you're in love with?" He swallowed down the bitter bile rising in his throat before forcing himself to give her a scornful look. "You don't even know what love is, Rosalie. You hop from man to man, falling *in love* with the one who's currently between your legs."

"Stop it," she whispered. "Stop being so mean. This isn't you."

"This is me," he said. "You agreed to keep it casual, remember? Now you think you can change the rules because you've realized you'll never be kinky enough for the lion? You and I both know that you're not in love with me. You're tired of being alone, and I'm just your second choice because I don't care that you don't want the kink. That isn't love, Rosalie, that's settling."

"You asshole!" She shouted at him. "You're the one who keeps acting like I'm yours. You called me your mate last night, you-you make me tell you I belong to you all the goddamn time! I'm not the only one who -"

He shook his head. "Just part of the dom/sub thing. I guess I should have been clearer about how that worked."

She stared at him, her face pale and tears brimming in her lovely eyes. "I love you, why are you doing this?"

He took a deep breath, pushed his snarling, growling polar bear down deep, and said the one thing he knew would guarantee to make her hate him. "You're boring in bed, Rosalie."

The tears slid down her cheeks, and she stared mutely at

him. His pulse racing and his polar bear screaming in rage and fury, he returned her stare, waiting for the love in her eyes to turn to hatred.

It didn't happen. Her body shaking, she wiped at the tears streaming down her face before giving him an oddly dignified look. "I want you to leave."

His chest tightened, and his throat closed until he could almost hear the air whistling in and out of it. He was frozen to the spot for a moment as his bear, roaring and snarling, made another push for control.

"Leave, Hudson," she said.

He made a choppy nod and threw her house key on the bed before lurching out of the room and staggering down the stairs. He stumbled out of the house, slamming the door before bending over and planting his hands on his knees. He concentrated on forcing air in and out of his shrinking lungs until the black spots in his vision disappeared.

Go back. Please, go back.

His polar bear had never sounded so lost and afraid. It made a soft, pleading whimper, and he turned around to return to his mate. He couldn't do this. He couldn't stay away from her. His polar bear would go mad.

She'll die. Is that what you want? Sooner or later, Corden will find you, and he'll take Rosie. He'll take her, and he'll hurt her, his inner voice whispered.

We'll keep her safe, his polar bear replied.

You couldn't save Samuel. She isn't safe with us. Do the right thing.

Hudson's hands clenched into fists, and he made a low sound that was a cross between a bark and a whimper before turning abruptly and striding away from Rosalie's house.

His body shuddered all over as his polar bear made a soul-crushing howl of agony before falling silent.

"LADY, ORDER A DAMN DRINK OR LEAVE," HUDSON SNARLED AT the wolf shifter leaning against the bar.

It was Saturday night, and just like last night, the bar was insanely busy. He'd never seen so many shifters packed into the place, and while he knew it was just his imagination, it seemed like every single one of them couldn't stop gawking at him.

He grimaced as the group of five female gopher shifters to his right leaned over the bar and, giggling loudly, stared at his crotch. It was the fourth time in the last ten minutes, and he glared at them.

Their giggles got louder and one whispered something to the others that he couldn't hear over the background noise of the bar. The five of them burst into peals of laughter so high-pitched it made his head ache.

He turned back to the wolf shifter, who was also leaning over the bar and staring at his crotch. He snarled loudly, and she gave him a toothy grin. "No need to be grumpy, big fella. You can't blame me for being curious. It was a hell of a lot of blurring needed."

He stared blankly at her. Before he could ask her what the fuck she was talking about, she reached out and traced her fingers over his forearm. "Hey, you feel like being tamed again, big guy? We can meet up after you're done work, and you can show me exactly what you can do with that big cock of yours."

He gaped at her before pulling his arm back. "Lady, you have ten fucking seconds to order a drink before I get your ass kicked out of the bar."

"God," she sniffed, "you don't have to be such an asshole.

You only into humans or something? Since when the fuck was a polar bear into humans anyway?"

Tired and on edge, with his temper frayed to the breaking point, he bared his fangs at her and growled so loudly that the giggling gophers fell silent. He caught the scent of the wolf's fear, and a mixture of shame and anger flowed through him.

Before he could say anything, Porter clapped him on the back. "Go take a break."

"I'm fine," he gritted out.

Porter shook his head. "Take a break, I said. Now, Hudson."

He stomped past the gophers, ignoring the way they all leaned over the bar again to stare at his ass as he stormed down the hallway. He shoved open the back exit and stepped into the cold night air, letting the door shut behind him.

He leaned against the rough brick, staring up at the night sky. Not two minutes later, the door opened, and Judd's scent washed over him.

"You okay, man?"

He pushed away from the wall and paced back and forth. "What the hell is going on, Judd? Tonight, and last night, it's been a fucking zoo in there, and the assholes won't stop staring at me. I've had six different shifters proposition me over the last two nights, and" he stopped and gave Judd a confused look, "do you know how many females have eyed my goddamn crotch? Like, just leaned over the bar and stared at it. What the fuck?"

Judd burst into laughter. "That's what happens when you become an Internet sensation and three-quarters of the shifters in this city see the size of your dick. I know you're with the little human and aren't interested in the ladies, but can you do me a solid and send them my way? Tell them black bear dick is just as big as polar bear dick."

Hudson stared blankly at his friend. What the hell was Judd talking about?

"If I were you," Judd continued, "I'd ask Porter for a raise before all the excitement wears off. You've made him some serious fuckin' quid in the last two days, thanks to that video."

"What are you talking about?" Hudson said.

"The video," Judd said. "The goddamn video that's on YouTube. It's so busy in here because everyone wants to see the beast. Hell, we're lucky Rosalie hasn't dropped by to see you. It'd probably cause a fucking riot if they saw the two of you together acting all lovey-dovey."

"What video?" Hudson said.

"Someone recorded what happened Thursday night and uploaded it to YouTube. You've got like half a million hits, man."

"What?" Hudson said through numb lips.

Judd pulled out his phone and typed for a few seconds before handing it to him. "Here, look for yourself."

He watched the video, dismay washing over him. He'd had no appetite over the last two days, and the acid in his empty stomach burned like fire as he returned the phone to Judd. His dismay was now edged with bright panic.

"Hey, man? You okay? You look like you're about to puke," Judd said.

"How many people have seen this?" He whispered.

Judd shrugged. "Like half a million or so. There's a meme going around on Facebook too. Beauty tames the Beast." He snorted laughter. "It's why all the ladies are so into you. Your dick might be blurred out, but they can still tell what you're packing. I'm surprised you and your lady haven't seen it. I know you ain't got a Facebook account, but she must, right?"

Hudson barely heard him. The panic was crowding into his chest and his polar bear was making low whines of distress.

Our mate. Our mate is in danger.

She's fine, he said soothingly. *She's fine. Corden has very little use for the internet. He won't be watching fucking videos on YouTube or Facebook.*

His bear whined again. It didn't believe him and renewed its vigorous efforts to get him to go to Rosalie. He hadn't eaten or slept since leaving Rosalie's house, and all his energy had been used to control his polar bear. It had been making a concentrated effort for over twenty-four hours now to gain the upper hand, and honestly, he wasn't sure how much longer he could keep it subdued.

He needed to leave the city and be in a place where he'd never see Rosalie again, but he couldn't go. His polar bear was on the edge of madness as it was. He had made a terrible mistake in thinking he could convince his polar bear that Rosalie wasn't their mate. If he left the city now and cut off any chance of ever seeing Rosie again, his polar bear would go completely insane.

Another shudder went through him. He wasn't sure what would happen to his human side if his bear went mad, but he had an idea that it would be terrifyingly... unpleasant.

"Hudson? Seriously, man, what's wrong?"

"Nothing," he said. "Nothing's wrong. I gotta get back to work." He pushed past Judd and opened the door. Rosalie would be fine. Corden wouldn't have seen the video, and after a few more days, it wouldn't be popular anymore, and he'd sink back into obscurity.

"MY MATE!" THE HOWL RIPPED FROM HUDSON'S THROAT, AND he sat straight up, his heart in his throat and the vision of Rosalie drowning in blood stamped into his brain. He staggered into a standing position from the couch.

His stomach heaved, and he lurched his way into the kitchen and leaned over the sink, vomiting up the fruit he'd forced himself to eat earlier.

"My mate," he croaked.

A beard grew on his face, and he straightened and growled deep in his throat as his eyes turned from dark chocolate to the black of his bear. "My mate," he said again.

He headed for the door as white fur sprouted on the back of his neck and down his arms. He stiffened and made a strangled cry as he reached for the door handle.

"No," he groaned. "You cannot."

He staggered back before turning and driving his fist through the wall. He punched the wall repeatedly, ignoring the pain that raced up his arm, ignoring the streaks of blood that turned the white paint a deep red.

When his bear retreated, and he finally had control, he leaned against the opposite wall and stared at the dozen blood-smeared holes that punctured the formerly pristine wall. He was panting and sweating, and he flexed his hand cautiously. It was broken, the knuckles swelling and bruising, but it would heal.

He flexed it again, almost relishing the sharp bite of pain, before returning to the kitchen. He pulled a bag of frozen peas from the freezer and set it on his knuckles, staring blankly at the kitchen table.

Our mate is in terrible danger.

He tried to ignore the insistent growls of his bear. He'd dozed off on the couch, and the nightmare had returned. A shudder went through him. Rosalie was okay and safe, and she would only stay safe if he stayed away from her. He couldn't risk –

You could kill Corden.

He froze, staring at his broken hand as his polar bear made another soft growl. *Kill Corden, and we can be with our mate.*

Excitement replaced the nausea in his belly. If he killed Corden, he could be with Rosalie. He could be with his mate. It was so simple. Why hadn't he thought of this before?

Maybe because Corden is dangerous? You're not thinking straight, his inner voice snapped. *Corden is powerful, and he has a lot of shifters to protect him. There's no way you'll get close enough to kill him, Hudson. Be reasonable.*

He dropped the bag of peas on the table and grabbed his phone with his left hand. It was just after two on Sunday afternoon. If he left now, he could be in Alberta by Monday night. He would kill Corden and then return to his mate. He would beg for her forgiveness. His mate was sweet-natured and kind. She would forgive him.

He clumsily texted Porter, telling him he wouldn't be at work this week. He gave no explanation. If Porter fired him, so be it. He'd find another job. It didn't matter what he did for a job. As long as he was with his mate, he would be content.

Stop! You can't do this. You're going to die, and Rosalie will never know how you feel about her. Is that what you want? You might be stronger than Corden, but you can't kill him alone. He has too many shifters to protect him, and -

His polar bear growled loudly, drowning out the protests

347

of his inner voice. As he headed up the stairs to pack a small bag, his beard thickened, and he grinned widely, revealing his razor-sharp fangs.

CHAPTER 20

"See you later, Magpie. Enjoy your Sunday afternoon, go home and bang your man or something equally fun."

Maggie untied her apron and stuffed it under the counter before smiling at her coworker, Simone. "I'm sticking around for a bit longer. Rosalie is meeting me here for coffee."

"Cool," Simone said. "You working the morning shift tomorrow too?"

Maggie nodded, and Simone scowled. "Man, we never get shifts together anymore. I'm going to complain to Colin."

Maggie laughed and poured herself a coffee before walking toward the table by the window. "I miss you too, Simone."

She sat down at the table and took a sip of coffee. The shop was having a rare quiet moment. Their last customer had just left a few minutes earlier. She could see Rosalie climbing out of her truck. As she walked across the parking lot, Maggie frowned inwardly. Rosalie had texted her Friday night to tell her that she and Hudson were finished but hadn't given her any details. Maggie had to practically beg her to meet her for coffee this afternoon.

Rosalie stepped onto the sidewalk in front of the coffee shop, and Maggie's heart sank. The curvy brunette looked tired and sad, and her face was drawn and pale. Whatever had happened between her and Hudson had –

Maggie's eyes widened, and her hand squeezed compulsively around her coffee cup when the black van roared to a stop behind Rosalie. The side door opened, and a huge man with a bald tattooed head and a long black goatee jumped out and picked up Rosalie.

His hand clamped over her mouth, and he threw her into the van before jumping in after her and slamming the door shut. The van took off with a squeal of tires and a cloud of black exhaust smoke.

Maggie staggered to her feet and stared wide-eyed at Simone. Simone looked up from the register. "Maggie? What's wrong?"

"Rosalie," Maggie said. "Someone just took her."

"What?" Simone gave her a startled look. "What do you mean?"

"Someone just took Rosalie," Maggie repeated. Her hands shaking, she pulled out her cell phone and called Porter.

"Hey, darlin', how was -"

"Porter! Porter, something really bad has happened," she said.

"It's okay, Maggie." Porter's voice soothed her even over the phone. "Tell me what's wrong."

HUDSON IGNORED PORTER'S CALL. HE'D BEEN ON THE ROAD for barely an hour and was in no mood to talk to the wolf shifter. His mission was to get to Corden, kill him, and return to his mate. It did not include explaining to his boss why he'd suddenly taken off without any explanation.

But when Judd called and then called again and then *again*, he picked up the call. "Judd, I'm busy, I'll -"

"Where are you?"

Something in Judd's voice made him pull into a passing gas station and park. "What's wrong?"

"They aren't together anymore. He won't be able to help."

He could hear Maggie's voice in the background, sounding both terrified and pissed off.

"Judd, what's wrong?" he repeated.

"It's Rosalie," Judd said. "Someone took her."

His blood turned to ice in his veins, and his ability to breathe was lost. He sat in his truck, his mouth open as he tried to gulp in air.

"Hudson? You there?"

"When?" he croaked. "How?"

"About an hour ago," Judd said. "Some guy in a van just snatched her from the goddamn sidewalk in front of the coffee shop. Do you know if she's in some kind of trouble or -"

"It's because of me," he gasped out. "They took her because of me."

"What do you mean?" Judd said.

"Corden. Corden has her."

"Fuck me," Judd groaned. "That guy is fucking insane. Don't tell me you're fucking mixed up with him, Hudson. Please."

"I killed his son," Hudson said dully. "I killed John after he killed Samuel, and now Corden is going to hurt my mate. I have to do something. I was on my way to Canada to kill him, but he-he found her. He found her, and now…." Hudson could hear the panic in his voice.

"Okay, calm down. Come to the bar."

"I have to find her. I have to find my mate before -"

"I know, man. But come to the bar. You can't deal with Corden on your own. You know that."

"I can't ask you to help me. He's dangerous and -"

"Don't I fucking know it," Judd said with a sigh. "Just get to the bar, Hudson."

"I'm about an hour away," he said. "I'll be there as soon as I can."

He ended the call and tossed his phone on the seat. Before he could turn the truck around, his phone rang again. He grabbed it, his hands shaking so wildly he could barely hit the answer button.

"Rosalie? Baby, are you -"

"Hello, Hudson. It's been a long time."

The low voice made his hackles rise, and his bear snarled in rage.

"Corden," he growled. "Corden, she means nothing to me."

The grizzly shifter laughed. "Doesn't she? The video I watched would suggest otherwise."

Hudson didn't reply, and Corden laughed again. "It was so easy to find your mate. I'll admit I don't have much use for social media, but it certainly made it a snap to find out who the little human was and where she lived. She's almost pretty for a human, but I'll admit I'm surprised you would fuck her."

"I didn't. She's nothing to me. Listen, I don't -"

"Don't fucking lie to me, Hudson! She is *swimming* in your goddamn scent, and I am not fucking stupid!" Corden roared into the phone. "Do you think I'm fucking stupid, Hudson?"

"No," he said. "I don't."

Corden took a deep breath and released it. "Good. Now, let's talk business. Do you know how surprised I was when an associate showed me the video of you and the little human? I've spent the last two years searching everywhere for you. They told me to give up. Told me you were gone, and I was a fool to waste time and resources searching for you. But it wasn't them who lost their son, was it, Hudson? It wasn't them who buried his broken and mangled body, was it? I vowed my revenge, and even though others around me insisted on giving up, I knew I'd find you someday."

The big shifter's breathing turned harsh. "And now here we are. Me in this disgusting city with its filthy mixture of humans and shifters. The air smelling like exhaust and rotting food, and the different smells of thousands of shifters and humans crammed into one tiny piece of earth."

Hudson could hear the disgust in Corden's voice. "You were wise to hide from me here, Hudson. I never would have thought that you would live in a place like this."

"Corden, this is between you and me, just let her go and -"

"Let her go?" Corden bellowed genuine laughter. "Do you think you can just tell me what to do, and I will do it? We may have been friends once, but that ended the day you tore my child's throat out."

"Corden, I -"

"Shut up, Hudson. It's time to listen. You come to me, and maybe I'll let your little human live."

"How do I know you haven't already killed her," Hudson said.

"I'm not a monster," Corden said. "But, it's a fair question. Human, speak to him."

There was silence, and then Corden's voice was faint but understandable. "Say something, you stupid little bitch, or I'll cut off your thumb."

Another few seconds of silence and relief swept through him when Rosalie spoke into the phone. "Hudson?"

"Baby, it's okay. I'm going to get you out of this. Just do what he says, okay? It'll be all right, sweet Rosie. Baby, I love -"

"She means nothing to you, huh?" Corden's voice mocked him. "Are you ready to meet?"

"Where?" Hudson said.

"Outside of the city," Corden said. "I can't breathe or think with this wretched stink surrounding me. The forest on the north side of the city. A river flows through the forest. Follow it north for two miles. There is a campsite, closed this time of the year, of course. Meet me there at nine tonight."

"How do you know about the campsite?" Hudson said.

Corden laughed. "I may not choose to live in such a vile city, but I know others who do. This city is a festering boil on the face of the earth, but that does come with perks. It was so very easy, Hudson, to find shifters willing to do just about anything for a pile of cash."

"You're not alone," Hudson said.

"Did you think I would be? I have thirty shifters watching my back," Corden said. "Remember that when you show up tonight. Anyone you bring with you, any friends you may convince to try to save your sorry excuse for a life, will die tonight."

Hudson didn't reply, and Corden laughed again. "What was I thinking? Samuel is dead. You don't have any friends, do you? Nine tonight. For every minute you're late, I'll cut off one of your pretty little human's fingers."

"Touch her, and I'll tear you apart, Corden. I swear to fucking God if you even -"

"Nine o'clock, Hudson."

The line went dead. Hudson threw his phone on the seat before slamming his hands on the steering wheel and roaring so loudly that the humans pumping gas gave him a startled look. He roared again before throwing the truck into drive and stomping on the gas. He tore out onto the road, gravel spinning beneath his tires, and headed back toward the city.

THE CLOSED SIGN WAS ON THE BAR WHEN HE PULLED UP TO IT. He jumped out of his truck and tried the door, ducking inside when it opened.

Judd was standing by the long, curved bar with Porter and Maggie, and he gave Hudson a grim look. "Hey."

"Hey, I…" He studied the group of shifters standing to his right. Bishop, Porter's brothers Mal and Heath, the cat shifter Katarina and a bird shifter whose name he couldn't remember were all staring gravely at him. "What are you doing here?"

"They're here to help," Judd said.

"No," Hudson replied. "It's too dangerous."

"Rosalie is our friend," Maggie snapped at him. "We're not just going to stand by and do nothing."

"You have no idea how dangerous Corden is," Hudson growled.

"Do we even know for sure that this Corden has Rosalie?" Bishop asked.

"He does," Hudson replied. "He called me from her phone. Let me talk to her for a moment."

"Okay," Mal checked his cell phone. "We know they're in a black van. Davis is on assignment, but I can get Garth and Fenton to start looking for the van. What are the chances of them finding it and Corden?"

"Slim," Judd said. "Corden's fucking smart and paranoid."

"He's leaving the city," Hudson said. "He wants me to

meet him at a campsite near the river somewhere west of the city."

Mal turned to Heath who was already studying his phone. "Do you think he means Mokora Falls Campgrounds?"

"Yeah." Heath showed Mal his phone. "It's right along the river."

Hudson swung around when the door to the bar opened, and the three shifters walked in. He bared his fangs, growling deep in his chest at the lion shifter. "What the fuck are you doing here?"

"I called Bria," Kat stepped in front of him and raised one eyebrow at him. "Do you have a problem with that."

"What's going on?" Bria said. "You said Rosalie has been kidnapped?" She gave Kat an anxious look as Jace put his arm around her slender shoulders.

"Yes," Kat said. "By a shifter who has a problem with Hudson."

"This is your fault?" Lincoln stared at Hudson.

Hudson curled his lip at him. "Get the fuck out of here. We don't need you."

Lincoln made his own low growl. "I'm not leaving."

"I said get the fuck out before I -"

"Before you what?" Lincoln snarled. "She might be with you now, but Rosalie has been my friend for two damn years, and I care about her. If she's in trouble, I'm going to fucking help, whether you like it or not."

Before Hudson could reply, Judd said, "What did Corden say to you, Hudson?"

"I'm to meet him at the campsite at nine."

"So, we go there, kill the asshole, and get Rosalie back," Judd said.

"He's not alone. He hired a bunch of mercenary shifters to protect him," Hudson said.

"Do you know how many?" Porter asked.

"He said thirty."

"Which means he's got at least fifty," the bird shifter said.

"Who are you again?" Hudson said.

"Ronin." The shifter grinned at him. "We met at the moving party."

Hudson sniffed at him. "What kind of bird are you?"

Ronin's grin widened. "Oh... a little of this, a little of that."

Hudson snorted in disgust. "We don't need you. You're too weak."

"Big guy," Ronin clapped him on the back, "it's real sweet of you to be concerned about little old me, but I'm stronger than I look."

"You'll just get in the way," Hudson growled.

"Yeah, well, my lady here is planning on joining in on the fight, and we're a package deal, so..." he winked at Kat, "you get her slashy claws and my sassy attitude."

Jace frowned. "If we know where he is, shouldn't we be calling the police?"

"If the police show up, I'll be arrested, and Corden will go free. He'll kill Rosalie the very next chance he gets, and I won't be there to protect her," Hudson said.

Jace raised his eyebrows at him. "Why exactly are you so certain you'll be arrested?"

Hudson shoved his hands into his pockets. "I killed Corden's son."

ROSALIE LEANED AWAY WHEN THE BALD AND TATTOOED SHIFTER sniffed at her. He was sitting next to her in the back seat of the SUV. She didn't know what type of shifter he was, but he was big, scary, and strong. He'd lifted her into the van and threw her into the back of it like she weighed nothing more than a feather.

They hadn't been in the van for very long. After only a half hour, they'd stopped, and the shifter had warned her not to scream before pulling her out of the van on some empty side street and marching her over to the SUV. He'd pushed her into the back seat, and a large silver-haired man had given her a cold smile from the front passenger seat and asked for her phone.

The shifter sitting next to her, sniffed at her again. "Christ, you stink," he muttered.

She kept her arms folded tightly across her abdomen and didn't reply. She'd thought by now that Hudson's scent would have worn off, but obviously, it hadn't. She stared blankly out the window of the SUV as panic bit and clawed at her insides.

Don't cry, Rosalie. Don't show them any weakness. It'll be okay. Hudson will save you.

She would have laughed if she hadn't been so terrified. Thinking Hudson would save her was stupid. The silver-haired shifter had held the phone out to her and made her speak to Hudson but pulled it away before she even heard Hudson's voice. Hell, for all she knew, Hudson told the shifter to just do what he wanted to her.

He wouldn't do that to you, Rosie. You know he wouldn't.

Up until Friday, she would have believed that. But now…

She closed her eyes and blocked out the memory of her last conversation with Hudson. She'd rehashed it enough over the last day and a half, she didn't need to think about it again when she was on her way to her own death.

Not just death, Rosie. Don't forget he said he'd cut off your fingers first.

She shuddered and blinked back the hot tears that were

threatening to slide down her cheeks. Right, torture first. How long would the shifter torture her before he gave up on Hudson coming to her rescue and finally killed her? She had no idea, and just thinking about it made her want to simultaneously vomit and pee her pants.

She studied the door handle of the SUV. The shifters hadn't bothered to tie her hands. Why would they? She was a weak human and the three of them were powerful shifters. In the movies, the kidnapped victim always tried to escape. They distracted their captors, and then opened the door at a red light and ran. It looked easy in the movies. Of course, they were on the edge of the city already and running out of red lights. If she didn't try it soon, she'd miss her chance.

She chewed on her bottom lip. Wasn't she supposed to have some sort of fight or flight instinct? She couldn't seem to muster either reaction. Instead, terror left her frozen to her seat. What if the door handle was locked? What if she managed to get out of the car and the shifter simply rolled down his window and shot her in the back? She hadn't seen any guns, but that didn't mean they weren't carrying them.

The shifter next to her suddenly rolled down his window. Cold air blew her hair across her face and her shivering increased.

The silver-haired shifter turned in his seat to stare at her for a moment before saying, "Roll up your window."

"I'm fucking gagging back here on the smell of polar bear," the tattooed shifter snarled.

"I don't care. Our guest is cold," the shifter replied.

Muttering a curse, the shifter hit the button for the window before glaring at her. "Fucking human stench is bad enough, let alone mixing polar bear with it."

"Enough," the silver-haired shifter said. He glanced at the

shifter who was driving. "How much longer until we get there?"

"An hour, maybe a little more," the shifter grunted.

The silver-haired shifter turned back to Rosalie and smiled at her. "Well, we've got some time. I don't believe I properly introduced myself. My name is Corden, and your name again is…?"

"Rosalie," she said.

"Right. Rosalie. Tell me, Rosalie, how did a human like you convince Hudson to take you as his mate?"

"I'm not his mate," she said.

Corden laughed. "There's no point in lying, my dear."

"I'm not," she said. "We were just… having sex and that– that ended on Friday. I don't mean anything to him."

Corden cocked his head at her and then gave her a cold smile. "For your sake, I hope that isn't true."

Fresh new terror. Freezing her up. Filling her lungs.

She sucked in a breath. "What are you going to do to me?"

"How did you and Hudson meet?" Corden asked.

She wouldn't tell him that Hudson worked at the bar, wouldn't give him any information on him. Maybe Corden already knew everything, but if he didn't, she wouldn't be the one to tell him how to find Hudson and kill him.

"Through friends," she said.

"It's strange that a human would have sex with him, don't you think? Considering who he is."

"Hudson is a good man," she said. "How… how do you know him?"

Corden studied his hands. They were big and covered in thick black hair. Gaudy gold rings were on each of his fingers, and he twisted one around and around as he said, "Hudson and I were friends once. I own a logging company, and Hudson worked for me. He was a good employee, strong and smart. He did his job and kept his mouth shut. Eventually, we became friends. I admired him, was even thinking about promoting him, grooming him to help John run the company when I retired."

"Who's John?" Rosalie said when Corden didn't say anything else.

Brief but intense pain slashed across his face. "John was my son."

"Was?" Rosalie whispered.

The gold ring twisted, turned, twirled.

"That good man of yours? The one you let into your bed and between your smooth little human thighs?" Corden's eyes glowed and brown and silver hair sprouted across his face. "He murdered my boy."

"Wait," Porter said, "so this Corden owns a logging company, but it's a front for drug smuggling?"

"Yes and no," Hudson said. "The logging company is a legitimate business and in Alberta, Corden is a powerful shifter. He's made a lot of money in the logging business, and he's used that money to influence and bribe and blackmail tons of different people. That includes the local sheriff's department. It was Corden's son, John, who ran the drug smuggling. Corden knew about it though, and I'm pretty sure that he used his connections once or twice to bail John out of trouble."

He glanced at Judd. "My best friend's name was Samuel. He was a brown bear shifter and we grew up together. We moved to Canada when we were in our early twenties and worked construction for a while. It's where I met Judd. Later, both Samuel and I started working for Corden's logging company."

"Where's Samuel now?" Maggie asked.

"He had a heroin problem. He started spending time with John, and it didn't take long before John had him hooked on other shit too. Eventually, he started running drugs for John across the border. But then Samuel double crossed him, kept some drugs that he was supposed to deliver."

"Shit," Heath said.

"Yeah." Hudson took a deep breath. "Samuel was an addict and he couldn't help it, but John, he... he took him out in the woods and he tortured him for two days. I eventually found his scent and tracked him down, but he was too badly injured, too... he died in my arms."

"Fuck, man." Judd squeezed his shoulder. "I'm sorry."

"John and his men were there." He stared at the group of shifters who were studying him silently. "He gave me the chance to walk away, he told me to leave and I wouldn't be killed, but I... I couldn't. Samuel was my best friend. So, I stayed. I stayed, and I killed all of them, including John."

"MY BOY WAS A GOOD BOY." CORDEN SMILED AT ROSALIE. "I knew about his little side business, of course, had even helped him out a few times when he got into some trouble. But, getting into trouble here and there doesn't make him a bad person. Does it?"

"No," Rosalie said in a low voice.

"Exactly. Everything was fine until Hudson's asshole of a friend, Samuel, double-crossed John. What kind of shifter does that? Huh? What kind of shifter takes advantage of someone who's trying to help them? Samuel was a degenerate, he was a useless piece of garbage who tried to take something that didn't belong to him."

Rosalie stared wide-eyed at Corden. He was speaking normally, cordially even, but there was madness in his eyes. Through numb lips, she said, "What-what did he take?"

"That's not important." Corden made a careless wave before twisting the rings around his fingers again. "What's important is that Samuel betrayed John. John did what any good business man would do, he pulled Samuel aside and demanded that he give back what he'd stolen."

Corden glanced out the window at the sky. "It looks like it might rain."

Rosalie wrapped her arms tighter around her torso. She didn't want to be, but she was fascinated by the story Corden was telling. "Did Samuel give it back?"

Corden smiled at her. "He did not, in fact, return what he had stolen. So, John was forced to take drastic measures. Did he go a little too far? Perhaps. But I can assure you, human, that he did not intend for Samuel to die. It was an unfortunate accident, brought on by Samuel's refusal to do as asked."

"He killed him," Rosalie whispered.

"No!" Corden's smile turned to a snarl and she swallowed down her whimper of fear. "Samuel's death was his own fault. If he hadn't fucked up so badly, he would be alive today. John was not a monster. Do you understand?"

When she didn't reply, he reached into the back seat and squeezed her knee with his powerful fingers until she moaned in pain. "Do you, human?"

"Yes," she said. "Yes, I understand."

"Good." He released her and then patted her knee in a grandfatherly way. "But Hudson, now he didn't see it that way. I thought he was smart, human. I thought he understood that there are consequences to actions, and that

Samuel's death was a product of his own actions. He didn't though. Hudson turned out to be nothing more than the mindless beast that everyone believed him to be."

Corden leaned over the seat again and she could feel his hot breath washing over her. "Hudson murdered five shifters that day, including my boy. He tore their bodies apart and splintered their bones until there was nothing left of them but puddles of blood and fur and flesh."

More hair pushed through Corden's flesh until his entire face was covered in a thick layer of silver and brown hair. "He murdered John in cold blood, and today? Today, Hudson will reap what he's sown."

"So, you've been running for two years, knowing that Corden would never stop looking for you?" Lincoln said in a low voice.

Hudson refused to look at him. "Yes."

"Then tell me why the fuck you thought it would be a good idea to start sleeping with Rosie," Lincoln growled. "You put her in danger because you wanted somewhere warm to stick your dick? What the fuck is wrong with you? Rosalie is innocent, and now she's going to die because you -"

"Shut up!" Hudson roared. He grabbed the lion shifter and, with an angry snarl, threw him across the bar. Lincoln crashed into a table and rolled onto the floor. He jumped up immediately, his clothes starting to tear as he began to shift.

"Lincoln! Enough!" Jace jumped in front of his friend and placed a restraining hand on his chest as Judd and Bishop grabbed Hudson's arms.

"Get the fuck off of me," Hudson growled.

Bishop bared his fangs at him. "This won't help get her back. Trust me, I know what you're going through and if you want your mate back, you need to keep it the fuck together."

Hudson stared at him for a long moment before relaxing his tense body.

"Okay?" Judd said.

"Yeah," Hudson said hoarsely. He glanced over at Lincoln. "Just keep that fucking asshole away from me."

"If she dies," Lincoln hissed at him, "I will fucking kill you."

"Lincoln," Jace gave him a look of exasperation, "knock it off."

"She is my mate, not yours," Hudson snarled. "She loves *me*. Not you. *You* mean nothing to her."

"Shut the fuck up," Lincoln said.

"Why don't you try to make me shut up, lion shifter?" Hudson asked.

Kat made a loud hiss. "Both of you shut up. We need a plan to rescue Rosalie. So, do you think, maybe, the two of you could stop comparing dick sizes for two fucking minutes?"

Ronin put his arm around her and gave her a lazy grin. "Kitten, I found the unaltered footage of that "Beauty tames the Beast' video. Trust me, Big White over there doesn't have anything to worry about when it comes to dick size."

His grin widened. "Not that I gave the video more than a cursory glance."

Heath rolled his eyes. "You added the *My Heart Will Go On* song to it, looped it on repeat and emailed it to all of us, including Kat's mother."

"Ronin, you didn't," Kat said.

"What? I can't help it if I'm a romantic. Besides, you knew about my Celine Dion obsession."

"I only found out after you moved in with me," Kat said.

"Kitten, she's a vocal powerhouse with crowd-pleasing ballads and a sexy French accent. Why wouldn't I love her?"

Ronin turned to Hudson. "She's a goddamn Canadian icon. You're from Canada, there's no way you don't love her. Am I right, big guy?" He held out his arms in a wide half circle. "You can admit it. There's no judgment in this friendship circle."

Hudson grunted in annoyance and Kat repeated, "We need a plan."

Hudson watched as almost all of the shifters turned to stare at Mal who was leaning against a table and staring at the floor.

"Mal?" Heath said.

Mal lifted his head and studied Hudson for a moment before pushing away from the table. "Here's what we're going to do..."

CHAPTER 21

Rosalie, her body shaking madly, leaned against the rough wood of the lodge. While she was grateful for the covered porch that kept her dry from the pouring rain, she was miserably cold. She'd thrown on just a thin cardigan over her shirt before leaving the house and she wished desperately that she'd been wearing a coat. She was going to freeze to death if she was out here much longer.

Uh, Rosie? You have a lot more to worry about than freezing to death.

That was true. She stared at Corden standing next to her before glancing at her watch. In exactly four minutes, she was going to have a damn finger cut off.

Her stomach was empty, but it tried it's hardest to expel the bile swirling around in it. She swallowed the bile down, her throat burning, as she stared into the darkness surrounding them.

They had arrived at the closed-for-the-season campground almost four hours ago. She'd sat in the SUV with the others, her hope of surviving the day growing dimmer with each vehicle that arrived over the next few hours, bringing more large and scary looking men. They were all shifters, she'd already figured out that Corden wasn't exactly a human enthusiast, and her hope that Hudson would show up to rescue her had switched to hope that he wouldn't.

There were at least fifty shifters in addition to Corden and the one that stood on the porch of the locked up main lodge with her. Hudson might have been strong and powerful, but he didn't stand a chance against that many shifters. If he came here to rescue her, he would die.

Despite what he said, despite that it was over between them, her chest tightened at the thought of Hudson dying.

Girl, you're gonna die too. You don't honestly think Corden is going to just let you walk away when Hudson shows up. Do you?

No, she didn't. She was hellishly aware of her impending death. But she would die regardless of whether Hudson showed up or not. Wasn't it better that only one of them died? If she had to watch Hudson being tortured and abused...

She gagged on more bile, and Corden stared down at her before giving her a brief smile. "Won't be long now, human."

Her eyes widened when he held out his hand, and the tattooed shifter slapped a small but wickedly sharp knife into the palm.

"Thank you, Tony." Corden smiled again at Rosalie. "Most of these shifters are just – what is it that humans call them... hired guns? But Tony has been with me for years now. Haven't you?"

"Yes, sir," Tony said.

"He's a grizzly shifter, like me. His father worked for me for many years and Tony is as loyal as his father was," Corden said.

Rosalie checked her watch. Two minutes to nine. "Uh, what type of shifters are, um, everyone else?"

She didn't give a rat's ass about the other shifters, but maybe if she kept him talking, it would spare her a few extra minutes until he chopped off a finger or two.

And then what? You can't just run off into the woods, Rosalie. You can't see them, but you know there are shifters hidden all around this damn campsite. Even if you could get off the porch and into the woods without Corden or Tony catching you, those hired goons can see in the fucking dark. They can smell you! You're already dead. You just don't want to admit it.

No, she supposed she didn't, but could you blame her?

"Oh, a little bit of everything, I suppose," Corden said. He leaned down and grinned at her until she could see his fangs gleaming in the dim light. "Tigers and lions and bears... oh my."

She clamped her mouth shut against the whimper that wanted to escape. "Where, uh, where do you find guys like that?"

Corden laughed before reaching out and grabbing her wrist. "Tony, the time, please."

"Eight fifty-nine, sir. Wait... nine," Tony said before smiling almost pleasantly at Rosalie.

"No sign of him," Corden said. "What a shame. Hold your hand out, human."

"No." Rosalie struggled to free herself from Corden's grip. "Please! Don't do this."

"I'm afraid I don't have a choice," Corden said gently. "Consequences have actions, remember? Now, hold out your hand or -"

"Boss," Tony sniffed the air, "he's here."

Still holding her wrist in a tight grip, Corden turned to stare into the darkness.

Rosalie's heart banged against her ribcage when Hudson, wearing a pair of jeans and a t-shirt, stepped out of the darkness. Tony raised his hand and the lights from the SUV blinked on, bathing Hudson in bright light.

He was soaking wet, the relentless rain bouncing off his granite body as he stared unblinkingly at Rosalie.

"Hello, Hudson," Corden said.

Hudson moved closer, stopping just a few feet from the steps to the porch and staring briefly at Corden before his gaze swung to Rosalie again. "Are you all right, sweet Rosie?"

At the sound of his deep voice, her fragile courage broke, and the tears flowed down her cheeks. She nodded, and Hudson smiled at her.

"Everything will be okay. I love you, my mate."

Her mouth dropped open in surprise, and she sucked in a sobbing breath of damp air as Corden made a snort of derision. "Touching, but a lie, I'm afraid. You and your fragile human mate will die tonight, Hudson."

"Let her go, Corden," Hudson said. "Let her go and I won't kill you."

Corden curled his upper lip at him. "Like you killed my boy?"

"He killed Samuel," Hudson said. "He tortured and killed him. John was a sadist who -"

"Shut up!" Corden snarled. "Speak my boy's name again and I will slit your mate's throat right here and you'll watch her bleed out."

Hudson stiffened and took a step back. "She has nothing to do with this. Just let her go."

"No," Corden said.

"Then you leave me no choice." Hudson gave him a look that was a mixture of sorrow and weary resolve. "You're going to die tonight, Corden."

Corden's lips curved up in a soft smile. "You and your mate are the only ones who will die."

"You can't defeat me," Hudson said. "You're too old, and your grief has made you weak. You're not as strong as you think you are. I'll kill you and," his gaze dipped briefly to Tony, "your little errand boy."

Corden's smile turned to a laugh as men appeared out of the darkness of the woods. They moved steadily forward toward Hudson as Corden raised his eyebrows. "I told you I was not alone, Hudson."

Hudson bared his teeth at Corden in a fierce grin. "Neither am I."

HIS POLAR BEAR WAS SNARLING AT HIM TO LEAP ONTO THE porch and kill the shifter who had taken his mate. Hudson held his bear back and stared steadily at Corden as the grizzly shifter shook his head. "You're lying. You have no one, Hudson. No one would risk -"

The scream of pain cut through the sound of the rain and Corden's voice. Hudson snarled at the shifter closest to him as the others turned toward the shriek. A brown bear shifter staggered forward, his body half shifted to his bear, before he fell to his knees. Kat, her golden coloured fur raised at the hackles and her long white fangs dripping with blood, stood behind him. She hissed softly as the bear shifter fell on his face. His back was torn open and Hudson could see the white of his spine as the pouring rain washed away the blood gushing out of his back.

There was shocked silence across the clearing as the shifters stared blankly at the jaguar. Kat yowled in satisfaction before, her tail flicking rapidly, stalked toward the closest shifter. He shifted to his animal form – a panther – and the two giant cats leaped at each other.

Corden's men quickly shifted as the three wolf shifters loped into the clearing. Moving as a pack, they surrounded two coyote shifters and easily took them both down, their teeth tearing and slashing into the howling coyotes' flesh.

A second panther, his fur gleaming with rain, crouched to pounce on Kat as she fought the first. Before it could land on her back, Bishop in his grizzly form caught the cat by its long tail. The panther dug its feet into the wet ground, but it was no match for the grizzly bear's strength. Bishop dragged it backward with a powerful jerk, and the cat screamed in agony when Bishop's sharp claws tore open its stomach.

A flash of gold fur caught his eye and Hudson turned to the left. The lion, his mane soaking wet and his green eyes flashing emerald fire, leaped onto the back of a giant black bear. He buried his fangs deep into the meaty shoulder of the bear. It bellowed and used one large paw to tear Lincoln off his back. Jace jumped onto the bear's chest, his large striped body knocking him onto the ground. He buried his fangs deep into the bear's throat and tore open the flesh.

Hudson caught the scent of grizzly only seconds before he was sent flying to the ground. He scrambled to his feet and turned to bare his fangs at the tattooed shifter. "Walk away, Tony."

"You fucking idiot," Tony snarled. "I liked you, man, and now? Now I gotta fucking kill you."

Tony shrugged out of his jacket, tore his shirt off and dropped it on the ground. The rain soaked into his tattooed flesh as his upper body swelled. He growled, his fangs starting to protrude from his mouth. "Why couldn't you have just -"

He suddenly screamed and dropped to one knee. Ronin stood behind him and he delivered another brutal kick to the back of Tony's other knee. His leg went out from him and he made a startled sound of shock as Ronin clamped one hand across his forehead and the other under his chin. He twisted Tony's head to the right with a brisk yank. Tony's body jerked, his eyes went blank and when Ronin released his head, his body fell forward with a harsh thud.

"Not bad for a bird, am I right?" Ronin grinned at Hudson.

When Hudson just stared in stunned silence at him, he laughed and blew him a kiss. "You're welcome, big guy."

He strutted off, giving Hudson another cheeky grin. "If you need me again, just – shit!"

The bird shifter stepped on a wet pile of leaves, and Hudson watched as his feet slid out from under him, and he landed in a graceless heap on his ass. Ronin bounced back up and gave him a sheepish look. "Yeah, I'm, uh, I'm gonna go… help my lady."

Hudson rolled his eyes and muttered, "idiot", before turning to the porch. "Corden, it's over. Give me my…"

Panic made his bear surge forward. The porch was empty, and he ran toward it. A black bear launched its large body at him. Hudson caught him and threw him to the ground before dropping onto him and ripping out its throat. He barely tasted the shifter's hot blood, barely heard its dying scream. He was up and running toward the porch again without a single look back. He lifted his shaggy head and inhaled before staring into the woods. His mate's scent was nearly buried under his own, but he found it easily enough. He dropped to all fours and ran past the lodge.

He ran toward the trees, pulling up short when the two

bear shifters appeared in front of him. They blocked his path and he made a low growl. They growled back but held their ground.

He shifted to his human form, staring at the shifters. "Step aside and I'll let you live."

The bigger of the two rose up on his hind legs before roaring at him. His polar bear growled viciously in return but before he could shift, he smelled Judd's scent behind him.

Judd, naked and bleeding from a bite wound on one thigh, clapped him on the back. "Go. I got this."

Hudson shook his head. "No, you can't take on both of them."

"The fuck I can't," Judd said. "Go."

"Judd -"

"I said I've got it, you ass." He grinned at Hudson. "Go save your girl."

Before Hudson could reply, Judd shifted to his bear form and with a fearless roar, charged the two shifters. As the three of them fought viciously, Hudson shifted to his bear form and ran into the woods.

"Move, you stupid bitch!" Corden snarled at her. His hand tightened around her upper arm until pain raced up and down her arm, and Rosalie cried out as he yanked her deeper into the woods.

"Let go of me!" She tried to hit him in the face and he growled at her before grabbing her by the hair with his other hand and giving it a brutal yank.

She screamed, and he snarled at her. "Move your fucking ass, or I will kill you right here. Do you understand, bitch?"

Her arm and scalp throbbing, Rosalie stared up at Corden. She had two choices – she could allow Corden to drag her into the woods and kill her before Hudson found them, or she could put up a fight and hope to God that he only broke a few of her bones and didn't outright kill her before Hudson arrived.

Be brave, Rosie.

She stared up at him and whispered, "Please don't kill me," before she burst into tears and let her body go completely limp. She sagged down, landing on her knees on the rain-soaked spongy ground, as Corden made a noise of disgust.

"Get up, you stupid fool." Standing above her, he wrapped his hand in her hair again and yanked her head up until she looked at him. "I said, get up before I -"

Rosalie, her body trembling, punched Corden as hard as she could in the crotch. His hand tightened mercilessly in her hair before it loosened and released her. His face paled, and she shuffled back on her ass like a crab, staring wide-eyed at him.

He sank to his knees, his hands covering his crotch as his mouth opened and closed like a fish. "Bitch," he wheezed as she climbed to her feet. "I'll... kill you for that."

Her heart pounding, she turned and ran back toward the campsite. It was pitch black in the woods, the moon covered by the dark clouds. As thunder boomed above her and lightning flashed in the sky, it briefly illuminated the fallen log in front of her. Moving too fast to stop or dodge around it, she made a feral scream of fear and leaped over it. She landed on her feet but the wet leaf-covered ground made them slip out from under her.

She landed on her ass with a loud grunt and immediately

ELIZABETH KELLY

scrambled to her feet. Before she could take off again, a large
paw came out of the darkness and slammed into her stomach. She flew backward, landing in a heap against the fallen
log, the back of her shirt rucking up and the wet bark
scraping bloody grooves into her skin.

The wind was knocked out of her, and she gasped for air
as she stared up at the large silver and brown grizzly
standing above her. He snarled at her before raising his paw
again.

She waited for the death blow, waited for those thick
sharp claws to tear her wide open. Before he could land the
blow, the giant, white polar bear came barreling out of the
darkness. He hit the grizzly like a freight train and the two of
them crashed against the ground.

There was no epic struggle, no violent fight for control.
Corden was large, but he was no match for Hudson's size
and strength. Hudson pinned him down easily and bent his
mouth to Corden's fur-covered throat. He tore open the fur
and flesh with a quick and savage ruthlessness. Blood
sprayed from the grizzly's jugular, and Corden made a single
soft growl before dying.

Hudson backed away from the dead shifter. Rosalie struggled to her feet and took a few steps forward as Hudson
shifted to his human form. He stood with his back to her and
his head bowed.

"Hudson?" She whispered.

He turned and wiped the blood from his mouth. There
was no triumph in his face, no victory in defeating his
enemy. Instead, there was only anguish and a weary remorse
that broke her heart.

"My mate," he said. It was almost a question, and the
combination of hope and resignation in his voice made tears
flow down her cheeks.

"Yes," she said. "Your mate."

Relief washed over his face, and he wrapped his arms around her hips and picked her up, burying his face into her neck.

She put her arms around his shoulders and hugged him tight, kissing his thick, wet hair. After a few moments, he set her down and took her hand. "Sweet Rosie, I -"

The howl of pain made them both freeze, and Hudson muttered a curse. "That's Judd. C'mon."

He took her hand, and they ran through the woods. They reached the campsite in only a few minutes, and Rosalie moaned in dismay when she saw Judd. The bear shifter was lying on his side, and despite the darkness, even she could see the blood that covered his naked body. The three wolf shifters had driven away the other two bear shifters, and Rosalie turned away when the jaguar and the tiger leaped onto their backs and delivered the death bites to the screaming, growling bears.

"Judd!" Hudson dropped to his knees beside the fallen bear shifter. "Judd, you're okay, man. You're okay."

Rosalie joined them, kneeling at Judd's head and stroking his dark hair as Hudson took his hand. "It'll be okay. You're gonna heal."

Judd shook his head and Rosalie winced when blood flew from his mouth. "Not gonna heal from this, buddy."

A loud whimper escaped from Hudson's throat and he shook his head. "Don't say that. You're not dying because of me. Do you hear me?"

Judd didn't reply, and Rosalie made a soft gasp when she peered around his large body. His back was ripped open and she could see torn muscle and ligaments, and the shattered bits of his spine.

"Can't feel my legs." More blood bubbled out of Judd's

mouth and Rosalie wiped it away. "Fuck, can't feel anything. Shouldn't dying hurt?"

"You're not dying," Hudson said. "We'll get you to the hospital."

"Found your girl," Judd said.

"Yeah, I did." Hudson squeezed his hand.

"Good, that's real good." Judd's eyelids drifted closed and Hudson squeezed his hand again.

"No! Judd, stay awake. Look at me!"

Judd's eyes popped open. "Glad you found your girl."

"Stay awake, Judd. Just -"

"Move, Rosalie. Let me see him!"

Hudson growled when Ronin dropped to his knees next to her. "Get away from him, bird."

"Rosalie, move!" Ronin pushed her to the side before bending over Judd.

"I said get away from him," Hudson growled.

"Hudson, he can help." Bishop appeared and grabbed Hudson's shoulder. "Come with me."

"No, I won't leave him."

"He's gonna help him," Mal joined them. "Trust us, Hudson. Let Ronin save him before it's too late." He helped Rosalie to her feet as Bishop dragged Hudson to his. "Rosalie, take Hudson over there."

She took Hudson's hand and tugged on it. "Hudson, honey, come with me." She didn't actually think Ronin could help, even if he had a medical background, she'd seen Judd's back. Nothing could repair that type of damage. But she didn't want Hudson to watch his friend die, so she tugged on his hand again. "Honey, come over here."

She led him a few feet away, wrapping her arms around his waist and holding him tight as Bishop and Mal knelt in front of Judd. Their big bodies blocked their view of Ronin and Judd, and Hudson jerked all over when Judd made a sudden loud bellow of agony.

"Judd!" Hudson pulled away from her, but before he could run to Judd, Porter and Jace were standing in front of him. They pushed him back, and Hudson snarled at them.

"Just wait," Porter growled as Judd's shrieks of pain filled the night air.

"He's killing him!" Hudson snapped.

"He's not, I promise," Porter said.

"Hold him still!" Ronin shouted. "Christ, don't let him thrash around."

"Judd!" Hudson shouted again. He shoved Porter to the ground and dodged around Jace before running toward Ronin and the wolf shifters. "Get the fuck away from him! Get away from...Judd?"

Rosalie dashed forward, grabbing Hudson's hand and staring in shocked disbelief at Judd. The bear shifter was sitting up. He was still covered in blood, but he was moving his lower legs and his arms.

"Fuck, that hurt. What did you do to me?" he said to Ronin.

Rosalie moved around him and stared at Judd's back. It was completely healed, the skin smooth and unblemished.

"How?" she whispered.

Hudson knelt next to Judd. "What happened?"

"I have no fucking idea," Judd said. He stared at Ronin again. "What did you do?"

Ronin grinned at him. "Let's just say we're even now for that time I broke your arm."

Hudson blinked at Judd. "The bird broke your arm?"

"Oh, you didn't tell him?" Ronin said. "I get it. It's embarrassing getting your ass kicked by a bird, huh?" He slapped

Judd on the back before standing and calling, "Hey, Kitten? You hungry? I could go for a taco. How about you?"

He wandered away, and Judd said, "Christ, I hate that damn bird."

"Me too, buddy," Hudson said. "Me too."

The two bear shifters grinned at each other before hugging.

Rosalie turned to Porter. "How did he do that? *What* did he do?"

"Ronin's a phoenix," Porter said. "He can heal injuries, even life-threatening ones."

"Holy shit." Rosalie stared at Ronin's retreating back as Jace joined her. He was naked, and she avoided looking at his lower body as he smiled at her.

"Hey, Rosie."

"Hi, Jace."

He pressed a kiss against her forehead. "I know you're supposed to be back to work tomorrow, but I'm going to be the greatest fucking boss ever and give you the day off. See you Tuesday, yeah?"

Her laughter turned into a hiccupping sob, and Jace kissed her forehead again. "It's okay, Rosie. You're okay."

She hugged him tight. "Thank you, Jace."

"You're welcome."

"Rosalie?"

She turned and stared at Lincoln. The lion shifter smiled tentatively at her. "You got a minute?"

She glanced at Hudson. He was still talking to Judd, and she took Lincoln's hand when he held it out to her. She thought with a weary sort of amusement that three weeks ago, she would have been thrilled to see a naked Lincoln standing in front of her. Now, she didn't have a lick of interest.

"You okay?" Lincoln asked.

"I think so. Why are you here?" she asked.

He gave her a small smile. "We're friends, Rosie. Aren't we?"

She nodded. "Yeah, we are."

Lincoln took her other hand and raised them both to his mouth before pressing a kiss against her knuckles. "I'm sorry, Rosie. Sorry for using you, sorry for taking advantage of you for the last two years. I'm happy for you, I am. You deserve to be happy."

She smiled at the lion shifter. "Thank you."

"Rosie." Hudson was standing a few feet behind her. He glared at Lincoln and held his hand out to her. "Come to me, my mate."

Lincoln squeezed her hands before dropping them. "See you at work, Rosie-girl."

She nodded and returned to Hudson, taking his hand and linking their fingers together as Mal helped Judd to his feet. She stared at the small group of shifters who had worked together to save her life and swallowed down the lump in her throat.

"Thank you." Her voice cracked, and she swallowed again. "I know just saying thank you isn't enough, but..."

"It's enough," Mal said.

"Although, if you wanna pay for tacos tonight," Ronin said cheerfully. "I wouldn't say no."

The large jaguar sitting next to him made a loud hiss before bumping him with her head.

"What?" Ronin smoothed a gentle hand over the jaguar's back. "You know I love tacos."

"C'mon," Mal said. "Let's get out of here."

"Man," Ronin said as he studied the dead bodies of the shifters that littered the campsite, "the first batch of summer campers are gonna be in for a big surprise when they show up."

Rosalie stared up at Hudson. He pushed a lock of her curly hair behind her ear before bending and pressing a kiss against her mouth. "Let's go home, my mate."

"Yes," she replied. "Let's go home."

SHE WAS WAITING FOR HUDSON IN THE BEDROOM AFTER HIS shower. Mal and Heath had driven them to her house, and she headed straight for the shower. She wanted Hudson to join her, but he'd shaken his head and disappeared downstairs.

After her shower, he applied antibiotic cream to the scrapes on her back with the careful precision of a surgeon before kissing her shoulder and sending her to the kitchen while he showered.

Fresh fruit and a sandwich were sitting on the table for her. She ate half the sandwich and an apple, petting Mr. Pibbles as he rubbed against her legs before she returned upstairs. All she wanted was to be in Hudson's arms.

The door to the primary bathroom opened, and Hudson appeared in a cloud of steam. He had a towel wrapped around his hips, and despite everything that had happened, despite the way her back was aching and the weariness in every muscle of her body, a small trickle of lust went through her.

He cleared his throat. "Did you eat?"

"A little." She patted the bed beside her. "Come sit down, Hudson."

He sat beside her, and she rested her head on his shoulder. He kissed the top of her head. "You should get some sleep."

"In a little bit. Hudson -"

"I'm sorry," he said. "I'm sorry for what I said on Friday. I didn't mean any of it. I knew that I couldn't be with you, couldn't make you my mate because of Corden, so I said terrible things to hurt you and drive you away."

She lifted her head, and he gave her a look of guilt. "I am so sorry for hurting you, my mate."

"Shh," she said. "It's okay, honey."

"It isn't," he replied. "I did not mean it."

"I know you didn't," she said.

"I love you." He cupped her face and pressed a kiss against her mouth. "I love you, and you are my mate, and I will never leave you again. I promise."

"I love you too," she breathed against his mouth.

He leaned back. "What about the lion?"

She shook her head. "I don't love him. I never loved him, and I know that now. What I felt for him was... it pales in comparison to how I feel about you. I love you, Hudson. You're my mate and I want to spend the rest of my life with you."

He took a deep and shuddering breath before lifting and sitting her on his lap. His big hand rested on her thigh, and he kissed her again. She parted her lips, moaning at the familiar taste of her mate when he slid his tongue into her mouth. He cupped her breast, teasing her nipple through the thin fabric of her sleep shirt.

When he pulled back, she made a whine of dismay. "Hudson, no."

"We should talk, sweet Rosie," he said. "We should talk about tonight, and why Corden went after you, and what happened to Samuel, and -"

She pressed her fingers against his mouth to silence him. "We will," she said. "We will talk about all of that. But not tonight. Tonight, I need my mate to make love to me. Will you do that?"

He nodded immediately. "Yes."

She smiled. "That's my good mate."

Keep reading for an excerpt of The Dragon's Mate (The Shifters Series Book Seven)

THE DRAGON'S MATE EXCERPT

"I knew it. You're fucking faggots."

Tyler's stomach dropped, and he pulled his mouth away from Corey. He looked behind him, and fear slipped into his gut. Jeff Howell and three of his football teammates were standing just behind them.

Corey's cold, shaking hand slipped into his, and Tyler squeezed it tightly.

"Get lost, Jeff," he said with a bravery he didn't feel. He glanced at Corey. The smaller boy's face was pale and pinched with worry, and Tyler's fear heightened.

"It'll be okay, honey," he said.

"It'll be okay, honey," Jeff mimicked in a high-pitched voice. He shook his head with disgust. "Jesus, you two are gross."

Tyler didn't reply. He had been schoolmates with Jeff since kindergarten, and he knew from experience the best way to handle him was to ignore his taunts. Although Tyler had never publicly announced he was gay and had done his best to quietly blend in, he'd been targeted by Jeff and his oafish friends for most of his life.

"Tyler, let's go." Corey tugged on Tyler's hand, and Jeff glanced at his friends. They spread out in a loose circle around them, and Corey moaned quietly with fear.

They were too far for anyone to help them. They'd ridden their bikes to the edge of the woods, and he and Corey had walked for nearly an hour into the trees to the long, wide river that wound its way through them. Tyler had grown up on the city's outskirts and spent many happy hours playing in the woods. Now, he lived with his father in an apartment in the city's downtown core.

Adrenaline was lighting sparks through his veins. Corey had moved to the city two years ago, and although Tyler was aware of him and admired how his lean, lithe body moved when he played soccer, he and Corey didn't start dating until this final year of high school. Corey, the captain of the school's soccer team, was failing Spanish, and Tyler was assigned to tutor him. It hadn't taken long for them to fall in love.

Tyler squeezed Corey's hand again. They had kept it quiet. In fact, many of the girls in their grade regularly swooned over Corey, and he had no idea how Jeff had figured it out.

"Why the fuck you'd want to stick your dick up his ass instead of some girl's pussy, I'll never fucking know." Jeff shook his head again. "Or are you the bottom? You strike me as the kind of guy who likes to take it up the ass, Wagner."

"You seem to know a lot about the lifestyle, Jeff," Tyler said. "Are you and your friends a little closer than you want people to know?"

Corey moaned again as Jeff's face turned bright red. "You'll pay for that, you fucking faggot."

"Original. Of course, I can't expect someone with your IQ to come up with better insults, can I?"

"Tyler shut up," Corey whispered.

Tyler shook his head. The fear on Corey's face, the way his body trembled, had buried his fear under a sudden, hot, throbbing pulse of anger, and he embraced the unfamiliar feeling.

"You and your idiot friends should leave, Jeff," Tyler said.

"Oh, we're not leaving until we teach you what happens to queers like you. What you're doing is sick." Jeff and his friends closed in on them. "We'll see how you feel about your little boyfriend when you're in the hospital with a broken -"

He took a step back when Tyler suddenly threw himself at him. He rammed his shoulder into Jeff's stomach, knocking the bigger boy backward as he shouted, "Corey! Run!"

He dropped on Jeff and swung his fist. His hand screamed in agony when it connected with Jeff's broad jaw, but he ignored it grimly and raised his hand again, smashing his fist into Jeff's nose.

Jeff howled with anger and threw Tyler to the ground beside him. He pounced on him, wrapping his large arm around his neck and hauling him into a sitting position as his nose gushed blood down Tyler's shoulder and arm.

He squeezed tightly as Tyler choked and clawed frantically at his arm. He released it enough for Tyler to drag in a whooping gasp of cold air.

"You and your boyfriend are going to burn in hell," Jeff whispered.

Eyes bulging, Tyler watched as Jeff's friends knocked Corey to the ground and began to kick him in the ribs and back.

"Corey!" Tyler tried to scream as one of the boys delivered a brutal kick to Corey's face, and his eyes rolled up in his head.

"What the fuck?" Jeff's hot breath puffed in his ear, and his arm relaxed around his neck.

"Corey?" Tyler whispered. Corey's limp body was rippling and changing, the clothes tearing away, and the boys watched in fascination as he shifted to a small, orange fox. Blood trickled steadily from the fox's nostrils as one of the boys reached down and prodded at it with the toe of his sneaker.

"Holy fuck." He turned to Jeff. "He's a paranormal."

Jeff grunted with surprise when Tyler nearly wiggled out of his grip.

"Let me go! He's hurt!" Tyler shouted.

Jeff tightened his grip until Tyler gagged. "It's not bad enough that you're fucking a dude, but he's a paranormal too? What is wrong with you?"

Tyler, his face going purple from lack of oxygen, reached for Corey. He had to get to him. He had to help him. He clawed again at Jeff's muscular arm as black roses bloomed in his vision.

"Let him go."

The voice was soft, but its tone was hard steel. Jeff dropped his arm from Tyler's neck and stood up. Tyler laid on the ground, gagging and gasping in air as Jeff scowled at the woman standing a few feet away.

"Get out of here, bitch. This isn't any of your business." Jeff wiped the blood from his nose with the heel of his hand.

"You're trespassing on my land. That makes it my business," the woman replied. She wore a long dark blue cloak with a hood, and she pushed the hood back to reveal her face as she glanced at the fox lying on the ground.

Tyler stared at the woman. She was tall, he guessed close

to six feet, and she had long dark hair with streaks of blue woven throughout it. Her skin was pale, and her eyes seemed to glow in the growing dusk.

"Fuck off!" Jeff clenched his ham-like hands into fists. "I'm not into hurting women, but I'm willing to make an exception for you."

"Lucky me," the woman replied. She eyed the others before shifting her gaze back to Jeff. "Go on. You and your little friends scurry off like the ugly rodents that you are. I grow tired of you."

"Bitch! You'll pay for that," Jeff huffed again. He glanced at the three other boys, and Tyler gave a hoarse shout of warning as Jeff suddenly rushed forward, and his friends followed.

The woman sighed loudly, and Tyler watched in stunned silence as she beat the shit out of his classmates.

The woman, who wasn't even breathing hard, bent and picked up the unconscious fox. Scattered around her, Jeff and his friends were lying on the ground, moaning softly, but she completely ignored them.

Tyler staggered to his feet and lurched after the woman as she walked into the woods.

"Wait!" He grabbed her arm and coughed hoarsely into the crook of his elbow. "He needs to go to the hospital."

"We can't take him like this. The hospital won't treat him until he shifts to his human form, and he's not going to shift while he's unconscious," the woman replied.

"Wh-where are you taking him?" Tyler squeezed her arm.

"To get him help." The woman frowned as she stared at

his hand. The knuckles were bruised and swollen. "Is your hand broken?"

"I don't know."

He glanced behind them at Jeff and the others. "What about them?"

"Leave them," she said dismissively. "They'll crawl home and lick their wounds."

She started walking again, and Tyler followed her, not knowing what else to do.

"Who are you?" he panted. The woman was setting a brisk pace, and he could barely keep up with her long strides.

"My name is Kaida."

ABOUT THE AUTHOR

Elizabeth Kelly was born and raised in Ontario, Canada. She moved west as a teenager and now lives in Alberta with her husband and a menagerie of pets. She firmly believes that a person can survive solely on sushi and coffee, and only her husband's mad cooking skills prevents her from proving that theory.

For more information about Elizabeth, check out her website at

www.elizabethkelly.ca

facebook.com/EKellyBooks
instagram.com/elizabethkelly_author
amazon.com/Elizabeth-Kelly/e/B00EOHZ0MS
bookbub.com/authors/elizabeth-kelly

ALSO BY ELIZABETH KELLY

Tempted Series

Tempted

Twice Tempted

Forever Tempted

Breathless

Tempted Trilogy (Books 1-3)

Red Moon Series

Red Moon

Red Moon Rising

Dark Moon

Alpha Moon

Pale Moon

The Recruit Series

The Recruit (Book One)

The Recruit (Book Two)

The Recruit (Book Three)

The Recruit (Book Four)

The Recruit (Book Five)

The Recruit (Book Six)

The Shifters Series

Willow and the Wolf (Book One)

Ava and the Bear (Book Two)

Katarina and the Bird (Book Three)

Porter's Mate (Book Four)

Bria and the Tiger (Book Five)

Rosalie Undone (Book Six)

The Dragon's Mate (Book Seven)

Rise of the Jaguar (Book Eight)

The Assassin and the Bear (Book Nine)

Elora and the Crow (Book Ten)

The Draax Series

Reign (Book One)

Rule (Book Two)

Rebel (Book Three)

Surrender (Book Four)

Survive (Book Five)

Salvation (Book Six)

Harmony Falls Series

Sweet Harmony (Book One)

Perfect Harmony (Book Two)

Forbidden Harmony (Book Three)

Redeeming Harmony (Book Four)

Absolute Harmony (Novella)

Beautiful Harmony (Book Five)

Reckless Harmony (Book Six)

Seasoned Romance Series

Bet Your Heart on Me (Book One)

Take a Chance on Me (Book Two)

Place Your Trust in Me (Book Three)

Individual Books

The Necessary Engagement

Amelia's Touch

The Rancher's Daughter

Healing Gabriel

The Contract

A Home for Lily

Saving Charlotte

Shameless

The Fairy Tales Collection

Broken

An Unlikely Seduction

Holiday Romance

The Christmas Wife

The Christmas Rescue

The Christmas Nanny

The Christmas Boss

Sordid Games